. . . AND INTO THE FIRE

Simon started to scan the area when an odd odor suddenly caught his attention, something acrid and vaguely familiar, yet distinctly out of place. Before he could put a name to it, it dissolved into the scent of Turkish tobacco and the realization that someone had stepped up close behind him.

"A beautiful place, no?"

Though he tried not to react, there was something about the ambiguous accent and impassive tone that sent a warning tremor rippling up his spine. "Sure is."

"The history, that is not so beautiful."

He turned, facing the man straight on. Despite the dark beard that covered much of his face, Simon knew by the eyes it was Jäger. "Oh?" He pressed and held the TRANSMIT button on the tiny two-way, opening the channel to Pilár. "Why's that?"

The man smiled, but without warmth, like an undertaker appraising his next client. "It is here they burned the heretics. During the Inquisition."

The words seemed to trigger some transcendental association in Simon's brain, attaching a name to the unknown scent that still lingered beneath the odor of tobacco: *napalm.* The word, and the memory it provoked, made his skin crawl. Though he tried to stop himself, he couldn't, and glanced down. A thin sheen of gelatinous dampness covered his slacks and shoes.

Jäger raised his cigarette and blew across the tip, making it glow. "This, I believe, would not be such a pleasant way to die."

THE COURIER

JAY MacLARTY

POCKET **STAR** BOOKS
New York   London   Toronto   Sydney   Singapore

This book is a work of fiction. Names, characters, places and incidents are products of the author's imagination or are used fictitiously. Any resemblance to actual events or locales or persons, living or dead, is entirely coincidental.

An *Original* Publication of POCKET BOOKS

A Pocket Star Book published by
POCKET BOOKS, a division of Simon & Schuster, Inc.
1230 Avenue of the Americas, New York, NY 10020

ISBN: 0-7434-6489-3

First Pocket Books printing June 2003

10   9   8   7   6   5   4   3   2   1

For information regarding special discounts for bulk purchases, please contact Simon & Schuster Special Sales at 1-800-456-6798 or business@simonandschuster.com

Cover design by Carlos Beltran

Printed in the U.S.A.

To
Louise Crawford,
dear friend and colleague,
who helped conceive the idea, did much of the research,
and pushed me forward.

ACKNOWLEDGMENTS

The author wishes to thank the following people for their help on this book:

For her invaluable insight into the world of chemistry and labs: Barbara Tucker, Ph.D.

For questions regarding foreign locales and languages: Edwin Marte, Mike DeVito, Roweena Schwani, Helen Feery, Dirk McBain, and Harold Leenderts.

To my readers: Mimi & James Blackmon, Lew Nelson, Philip Smith, Julie Salazar, and Mary Leman.

With special thanks to:

> Elaine Nelson, who read the manuscript twice in her unrelenting quest to find and destroy my grammatical misdeeds;
> and my daughter, Lisa MacLarty, a fine writer who understood the process and never failed to be honest.

Finally, I am indebted beyond measure to the members of my dedicated critique group:

Liz Crain   Louise Crawford   Gene Munger

for their intellectual companionship and uncompromising honesty, and who, because they were always there, always asking for "more," forced this book to completion.

THE COURIER

Madrid, Spain

Sunday, 3 November 11:45:59 GMT +0100

Though eager to get home, Simon couldn't help being amused. For someone who spent half his time fighting his way through airports filled with nervous travelers and egocentric custom agents, he'd learned to expect delays, irritations, and the unusual. But this bordered on the bizarre: 438 passengers on the tarmac of Madrid Barajas Airport waiting to identify their luggage as it came back off the Boeing 747. Thirty minutes earlier, and two minutes prior to takeoff, Security had discovered an extra bag and was now determined to match it with a passenger—a primitive, yet effective deterrent to nonsuicidal bombers. Simon chuckled to himself—in the high-tech world of computers, X-ray scanners, and bomb-sniffing machines, the ultimate safety measure came down to each passenger having to step forward, stick out a finger, and point.

Under the stark glare of six high-intensity mercury flood banks, the international conglomeration of travelers instinctively migrated into groups of common language. Though Simon spoke only English and Russian fluently, he had no problem interpreting the litany of complaints that reverberated around him: everyone carping about the delay, their loss of holiday time, the meetings missed, and the inefficiency of Iberia Airlines. No one, however, had any desire to get back on the plane before the extra piece of luggage had been identified or left behind.

Simon spotted his as it came down the ramp—an indistinct, scraped and scarred, gray nylon carryall—without any identifying marks except for the claim sticker and a small ID tag with his New York address. Though the bag was well constructed and expensive, any evidence of quality had been removed, so as not to attract the attention of dishonest baggage handlers. It still amazed him how many intelligent people advertised the value of their belongings by packing them in expensive bags. They might as well have attached a sign to each piece: "Open me—I'm full of good stuff." He stepped forward, pointed out his bag, waited as the security officer matched the tag number to the one attached to his ticket, then moved over to join the *cleared* passengers, grouped together near the tail of the plane.

Off to the left, the huge terminal building glowed with light, its restaurants and shops and lounges deserted at such a late hour, but Security wasn't about to let the passengers wait inside where somebody could possibly slip away. As Simon burrowed his way into the crowd, looking for a friendly face, his satellite-linked cellular began its irritating vibration. He reached down, unclipped the tiny unit from his belt, read the familiar number that pulsated across the display, extended the aerial, and growled into the receiver, "Simon says: Leave me alone." Of course he knew it was his sister Lara, the last survivor of his immediate family, his office manager and sole employee, his counselor and confidante and conscience. "It's almost midnight. All sane people should be in bed." He worked his way toward the edge of the crowd, not wanting to disturb anyone with his conversation.

"Hello to you, too, Boris. I take great umbrage at all remarks regarding sanity. May I remind you that we come from a long, proud line of the functionally disabled. Besides, it's not even six o'clock here at the center of the universe."

"If New York is the center of the universe, God is a sadist. And don't call me Boris." It was a useless request; whenever Lara wanted to needle him, she would yank the name from their antediluvian family archives. Their mother, a Russian immigrant born Anna Pasternak, clung to the improbable belief she was somehow related to the great author Boris Leonidovich Pasternak, and in a fervor of motherland nostalgia had named her daughter Lara, after the *Doctor Zhivago* character, and her only son, Boris Leonidovich Pasternak Simon, a mouthful that had haunted Simon throughout his childhood and adolescence. At the age of eighteen, in his first great act of familial disobedience, he legally had it changed to Simon Leonidovich, a compromise he could live with, yet not overly offend his alcoholic father or the delusionary fantasies of his mother.

"I'm surprised you answered," Lara said, taking on her familiar businesslike tone. "What happened? Miss your flight?"

"I wish. We're sitting on the ground in Madrid while Security tries to confirm the bag count."

"You have all the fun."

"Yeah, right, I can hardly stop chuckling. What's up?"

"You were supposed to check in. I thought something might have gone wrong."

"What could go wrong? Pick up a book from the New York Public Library, deliver it to the Prado Museum in Madrid. What could be easier than that? Any idiot could do it."

"Oh, for God's sake, Simon, a Gutenberg Bible is not just a book. It's a priceless work of art."

"Of course it's a book. A novel I think."

"Don't be a smart-ass. One of these days God's going to give up on you, Simon Leonidovich. Then you'll be sorry."

"Don't worry about me and God, we have an arrangement."

"An arrangement?"

"Right. I don't ask for anything, He doesn't give me anything."

"You're hopeless. You should have called me."

"Come on, Sissie, loosen up. It's Sunday, you shouldn't have to deal with this stuff when you're at home." It was an ongoing argument. Lara insisted on handling all calls, and since they did business all over the world, it meant she had to stay "connected" twenty-four hours a day. "There's no reason we can't use the answering service at night."

"We're not going to discuss this, Simon."

"I can discuss whatever I want." But he knew that nothing he said would change her mind. He paid her triple what most office managers made, and she felt obligated to justify her salary. It was an unnecessary and totally self-imposed burden. "I know it's hard, Sissie, but you might try to remember that I'm the boss."

"Uptight is what you are. You need to get laid, Simon."

He wanted to tell her the same, suspected she hadn't been to bed with a man in the four years since her husband died, but she was still his little sister—it didn't matter that she was thirty-two years old—and he couldn't say it. "What I need is a good night's sleep."

"Then turn down a job once in a while."

It was a useless reprimand and she knew it, he could hear it in her voice. That was one of the problems with his business: he didn't want to deal with a big office and lots of employees, so he tried to limit his client base, but the more his reputation grew, the more people sought him out. He kept bumping his fee, hoping to discourage business, but it only seemed to enhance his image as "the man who could deliver anything, anywhere."

A container of brown snakes from Australia to the CDC in Atlanta. *No worries.*

A crate of diamonds from Cape Town to New York. *Easy.*

A human heart from London to Moscow. *Before it skips a beat.*

Work had become both burden and mistress, something he couldn't turn his back on, and promising to do so would only be a lie—to Lara, as well as himself. "Simon says: Take a night off. I'll forward the phones to my seat location as soon we're airborne."

"Love you, Boris. Don't forget."

"You too, sweetheart. Give the kids a kiss." He pressed the END button, then realized he didn't have a clue what she meant by "don't forget." Not the phones, he was sure of that. He considered a quick callback, but decided against it, confident he'd remember before he reached New York.

CHAPTER ONE

Södertälje, Sweden

Sunday, 3 November 11:50:59 GMT +0100

Pär Olin placed the last slide beneath the lens of his Darkfield and adjusted the focus. He felt slightly nauseated, that familiar motion sickness he got from staring into the ocular tubes of his microscope and moving slides back and forth. Without shifting positions, he methodically began to compare the number of necrotic spots with the data on his monitor. Though few in number, there was no denying the growing presence of dead and dying cells. It would take time—eight or nine years—but every long-term user of Mira-loss would eventually die an excruciating death, their livers dissolving into an amorphous mass of useless tissue.

He transferred the slide to his camera-equipped Brightfield, carefully adjusted the focus, and snapped the shutter, automatically storing the image on his computer. Finally done, he leaned back and closed his eyes. Instantly thirty-three million screaming faces began to play across the back of his eyelids—Edvard Munch's *The Scream* multiplied by the face of every Mira-loss user. Night or day, there was no escape from the nightmare. If only he could open his eyes and find it was all a dream. But it wasn't. It was real, and it was his nightmare to deal with.

He glanced at his watch, surprised to see he'd worked fifteen hours without a break. Another fifteen hours of overtime for which he'd never receive so much as a single krona or a simple *thank-you*. Another Sunday away from his children. Not that he had much choice; not if he hoped to finish his analysis and avoid Karl Langerkvist, the director of research, who had dismissed his preliminary report as *flawed,* and since reading it had kept Pär busy on other projects—Karl's bureaucratic way of quashing the research without issuing an order. Once a respected scientist, Karl had turned into a fat-and-happy bureaucrat with the success of Mira-loss, a man who refused to accept anything that might jeopardize his position with the company. And nothing would do that faster than Bain-Haverland being forced to pull its miracle weight-loss drug off the market.

Not that Pär had any illusions about his own career; the reward for bad news was rarely good. In fact, he couldn't remember the last good thing that happened in his life. His beautiful and bright Inga, her body and mind ravaged by cancer, dead at the age of twenty-nine; Erik and Lena, barely out of diapers, left without a mother. And now this.

At least the research was over.

Exhausted, he placed his palms on the cool surface of his workbench and levered himself to his feet. The huge lab—normally a buzz of noise with compressors kicking on and off, centrifuges whining, and air-changers humming overhead like angry bees—seemed ominously quiet, as if it too could sense the end of something. Pär worked his way through the maze of black counters and gunmetal stools, toward the windows and the lights of Stockholm in the distance. *Now what?*

But he knew.

Though she'd been dead three months, he could still hear Inga's whispered advice: *You can't worry about your job when thousands will die.*

No, he could never live with that.

He felt like a man trying to skate over thin ice with a thousand-pound secret on his back. He had to pass the burden to someone else before it killed him. *But who?*

He knew the answer to that, too.

Without the support of Karl, there was only one person he dared trust with the information: Grayson Haverland, the CEO of Bain-Haverland and the man personally responsible for bringing Mira-loss to market. The man had an impeccable reputation as both a scientist and administrator, but most important, a reputation for fairness and honesty. And that was all Pär needed, a fair hearing. His study would accomplish the rest: removing Mira-loss from the shelves.

He glanced over his shoulder, through the glass wall of Karl's office to the large side-by-side chronometers—one labeled STOCKHOLM, the other LA JOLLA. As he watched, 11:59 dissolved into 00:00 and another day passed behind him, Sunday to Monday. In California the time read 15:00, where it was still Sunday afternoon. Inga's soft voice prodded his subconscious: *It's time, Pär.*

Yes, no time like the present to solve yesterday's

problems. Or was it no time like yesterday to solve today's problems? Too tired to think through the riddle, he returned to his desk and picked up the phone before the whisper of Inga's voice faded—along with his nerve.

For more than twenty minutes, dragging the phone cord behind, he paced his workstation as his call was transferred from one person to another. No one with authority seemed to work on Sunday in California, his request to speak with Grayson Haverland meeting with varying degrees of discourtesy and disbelief. Losing confidence, he removed the tiny laminated picture of Erik and Lena from the pocket of his lab coat and placed it next to the phone. He was doing it for them— for all the children who would eventually lose their parents to Mira-loss. The horrifying statistics—one new user every minute of the day—only increased the urgency. Twenty more in the time he'd been on the phone. It made him angry and gave him the strength to resist every suggestion to "call back tomorrow" or to "speak with someone else."

Finally, after another round of frustrating holds and waits and transfers, a new voice echoed over the line. "Who's this?"

Tired and losing patience, Pär snapped back, "This I've explained. I insist to speak with Dr. Haverland."

Insist! The word annoyed Haverland nearly as much as the idiot who forwarded the call—someone he would find and deal with before the day was over. "This *is* Grayson Haverland." He took a deep breath and softened his tone. "And who is this?"

Surprised, the man's insisting tone melted into a

hesitant stammer. "Pär Olin . . . in Södertälje. Excuse
please my interruption. We met when you last year
came to Sweden."

"Oh, yes, I remember." He didn't, of course. How
could he, having met over two hundred employees in
two days? But that was one of his strengths, making
everyone feel as if they made an impression. He decided to take a chance. "Dr. Olin, isn't it?"

"*Ja.* I am most pleased you remember."

Haverland motioned to the other members of his
foursome, indicating they should tee off, then moved
off to the side so as not to bother them. "I do hope this
is important, Dr. Olin. I'm down eight skins and not in
the best of moods." Actually, he felt wonderful—it was
a beautiful day, the blue Pacific and the rolling green
hills of Rancho Santa Fe a satisfying reminder of
everything he'd attained in life—but he didn't sub-
scribe to that chummy camaraderie so many techno-
age executives affected with their employees. He liked
to keep his people on their toes and slightly off balance.

A moment of silence followed, the caller clearly not
understanding the meaning of skins. "*Ja,* it is most important."

"Get on with it, then. We've got four holes to play
and we're running out of daylight."

Another irritating silence followed before the man
sputtered out, "Your pardon, please. Would this be
playing golf, sir?"

"Of course I'm playing golf. What do you—" He
reined in his temper. "Please get on with it, Doctor."

"Very sorry, but is this a cellular instrument on
which you are speaking?"

Haverland understood the inference but discounted the danger of anyone overhearing or caring about their conversation. The problem, he suspected, involved some complaint against Karl, his director of research. Anything else and Karl would have called himself. "Yes, of course I'm on cellular."

"A discussion in such a manner would not be advisable, sir."

That suited Haverland just fine; he had no desire to mediate an employee dispute on a Sunday afternoon from the fifteenth tee box of the Rancho Santa Fe Country Club. He mouthed the word *sorry* to the three men waiting on the tee. "Understood. Why don't you call me in the morning? At the office."

"This delay would not be advisable," Olin answered quickly, his tone suddenly emphatic.

"This has something, I assume, to do with Karl Langerkvist?"

"Nej."

Haverland felt the first touch of alarm, like a tuning fork at low pitch tingling the hair on the back of his neck. "Please refresh my memory, Doctor. Your department?"

"PNU."

That was not what Haverland wanted to hear, PNU being the in-house euphemism for Phase IV Pharmacovigilance Unit, the group responsible for tracking post-release safety problems. In the business of pharmaceuticals, there was no greater nightmare than having something go askew once a drug had been released. Though he knew better than to pursue the matter by cellular, he couldn't resist one final question. "And exactly which drug are you tracking, Doctor? Use the lab name, please." Only one answer, he decided, would keep him from finishing his round. Anything else could wait.

"M-L One."

He felt the blood drain from his legs, and for an instant thought they might actually fold up beneath him. He turned away from the tee, afraid what his face might reveal, and struggled to speak past the acid that suddenly clogged the back of his throat. "Give me your extension, Doctor. I'll call you back in five minutes."

Though difficult, he managed to hide his concern behind a look of irritation as he turned back to his playing partners. "Sorry, guys, you'll have to finish without me."

Bill Shingleford, the president of MedTech Software, snorted. "What's the problem, Grayson, can't push enough pills during the week to keep up with your losses in golf? You have to work Sundays now?"

Everyone laughed and Haverland forced himself to join in. Though they were all worth at least fifty million, he was the only one to make *Forbes*'s annual "List of Billionaires," and they teased him relentlessly. "A little crisis at home." He rolled his eyes, as if it were nothing of consequence. "You know how it is—family first." That, of course, was not true, either. The family had never come first, but that was something he couldn't help. It just was. You couldn't build a great fortune without compromises and sacrifices, something the *Now* or the *It* or the *Whatever-the-hell-they-called-themselves* Generation didn't appreciate. Especially his children, who considered him cold and aloof. He felt rotten about it, but consoled himself in the knowledge that they would someday understand. A person had to take the long view, like Rockefeller and Mellon, to build an American dynasty.

Robert Maitland, the chairman of Allen Labs, narrowed his eyes. "Don't try and shit me, Grayson."

Haverland felt another surge of acid climb into his throat. Maitland was the last person who needed to hear about a problem, not with the merger of their two companies hanging in the balance. "What do you mean?"

"You're just trying to sneak off without paying."

Relieved, Haverland affected an embarrassed expression. "You got me, Rob. I'm tapped out. You'll have to let me slide on the skins."

David Dillard, an investment banker and the fourth member of the group, stuck out his hand, palm up. "In your dreams, Doc. My wife takes enough of those damn weight-loss pills to keep that new jet of yours flying on champagne."

Haverland pulled out his money clip, peeled off eight one-hundred-dollar bills, apologized again for having to leave, and headed toward the clubhouse and a private phone. Just the thought that something might diminish the value of Mira-loss made his stomach clench, forcing a reflux of bitter acid into the back of his throat. Though a billionaire on paper, every cent he had was tied up in Bain-Haverland stock, which, as an insider, he couldn't sell without SEC approval. Any problem with Mira-loss, even a whisper, would kill the merger with Allen Labs and send the stock into a nosedive.

Despite the perpetual coolness of the lab, by the time Pär finished summarizing his study the back of his shirt was damp with nervous perspiration. His final words were met with the silent hum of long distance. *"Hållo.* Are you there, sir?"

Haverland's voice came snapping back over the line. "Yes, of course I'm here. Why is it, Doctor, you're the one calling with this information? Where is Karl Langerkvist?"

Pär hesitated, struggling to think of some discreet way to answer without discrediting Karl. "Uh . . . it's most early in the morning here, sir. He would most probably be sleeping." *Dumb—Dumb—Dumb,* he knew it the moment he spoke the words.

"Holy Mother of God, you're telling me Mira-loss is going to kill thirty-three million people and Karl Langerkvist is home snuggled in bed!"

Pär stared at the tiny picture of his children, trying to gather strength from their innocent faces. "The work is just now finished. Dr. Langerkvist has not been yet made aware of these results."

"So why is it you called me, here in the United States, before calling him?"

Pär tried to think of some way to explain, to say it without bringing into question the validity of his research. "It's for the reason that—" He took a deep breath and let it out slowly. "Dr. Langerkvist is not so aware of my work."

"He doesn't know what you're working on? How is that possible?"

"He knew, but—"

"But what? What exactly are you trying *not* to say, Dr. Olin?"

There was no way to avoid it. No way to soften the truth. "My preliminary report he did not so much agree with."

"Ahh."

Pär expected an eruption, at the very least a severe reprimand for going over Karl's head, but the sound was more of relief than anger.

"So," Haverland continued, "you completed the research on your own?"

"Ja, ja. I must."

"Of course you did. Any good scientist would."

Pär wasn't sure how to respond. Was Haverland being complimentary or contemptuous? Though comfortable with English, he'd never been able to grasp the nuances of American sarcasm. He settled on a neutral response. *"Ja."*

"And who else is aware of your findings?"

Pär hesitated, not liking the question, but unable to think of any way around the truth. "No one."

"You understand, of course, we have to check your research? We couldn't very well pull Mira-loss off the market without verification."

"At least six times each test has been validated."

"I don't doubt your work, Doctor. But we must keep in mind the ramifications this kind of news might have."

"Ja, this I understand, but—"

"We wouldn't dare make a premature announcement. The FDA would crucify us. Not to mention the SEC, our stockholders, and the thousands of people who benefit from Mira-loss."

Benefit? Pär doubted anyone would remember the benefits when their livers turned into blood pudding. "But—"

"Of course we'll start the cross-verification immediately. This is too important to delay even a day. I'll organize a team tonight, and we'll start the minute we receive your data."

Though encouraged by the man's take-charge attitude, Pär didn't like the thought of being excluded from the process.

Haverland seemed to sense his hesitation. "Of course we'll need your help here in La Jolla."

California! He glanced down at the picture of Erik and Lena. What a wonderful experience it would be for them, something to take their minds off "Mamma." Only a few miles from San Diego, with its world-class zoo and beautiful beaches, and less than two hours from Disneyland. He could almost see them laughing again, their somber expressions wiped away by Mickey Mouse and Goofy. *"Ja,* I would be most honored."

"Excellent. I'll speak with Karl about the arrangements. When can we expect the files?"

"It would not take more than one hour."

Haverland's response was immediate. "No, this information is too sensitive for the Internet. And we'll need the slides. Better send it hot. Directly to me. Wouldn't do to have anything get lost."

Pär recognized the term—*hot*—their in-house expression for private courier, a service they used infrequently, only to transfer the most sensitive specimens back and forth between Sweden and California. Never, as far as he knew, had they used the service to transfer files. Haverland was clearly taking the matter seriously. *"Ja."*

"Make sure everything's encrypted and copy protected." Haverland's voice dropped slightly. "For the time being let's keep this between us."

"You will not be speaking to—"

"And Karl of course."

"He will not be pleased."

"Don't worry about Karl. He obviously doesn't appreciate your brilliant work. We don't need that kind of attitude, do we?"

The overly gratuitous remark made Pär uncomfortable. There was nothing brilliant about it—he had simply done his job, using good scientific principles, something he now doubted the company had done before marketing the product—but that was not something he dared mention.

"And, Doctor—"

"Ja?"

"Good work. Terrible news, but good work. If this checks out, you'll be responsible for saving countless lives."

Again, Pär felt uneasy about the compliment, questioning the sincerity. *"Tack själv.* It is my regret to bring you this report."

"Not your fault. Don't you worry now, we'll survive. Anything else, you call me direct. On my private line."

"Ja." He copied down the number and that of WorldWide SD, the private courier service used by the company, then slumped into his chair as the line went silent. *We'll survive.* Was it possible? Could Bain-Haverland withstand the loss of their number-one product?

Inga's soft voice whispered through his head: *You're a good man, Pär Olin.*

Feeling better, he reclipped the picture of his children back onto the pocket of his lab coat and dialed the number for WorldWide SD. Maybe now he could sleep—close his eyes and not see those terrible screaming faces.

But something deep inside told him otherwise.

CHAPTER TWO

Madrid, Spain

Monday, 4 November 00:40:38 GMT + 0000

The inmates, Simon saw, were growing restless. Everyone who had a cell phone was using it, trying to make alternative flight arrangements, informing friends or business associates about their delay, or simply taking the opportunity to gripe to some unfortunate, sleepy soul about the ordeal. To make matters worse, the air had gone heavy with a thin mist that threatened to become rain. If Security didn't find the bag soon, they would have to break out the riot gear.

A few minutes later, when the mist turned into a steady drizzle, the head of Security finally recognized the problem and gave the go-ahead for all *cleared* passengers to reboard. Flanked by a cadre of security guards, they were herded like cattle toward the front of the 747. As they neared the steps leading up into the Goliath of all passenger aircraft, Simon turned and smiled at the middle-aged woman behind him. *"Buenas noches."* He motioned for her to move around him. *"Por favor."* The flight to New York would take eight hours, and he wasn't eager to spend any more time than necessary in his seat.

She answered in heavily accented English, "Thank you, Señor."

As the woman stepped past him, the phone on his belt began its familiar dance. The fact that it was Lara's number that scrolled across the display didn't surprise him. "Caught me again."

"Still sitting on the tarmac, I presume?"

"Yeah, but it started to rain so they're letting us back on the plane. At least the ones who finished identifying their bags. The others are crouched under the wing, trying to stay dry. What's up?"

"A job. Can you write?"

"Not really. Some pimply-faced kid with a gun and a uniform is staring at me like I'm plotting the overthrow of the monarchy. I assume you've sent the details." He really didn't need to ask; Lara was like a Cray supercomputer when it came to efficiency and speed.

"Is a frog's ass waterproof?"

"Smart-ass. What's the job?"

"He didn't say and I was too busy trying to drown the kids in the bathtub to ask. I told him you'd call him back within the hour."

"And how are my two favorite little people?"

"Hyperactive aliens from another galaxy is more like it. I think Mrs. Anderson feeds them M&M's for lunch. I'm exhausted."

"Then go to bed. I'll call the guy as soon as I'm in my seat. Love you."

The woman ahead of him, who had just reached the first step, looked back over her shoulder and smiled. *"Tu esposa?"*

It took a moment to switch his thoughts from English to Spanish, and another half second to translate the question into "your wife?"—a concept he was not good at, at least the one time he tried, a brief and painful experience. He smiled back and nodded, not about to explain that he didn't have a wife, didn't have a girlfriend, couldn't remember the last time he had a date, and that the best relationship he had going was with a group of asexual cybernuts. *Not good*—but what could he do?—his constant travel torpedoed every chance he had for a serious relationship. To avoid the loneliness he worked harder, a vicious cycle he seemed incapable of escaping.

Ten minutes later he had his laptop connected into the seatback phone and his e-mail downloaded. He quickly scanned the list of messages, knowing the flight attendant would make him shut down during takeoff. There was the usual accumulation: a couple of tech jokes from an old high-school sweetheart, a shipping confirmation from Amazon for some books he'd ordered, and the CONTACT message from Lara. The man's name, Pär Olin, was unfamiliar, along with his company: Gotland Research. The country code, 46, which followed the international access code of 011, signified Sweden, but neither the city code or telephone number rang any bells. He clicked the WorldWide icon on his toolbar, typed his password, and within seconds had access to his office computer. He input the telephone number along with the names Olin and Gotland and hit SEARCH. Instantly the word MATCH began to stream across the top of his monitor, followed a moment later by a small dialog box.

Gotland Research: Södertälje, Sweden—
subsidiary of Bain-Haverland, La Jolla, CA

He clicked the box, opening the record. He'd worked for the company once, transporting a small container of radioactive tissue from their research lab in Sweden to their main facility in La Jolla, California. Boring work, not the kind of thing he liked to do. He minimized the screen, exposing his regular tabletop, and clicked his EarthTime icon, confirming what he already knew: Södertälje and Madrid were in the same time zone. Whoever Pär Olin was, the man was working awfully late or awfully damn early.

Closing the program, he clicked his Atlas icon and typed SÖDERTÄLJE. The giant globe that dominated his screen instantly rotated toward Europe, then zeroed in and enlarged the area over Stockholm, including the nearby city of Södertälje. He highlighted the name and clicked his CNN-Weather link. Within fifteen seconds he had the current weather and twenty-four-hour forecast.

He glanced up, surprised that the first-class section was now over half full and the line at the door was backing up. The mystery bag had obviously been identified. *Not much time*—not more than ten minutes before the flight attendant would make him stow the laptop. *Decision time*—call now and risk an interruption, or wait until they were airborne. The answer seemed obvious, Olin wasn't working in the wee hours of the morning because he enjoyed long Swedish nights, he had something important to get out. With a little luck—he glanced out the window and the dark sky beyond—and a bit of divine intervention, he might still have time to book the job and get off the plane. A flight between Madrid and Stockholm wouldn't take more than five hours; a connection via New York would be a two-day stint in aluminum purgatory—something he didn't want to even think about.

Pulling a jumper cable from the inside pocket of his security case, he quickly made the connection between his cellular and laptop, enabling him to record the call. It was a habit that helped eliminate misunderstandings, something that often occurred when people spoke different languages. If he agreed to take the job, the information would be transferred onto an Assignment sheet and electronically forwarded to Lara and his bonding agent.

Still connected to the Web, he clicked his Travel-Wizard icon, waited for the site to check his password, then punched in Olin's number. As the call magically worked its way from satellite to satellite and down through an international network of land lines, he slipped his translation DVD into the laptop, just in case Olin didn't speak English. If necessary, his words could now be translated directly onto the screen.

The phone rang three times, then was answered by machine. Simon punched in the extension number, interrupting the message. Instantly a man's tinny voice echoed back over the line, as if he'd been waiting with his hand on the receiver. *"Hållo, Det ar Pär Olin."*

The plane made a small movement and Simon had the uncomfortable feeling he had just taken the first step on his flight to hell. *God hates you, Simon*. He clicked the RECORD icon on his toolbar. *"Kan du Engleska, Herr Olin?"*

"Ja."

"This is Simon Leonidovich, from WorldWide SD. Returning your call."

"Ja. Thank you. I am here waiting."

"You get to the office early, Herr Olin."

There was a slight hesitation, as if the man didn't understand. "Oh. *Ja.* Very early here."

Judging from the exhausted tone, Simon suspected it was late rather than early in the day for Mr. Pär Olin. "Looks like it's going to be a beautiful morning. Warmer than usual." It was part of his schtick, to say something specific to the client's time and location, as if he were right down the street. He didn't do it to deceive, but to instill a degree of confidence in the knowledge that he was always available and no farther away than a phone call. "What can I do for you?"

"We need for you to deliver a package."

Already dreading the answer, Simon asked the perfunctory question. "When?"

"Most immediately."

Somewhere in the back of his mind, Simon thought he heard God chuckle. He began to run through his normal litany of questions: the value of the product to be delivered, the size of the package, the level of security required, whether the item was explosive, contagious, or radioactive. Etcetera—etcetera—etcetera. As he asked the questions, he recalculated his arrival time in New York and added two hours. Using that as the "Requested Departure Time" he typed NEW YORK/KENNEDY into the FROM box on his TravelWizard screen, STOCKHOLM into the TO box, and hit SEARCH. The words WE ARE SEARCHING THE RECORDS OF ALL AIR-LINES TO FIND FLIGHTS THAT BEST MEET YOUR TRAVEL RE-QUIREMENTS began to scroll across the monitor. Fifteen seconds later, just as he finished the questions, a list of available flights appeared on the screen. He was half tempted to lie, but that wasn't his nature, so he picked the best connection and committed himself. "The earliest I could be there would be ten A.M., Tuesday morning." The line hummed quietly and for a moment Simon thought God might have looked away, distracted by some cosmic catastrophe more important than punishing Simon Leonidovich by trapping him in an aluminum tube seven miles above the earth for the better part of two days. "If you need someone sooner, I could recommend an excellent firm in Stockholm." *Simon says: Go for it—please!*

The first-class flight attendants were now working their way through the cabin, checking seat belts and making sure all the passengers had their bags properly stowed. The one coming down Simon's aisle was a real looker: mid-thirties, tall and slender, with beautiful olive skin and big dark eyes. If God was good, Simon thought, Pär Olin would agree to use the Stockholm firm. If God was compassionate, this exquisite Spanish beauty would find something irresistible about Simon Leonidovich; and if God could still remember his youth, by noon Simon and the object of all his lustful thoughts would be feasting on stone crab at Tavern on the Green, and shortly thereafter, each other.

The voice of Pär Olin interrupted the fantasy. "That will be most fine. Please inquire for me at the security desk."

Damn, that was the problem with God, no sense of humor. "Wonderful, you'll have a copy of the contract within the hour. Please sign and fax it back to the number on the cover sheet. Look forward to meeting you, Herr Olin." A courtesy, not a real lie. He unglued the phone from his left ear, pressed the END button and dropped it into the seat beside him. At least that was a blessing. Maybe God was sending him a message: I've given you an extra seat, Leonidovich—sleep, you're too old for young beauties.

The beauty in mind suddenly hovered overhead. "We're about to depart, Señor. You'll need to shut down and stow that under the seat."

From what he saw and heard in those two brief sentences, Simon concluded a number of things: though she spoke with a Castilian accent, the syntax was clearly American, an indication she had worked or studied in the States; a first-class assignment on an international flight suggested a degree of sophistication and competence; but what he found most interesting was the lack of a wedding ring, though he knew from experience that didn't necessarily mean available. "Sure, no problem."

He quickly highlighted the flight he wanted, clicked the RESERVE option, moved his pointer to SHUTDOWN, and clicked again. The minute they were airborne he would go back on-line, confirm his reservation, and book a return to New York, with a quick stopover in San Diego to deliver the package.

He slipped the laptop into his security case, placed it under the seat, leaned back, closed his eyes, and tried to better his relationship with the Almighty. *I'm not asking for much, God. A sudden case of pilot aviopho-*

bia would be sufficient. Just enough time to get off this damn thing. Whataya say, Big Guy?"

Two minutes later they were airborne.

Losing confidence in all things theological, Simon recalculated his schedule: eight and a half hours to New York, two and a half hours to shave, shower, change clothes, and catch his plane to Stockholm. The ultimate flight to Hell. If he slept now, he'd never be able to z-out on the New-York-to-Stockholm leg, and since he never slept with a package in hand, it meant he would need to stay awake until they left New York. Eleven hours. *Ugh.* Jobs like this made his ten-thousand-dollar-plus-expenses minimum sound cheap.

A few minutes later, when the Spanish beauty began to take drink orders, he decided to give God a chance to redeem Himself. But the man across the aisle, a good-looking, dressed-for-success businessman, obviously had the same idea and the first opportunity. As Mr. Biz turned on the charm, Simon gave up his fantasy of making a connection. It was one of his credos—*know your limitations*—and competing for women was not one of his strengths. Not that he was bad looking—Lara claimed he had a smile women couldn't resist—but it didn't matter, he just didn't have any confidence when it came to women. Realistically, his chances for finding someone didn't look promising: he was about to hit the big 4-0 and needed to lose a good fifteen pounds. The aging process was inevitable, and as long as he ate a third of his meals at 40,000 feet, he didn't see much hope for losing the weight. Not that he was in bad shape; he could walk all day and often did, using his digital camera to record the many exotic places he visited. It was a hobby and adventure he would have enjoyed sharing with someone, but the best relationship he had going at the moment was with his computer, which he pulled out from under the seat, plugged into the telephone, and booted. When his tabletop popped into view, he swiped his American Express through the card reader and dialed his server.

Across the aisle, the flight attendant giggled, apparently dazzled by Mr. Charm's line of bull. But a moment later, when she turned and rolled her eyes, Simon realized God might have left a slight crack in the door of opportunity. "Can I get you something, Señor Leonidovich?" Though she stumbled awkwardly over the pronunciation of his name, the warm tone of her accent made it almost sound better. "A glass of wine or a mixed drink?"

He gave her a friendly smile, impressed she would even attempt to remember the names of her passengers. "That's Le-on-o-vich. The *d* is silent. Looks harder than it is. Easier yet if you call me Simon."

"Okay, Simon. I'm Pilár. What would you like?"

He tried to ignore his lascivious thoughts and concentrate on the burden of staying awake for eleven hours. A perfect time to go for the gusto, though it clearly violated his no-caffeine, anti-jet-lag routine. "Any chance for an espresso, Pilár?" Nice name, he liked the way it rolled off his tongue.

"I would be delighted to fix you one."

Delighted. God was making a comeback. He reached down and pulled his travel mug from the side pocket of his carryall. "I'll take a double with a shot of Monin if you have it."

A glimmer of incomprehension flashed through her

eyes before she surmised the mug's purpose and moved off toward the galley. Simon logged back on to his travel site, confirmed his reservation, faxed his standard contract to Pär Olin, then shot a quick e-mail to SAS, letting them know he'd collect his ticket at the gate.

A few minutes later Pilár leaned over the empty seat and placed his mug on the console that separated the wide leather chairs. "That's smart, Señor. You would not believe how many laptops I have seen smothered in coffee."

"Yeah, really brilliant. It only took me a glass of Heineken and a thousand-dollar repair bill to figure it out."

She nodded knowingly. "It is not an easy thing to outwit the Irish; they're very clever."

He tried to keep the confusion off his face. "The Irish?"

She smiled mischievously, her voice taking on a playful tone. "I'm convinced of it—laptop leprechauns. You know the ones, living down there in Motherboard Land, just waiting for the perfect moment to flash FATAL-ERROR across your screen." She leaned down and lowered her voice. "They be thirsty little devils, I can tell you that. Like nothing better than a cold glass of beer over the keyboard and down the hard drive."

He laughed, liking her humor. "You're right, they do sound Irish." He also liked her perfume: a soft, fresh smell, like wet grass after a spring rain. "You speak pretty good computer, Pilár."

"Just enough to get myself into Computer Hell once or twice a month."

"Ah, an expert."

*   *   *

As the cabin grew quiet and the other passengers folded into awkward positions of stratospheric slumber, Simon worked to keep his eyelids above the horizon of his screen. Shortly after four A.M. Pilár slipped into the seat beside him. "Mind?" She spoke in a whisper, obviously not wanting to disturb the other passengers.

He smiled—feeling an unfamiliar confidence from their earlier conversation—and answered back in the same low voice. "Mind? I want you to bear my children and be there when I'm old and gray."

She laughed softly, the sound tinkling like a glass wind chime. "How exciting. That's the fourth proposal I've had since takeoff. A new record."

"And how do you respond?"

She pointed to his monitor and fluttered her long eyelashes. "I say, but, Señor, you already have a wife and children."

He glanced at the screen, at the picture of Lara and the kids. "I'm working on a family album. That's my sister and her children." He pointed to his niece. "That's Allie. She's five." He moved his finger to the right. "And that's Jack Junior. He's seven."

"Good story. Do American girls fall for such lines?"

He knew better than to overexplain; it would only make him sound guilty. "Must not. It's the only story I've got and I don't have anybody waiting to buy it."

"She's pretty."

Simon studied the picture. He never really thought of Lara as pretty, more like a Roman candle lit at both ends, all sparkle and energy. "I guess so. She's aged a bit over the last few years. Her husband was killed in a car accident."

"Oh, no!" She reached out and briefly touched his hand. "I am so sorry."

He nodded, hoping to feel her touch again, and that it would last a bit longer the next time. *Simon says: Don't rush things.* "What about you? No husband?"

She made a face, as if she'd just taken a bite of lemon. "As you say in America, been there, done that."

"Yeah, me, too. A three-month nightmare."

"Three months!" Her hushed voice squeaked with shock. "You are not exactly the stable type, Señor."

"It was over in less than a week." He tried to smile but felt it dissolve into a grimace as the memories came flooding back. "But I wanted to give it a chance."

"So it was her fault?"

He shook his head, noting the edge in her voice. "Nope. Mine. Got love and lust all mixed up."

She studied his face, her expression a mixture of interest and skepticism. "I'm sure there was plenty of blame to go around."

"I was older. Should have known better."

"Most men blame their wives."

He almost said, "I'm not most men," but knew it would sound self-serving, so he simply shrugged.

"I think you are an honest man, Simon Leonidovich."

God is good. "And I think you are insightful and beautiful and brilliant."

She leaned closer, her words barely a whisper. "And I hear that a dozen times a day."

The intimate tone of her accent and the spring-grass scent of her skin made him feel like an awkward teenager. "So how do I impress you?"

"Don't try."

Ha, not impressing beautiful women was one of his specialities. "I can do that. Where do I start?"

"Lunch?"

God is great. "Wonderful. When?"

She smiled. "What's wrong with today?"

"Not a thing. How does the Källaren Aurora sound?"

Her smile melted into confusion. "I've heard of it. But I thought it was in Stockholm."

"Bingo."

The confusion dissolved into astonishment. "You're going to Stockholm? Today?"

" 'Fraid so."

The astonishment turned to incredulity. "You're flying through New York to reach Stockholm?"

"God is punishing me."

"He is doing a very fine job. Do you deserve it?"

"Probably." He gave her a teasing smile. "Sometimes I have bad thoughts."

"Bad thoughts? What kind of bad thoughts?"

"Can't say."

She nodded knowingly, her voice dropping lower. "Do these thoughts involve getting naked?"

Beautiful, smart, and clairvoyant. "I refuse to answer on the—"

She reached out and playfully punched his shoulder. "You're a bad man, Simon Leonidovich. A very bad man."

"But honest."

"So, when do you get back to New York?"

He reached over and clicked the calendar icon on his Quick-launch toolbar. The current date popped into view, along with the instant realization of what Lara meant by *Don't forget*. "Uh-oh."

"What is it?"

"My birthday."

"When?"

He was almost too embarrassed to say. "Today. Forgot all about it. My sister has a party planned. She'll kill me."

Pilár shook her head, clearly not impressed. "Why don't you give me a card? I will call you the next time I am in New York."

"Sounds like a plan." He pulled a card from his pocket, knowing he'd never hear from her again. He couldn't blame her: a man who couldn't remember his own birthday and couldn't hold a marriage together more than three months.

She studied the card, as if she really intended to call. "WorldWide SD? What's the SD stand for?"

"Special delivery."

"You work for a delivery company?"

He resisted the impulse to say he owned the company, knowing she met more than her share of successful businessmen. "Yup."

"Like UPS?"

"Exactly." He couldn't think of anything more dissimilar.

She pushed herself out of the seat. "It is time to prepare for breakfast. I will give you a call, *sí?*"

"Absolutely. Great." He felt terrible, knew she'd never call, and even felt worse about forgetting Lara's party. He dreaded telling her, but knew it wasn't the kind of thing he could avoid with an e-mail. He waited until the final approach into Kennedy before calling. "Morning, Sissie."

"You're not coming," she said, disappointment and acceptance in her tone.

"Couldn't squeeze out of it." *Not exactly true.* "But I tried." *Not hard enough.*

"Oh, Simon."

He hated that. Hated to disappoint her, and hated worse that she always forgave him. "Tell the kids we'll go to Disneyland for Christmas."

"You can't buy them, Simon."

"I know that!" But understood that was exactly what it sounded like.

"For God's sake don't forget Thanksgiving."

"I won't. Promise."

"I've invited someone I think you'll like."

He groaned inwardly, recalling the last woman she'd set him up with—nice, but no sparks. "I'm dating someone."

"Bullshit."

He glanced over at Pilár, who was making her final pass through the cabin before landing. "I'm *thinking* about dating someone."

"You're always thinking about it, Simon. Is she?"

No, he was sure she wasn't. "I'm thinking I should look for an office manager who keeps her nose out of my personal life."

"Ha! You forget Thanksgiving, Boris, and you'll be looking for an office manager all right."

She disconnected before he could answer. *Damn.* What a fine day this was turning out to be: another relationship missed, another day trapped in aluminum, another year older.

Happy fucking birthday, Simon Leonidovich.

CHAPTER THREE

Södertälje, Sweden

Tuesday, 5 November 08:00:23 GMT +0100

Pär arrived at work Tuesday morning feeling better than he had in weeks. Within an hour the files would be on their way to La Jolla, the burden of responsibility off his shoulders. Even more exciting was the thought of living in California, getting his children away from the well-intentioned but somber expressions of their grandparents and the reminders of their mother's death.

As he entered the building the night shift of researchers and animal-care people were coming down the stairs and exiting the elevator, their usual end-of-shift banter echoing through the cavernous chrome and glass lobby. But instead of the normal rush toward the exit they were being held back by a line of employees waiting to clear Security. Normally, the procedure entailed a perfunctory "walk and wave" past the guards, who were nothing more than uniformed gatekeepers, there to assist visitors and discourage animal-rights zealots from invading the lab. For some reason they were now searching through bags and purses and patting down anyone wearing loose-fitting clothes.

"What's going on?" he asked as a guard opened the side gate.

"New procedures." He rolled his eyes, as if he considered it foolishness. "Nothing's to be removed from the labs."

That was standard, had always been the policy, but never before did it include any kind of formal search. "What happened, we missing some equipment?"

The guard shrugged. "Nothing I've heard about."

"So why . . . ?"

"Don't ask me." He shook his head. "Americans." He might as well have said *dog shit*.

"This was La Jolla's idea?"

The guard motioned Pär forward as other people tried to squeeze past. "Got the order an hour ago."

Pär moved toward the elevator, his buoyant mood evaporating like an early-morning fog over the Mälaren. To think the changes had anything to do with his research seemed foolish and paranoid, yet he couldn't stop the thought. He crowded into the elevator with a group of coworkers.

"Americans are so clever," complained a young female cytotechnologist. "Lose something in California—search in Sweden."

The man next to her chuckled. *"Ja.* All Americans steal, so they think everyone does."

Though spoken in jest, Pär thought it made sense. Something had been lost in La Jolla, so the security people had implemented new procedures company-wide, a typical American reaction. By the time he reached the third floor he almost believed it.

He stepped off the elevator and took a deep breath, hoping to find some comfort in the strange and oddly satisfying odor of chemicals and cultures. Karl, who was rarely there at such an early hour, poked his head out of his office and gestured—not a friendly "good-morning" wave, but an angry "get-in-here" motion that left no doubt as to his mood.

Though Pär had been expecting the confrontation, he dreaded the thought of facing his former mentor. Before the success of Mira-loss had corrupted his values, Karl had been a good scientist. Now he considered any question about Mira-loss an attack against him and his reputation.

"Just had to do it," he snapped the moment Pär closed the door. "Just had to call La Jolla."

"I didn't have a choice."

The knob in Karl's throat moved up and down, his cheeks flaming. "Didn't have a choice?" He threw out his arms in a gesture of disbelief. "What do you think I'm here for?"

Pär forced back his urge to respond, to remind Karl of their previous conversations, but there was nothing he could say that would alter the facts.

Karl tapped his index finger on a stack of thermal-fax sheets. "Haverland, no less. Who the hell do you think you are, Jonas Salk?" He circled the desk like an angry jackal looking for something to kill. "Word gets out about this and we'll be out of business within a week."

"Is that all you're worried about, Karl? Your job? You don't care about the lives of thirty-three million people?"

"That's crap and you know it. You found some bad tissue, nothing more. You can't just assume it was caused by Mira-loss."

"Assume!" He took a deep breath, trying to control his anger. "I didn't assume anything. There's a direct conn—"

"You can't prove it. You can't draw a straight line between Mira-loss and one single case of liver damage."

"Prove! Listen to yourself, Karl. You sound more like a lawyer than a scientist. Maybe I can't draw a straight line from one to the other, *not yet*, but I know how to draw a circle, and I can guarantee you it's a noose around the neck of every Mira-loss user. I can even remember the day when Karl Langerkvist would have been the first to see it."

Karl stabbed a bony finger within an inch of Pär's nose. "Don't you get sanctimonious with me, you little bastard. You won't be so smug when—"

The intercom buzzed, followed by the hollow sound of a woman's voice. "Dr. Langerkvist, you're needed in the lobby. One of the technicians won't allow the guards to check her purse."

Karl shouted at the gray box, "That's their job! Just tell them to do it!"

"I'm sorry," the woman answered in a low squeak. "But they don't want to. They don't think it's polite."

"Polite!" He turned on Pär and lowered his voice, "See what you've done?" He turned back to the intercom. "Okay, I'll be right there." He started toward the door. "You wait here. I'm not through with you yet."

Though his words confirmed what Pär already suspected—that the new security measures were connected to his research—he was more concerned with what Karl hadn't said: "You won't be so smug when—" *When what?* He glanced over at the thermal-fax sheets, knew the answer was there, but didn't have the nerve to look, not in the fishbowl of Karl's glass-enclosed office. He sat down on the edge of the desk and stared out over the lab. Most of the researchers and cytotechnologists were already at their stations, the majority of them peering into microscopes or staring at computer screens. He leaned back on one hand, and casually turned his head, his eyes darting over the top sheet: 1 of 4 pages from the desk of Grayson Haverland.

Do it, Inga whispered.

He took a deep breath and slid the sheet to one side. The second page contained a long list of questions, all dealing with the M-L One study and asking for Karl's evaluation of the research. Though Pär felt some irritation at having his procedures so openly questioned, the query seemed both reasonable and prudent. In fact, he had to admit, it would have been negligent for Haverland not to have asked.

He glanced toward the lab, quickly checking the room and floor indicator over the elevator, then turned to the next page. New security procedures were mapped out in detail, Haverland expressing concern about "premature leaks of information," but the words "before the research is confirmed" gave Pär a renewed feeling of confidence. The man clearly intended to do the right thing, no matter what the consequences. That was all Pär wanted, a fair assessment of his work, which he had every confidence would confirm his findings. Satisfied, he almost skipped the last sheet, but Inga, always the daring one, prodded him on: *Look.*

The last page contained a list of new computer access codes, effective at noon that day. Another prudent move, Pär thought, as he scanned down the long list of names and the security level assigned to each. He missed his name the first time through, was about to start down the list again when the light over the elevator blinked on. He quickly restacked the pages and slid into a chair as a new wave of paranoiac adrenaline surged into his bloodstream. Had he missed his name, or wasn't it there?

Karl stomped into the office and slammed the door, the glass bowing like a wave about to crash onto the beach. "A box of paper clips! Crying her eyes out, thinking she's going to lose her job for taking a box of lousy paper clips." He glared at Pär. "You created this mess and now I've got to deal with it."

Pär looked at his watch, hoping to send Karl a message and avoid what was clearly going to be a useless debate. Karl immediately glanced over his shoulder at the two huge chronometers behind his desk. "Is the package ready?"

"Not quite."

"Not quite?"

"The slides are packed. I still need to copy the computer files."

"So what are you doing here?"

Pär pushed himself out of the chair, asking himself exactly that question: why was he there, and where was he going? The vision of La Jolla was fading like an old photograph, going from palm green and Pacific blue to muted shades of Scandinavian gray. He needed to be alone, to think, to figure out the meaning behind the words of Haverland's memo and Karl's cryptic "you won't be so smug" comment, but Karl followed him out of the office and across the lab. Losing patience, Pär turned on the man, "Now what?"

Obviously conscious of others within earshot, Karl smiled pleasantly. "I'll verify the slide count while you copy the files."

"I've already verified the count."

"I'll double check for you." Still smiling, he glanced around. "Glad to help."

Pär unlocked the slide drawer attached to the underside of his lab table, lifted out the long, narrow shipping tray, and set it on the counter. Karl reached over and pulled it toward him, a gesture that left Pär feeling hollow and breathless, as if someone had reached inside his chest and wrenched out one of his lungs. Everything seemed to be out of control, slipping beyond his grasp.

He pulled on his lab coat, entered his password into the computer, and began to highlight the folders he needed to copy, a total of 8.3 gigabytes. Pulling two Magneto disks from his supply drawer, he slipped the first one into his optical drive and hit COPY. Instantly a list of files began to flash across his monitor, months of work pouring onto the five-and-a-quarter-inch disk. In less than a minute a small dialog box popped onto the screen:

Disk Full
Insert Disk 2

After ejecting the disk, he marked it "1 of 2," inserted the second disk, and hit ENTER.

"You didn't list your notebook," Karl said, looking up from the inventory summary.

For a moment Pär could only stare. Without the slides or computer access, his notes became his last and only link to M-L One. Without them, he had nothing, no way to defend or prove his research. "They don't need it."

Karl smiled, the expression in total contrast to the uncompromising edge in his voice. "Of course they do."

Though he knew better, Pär also knew it was useless to argue; as long as he worked for the company, they owned everything he did or dreamed or thought or wrote. He unlocked his file drawer and handed Karl the notebook, avoiding his eyes and any look of triumph.

Copy Complete

Marking the second disk, he wondered if he was just being paranoid—that or M-L One and the loss of Inga had warped his perspective. Perhaps he was twisting innocent precautions into evil intentions. He couldn't fault the company for wanting to prevent leaks of information, or even for changing his computer access—not if he was *really* going to La Jolla. So why did he feel so uneasy?

"How many disks?" Karl asked, his pen poised over the inventory sheet.

"Four." It was an instant decision, almost involuntary, but once the word popped out of his mouth he felt energized, committed to making an extra copy for himself. He wasn't sure how, with Karl watching, but he had to try. Inga would approve. He pulled two more disks from the drawer and began to repeat the process.

Karl slid the inventory sheet down the counter. "You sign it. I don't want my name associated with this mess."

Struggling not to show his nervousness, Pär scratched his name across the bottom of the sheet, acutely aware of *4 Disks* listed in ink above. "I think I can handle it from here, Karl. I'm almost through."

Karl didn't move, clearly intending to see the package out the door, and Pär resisted the urge to say more, realizing the man would do exactly the opposite of anything he suggested. The phone buzzed just as the COPY COMPLETE message popped onto his screen. He reached over and hit the speaker button. *"Ja."*

"WorldWide SD here for a pickup."

"Be right down." *Now what?* How, with Karl watching, could he keep the disks out of the shipment? He popped the last disk out of the drive, his mind racing. The courier would be the last person to get anything out of the building, and that, Pär suddenly realized, represented his opportunity. Somehow he had to get rid of Karl. *Be bold,* Inga whispered.

But how? Then it hit him. A long shot as the Americans would say, but a shot. He laid all four disks on top of the slide box, added his notebook and inventory sheet to the pile, and pushed it toward Karl. "All yours."

"Mine?"

"You don't need me just to sign it out."

Karl hesitated, obviously not wanting to put his

name on anything to do with M-L One. "I wasn't going down." His eyes told a different story. "I just wanted to make sure you didn't forget anything."

Trying to look disgusted, Pär scooped up the materials. "I've got better things to do." He could feel Karl's eyes all the way to the elevator.

He considered getting off at the second floor and trying to rewrite the inventory, but suspected Karl would be watching the floor indicator on the elevator. That left only two choices: to change the number of disks on the summary sheet, or stick the form in his pocket. An alteration might attract attention—4s didn't make good 2s—and if discovered, would clearly expose his deception. The second choice seemed the safer option, and he quickly stuffed the sheet into the pocket of his lab coat. If La Jolla asked for an inventory, he could prepare and fax a new one.

He stepped off the elevator, confident he'd made the right decision. The next step, getting the courier to accept two packages without drawing the attention of the security guard, would not be so easy. He couldn't send it to anyone close, that would seem odd, and if he tried to send the courier out of his way, he might refuse the shipment. *Where to? Who to?* He needed time to think and didn't have any. Trying to appear more confident than he felt, he stepped briskly toward the security desk. The courier was not the formidable Schwarzenegger type Pär expected. If anything, the man looked remarkably ordinary: not very tall, a little overweight, with dark friendly eyes, his black hair lightly peppered with gray near the temples. Pär stuck out his hand and smiled. "Mr. Leonidovich. I am Pär Olin."

Despite the smile, Simon had the distinct feeling Pär Olin was about two beats short of popping a heart valve, which, judging from the dampness of his palm, was rapping out a solid 200 beats per minute. For someone so young, his blue eyes seemed hauntingly old, his longish blond hair less fashionable than overlooked, a man without a wife to remind him, and too harried to remember himself. A tiny picture hung from the pocket of his lab coat: a small boy and girl with their dog, Olin behind them. There was something melancholy about the scene that reminded Simon of his own family—Lara and the kids and the missing parent—a sadness that spoke of death, not divorce. "Good morning. Nice to meet you, Herr Olin."

"Your pardon, please—" Olin's eyes shifted toward the guard. "I must, if you please, see your identification."

"Of course." Simon fished a business card out of his pocket. The guard had already checked his credentials, but he suspected Olin knew that. "Will that do?"

Olin barely looked at the card, then slipped it into his pocket. "New York. Most convenient."

Convenient? Either the guy had no sense of where La Jolla was on the American continent, or an odd sense of humor.

Olin gestured toward a small table a few feet away. "Please, we sit here?"

The guard frowned, the procedure clearly a departure from normal, but said nothing. Olin placed his materials on the table, stacked the two extra disks off to one side, and sat down. Simon pulled a transmittal sheet from the pocket of his security case and took the chair opposite. "What do we have here?"

"One box of slides. One notebook. Two storage disks."

"Are the disks encrypted? I need to know for insurance purposes."

"*Ja*—192-bit block cipher."

Simon pointed his pen at the other disks, for some reason knowing he wasn't going to like the answer to his next question. "And those?"

"*Ja.* Encrypted."

"But what—"

"The other delivery," Olin interrupted. "To New York."

Other delivery? Had he zoned-out during their conversation, or was he staring at Pilár Montez and having lustful thoughts when he should have been paying attention to business? "I don't recall you mentioning a drop in New York."

"*Nej?* This would be inconvenient?"

It wasn't, he was going directly home after the La Jolla drop, but it bothered him that he couldn't remember. He was tempted to boot his laptop and listen to the tape. "It's not that—"

Olin interrupted, his voice tight with anxiety. "This is most important. Many people—" He hesitated, searching for the right words. "Lives. How do you say? Affected?"

From the desperate look in the man's eyes, Simon had the feeling *affected*, if anything, was an understatement. "Many lives could be affected?"

Olin nodded, the look in his eyes going from desperate to pleading. "Most affected."

"Okay." What did it matter? His mistake or not, the materials needed to be delivered and he wasn't going to refuse them. "One delivery to La Jolla, one to New York. No problem."

Pär took a deep breath and leaned back, bubbles of relief bursting in his chest. Despite his intense desire to look at the guard, he forced himself to keep his eyes on Leonidovich. The man pulled another transmittal from his case along with two large plastic bags. He filled out the CONTENTS area of the transmittals and slid them across the table. "Fill in the address and sign here." He made a small check mark next to the signature line on the right-hand side of the sheet.

Pär filled in the Bain-Haverland address for the La Jolla package, then signed both sheets and shoved them back. "The New York business, they have been moving recently. I must call back to you their location."

Simon didn't like it, hated accepting anything without full documentation—it was the type of thing that sent custom agents into a frenzy of suspicion. "You can't reach someone now?"

Olin shook his head. "*Nej.* I tried, but the time there is four in the morning."

It was exactly the answer Simon expected, but wondered why the man hadn't called the day before. He didn't seem the type to overlook things. "Can you get me the information before I reach the States?"

The man smiled, a tight, nervous expression that reminded Simon of a baby with gas. "*Ja.* I can reach you on the plane, no?"

"You can e-mail the information." He pulled another business card from his pocket, laid it on the table and pointed to his e-mail address. "We prefer a written record."

Olin nodded, his fingers shaking a bit as he picked up the card. "*Ja.* I understand."

There was something about the situation Simon didn't like, especially Olin's nervousness, yet nothing about the shipment seemed remarkable. Though tempted to question the man further, the more he looked into his sorrowful eyes and thought about that sad little picture hanging from his pocket, the less he wanted to know. He slid the two storage disks into a security pouch, pulled off the safety strip—its control number corresponding to the one on the bag—then quickly folded the flap over onto the quick-drying glue, making it impossible to open without cutting. The clear plastic would usually satisfy the curiosity of paranoid custom agents. He repeated the procedure with the La Jolla package, attached the safety strips to their respective transmittals, signed both sheets, removed the second copy for himself, and extended the originals to Olin.

The guard immediately stepped forward. "I will take those, Doktor."

In that moment Pär thought of many things: his incredible luck to have come so far, to have copied the disks and gotten them past Karl, and then to convince the courier to make an extra drop. Was it possible he could now convince the guard into believing the papers were to be filed in the lab? He glanced over at the watchful, intelligent eyes of Leonidovich and decided not to risk it. The receipts would likely get buried in a mountain of bureaucratic paperwork. "*Ja.* Of course."

The courier lifted his security case onto the table. Though somewhat scarred from wear, it looked exactly like the bags pilots always carried, black rectangular cases with a fold-over top. He placed the security bags inside, closed the top, connected a thin black strap hanging from the handle to his left wrist, then reached down and did something to one of the small rubber feet. "You have a gun, *Ja?*"

Simon shook his head. That was the question everyone asked first. "Nope."

"Why could not someone cut the strap?"

And that was always the second question. "Titanium weave. Be easier to cut off my hand."

A look of confusion flashed across Olin's face, then froze into an expression of genuine astonishment. Simon laughed. "I'd give up the case first."

"Ah. Good for Leonidovich—bad for my documents."

"Don't worry about your package, Herr Olin. This case gets more than a few feet from Papa, it starts to miss me real bad."

Olin stared intently at the case, like Superman struggling to activate his X-ray vision. "This I do not understand."

Simon smiled and stuck out his hand. "Have a nice day, Herr Olin. I'll be expecting that New York address before I reach California."

Contrary to his first impression, Pär suddenly had the feeling his research was in very good hands. *"Ja.* I will send it to you most direct." Now all he needed was to figure out where to send the disks and how to get them back.

CHAPTER FOUR

New York City

Wednesday, 6 November 15:00:52 GMT –0500

Simon glanced down at his watch, more to check the day than the time. The three-day game of Intercontinental Hop and Skip had turned his brain into a fuzz ball.

Wednesday, 3 p.m.

He handed the cabbie a twenty for the sixteen-dollar fare and stepped onto the curb. The cold November air burned across his skin, the distinctive street smell a welcome relief after the stale diet of canned air, giving his brain a needed shot of adrenaline. He took a deep breath and started up the five steps to the front door of his building.

By mutual consent of the tenants—a conglomeration of multinational firms—there was no sign or listing that might encourage walk-in trade or indicate the old brownstone was anything other than a typical New York co-op. Passing his keycard through the reader, he shouldered his way into the lobby, his security case in one hand, his carryall in the other. He started toward the elevator, then reversed course and headed for the stairs, determined to lose five pounds before Thanksgiving.

By the time he reached the third floor and the door to his suite, his face was damp with perspiration. Except for the small, gold nameplate and a twelve-button security pad, there was nothing about the faux-wood steel door to indicate the brightly lit, high-tech offices that lay beyond. He punched in his code and pushed open the door.

Dressed in her normal winter attire—black jeans and colorful ski sweater—Lara was stretched out on the floor beneath the short wing of her L-shaped command center, staring intently into the open side of her computer and mumbling Russian profanities. Either her head mike was turned off, or she was now giving tech advice to one of their Cyrillic clients, something that wouldn't have surprised Simon in the least. "You learn that from Mom?"

She jerked up, banging her head on the thick glass desktop. "Ow! You shit!" For emphasis she repeated the curse in Russian. *"Ti takoyeh dyermo,"* then scrambled to her feet, crossed the room in three quick strides, and enveloped him in a motherly hug. "Thought maybe you got skyjacked."

He kissed her on the forehead, through her coppery bangs, helpless to do more with his hands full and his arms immobilized. "I feel like I was. It's been a long two days."

She pulled the wand of her microphone down beneath her chin and stepped back. "You look like crap."

"Thanks. I appreciate your loving support."

"You know what I mean." She gave him a slow head-to-toe. "You promised to buy some new clothes."

"I will," but knew that he wouldn't. It was all part of his blend-into-the-environment philosophy. Over the years he had learned how to make the subtle but important changes in dress that differentiated a local from a tourist. In his line of work it didn't pay to draw attention to oneself or the things he carried. "Soon."

She shook her head in mock disappointment, knowing better. "I expected you two hours ago. I was worried."

"I can tell. Worried sick."

"I was. Thought maybe you'd run off with some hot flight attendant."

"Never happen."

She gave him a sly look. "Oh?"

"What's that supposed to mean? Oh?"

"Nothing."

He knew better. With Lara *nothing* always meant something, but he was too tired to wheedle the information out of her. He dropped his bag and swung the security case up onto the long arm of her desk, ignoring the flash of irritation that passed through her eyes. An organizational freak, she didn't like anything to disrupt the order of her *Star Wars* command center, a spot from which she could dictate directly into her computer while simultaneously scanning, faxing, e-mailing, and electronically filing documents. Removing the wrist cuff, he sequenced through the unlocking procedure—right latch toward the handle, foot lock one-half turn clockwise, left latch outward—snapped open the case, and handed Lara the plastic pouch. "Throw that in the safe, will you?"

She turned the bag over in her hands, eyeing the disks. "I thought you were going to drop this on the way in."

"Yeah, so did I."

"So . . . ?"

"Supposedly the company moved and the shipper's having problems coming up with an address."

Lara swung the tiny mike up from under her chin, toggled the three-way switch on her belt to COMPUTER, and started across the room, dictating as she went. "Lara says—two, seven, Y, seven, two—open sesame." The grid beneath the under-counter refrigerator slid silently to one side. She toggled her microphone switch to MUTE. "What do you mean, *supposedly?*"

"Something doesn't feel right."

She placed the package in the safe, stepped back, and toggled the switch back to COMPUTER. "Lara says— two, seven, Y, seven, two—clam up." The heavy steel grid moved back to its locked position. "In what way?"

"The guy had two packages. Claimed he mentioned it, but I checked the tape and he hadn't."

"Maybe it was just a language thing."

"Yeah, that's what I thought. Now I'm not so sure."

She wiggled her fingers impatiently, as if to draw the information out faster.

"The guy was nervous as a tick when I picked up the package and sounded worse by the time he called me back. Kept explaining how much trouble he was having getting the address and wanted us to hold the package until he got everything straightened out."

"So? We hold shipments all the time."

"I offered to help him locate the company, but he wouldn't give me a name. Said he thought they might have changed names. Didn't want his package going to the wrong place."

"What's odd about that? That's why people pay your ridiculous fee, so nothing gets into the wrong hands."

"I guess you're right." But he still had doubts and intended to do some checking on his own.

She stared into his eyes, reading his uncertainty. "You're suspicious of everything. No wonder women don't trust you."

"It's my job to be— What the hell's that supposed to mean? Women don't trust me."

She dropped to her knees and stretched out alongside her computer. "Nothing. Forget I said it."

"Don't start with that nothing crap. Spit it out, Sissie."

"I don't have time to discuss your failures with women, Simon, that would take *ho—urs.*" She stretched out the word like a strand of taffy. "And I need to get this new burner installed before I go home."

He reached for her feet, intending to drag her out from beneath the desk, but she saw it coming and pulled her legs into a fetal position. "Get away! I'll tell you tonight." She looked up at him, through the glass desktop. "You are coming? The kids have been waiting two days to give you their presents."

"And my favorite Golden Galliano sponge cake, I hope."

"The cake was delicious. Thank you very much."

"You didn't save me a piece?"

She smiled, the thick glass transmuting her image into a ghoulish grin. "You need to lose weight."

He wasn't about to admit he'd already decided to go on a diet. That was something he had to do on his own, and knew if she jumped on his lose-weight bandwagon he'd leap off the other side. "Sorry, I can't make it tonight." He turned and started toward his office, not wanting her to see his face. "Maybe later this week."

She was out from under the desk and in his path faster than a starving cat after an open can of tuna. "Don't you say that, Boris. Don't you even think it."

It took an effort not to laugh, but he managed. "Hey, I just flew halfway around the world and back, celebrated my fortieth birthday at forty thousand feet with four hundred grouchy, jet-lagged zombies, crossed so many oceans and time zones my body clock thinks I'm a lost pelican, and all I get from you is how overweight and untrustworthy I am. Who needs the abuse?"

She ran to her desk, pulled a small gift-wrapped box from behind her monitor, and ran back. "Happy birthday, Boris Leonidovich Pasternak Simon."

He turned the tiny package over in his hand, intrigued by its hefty weight. "My forgiveness cannot be bought with cheap gifts."

"Cheap! That little goody set me back half-a-week's pay."

He set the box on the desk, knowing she wanted him to open it immediately. "You'll have to do better."

She sighed, giving up the battle. "We had an interesting visitor stop by the other day."

"Ah so. Judging from your previous remarks and that shitty grin, I'm guessing a female-type visitor."

"You got it."

"One of your just-happened-to-be-in-the-neighborhood, she's-perfect-for-you setups, I presume?"

"Nope."

That surprised him. Office visitors were rare and *interesting* female types nonexistent. "A new client?"

"Nope."

"A personal visitor?"

"Yup."

"Will you stop with the monosyllabic crap? Who?"

"A real beauty."

That meant nothing—Lara had a way of judging other women that defied male logic—a lesson he'd learned the hard way. "Define beauty."

"Olive-colored skin and big dark eyes."

"Sounds like E.T."

"Tall and slender."

"You have my attention."

"A Spanish accent."

The possibility hit his tired brain like a jolt of espresso. "Pilár Montez? Iberia Air?"

"Bingo."

He tried to hide his excitement but couldn't. "Really? Why?"

"You must have given her that magic smile."

"Don't give me that magic-smile crap. My smile's no different from anyone else's."

"You just don't get it. It's not just your smile, it's the way you listen. It makes a girl feel special—all warm and fuzzy."

"I'm not interested in warm and fuzzy, I'm looking for hot and passionate."

"That's your problem, Simon, you don't understand

women. When a woman feels warm and fuzzy about a man, that's when she gets all hot and passionate."

"Which is not a subject I care to discuss with my sister. Why'd she come by? Really?"

"Well, despite your dazzling smile, she thought you might be married. Decided to check out your story."

"Figures. I wasn't exactly smooooooth."

"So I heard." She crawled back alongside her computer. "Lucky for you."

"What's that supposed to mean?"

"She hears smooooooth all the time. She liked the fact that you weren't."

"She really liked me?" He sounded like a teenager but couldn't help himself. "You sure?"

"She didn't drop by to meet me, you dummy." Then she smiled, just a little, enough to let him know Pilár had passed the sister test with flying colors.

"Thank you, God."

She cocked an eyebrow. "You don't believe in God."

"I've decided to give Him another chance." *Just kidding, God. Always knew you were there.*

"I'm sure He's ecstatic."

"Should be. I'm a good guy to have on the team." Now all he needed to do was deliver Olin's second shipment, drop a few pounds, and free up some time— just enough to find out what kind of *team* he could make with Señorita Pilár Montez. A tough assignment, but now that he was back in God's gratuitous good graces, it no longer seemed insurmountable. *Nope,* not too tough at all. *Easy breezy.*

CHAPTER FIVE

La Jolla, California

Friday, 8 November 16:51:43 GMT −0800

"Get in here," Haverland ordered, "we've got a problem."

Edgar Tripp gave the intercom a one-finger salute, then slowly pushed himself out of his chair. Despite the command, he took a moment, carefully adjusting his vest before slipping into his Armani suit-coat: a navy-blue worsted with pinstripes, nipped at the waist. There were days, most actually, when he would have preferred chasing ambulances to playing in-house legal lackey to the King of Bain-Haverland. *Seven more weeks*—once the merger with Allen Labs was complete, then he'd tell His Royal Highass exactly where to stick his imperial scepter. He took a deep breath, composing himself for what he suspected was nothing more than his daily dose of irritation, and pulled open the door that separated their offices.

Haverland immediately reached over and snatched up his receiver, cutting off a speakerphone conversation. Typical, Tripp thought. "Get in here quick," then keep me in the dark and feed me shit—the company mushroom. Determined not to show his annoyance, he ambled over to the floor-to-ceiling windows that overlooked the Pacific, one ear cocked toward Haverland and what he was whispering into the phone. The laser fax built into the side of his custom-made rosewood desk was humming out reams of paper, drowning out most of the words, and Tripp gave up the effort.

The sky glowed with streaks of orange and red, the sun hovering over the horizon like a giant neon tangelo. A perfect California sunset, most tourists unaware they were witnessing a pollution light show and filling their lungs with carcinogenic hydrocarbons. Located on the bluffs high above Black's Beach, the Bain-Haverland Research Center commanded a spectacular view of coastline, from La Jolla to Del Mar. An atrocious waste of money, in Tripp's opinion, but nothing less would satisfy the ego of their illustrious leader. Not that King Grayson cared about the view. It was the proximity to their esteemed and world-renowned neighbors—the Scripps Institute of Oceanography and the Salk Institute of Biological Studies—that gave cachet to Haverland's grandiose vision of himself: paragon of science, savior to a world living on the edge of obesity and premature death. Tripp knew better, understood Mira-loss for what it was—a quick fix for the fatties of the world—and a way to get outrageously couldn't-spend-it-in-a-lifetime rich before the next "miracle drug" hit the market.

By the time Haverland slammed down the phone, the huge desk was buried beneath a blizzard of fax paper. "This could be bad." He motioned toward a gray leather chair.

Tripp ignored the imperial wave and lowered himself into the chair opposite. It was a game they played, based on the rules of distrust and mutual disdain. As the only players, they put up with each other out of need: Haverland to fulfill his royal duty as self-promoting company shill, Tripp to clean up the messes and guard the secrets. "Bad how?"

"There may be a problem with Mira-loss."

Tripp felt a sudden chill, as if he'd just walked past the door of an open refrigerator. He nodded, determined not to show his anxiety. "Lay it out."

Fifteen minutes later he knew the worst of it: no *maybe* about it. The research didn't worry him, that would take time to confirm, and might prove wrong—but any *hint* of a problem, real or imagined, would kill the merger. The price of Bain-Haverland stock would plummet, leaving him holding the bag on three million dollars' worth of options he'd secretly parked with a distant relative. His escape money. His fuck-you-Haverland money. He took a deep breath, fighting back the panic. "Is that it?" He knew better; Haverland always held back. "You've told me everything?"

Haverland shuffled through the sheets of fax paper, found the two he was looking for, and shoved them across the desk. Tripp glanced back and forth, comparing the two documents, transmittal copies for two shipments with WorldWide SD. The first listed four items—a box of slides, one notebook, and two Magneto disks—to be transferred from Södertälje to La Jolla. The second listed only two items: two Magneto disks. The address lines below SHIP TO were blank. Having a conversation with Haverland was like shadowboxing, sweaty and time-consuming, with little satisfaction. "So?"

"It looks like Olin made a second set of disks. Shipped them out the same time he sent the packet here."

Jesus, it was like a bad dream coming to life in segments. "Shipped them where?"

Haverland shook his head. "We don't know. Olin doesn't know we're aware of the shipment, and Karl thought it best not to tip him off."

Tripp nodded, trying to think through the options but unable to get past the thought of going broke, his fuck-you money lost, along with the opportunity to escape his subservient life at the foot of King Grayson.

Haverland leaned back in his chair, reading the anxiety on Tripp's face and knowing exactly what the man had done. Another nudge, and he'd do anything to save himself. And in the process, Bain-Haverland. "If those disks end up on the desk of some reporter, it'll look like we were trying to bury the research."

"What good will that do Olin? More likely he'll try to blackmail us."

Typical. Tripp could never understand anyone who didn't try to profit from a situation. Haverland knew better; his conversation with Pär Olin had convinced him of that. "I don't think so." He leaned forward, activating the RECORD button beneath the lip of his desk, and pushed himself to his feet. "We'll have to break the story ourselves."

"What!" Despite his intentions, Tripp couldn't contain himself. "Are you nuts?"

Normally, Haverland would never have let such a comment slide, but in this case it was the one he hoped for and wanted. "What choice do we have?"

"That's not a choice. That's suicide."

"It's not good, I'll grant you that, but we have insurance."

"Forget insurance," Tripp snapped, his voice rising to a womanish pitch. "We're talking about thirty-three million users. Thirty-three million potential claims. Thirty-three million potential *death* claims. Our carrier would file for bankruptcy protection ten minutes after we made the announcement."

Haverland feigned a look of surprise. "But Karl assures me the research is flawed. Our pre-release studies were impeccable. No long-term negative effects."

Tripp remembered things differently: shortcuts taken and reports altered as they rushed to get Miraloss approved. That was the problem with monarchs: they saw everything through the prism of their own self-importance. "Doesn't matter. Every lawyer in the country would give his left nut for a part of this action. Within twenty-four hours we'd have class-action suits in every state."

"But the facts are unconfirmed."

Tripp rolled his eyes. "Facts have nothing to do with it. This is America; anyone can sue anyone."

"But that's crazy." Haverland circled the desk, trying to appear as if he were thinking through the situation for the first time, but staying close enough for the hidden microphone to pick up his voice. "There's risk with any drug. Everyone knows that. Our patients understand that."

Tripp wanted to shout *customers*, not *patients*, but thought better of it. He would need a very large pile of fuck-you money before he dared belittle Haverland's Nobelistic view of himself. "Doesn't matter. The FDA will make us pull Mira-loss off the market pending an investigation."

"Do you have any idea what that would mean?" Haverland shook his head, as if the thought were beyond comprehension. "Without Mira-loss many of our patients would die of heart disease and stroke."

Tripp knew the argument: weight kills, better to take the drug and accept the side effects. For the genuinely obese that might be true, but recent studies had shown that more than fifty percent of Mira-loss customers were considered "normal and healthy" and were using the drug to achieve supermodel thinness, a point His Kingship always avoided.

"We can't let that happen," Haverland continued, his voice rising dramatically, as if addressing a review panel of the FDA. "It's our duty and responsibility to our patients. We can't let them fall victim to the hyperimagination of a well-meaning but delusional man."

"Delusional?"

Haverland bobbed his head emphatically. "Absolutely. Karl told me the poor man recently lost his wife. He's not thinking straight."

Poor man ... What a colossal load of bull. "It doesn't matter if the man is bonkers or his research is full of shit. That's not the problem."

Haverland took a deep breath and dropped back into his chair. "You're right. We need time to prove the study is flawed, and it doesn't look like we'll get it."

Tripp might have objected to the *we* if it wasn't so true. If Bain-Haverland went down, he sank with them. "We'd have time if we got the disks back."

Haverland leaned forward, his finger poised over

the RECORD button, afraid Tripp might mention the merger. "I absolutely refuse to do anything improper."

"Nothing improper about it. The disks belong to Bain-Haverland."

Haverland nodded. "What do you advise?"

"Leave it to me."

Those were the words Haverland had been waiting to hear. If the disks could be recovered quickly, they would have time to prove the validity of Olin's research. If it was wrong—*great*. And on the off chance Olin was right, and Mira-loss did contain some kind of formulaic flaw, they would fix it before anyone realized there was a problem. *No harm, no foul.* "You're the lawyer." He toggled the RECORD switch to OFF.

Tripp tapped his thin, perfectly manicured finger on the WorldWide transmittal. "These people know where the disks went. Finding out should be easy enough. Getting them back—that'll be the trick."

"What do you have in mind?"

"Don't worry about it." *Nobody*, least of all some pissant Swedish scientist, was going to fuck Edgar Tripp out of his fuck-you money. "I'll handle it."

"Don't do anything precipitous."

"I'm not stupid."

Haverland cocked an eyebrow, as if seriously questioning the thought. "Need I remind you of past difficulties."

Past difficulties. The words burned a groove into Tripp's memory, a lightning bolt to his darkest secret, and it was all he could do to control his anger. "That was an accident and you know it."

"An accident!" Haverland shook his head, as though trying to erase the absurdity. "It's not bad enough you were playing fiddle and fondle with a twelve-year-old, you had to go and give the kid drugs."

"I didn't give him drugs and you know it. A couple beers, that was all. I didn't know anything about the drugs until he went into convulsions. How was I to know the little bastard had a weak heart? Give it a rest, that was six years ago."

Haverland shrugged, as if to emphasize that that was hardly the point. "The case is still open, I believe."

"Much to your delight."

"Now, how can you say that? I've protected you."

"Yeah, sure, Grayson, you're a real buddy. Excuse me while I regurgitate."

"You know better than to get smart with me, Edgar."

Yeah, he knew, the *secret file*. One little mistake and the bastard thought he had a legal lackey for life. "Go piss up a rope."

"Now, Edgar, don't be ungrateful. It's better than practicing law from the pedophile ward at San Quentin."

CHAPTER SIX

New York City

Friday, 8 November 20:04:58 GMT –0500

Leaning against his office window, Simon aimed the viewfinder of his digital camera toward a yellow cab three blocks away and touched the autofocus button. Instantly the back end of the taxi ballooned onto the LCD screen. *Nice!* He moved the crosshairs down to the license plate and touched the button again. The plate expanded onto the screen, the numbers as clear as the embossed *SL* on his gold cufflinks. *Very nice!* His birthday gift from Lara, the 12-power lens would add an exciting new dimension to his photography.

Growing impatient, afraid they would miss the opening curtain, he shouted toward the door dividing their offices. "How you doing?"

"Don't rush me," Lara yelled back, her words muffled by the door, "or you'll be going alone!"

Though he knew she was looking forward to the evening—a rare break from the kids—he had learned long ago that any attempt to hurry his headstrong sister would only slow her down. "I wasn't rushing. Just checking."

"An office isn't the most convenient place for a girl to dress and put on makeup."

"Don't blame me. You could have changed at my place."

She cracked the door, apparently tired of shouting. "I don't feel comfortable going into a man's hotel room."

"For God's sake, Sissie, I'm your brother."

"The staff doesn't know that."

"Who cares what they think? And it's not a room, it's a suite. And it's my home."

"It's not a home, Simon. Homes come with kitchens and dining rooms and family rooms."

It was an old argument, one he should have avoided, but couldn't help himself. "You're just jealous. I have two dining rooms, a chef on duty twenty-four hours a day, a laundry, and full-time maid service. You should be so lucky."

"It's not the same."

"You're right—it's better. I'm gone for weeks at a time and I don't have to worry about someone watering my plants or breaking down the door to steal my goodies. What more could a man want?"

"Someone to take out besides his sister."

Ouch. "I tried to reach Pilár. I never heard back."

"Of course not. What self-respecting woman would go out with a man who lives in a hotel?"

"She doesn't know where I live." *Unless you told her.* "And she wouldn't have come by if she wasn't interested." The last came out sounding like a question, and he quickly tried to cover it up. "I haven't seen anyone hanging around your doorstep lately."

The door swung open. "And just look what they're missing."

It had been so long since he'd seen her in anything but jeans and a ski sweater, the transformation momentarily left him speechless. She had pulled her hair back into a sophisticated French twist and covered her long legs in black silk, her slim figure in a flattering black chemise. "Wow, you look hot."

"*Hot* is not an appropriate way to describe your sister, Simon."

Despite her words, he could tell she was pleased by his reaction. "I'd forgotten what a knockout you were."

"Thanks, I'll take that as some kind of bumbling male compliment." Her hazel eyes glinted with amusement. "You don't look so bad yourself."

He shot his cuffs and did a little spin, showing off his tux. "Still fits."

"Right. As long as you don't try to button the coat."

"Give me a break." He resisted mentioning the diet, especially his decision to give Mira-loss a try. Like most naturally thin people, Lara had little compassion for the struggles associated with weight loss. "I'm not that—"

The sharp buzz of the phone interrupted. Simon glanced at his watch. "Don't answer it," but knew that she would. It was part of their mystique: worldwide availability—anytime, anywhere.

Lara snatched up the receiver. "WorldWide SD," and immediately began logging the call on a pad next to his phone. "One moment, please. Let me see if Mr. Leonidovich is available." She punched the HOLD button. "A guy by the name of Edgar Tripp. From Bain-Haverland. Wants to speak"—she rolled her eyes—"to the man in charge."

Simon slid into his chair and quickly spread out the documents he'd downloaded off the Web. His search on Olin had produced only one hit: a newspaper article relating to the death of Inga Olin: survived by two children, Erik and Lena, and her husband, Pär, a twelve-year employee of Gotland Research. The search on Gotland produced almost nothing in English, but there was a library of information on Bain-Haverland: a modestly successful company until the release of Mira-loss, which shot them into the big time and turned their CEO, Dr. Grayson Haverland, into one of America's richest men. The testimonials to the "miracle" of Mira-loss had been enough to convince Simon to give the stuff a try. He reached over and pressed both the SPEAKER and RECORD buttons on his computer inter-link. "This is Simon Leonidovich."

"Yes, Mr. Leonidovich, this is Edgar Tripp from Bain-Haverland. I'm calling about a shipment from one of our subsidiaries. It was picked up Tuesday."

Simon found Tripp's name on the Bain-Haverland profile sheet—Edgar Tripp: corporate attorney, member of the Board—and knew his instincts had been right. Pär Olin was a man in trouble. "Yes, how can I help you?"

"I would just like to confirm the delivery of that shipment."

I would just . . . Something about the casual tone didn't ring true. He decided to play dumb. "What's the name of your subsidiary?"

"Gotland. It's a research lab in Sweden."

"One moment, please." He shuffled loudly through a stack of papers near his phone, as if searching for the file. Lara gave him an admonishing look, clearly thinking his suspicious mind had taken a leap off Reality Mountain. "Yes, here it is. Delivered to your La Jolla office that same afternoon."

The speaker hummed with silence for a long moment before Tripp's voice reverberated back over the line, "Oh, yes, of course. Very prompt. However, it's the other package I'm calling about. The destination on our copy of the transmittal was blank. An inadvertent oversight, I'm sure. I just need to confirm the address and delivery for our records."

Just, again. Why would the company lawyer be involved in something he himself characterized as an *inadvertent oversight?* And why didn't he call Olin for the information? Didn't make sense. "I don't mean to be difficult, Mr. Tripp, but my clients expect confidentiality. I really don't know who you are."

"I work in the bookkeeping department. You know us bean counters"—a low self-deprecating chuckle echoed from the speaker—"need to have all the *i*'s dotted and *t*'s crossed."

Simon pointed to Tripp's title as Lara circled around the desk. Her lips parted in surprise as she read Tripp's corporate profile. "I'm afraid," Simon continued, "that's not quite good enough. Anyone could tell me that."

"You're right," Tripp answered, not sounding the least offended. "Why don't you call me back at our La Jolla office? That way you'll know the call is legitimate."

Simon didn't like it, everything felt wrong—from Pär Olin's initial nervousness to Edgar Tripp's casual tone—but he couldn't think of any legitimate reason not to agree. "Okay."

"You have the number?"

"I do. Your extension?"

Tripp hesitated an instant too long, as if unable to remember his own extension. "One hundred."

Not a number easily forgotten. "I'll call you right back." He disconnected and immediately dialed the Bain-Haverland number. A voice-mail recording answered, and he hit 0 for the operator. "Mr. Ashton, please. Extension one hundred."

There was a momentary pause, the operator obviously searching her list of employees. "I don't believe we have a Mr. Ashton, sir."

"Really? Maybe I got the name wrong. Who's at extension one hundred?"

"Dr. Haverland."

Simon had the sudden feeling he had a bomb locked in his safe; one wrong move and it would explode in his face. "Sorry, I must have written down the wrong number." He clicked off and immediately hit REDIAL. When the recorded message started into its spiel he punched in 100.

"Bookkeeping department. Edgar Tripp here."

"Mr. Tripp, Simon Leonidovich."

"Yes, Simon, thanks for getting right back. I certainly do appreciate your help."

Simon now, like they were a couple of old chums. "I'm not sure I can help you, Mr. Tripp."

"What do you mean?" his voice taking on an edge. "I thought you agreed—"

"I agreed to call back. Whether I can help is another matter."

"I don't understand."

"I can tell you how to get the information. I can't give it to you."

"I don't understand. Why?"

"Because Bain-Haverland was neither the shipper or the consignee." A stretch, but technically true, and for some reason Edgar Tripp didn't sound like a man Simon cared to get on a first-name basis with.

"That's nonsense. We own Gotland Research."

That was exactly the answer Simon expected, and he couldn't wait to hear the answer to his next question. "So why don't you just ask them for the details?"

The line hummed softly, as if Tripp had hit the MUTE button on his phone. Simon leaned toward Lara and whispered, "He's talking to Haverland." She nodded.

A good ten seconds ticked by before Tripp's voice came booming back over the speaker. "That's ridiculous, it's the middle of the night over there! We're a client. There's no logical reason for you to deny us the information."

The more the man pushed, the less inclined Simon was to say anything before he talked to Olin. "I'm sorry, but I assure you my position is both prudent and responsible." He gave Lara a wink. "I'm sure your legal department would agree."

"And I'm sure you won't be doing any more work for Bain-Haverland."

"That's regrettable." Actually he didn't regret it at all, and couldn't resist letting Tripp know it. "If you'd like, *Edgar,* I'd be glad to refer your business to a firm that doesn't take the matter of confidentiality so seriously."

"Fuck you, Leonidovich!"

Lara reached over and pressed the SPEAKER-RECORD buttons on the inter-link as the word DISCONNECT scrolled across the phone's LCD panel. "I don't think Mr. Tripp likes you very much."

"You think? For a while there I thought we were going to be best buds."

"What do you think is on those disks?"

He'd been asking himself the same question all afternoon. "If Haverland's involved, it's important." He stood up, clipped his cellular to the side of his cummerbund, and hit FORWARD on the phone-computer inter-link. "Let's move. We'll miss the curtain."

"You think this guy in Sweden is stealing secrets?"

"Maybe," but he didn't think so. Olin didn't seem the larcenous type. But two things Simon knew with absolute certainty: he had something valuable in his safe, and things were going to get complicated before they got easy.

CHAPTER SEVEN

La Jolla, California

Friday, 8 November 17:12:49 GMT –0800

Haverland tried to control his anger but couldn't keep the sarcasm from his voice. "You handled that well."

Tripp responded with a look sharp enough to slice steel. "That guy's an idiot. He pissed me off."

Haverland had a distinctly different opinion of who the idiot might be. Tripp could usually be counted on to solve the difficult problems—the ones that required legal shortcuts and *special* handling—but his temper had clearly ruined whatever chance they had to shmooze the information out of WorldWide.

Tripp stood up and began to pace, his gaunt, effeminate stature contributing to the impression of restless energy as he moved back and forth across the room. "We could drag his ass into court . . ."

Haverland hiked an eyebrow—that was all they needed, public attention.

". . . but why bother?" Tripp continued, glancing at the transmittal sheet in his right hand. "The researcher—" He scanned the sheet, looking for the name. "Olin. He knows where the disks are. And I still think he's going to try and blackmail us. We'll have to deal with the bastard sooner or later."

The blackmail theory, Haverland suddenly realized, might be of use. Without the disks Olin could be painted as a man who had slipped over the edge: a distraught widower and disgruntled employee, intent on extortion. Faced with that, the threat of it, he wouldn't dare go public. *Not without the disks.* He leaned forward, activating the RECORD button beneath the lip of his desk. "I want Olin on the team."

Tripp stared back across the desk, eyes blank, like a stopped clock. "Team?"

"The verification team." Tripp opened his mouth, but Haverland waved him off. "I know, I know, you think Olin's just trying to blackmail us with bogus research. Maybe you're right, but we have to be sure. We have an obligation to our patients." He saw but ignored Tripp's contemptuous frown. "Besides, Dr. Olin will never accept any contrary result unless he's part of the verification team."

"Let me get this straight. You want to offer this guy a position here in La Jolla?"

"Of course." He turned his head slightly, making sure the microphone would catch every word. "We have nothing to hide. If he's not trying to blackmail us, what else could he want?" He cocked his head, as if giving the question consideration. "A quick verification of his work, that's what. So we'll give it to him. We know there's nothing wrong with Mira-loss. All we have to do is prove it. And if we find some type of anomaly, we'll fix it, that's all. No problem. We'll expedite everything. Should be able to wrap everything up within a few months." He toggled the RECORD switch to OFF and leaned back, pleased with what he'd gotten.

Stunned, Tripp wasn't sure how to respond. In a few months he intended to be on the beach in Rio, drinking piña coladas from the navel of some bronze-skinned cabana boy. "I think it'll take a bit more than that."

"Like what?"

"I'm not sure. We all have a price."

Though Haverland didn't appreciate being heaped into the crucible of human mediocrity, he knew it was true—only the price varied. For the Nobel, he would have handed his soul to the Devil. Tripp had a weakness for young boys. And Olin? What did he want above all else? "We could offer him a substantial raise."

Tripp shook his head, not so much in answer as disbelief. "Right. That and five million bucks in a Swiss account."

"He's not going to say anything before his research is verified."

"Bullshit."

"Not without evidence."

That, Tripp realized, was as close as King Grayson would come to lowering the drawbridge and ordering his knights into battle. "I'll get the disks, you can bet on that."

"How?"

"I know someone." Actually he knew the man only by reputation. "He specializes in lost property. Kids or diamonds. You lose it, he finds it, no questions asked. Once he explains the situation, I'm sure Olin will see the benefits of returning the disks."

Haverland shook his head emphatically, so hard his jowls lagged behind his chin. "I don't want to involve anyone else in this. You handle it."

Like a steaming pile of horseshit, Tripp could smell the trap, and knew better than to step into it. He needed to put a buffer between himself and Olin, just as Haverland was trying to do with him. "I'm a lawyer, I can go after the disks in court . . ."

Haverland scowled. "Not an option."

". . . or negotiate some kind of deal."

"What's wrong with that?"

"Nothing, unless you're right, it's not money he's after."

Of that, Haverland was sure. "Which means?"

"Those disks would be in the hands of the FDA before I could spit two words."

"I see." What he saw was a vision of his fortune and reputation dissolving into thirty-three million lawsuits. "And this I-know-someone can somehow prevent that?"

"Yes."

"I refuse to be involved in anything illegal."

"Nothing illegal about it. Olin stole our property. We can either go to court or exercise the right of self-help. Your call."

"Right of self-help?"

"An injured party, or his representative, acting to enforce their rights outside the legal system."

"That's legal?"

"It's not used much, but it's legal."

"So why isn't it used?" Haverland demanded.

"Lawyers hate it." In truth, most lawyers loved it when people did things on their own, trampling over the rights of everyone involved and getting themselves into even bigger messes. "So they don't advertise the option."

"And this person can be trusted?"

Tripp nodded empathically, though *trusted* was the very last word he would have chosen to describe the man he knew only as Retnuh.

CHAPTER EIGHT

Taormina, Sicily

Saturday, 9 November 16:35:29 GMT +0100

The housekeeper hovered at the step-down leading onto the veranda, hesitant to speak or intrude before being acknowledged. The man with many names, but who thought of himself as Eth Jäger, The Hunter, let the old woman wait, enjoying the last soaring notes of *La Bohème* before pressing the PAUSE button on his remote. "*Parlare,* Maria."

"Will that be all, Patron?" She smiled sheepishly, clearly pleased with her latest effort at English.

"*Sí, grazie,* Maria. That was very good. We will practice more tomorrow."

She nodded and backed away. "Thank you, Signore."

She was a good woman, honest and hardworking, and it pleased Jäger to help, though he couldn't understand why anyone would want to learn another language at such an advanced age and without reason. Not that it surprised him. In his observation most people floundered through life without a blueprint. Nothing could have been more alien to his own personality.

He never did anything without planning or purpose, never acted without premeditation, and never took chances or unnecessary risks. And he never failed.

He waited for the sound of the door and the dead-bolt clicking into place before reactivating the music and turning back to what he considered the best vista on the island. Beneath his feet the land dropped into a steep, green cliff, a vivid tangle of wildflowers and underbrush, all the way to the sea sixty meters below. Just beyond the railing, almost within reach, a single white gull hovered on the warm air currents rising off the water.

He leaned back, savoring the view and the rich flavor of his Fatima, one of only four cigarettes he allowed himself each day. It was his favorite hour: the villa silent except for the hushed aria by Pavarotti, the late-afternoon sun shimmering off the water in multifarious hues of orange and crimson before fading into the shadow of Italian coastline forty kilometers across the strait. Following some ancient weather pattern, a warm, soft breeze swept over the Mediterranean and curled northward into the Ionian, churning tiny whitecaps across the aquamarine sea. Though too high to hear the waves, Jäger could smell the water and feel its rejuvenating effects seeping into his pores. The rude buzz of the phone couldn't have come at a more invasive moment.

For a brief instant he considered letting it go, yet knew that he couldn't, the possibility of an exciting hunt stronger than his addiction for Turkish tobacco. In one quick motion he hit the MUTE button on his remote, cutting off Pavarotti's Rodolfo in mid-lyric, and swiveled toward his laptop. A map of the world popped onto the screen as the computer answered the call and began its trace. The caller would receive a steady and false ring, giving no indication of the connection or the electronic bloodhound that was now sniffing its way back through the maze of circuits and satellites. How Jäger answered, and what language he spoke, would depend on where the transmission originated. The string of dots quickly traced their way from Sicily to Italy, up through western Europe and across the Atlantic to America—a place where they knew him only as Retnuh. Afraid the caller might lose patience before the bloodhound finished its task, Jäger snatched up the extension. "To whom do you wish to speak?" Though he spoke the language reasonably well, he took special care to mask his accent behind a proper British vernacular.

A moment of silence followed, the typical intercontinental delay, before a man's voice echoed back over the line, the tone distorted only slightly by the security scrambler. "I'm trying to reach Mr. Retnuh."

Jäger never took his eyes off the screen and the trace monitor at the bottom, ready to terminate the call at the first indication of a counter-trace. "This is Retnuh. And you are?"

A hesitation beyond the normal satellite delay. "I prefer to handle this anonymously. I don't believe a name should be necessary."

It was a common request, one Jäger never agreed to. To do his job he needed to understand the facts as well as the players, without which mistakes could be made—an unacceptable scenario. "Of course, completely unnecessary," he agreed, not about to give the man time to think, "unless you wish to continue this call beyond the next five seconds. Four—three—two—"

"Tripp! The name's Tripp."

Jäger hoped it was true—the one thing he could not abide was a liar—and this he would know soon enough. "Please continue, Mr. Tripp."

"You were recommended to me."

The dots now extended from New York to Los Angeles and down to San Diego, closing in on their target. "By whom?" He placed a finger on the DISCONNECT, ready to terminate the call should the reference prove unacceptable.

"Jake Cayhill."

It took only a moment for Jäger to pull the name, and the hunt associated with it, from memory. An Iranian millionaire living in California had suddenly decided he no longer appreciated the independent attitudes of his young American wife, and without warning had decamped to Iran with their two infant daughters. Cayhill, a lawyer from Los Angeles, had hired Jäger to find and bring them back, a job he accomplished quickly and efficiently, for a modest fee of $500,000. Everyone, with the exception of the husband, had been satisfied. Unfortunately, that was the way of business, there was always a loser, and the reason Jäger guarded so carefully his own anonymity, lest he become the hunted. Satisfied, at least temporarily, he pulled his finger back from the DISCONNECT. "Continue, please."

"I understand you find things."

"Yes."

"My firm is interested in your services."

Firm, not company. Architects, engineers, and

lawyers used the term. "And what exactly are you looking for?"

"I would like to discuss the fee. I mean—" The man cleared his throat. "What would be normal?"

Americans, they always wanted to discuss price first. "Nothing about my fee is normal." A large bull's-eye with the words TARGET ACQUIRED suddenly bloomed onto the monitor, followed by a telephone number and the name: Bain-Haverland Pharmaceuticals. Jäger highlighted the name and clicked the SEARCH button on his Web toolbar. "The price depends entirely on the value of the property and the difficulty of acquisition."

"It's not really valuable. Some research material was stolen from my company. We want it back. It's that simple."

Jäger knew better—nothing was simple if they needed The Hunter to find it. "Give me details." He listened without comment to Tripp's story, jotting down the important names and information, but concentrating more on the man's tone and voice fluctuation, hunting for what lay buried beneath the words. By the time Tripp finished his tale of the disgruntled employee and the stolen disks, Jäger had scanned the Bain-Haverland material on his screen and identified Tripp as the corporate attorney. "How much time would I have?"

Tripp's response was immediate. "We're out of time."

As expected. Though the assignment sounded easy enough, the lack of preparation would magnify the risk—increasing his fee exponentially to the lack of time. "My fee is payable in advance."

"What if you don't recover the disks?"

"The money will be returned. Less expenses, of course. The price is fifty thousand—"

"Fifty thousand!"

"Pounds sterling."

"That's"—the line hummed softly as Tripp did the math—"almost eighty-five thousand dollars."

"Plus expenses," Jäger reminded him. "Nonnegotiable."

"That's a little steep."

Jäger said nothing, letting the silence speak for him, knowing the next words out of Tripp's mouth would provide the best clue to the disks' value. The sun disappeared behind Mount Etna, the coastline of Italy losing contour as it faded into the blue-gray horizon of sea and sky.

"Okay, fifty-thousand pounds. Half now, half when you deliver the disks."

Americans, they had no style, no sense of fairness. Once he had the disks, he would teach this man a lesson. "You will wire the funds to this account." He dictated slowly the twelve-digit number of his Zurich account. The entire amount, less an 8-percent transaction fee, would automatically and immediately be transferred to a corporate shell in Luxembourg, the ownership hidden behind anonymous bearer bonds, of which he owned 100 percent. "I'll begin work upon confirmation."

"Couldn't you start immediately?"

"No." Of course he could, and would, but he had no intention of letting Tripp know that. "You have chosen not to trust me with the full amount. Do not expect what you will not give." He reached over and pressed the DISCONNECT. The man would think twice before he again dictated terms to Eth Jäger.

He leaned back, considering the two names on his notepad: Pär Olin and Simon Leonidovich. Which was the weaker prey, the one who would lead him to the disks?

CHAPTER NINE

New York City

Monday, 11 November 12:34:46 GMT −0500

Lara dropped the deli bag on the corner of her desk and pulled off her windbreaker. "Brrrr. I hate this time of year. Wish it'd just snow and get it over with."

It was actually warm for November, but in the four years since Jack's death Simon had learned to recognize Lara's preholiday depression and knew better than to argue. He opened the small refrigerator, trying without success not to think about the disks lying in the safe beneath. "What do you want to drink? One of these Cook Island things?"

"Don't give me that face. It's good for you."

"Ugh."

She looped the omnipresent head mike around the back of her neck and opened the bag. "What's with the salad and low-cal dressing? You on some kind of special diet?"

"Nope." Just the normal kind, rabbit food, no wine, and a Mira-loss pill with breakfast. In two days he'd managed to *gain* three pounds. He realized it was probably just some metabolic reaction to his traumatized body clock, and unrealistic to expect instant results, but couldn't help himself. "Wasn't hungry." *Starved* was what he was.

"Don't try and bullshit your sister." She took the salad and her 2000-calorie gut-buster, a corned-beef and kraut sandwich smothered in Russian dressing, and placed them on the small table next to the window. "That salad has Pilár Montez written all over it."

"Don't recognize the name."

"The woman you've been calling night and day since you got back."

"Oh, her." He slid the bottle of Noni juice across the table and sat down.

"Don't pout, Boris, it doesn't become you."

"Yes, Mom."

"Trust me, she'll call."

"Trust you! Ha, this from the woman who set me up with Rita Nincompoop."

"Don't be an ass, Simon. Rita Nitenbaum's a very nice person."

He poured the watery Italian over the top of his salad, feeling less hungry by the drip. "Why do women always substitute the word *nice* for *asexual?*"

"She's not asexual. Rita's a little plain, that's all."

"Can't argue with that. The woman's *plain desperate* is what she is."

"She's not *desperate.*"

"How would you describe someone who rides the subway at night in search of a *meaningful* relationship?"

"That's cruel, Simon, especially from a guy who hasn't *had* a meaningful relationship since—" She waved a hand in the air, as if to ward off a swarm of gnats. "It's been so long I can't even remember her name."

The truth of it, sad though it was, made him laugh. "Me neither. Maybe I should give Rita another shot."

"Forget it, the woman's pathetic."

So often the case with women, especially his sister, Simon felt as if he were on a bungee cord, being jerked first one way and then the other. "Would you kindly make up your mind?"

"I have. Pilár's got my vote."

"You don't get a vote."

She stabbed a huge kosher pickle off the side of her plate and waved it at him. "As long as I know your secrets, I do."

"I don't have secrets."

Her hazel eyes sparkled with mischief. "How about playing *doctor* with Kimmy Kabata?"

"Doesn't count, I was only nine."

"Yeah, but she was fourteen."

Going on twenty. And what a fine memory it was, until Sissie walked in and ruined his first in-depth examination of the female anatomy. "That was strictly a career thing. I was thinking of becoming a gynecologist."

"I'll bet you were." She took a sip of Noni juice, her expression turning serious. "Want some good female advice?"

He wasn't at all sure such a thing existed. "No," but knew that wouldn't stop her.

"Show up at her door with a dozen long-stem roses."

"That's brilliant. She lives in Madrid."

"And what woman could resist a man who flew halfway around the world to give her flowers?"

"She'd think I was some kind of pervert."

"She already knows. I told her about Kimmy."

"I wouldn't be surprised."

"She was very understanding."

A feeling of dread blossomed in the pit of his stomach, like bread dough rising. "You didn't *really* tell her?"

"It came up in conversation."

"And which conversation was that?"

"The one about your sex life."

"Oh, God, give me strength."

"Don't blaspheme, Simon."

"Trust me, that was a prayer."

"Pilár thought it was funny."

His sex life, or getting caught between the legs of Kimmy Kabata with a flashlight? He didn't want to know. "What is it with women and this need to share?" He held up a hand, stopping her before she could answer. "No, don't try to explain, it will only confuse me."

She took a bite of her sandwich and turned to the window. "You could return the disks to Gotland on your way over."

Though she tried to make the suggestion sound spontaneous, he realized she had worked the conversation around to this very point, obviously wanting to get rid of the disks before the company ended up in the middle of some legal confrontation over ownership. A concern he shared. "Who says I'm returning them to Gotland?"

"What else can you do?"

He'd been asking himself the same question for two days. "I could turn them over to Bain-Haverland." He'd already decided against it but wanted to hear her argument.

"But you won't."

"Why not?"

She scrunched up her nose. "Doesn't smell right."

His opinion exactly, though he wasn't sure why. His check of the company had turned up nothing but glowing reports, along with that of its CEO, Grayson Haverland, a respected scientist and administrator, with a reputation for both fairness and honesty. "That's how I'm supposed to run the business? Wait for your nose to twitch yippidy-up or yippidy-down?"

"Female intuition."

"Hard to argue with that logic. Maybe I'll give them back to Pär Olin."

"But you won't."

This was starting to sound familiar. "Why not?"

"Because he's stealing company secrets."

Made sense. Everything pointed to it. So why didn't he believe it? Because of something as nebulous as female intuition—his gut—told him otherwise. And his gut told him Pär Olin was an honest man. "No, I don't think so."

"Wake up and smell the manure, Boris."

"It smells, but I think it's coming from this side of the pond."

"So why hasn't Olin returned your calls?"

"I have this hunch he's not getting my messages."

She cocked an eyebrow. "A hunch? Is that something like female intuition?"

"It's more sophisticated. Female intuition is little more than a guess. A hunch comes from experience."

"Bullshit."

"That, too."

"I don't understand why you believe this Olin character."

Part of it, Simon knew, came from that sad little picture hanging from the man's pocket, the glimmer of loss and unshed tears so typical of Lara and the kids without Jack. But that was not something he could say or explain, and not enough to justify his feelings. No matter how he spun the facts, he couldn't think of any logical and honest reason for Olin to hide the shipment from his own company, the ones who were paying the bills and supposedly owned whatever was on the disks. "I don't like it, Sissie. Nothing feels right."

"So?"

"I'll give Olin until Monday morning. If I don't hear something by then, I'll return them to Gotland."

"Good decision. And deliver some flowers on the way back."

"She's probably flying. I'd never catch her."

"She's off Monday through Wednesday next week."

"Now, how would you know that?"

"I hacked into Iberia and got the flight-attendant's schedule."

"You're a bad girl, Sissie."

"Yup."

"Do I have time? What do we have booked?"

"Just that jewelry thing from Bolivia. No big deal, I could lay it off to Manhattan Express."

He hated referring clients elsewhere, but the thought of seeing Pilár Montez made his heart go giddyup. "What else?"

"Nothing till December. And nothing big until the 'Treasures of the Vatican' move the end of January."

That was the kind of job he lived for: transporting an exhibit of priceless religious artifacts from Rome to the Metropolitan Museum of Art in New York. "Where are we on that?"

"Everything's set. Packers, movers, armored transport, DC-8 cargo plane, insurance—"

"How much?"

"Eighteen million. The Vatican set the value, the Met pays the bill. I had to divide it between four carriers."

"Sounds good."

"I did my part. Now, if you can manage not to lose anything . . ."

"A good altar boy never loses—"

"You haven't attended mass in fifteen years."

"Yeah, but I still remember the first commandment."

"What's that?"

"Thou shalt never under any circumstances piss off the Pope."

"Good rule, but if you give those disks back to Olin, I think it's Grayson Haverland you better be worried about."

"I didn't say I was giving them back to Olin."

"I can read it in your eyes. You like the guy and you're determined to help him."

Women, always thinking they had a handle on the human psyche. Of course she was right, that was the exasperating part. He stabbed a piece of lettuce, avoiding her eyes.

"You do it, Boris, and we're going to end up in one hell of a mess, I can feel it."

"More female intuition, I suppose?"

"Nope. A hunch."

CHAPTER TEN

The village of Grönslätt, south of Södertälje, Sweden

Thursday, 14 November 07:44:38 GMT +0100

Jäger glanced around at the barren trees and nondescript boxlike structures, feeling more conspicuous with each passing minute. The sunrise reflecting off the metal and red-shingled roofs gave the neighborhood a celestial glow, like a *Star Trek* planetscape. Except for his rental, a nondescript Volvo, there wasn't a single car parked on the street. Normally he would have switched to another location before someone noticed an unfamiliar vehicle with a stranger behind the wheel, but the neighborhood was so quiet and motionless any movement would only magnify his presence. He turned his attention back to the small house at the end of the block, waiting for the scientist to show himself.

At 7:50 a gray-haired woman emerged from the house next door. She crossed the brown, frost-burned lawn and entered Olin's front door without knocking. *The grandmother,* the one who cared for the children during the week. In two days he had accumulated quite an extensive file on Dr. Pär Olin: his education, his work, his family. The facts. What he didn't have, and had no time to research, were the intangibles—the stubbornness, the desperation, the hidden courage of the man—and that made Jäger nervous. He felt exposed and underprepared. The hunt had been easy, the trap set, but there had been no time to plan for contingencies. He didn't know Olin, the man, and couldn't anticipate his reaction. It was not the way Jäger preferred to work.

He remembered all too well how messy things had gotten the last time he rushed a job. He chuckled to himself—*very messy*—the fat man from Chicago and his tiny gold coin. It had taken Jäger a month, zigzagging back and forth across South America, before he finally found the blubbery fool hiding in a remote seaside bungalow near São Paulo. Even then, trapped with no way to escape, the man refused to give up his stolen treasure: a Greek daric, worth over a million dollars.

"I earned it." His eyes, like a pair of black marbles set in dough, glinted defiantly. "Thirty-two years I cleaned up after that old fart. His wives and girlfriends, too. Then the bastard replaces me with someone younger. He owes me."

The man's justifications meant nothing to Jäger. He was The Hunter—*find and retrieve*—the reasons did not concern him. "You are most fortunate, I am a reasonable man. The police would not be so understanding. You will now give me the coin."

The fat man shook his head, his jowls sloshing back and forth beneath his chin. "The old bastard has more'n a thousand pieces in his collection. What's the difference one coin more or less?"

Jäger flashed his stiletto. "I will not ask again."

The man hesitated, as if considering his options, then reached in his pocket and retrieved a flat silver case, about the size of a matchbook. He opened it, extracted the coin, stared at it for a long moment, then popped it into his mouth and swallowed. "Fuck you, too."

Such obscene arrogance Jäger could not abide—it was a matter of respect. He stepped close, locked the man's eyes in a rigid stare, and with one smooth stroke ran his knife beneath the fool's huge belly. It took a moment before the man realized anything had happened, then his head dropped and his eyes bulged. "Oh, my God!"

Jäger stepped back, watching as the man struggled desperately to hold back the flood of intestinal snakes that began to crawl through the gaping wound. Within seconds he was sitting in a pool of blood, his insides spread out between his legs. "Please help me." His voice quivered, like a child about to cry. "Call a doctor."

Jäger smiled and shook his head—that was out of the question. He considered putting the sputtering fool out of his misery, but rather enjoyed the spectacle. Retrieving the tiny coin from the stomach of such a blubbery, squirming mass of protoplasm did, of course, make things more difficult—*very messy indeed*—but that was a small price to pay for such entertainment. He hoped Pär Olin would not be so foolish, though the lack of preparation did add an enticing degree of unpredictability and excitement to what seemed to be a simple job.

At precisely 8 A.M. Olin opened the door and stepped out onto the stoop, his blond hair curling over the collar of his overcoat. The old woman filled the doorway behind him, a young girl in her arms, a small boy at her side. Olin turned, gave the girl a kiss, then leaned down and scooped the boy into his arms. Jäger watched the scene through his miniature eight-power scope: a typical see-Papa-off-to-work routine. Typical, except for Grandmamá and the dark shadow of exhaustion that circled the eyes of Olin's otherwise boyish face.

Hoping for some additional clues into the scientist's psyche, Jäger watched carefully as Olin opened his garage, backed his white Saab onto the ash driveway, got out and closed the door, climbed back into his car, and then sat there—one of those people who followed the rules, who took the time to read the owner's manual and abide by the manufacturer's recommendation to "properly warm up your vehicle." It told Jäger much about the man, but led to more questions than answers. There seemed to be nothing remarkable or daring in his personality. Nothing to indicate why he would steal from his company. Perhaps, as Tripp claimed, it was the strain of his wife's death and the financial burdens that followed, but for some reason Jäger didn't believe it. Not that he cared much about the *what-for*s and the *why*s, that was not his job, but he didn't like working with only half the facts—that was dangerous. Without the facts he had no way to judge the risks and rewards. What motivated Olin to steal the disks? How far would he go to keep them? To protect his family?

Uncomfortable with what he didn't know, but not overly concerned, Jäger reached forward and activated the tracking receiver he'd attached to the underside of

Olin's rear bumper. The tiny screen bloomed to life: a red dot identifying the Saab, the digital readout indicating a distance of 120 meters. He waited patiently, until Olin backed out of his driveway and turned the corner at the end of the block before following. He had no reason to stay close, wanting only to track Olin's route between home and work and identify the most remote location along the way. He planned to make his move that evening, when Olin returned home, long after the conveniently early sunset at 3:23. His plan was simple: isolate the man, make him feel exposed and vulnerable, scare him half to death, get the information.

Olin headed north on the main highway leading toward Södertälje, the traffic growing more congested with each passing kilometer. Jäger stayed well back, tracking the route on a map taped to the Volvo's dashboard. After ten minutes they had covered nearly half the distance to the research center, then Olin made an unexpected turn onto an unmarked side road with no traffic. Jäger narrowed the gap to 1200 meters, trying to maintain visual contact without getting too close. After a few kilometers the pavement disintegrated into a hard gravel composite and narrowed severely, cutting northwest across a floodplain, water on one side, marshland on the other.

Surprised by the obscure route, but not wanting to let an opportunity slip by, Jäger closed to within 800 meters. A glance in the mirror confirmed there were no cars approaching from either direction. Without hesitation he reached over and pressed the red button on the remote cutoff switch, temporarily disabling the Saab's ignition.

* * *

It was Pär's favorite stretch of road, the one place he could carry on a conversation with Inga and not have people stare at him like he was some kind of lunatic who talked to himself. Absorbed in telling her of his decision to have Leonidovich deliver the disks to the FDA, he barely noticed when the car began to slow. It was something he did often, getting lost in conversation and forgetting to drive. It wasn't until he stepped on the gas that he realized the engine was dead. He pulled over onto the narrow shoulder, two wheels still on the road, and turned the key, but there was no response, not so much as a click. He didn't notice the black Volvo pull alongside until the driver tapped his horn.

"A problem?" the driver shouted in English.

Olin nodded and rolled down his window. *"Ja. Kaput."*

"Hop in. I'll give you a lift."

"Thank you."

Grateful for the timely rescue, Pär quickly locked his car and climbed into the Volvo. "I am most grateful. This road is not much used."

The man, dressed in black slacks and a dark brown leather jacket, shifted sideways on the seat and smiled, seemingly in no hurry to proceed. "Yes. I was wondering why you took it."

The question struck Pär as odd, as if the man had been thinking about him personally, but assumed it was only a misunderstanding of language. "Not so very much traffic."

The man glanced back and forth down the road. "None."

There was something about the dusky-skinned

stranger that made Pär uncomfortable, his smile and easy manner at odds with his dark, calculating eyes. "*Ja*. Your arrival is most fortunate."

The man smiled again. "I followed you."

Pär felt as if the air had been sucked from his lungs, his heart frozen in mid-beat. "This I do not understand."

"I think you do. Where are the disks?"

Pär tried to look the man in the eye, but couldn't. "I do not know what this question is concerning."

"You insult me with lies." He glanced down the road again, first in one direction, then the other. "You make a complication that is unnecessary. You have something that belongs to someone else. They want it back. You return this property to me. All is forgiven." He motioned with his hand, like a priest bestowing absolution. "No harm done. Life goes on."

Olin knew better; for him, maybe, but not for the thirty-three million users of Mira-loss. And that was not a responsibility he cared to live with. "You do not understand—"

The man sliced his hand through the air, cutting off the words. "I have no interest in explanations. Where are the disks?"

Pär wanted to lie, but knew the dark eyes would catch it, like two cosmic black holes that sucked everything in and let nothing out. "I turned them over to a courier service."

"I warned you—"

"It's true."

"A lie of omission," the man snapped, growing impatient. "I am a reasonable man, Dr. Olin. I will allow that one infraction. Do not disappoint me again. Where are the disks?"

At that moment Pär believed two things: the man was truly evil—and before he did anything, those dark eyes would glance at least once more down the road. He held his breath and waited, the silence hanging between them like a dark cloud of cold air. The man seemed to realize he wasn't going to get anything more and took a deep breath, as if to prepare himself, and glanced back over his shoulder. Pär scrambled from the car and ran, only to realize there was no place to go and not so much as a tree to hide behind.

He ran as hard as he could, expecting at any moment to hear the car swooping down upon him, but he heard nothing, save the pounding of his own feet on the roadbed. He glanced back, could see the man sitting behind the wheel, calmly smoking a cigarette. A few moments later he heard the sound of the engine as the car began to move. He ran harder, measuring his chances in the cold water against sinking into the muck of the marsh. Neither choice offered much hope for escape, and he decided to try and dodge past the car, to get back to his Saab and lock himself in. Maybe it would start. Maybe the man only meant to scare him.

He turned and waited, determined to hold his position as long as possible, then fake one step to the left and dive to the right. The car was nearly on top of him, the engine growling like a primal beast about to strike, and then before he could move, the car swerved to the edge of the road, momentarily freezing him in place. The left fender brushed past his leg, and for a brief instant Pär thought he was safe—the instant before the driver's door popped open, catching him square in the chest. He heard the impact more than felt it, the sound like pencils snapping.

He surfaced into consciousness like a bubble floating up from the deep, the man with the dark eyes hovering over him like Mephistopheles, his breath heavy with the smell of Turkish tobacco.

"You stupid man. Where are the disks?"

Pär shook his head, knowing he was going to die and there was nothing more the man could do to him. A Polaroid suddenly appeared before his face: a picture of Erik and Lena with their Grandmother.

"You would like for me to visit your house?"

Pär understood the threat, and realized the location of the disks no longer mattered, that without instructions Leonidovich would return them to the company. "WorldWide." The effort to speak stabbed at his chest.

The man glared down at him. "Where were they sent?"

Pär gathered his strength, determined to save his children. "The courier is holding them." The sky seemed to grow brighter and he suddenly felt warm all over, as if Inga had taken him into her arms.

CHAPTER ELEVEN

La Jolla, California

Haverland rolled over and snatched up the receiver before the ringing woke his wife. The luminescent numbers on the clock read 1:12, so he expected trouble—another *incident* with his spoiled eighteen-year-old daughter. "Yes."

Edger Tripp's irritating falsetto whispered back over the line. "We need to talk."

The *incident* scenario instantly escalated into *catastrophe.* "Let me get to another phone. Where are you?"

"No. In person."

Haverland hated demands, especially from Tripp, but resisted the temptation to argue. The disks, he had a feeling, had landed on the desk of some reporter. "Where?"

"The office."

It took him only twelve minutes to pull on a sweatsuit and make the short drive. Tripp was waiting, looking as he always did, all prissy and perfect in a three-piece Brooks Brothers' suit. Just the sight of him, and the thought of what he did with his pubescent boyfriends, made Haverland's skin crawl. He dropped into his chair, girding himself for the worst. "Okay, who's got them?"

"Leonidovich."

It took Haverland a moment to remember who Leonidovich was, then another second to adjust his thinking from worst-case scenario to best. "The courier? He still has them?"

Tripp nodded, though he didn't look especially thrilled. "Been holding them all along."

"So what am I missing here? Just demand them back."

Tripp glanced toward the dark windows, avoiding eye contact. "It may not be that simple."

"Why not?"

"These kind of companies are all dot the *i*'s and cross the *t*'s. I doubt he's going to give them up without Olin's approval."

"Screw Olin! He agrees or we have him arrested for theft. Either way we get the disks."

"He's dead."

Haverland felt the words as much as heard them, his momentary elation dissolving quicker than spit in the desert. "How?"

"A car accident. Hit-and-run."

"How do you know this?"

"Retnuh called. He was there."

"There?" Despite his heavy sweatsuit, Haverland felt a chill run through his body. "Saw it or caused it?"

Tripp shifted his attention from the window to his manicured nails. "Didn't ask. Some things you don't want to know."

Haverland recognized lawyer-speak for deniability,

but doubted that would be good enough if Retnuh was picked up by the police. "Where the hell did you find this guy, your favorite fag-and-fondle bar?"

Tripp's head jerked up, his eyes burning with hatred. "I've never met him. Everything was handled over the phone."

Though he tried not to show his relief, Haverland felt his pulse drop back to pre-stroke level. "He's never seen you?"

"No."

"What did you tell him?"

"To get the disks."

"That's all?"

"Of course that's all! What the hell do you think?"

"Can the money be traced?"

Tripp adjusted his tie, nervously fingering the dimple below the knot. "Not a chance."

His words had the hollow ring of wishful thinking, making Haverland all the more nervous. "You'd better be right—it's your butt hanging out there." The words conjured up an ugly vision of Tripp's sexual proclivities, and he regretted them instantly.

The fire in Tripp's eyes intensified. "I didn't tell him to kill the guy!"

"But you think he did?"

Tripp hesitated, then slowly nodded.

Haverland pushed himself out of his chair, needing to move, to think, to consider his options. He was half tempted to go to the police, tell them what he knew and exonerate himself from any crime—except he had no real knowledge of a crime. Why risk his reputation and fortune on a suspicion? He paused at the window, taking in the vista of lights that defined the village of

La Jolla—the ultimate symbol of wealth and success—and knew he'd rather die than give it all up. He closed his eyes and tried to focus. On the positive side, Olin was dead, unable to spread his lies about Mira-loss. On the negative side, he might have talked to colleagues or friends about his study. Talk could lead to questions . . .

Questions to speculation . . .

Speculation to suspicion . . .

Suspicion that would eventually lead to Retnuh. And if they found Retnuh, they would find Tripp. The thought of it made his stomach clench. He needed to break the link, and the link was obvious. "We need those disks."

"Retnuh was on his way to the airport. He assured me he'd have them within twenty-four hours."

"Forget that bozo, I'll get them myself."

"You," Tripp snorted, as if the word gave him a bad taste. "That's not a good move."

"You'd rather end up with another body? Forget that. I'm going to do this myself and I'm going to do it right."

"What makes you think Leonidovich will give you the disks?"

"Because you're going to give me enough legal shit to scare the bejesus out of him. You can fax it to me on the plane."

"He didn't scare when I talked to him."

"Because you sound like a goddamned pussy." He crossed to his desk, ignoring Tripp's angry glare, and snatched up the phone. Having a plane with a travel wardrobe and pilot on call twenty-four hours a day had its advantages. Five minutes later everything was arranged. "Start working on those papers. I want to see a draft within the hour."

Tripp nodded, though he didn't look at all happy about the plan. "What about Retnuh?"

"Call him off."

"What about his money?"

"I thought you paid him?"

"Half. The other half was due when he delivered the disks."

"Well, he's not going to deliver the disks. The last thing we need is to make a payment after Olin ends up dead. How do you think that would look?"

"Retnuh's not going to like it."

"So what? What's he gonna do?"

That was something Tripp didn't want to think about.

CHAPTER TWELVE

New York City

Like a soldier heading into battle, Lara marched into Simon's office and planted herself in front of his desk. He knew what she wanted—to get rid of the disks before WorldWide got caught up in some kind of legal morass—but he was still undecided about what he should do and tried to ignore her. But of course that was hopeless; ignoring his sister was like trying to ignore an irritating fly that kept dive-bombing the end of your nose. "What?"

"It's ten o'clock."

He knew what she meant by that, too, but hated being pushed into something he didn't want to do. "So?"

"You said you'd give him until Monday. It's Monday."

"It's still early."

"Don't play dumb with me, Boris. It's four in the afternoon over there and you know it."

He knew it all right, had thought of little else for the last hour. "Okay, call him."

"What for? I left four messages on Friday and one an hour ago. The operator made it clear she 'had the message.' I say give the damn things back to Gotland and be done with it."

"I told you, I don't think he's getting my messages."

Her brows drew together. "Oh, right. One of your hunches."

"No, not a hunch. Instinct."

"Well then, that's different. I'll call immediately."

He ignored the sarcasm. "Sweden's next door to Russia. Why don't you overwhelm the operator with some of that Slavic Pig Latin you're so good at? Tell her you just *have* to talk to your nephew, Pär Olin. That it's a matter of life and death."

She hesitated, the chance to practice her Russian an obvious temptation. "I hardly think that's necessary."

"Humor me."

She shook her head.

But he knew she would; all it would take was one more nudge: the magic panacea. "Please."

She gave him a good-natured "humph," just to let him know he owed her one, and marched back to her office. He could hear her punching in the long sequence of international numbers, and a minute later jabbering away in a convoluted mishmash of Russian, English, and Swedish. Her tone seemed sincere and convincing, her natural talent for language and dialect impressive. But after a few moments her enthusiasm seemed to abate, her voice going low, without animation, and he suspected the ruse had failed. She disconnected and stepped into the doorway that separated their offices. "You're not going to believe this."

"What?"

"Pär Olin. He was killed this morning."

Though he hardly knew the man, the news hit Simon unexpectedly hard. There was something about him—something good and honest and sad. "How?"

"Car accident. Hit-and-run."

He didn't know why, probably some mindless prejudice against the violent nature of his own country, but a hit-and-run in Sweden seemed oddly out of place. "They get the driver?"

Lara shook her head. "Not yet. Best I could understand, some truck driver came along right after it happened. Apparently the guy panicked when he saw the truck. Jumped in his car and skedaddled."

There were moments, more frequent as he got older, when the evolution of intelligent life seemed to be spiraling in the wrong direction. "God sucks."

Lara frowned, her customary reaction to his ongoing battle with the Deity, but seemed to realize this was not a good time to debate the issue. "Guess that settles who gets the disks."

"Guess so." As much as he would have liked to have known Olin's motivation for taking them, he couldn't think of a legitimate reason not to return the disks to Gotland. "Go ahead and make the reservation."

"What about Spain?"

He shook his head, in no mood to think about romance. "Not this trip."

"Come on, Simon, I know you liked this Olin guy, but there's nothing you can do about it. Accidents happen."

"I feel bad is all. The guy had two kids."

"And was stealing from his company."

He didn't believe it, but knew he'd probably never learn the truth, and didn't have the energy to argue the point. "Stockholm and back. No side trips."

She expelled an exasperated sigh and turned back to her office. "You always let the good ones get away, Boris."

The unexpected visitor not only caught Simon off guard, but forced him to focus on something other than Pär Olin's children and the vagaries of God. Flashing her own inquisitive look of surprise, Lara showed the man into Simon's office. "This is Simon Leonidovich, the courier who handled the Gotland shipment." As agreed, she never mentioned that Simon owned the company, was the *only* courier, or that their relationship was anything other than professional. "Mr. Leonidovich, this is Dr. Grayson Haverland."

Simon stood up, barely able to conceal his surprise. "Doctor."

Haverland extended a huge smile along with a firm handshake. "Mr. Leonidovich, my pleasure." His voice boomed with enthusiasm. "I'm so pleased to make your acquaintance."

Knowing this was the man behind the call from Tripp, Simon was not inclined to accept the Mr. Congeniality act too quickly. Everything about Dr. Grayson Haverland exuded power and wealth, from his ultra-thin Patek Philippe watch to his Italian suit and tightly knotted Johns Hopkins tie—the kind of man who wanted to be recognized and never tired of platitudes. Simon pumped his hand in mock wonderment. "Aren't you the fella who invented that awesome new drug for losing weight?"

Though his eyes sparked with egotistical gleam, Haverland responded with a modest dip of his steel-gray mane. "My company."

Simon glanced over at Lara, repeating the information as if she were deaf. "This here's the guy who invented Miracle Loss."

"How nice."

"Mira-loss," Haverland corrected.

Lara retreated toward her office, letting Simon know with a couple of well-aimed eye darts that she was not impressed with his Okie impersonation. Undeterred, he gestured Haverland toward a chair. "Take a load off."

Haverland laid his black leather folio on the edge of the desk and sat down, his back straight as a Marine at attention. Simon dropped into his own chair with a nonchalant thud. "Been taking your miracle stuff myself." He leaned forward, as if to share a secret, and lowered his voice. "So far I've gained three pounds."

The doctor's tanned face clouded with concern. "Really? When did you first begin the regimen?"

"Four, maybe five days ago."

Haverland smiled knowingly, the perfect you're-going-to-be-fine expression every patient wanted to see. "That's normal. It usually takes a few days for the body to achieve homeostasis."

Simon added the word *pedantic* to his growing list of impressions. Anyone who used the word *homeostasis* to explain a simple metabolic adjustment couldn't be trusted to speak the plain truth. "Homeostasis?"

"Equilibrium. Give it another week, you'll see results."

Simon took a deep breath and released it, exaggerating his relief. "That sure is good news. I was starting to worry." He leaned back in his chair, inwardly preparing himself to hear for the second time about the death of Pär Olin. "Guess you must be here about that shipment from Sweden."

Haverland nodded thoughtfully, a look that clearly stated the affair was far more complicated than Simon could imagine. "Yes. I understand you still have it."

Simon struggled not to show his surprise. That information could only have come from Olin. What was so important about the disks that would motivate one of America's richest men to deal with the matter personally? More puzzling was his failure to mention Olin's death. "Yup, sure do. Been waiting for Mr. Olin to confirm the delivery location."

"I'm afraid that won't be coming."

"Oh?"

"I'm sorry to say Mr. Olin took the disks without authorization. He confessed an hour ago."

From the morgue? This time Simon didn't attempt to hide his surprise. "He stole them?"

"I'm afraid that's correct."

"Well, I'll be . . ." Simon hoped he looked as confused as he felt. "You just never know about people, do you?"

"No, you don't." He shook his head slowly back and forth, as if the matter caused him great disappointment. "He was one of my most trusted employees."

My? Simon had a hard time believing the renowned Dr. Grayson Haverland would be so personally involved with one of his Swedish researchers. "And now he'll be going to jail?"

Haverland hesitated an instant too long before answering. "I'm afraid he will." He squeezed out the words with a deep exhale, like the final *whoosh* of air from a balloon.

Simon nodded, knowing the man was lying through his pearly whites. "So you're here to pick up the shipment?"

"Yes."

"Good, I sure don't want nothin' to do with stolen property."

Haverland seemed to relax, as if the drill sergeant that held him so rigidly at attention had suddenly bellowed: *At ease!* "I'm sure you had no idea."

Simon shook his head emphatically. "No siree. That's something we have to be very careful about in my business."

"I'll bet you do," Haverland responded, his voice lifting in relief. "I never thought of that."

"Course, you could have explained all this over the phone. I'd been glad to deliver the package to your office in California." He gave the man a questioning look, as if worried about payment. "That's what we get paid for."

"And of course you will be paid," Haverland answered quickly. "No reason you shouldn't collect your fee just because I happened to be in New York."

"Oh, you were in the city?"

Haverland nodded. "Just for a couple days."

With each ever-so-casual statement, Simon trusted the man less. "Hope the rain didn't upset your plans."

"Not a bit, it was a pleasant change from California."

That was the second lie Simon was sure of—it hadn't rained a drop. Combined with his other suspicions, it was enough to convince him Haverland shouldn't get the disks. "Of course, I'll still need some kind of documentation before I release the shipment." He didn't doubt for a moment that was exactly what Haverland had in his folio. "You understand. Proof of ownership, something like that."

Haverland smiled, waving off any suggestion of a problem. "Of course I understand. I appreciate the fact you're so careful. It speaks well of your company."

"Your Mr. Tripp didn't think so."

Haverland snorted, as if the mere mention of Tripp's name gave him a bad taste. "I've met the man. Typical bookkeeper, doesn't understand the realities of business."

Simon bobbed his head emphatically, as if he couldn't agree more. *Lie number three.*

Haverland reached over and opened his folio. "I think you'll find everything here. Affidavits from both Bain-Haverland and Gotland Research regarding my position. A power of attorney from each. A copy of Mr. Olin's employment agreement, vesting interest in his work product, intellectual or otherwise, to the company." He rolled his hand in a circular motion. "Etcetera, etcetera." He laid the stack of documents on the desk. "And, of course, a full release for your company, absolving WorldWide of any complicity in the matter."

"Sounds good." Simon shuffled through the stack of papers, trying to appear somewhat overwhelmed by the mass of legal documents. "Sure does look okay to me."

Smiling confidently, Haverland bobbed his head. "I

could tell you were a no-nonsense–type person. If you'll get the disks, I'll sign the documents and we can put this unfortunate matter behind us."

"Great. I'll have them here first thing in the morning."

Haverland leaned forward, as though not sure he'd heard correctly. "Pardon me?"

"Obviously we don't store shipments here." Why that would be obvious he didn't have a clue, but it sounded good. "Like I said, I could have it here first thing in the morning, or if you're heading back to California today I could deliver it there by tomorrow afternoon." He gave the man a big commercial smile. "It's all part of the WorldWide service."

For a moment Haverland hovered on the edge of his chair, like a huge moth stunned by a thousand-watt light, then finally managed to regain his composure. "No. No, I'm actually going to be here until tomorrow. Would nine o'clock be convenient?"

"That'd be great." By nine o'clock he planned to be on a plane to Stockholm.

"What's this about you taking Mira-loss?" Lara snapped the minute Haverland was out the door.

The woman had ears like a bat. "I was just chumming up to the guy."

She shook a finger at him, like a schoolteacher admonishing a disobedient student. "It's not nice to lie to your sister, Boris."

"You're the one who's always telling me I should lose weight. Thought I might give the stuff a shot."

"I don't like the idea of taking drugs to lose weight."

"Of course *you* don't. You weigh a hundred and twenty pounds on a fat day."

"One hundred and twenty pounds!" She leaned forward on his desk, her palms squeaking across the glass. "I do *not* weigh one hundred and twenty pounds."

"Point made. Get off my case."

"We'll discuss it later," she warned, her expression shifting to business mode. "You *are* going to give him the disks?"

"Is Buddha Catholic?"

She shook her head, as if to erase the heresy of his words. "I was afraid of that."

"I caught the guy in at least three lies, Sissie. He didn't say anything about Olin being killed. Actually claimed he confessed an hour ago to stealing the disks." He held up two fingers to emphasize the point. "He told me he'd been in the city all weekend. I know better." He extended a third finger. "And he claimed Tripp was a bookkeeper he barely knew. We know he's the company lawyer and sits on the board. I don't care if the guy is a famous doctor. And I don't care if he's worth a billion dollars. He's nothing but a lying son of a bitch as far as I'm concerned."

Lara uttered a heavy sigh and flopped her arms in resignation. "So what are you going to do?"

"I'm turning the disks over to the Swedish police. Haverland claims they're stolen. If that's true, he'll get them back. If not, the police can deal with him. As of tomorrow it's out of our hands."

"Along with our ten-thousand-dollar fee."

"No sweat. It was only your Christmas bonus."

"Thanks a bunch."

He gave her a big smile. "It's the thought that counts."

"That's a relief. I was thinking of getting you a Z3 Roadster."

"And I appreciate the thought. I'll drive it in my dreams."

"And while you're tooling around in the clouds, who gets to tell Dr. Haverland of this decision?"

"That's why I pay you the big bucks."

"Thanks a heap," she said, flashing a sarcastic happy face. "You told him he could pick them up in the morning."

"No, I didn't."

"You implied."

"He assumed."

"He's going to sue our ass."

"No, he's not. What are his damages? Going to the police is the only safe thing I can do."

"You could turn them over to the police here."

"Haverland would have them back within a day."

"They *do* belong to his company, Simon."

"I'm not so sure about that. But it doesn't matter. Our client is Swedish and that's where I'm taking the damn things."

"We no longer have a client."

Something he was trying hard not to think about, but unable to forget that tiny picture hanging from Olin's pocket. "I still have an obligation."

"Is that the reason?"

"Of course it is." At least that was part of it. That and Olin's claim that many lives could be affected. *Most affected.* "It's the right thing to do." And doing something, he wasn't sure exactly what, for two orphans seemed the right thing to do.

CHAPTER THIRTEEN

New York City

Thursday, 14 November 21:45:26 GMT −0500

From his table in the back corner, Haverland surveyed the dimly lit room, especially the women at the bar. They were dressed remarkably the same: short skirts and sheer tops with push-up bras. He could barely distinguish one from the other through the haze of cigarette smoke. None of them had the innocent look and pubescent body that could still arouse him, but he knew from experience the assortment would change and he'd find someone before the night was over. Feeling omnipotent, knowing he would have the disks by morning, he was tempted to celebrate with a ménage à trois, a fantasy he'd never had the nerve to indulge. Absorbed in the thought, he didn't notice the man in dark slacks and brown leather jacket until he was hovering over the table.

"See anything that makes your tongue hard, Doctor?"

Startled and offended, but more concerned that someone would recognize him in such a seedy place, Haverland tried to bluff. "You must have me confused with someone else."

The man responded with a granite-like stare. "I'm never confused, Doc."

No one ever called him *Doc*, an epithet he hated and never allowed anyone to use—until that moment. In some instinctive way he knew this man was dangerous. He started to rise, but before he could move an inch the man pushed him back into the chair. "Stick around, Doc. We need to talk."

Haverland glanced toward the bar, considered yelling for help, but the thought of causing a scene and having his name end up in the tabloids was not a risk he dared take. "Who are you?"

The man slid into the chair on the opposite side of the small cocktail table. "Retnuh."

Haverland tried to conceal his surprise. "Like I said, you must have—"

The man interrupted, a slight movement of his right hand, a warning. "I do not like people who lie, Doc."

Knowing he needed to establish his authority, Haverland forced himself to return the man's cold stare. "And *I* don't like people who call me Doc."

Retnuh tilted his head, in a kind of mocking amusement. "And what do you think of people who renege on their agreements?"

"I don't know who you are or what you're talking about."

Retnuh leaned forward, his voice low and threatening. "You lie to me again and you will end up like that idiot in Sweden."

Though frightened by the threat and what sounded like an outright admission of murder, Haverland now felt confident the conversation wasn't being recorded. "What do you want?"

"My money. All of it."

There was something about the man's dark eyes and slicked-back hair that Haverland found unnerving—like staring into the face of a cobra about to strike. "You'll get it. You have my word."

"I'm not interested in your word, *Doc*."

"I understand. You found the disks, no reason you should be penalized just because we made other arrangements." The argument, he realized, was exactly the one he'd used to placate the courier.

Retnuh leaned back in his chair, pulled a slim gold case from the inside pocket of his jacket, and snapped it open. "Other arrangements?"

Haverland hesitated, not wanting to say more. "I prefer you not smoke."

Retnuh studied the layer of cigarettes, as if trying to distinguish one from the other, made his selection and snapped the case shut. With methodical precision, he gave the cigarette two sharp taps on the case, slipped it between his lips, pulled a gold lighter from his pocket, and with a deep and satisfying breath, filled his lungs with smoke. The pungent odor of Turkish tobacco wafted through the air. "What arrangements?"

Haverland watched the smoke curl slowly out of the man's nostrils, masking his face in a ghoulish haze, and gave up the thought of resisting. "I'm to pick them up in the morning."

"From Leonidovich?"

"Yes."

"That's unfortunate."

A bewildered frown furrowed across Haverland's tan forehead. "I don't understand."

How, Jäger wondered, could such a stupid man be

worth a billion dollars? Not to relieve him of at least a million would be unforgivable. "Leonidovich"—Jäger glanced at his watch—"will be on a plane to Stockholm in exactly twelve minutes."

"But—" Haverland's mouth opened and closed, like a parrot struggling to learn words. "But he agreed."

"This I doubt. Simon Leonidovich is not a man to lie."

Haverland thought back, replaying the conversation in his mind. It was true, he hadn't specifically promised to hand them over, not in so many words, but doubted Leonidovich was smart enough to intend such a deception. "I don't believe you."

Jäger decided to let the remark slide—not indefinitely, but for the moment. "Believe what you will." He dropped his cigarette into Haverland's untouched drink and pushed himself up from the table. "This is no longer a matter of my concern. I will expect the remainder of the money to be in my account by noon tomorrow."

"Wait!" Haverland motioned toward the chair. "Please. One more minute."

With a show of impatience, Jäger allowed himself to be coaxed back. "One minute." He knew it would take at least five.

Haverland leaned forward, his voice frantic. "What do you mean, wouldn't lie? You know the man?"

"He has a reputation."

"He works for a courier service, for God's sake! What kind of reputation is that?"

The man was a bigger fool than Jäger imagined. "He doesn't work for anyone. He owns the company."

Haverland blinked and sat back, like someone had

snapped a flashbulb in his face. "That backwoods hick owns the company? He didn't mention that."

"Of course not." Jäger shook his head, trying to make the man feel stupid and out of his depth. "But I'm sure you did. The famous Dr. Grayson Haverland arriving to pick up a package. You don't suppose that made him suspicious?"

Haverland glared back, his face pale with suppressed anger. "I get the point. But it doesn't explain why he's taking the disks to Sweden."

"I don't concern myself with why."

"But you have an idea?"

In truth he had half a dozen, one no better than the other, but chose the one that would scare Haverland the most and stated it as fact. "The researcher gave Leonidovich an alternate delivery location in case something happened to him. That's where he's taking them."

"But I didn't tell him Olin was dead. I told him the disks were stolen."

"That was foolish. You should have told him the truth."

"The truth!" Haverland could barely contain his anger, that a cold-blooded killer would lecture him about the truth. "The truth would put you in the electric chair."

Jäger feigned a look of surprise. "Really? If you believe such a thing, why not go to the police?" The man's silence only confirmed what Jäger already suspected: the disks were far more valuable than the life of one insignificant researcher. Exactly how valuable, he intended to find out. "The truth *is*, Herr Olin was killed in a motorcar accident. Some"—he hesitated, searching for the word in English—*"insignificante?"*

"Insignificant?"

"Sí. Some insignificant person from your company should have been sent to pick up the shipment. And that is your truth."

Though Haverland didn't believe Retnuh's proclamation of innocence, he realized that's exactly what he should have done. "It wasn't that simple," but he couldn't remember exactly why. "Could you still get them?"

Though he had a plan to do exactly that, Jäger hesitated for effect. "Yes, but it would not be easy. Leonidovich knows something is wrong."

"There's nothing wrong," Haverland snapped. "The property is ours."

Jäger leaned forward, keeping his voice low. "I do not care if you're selling nerve gas to Saddam Hussein. You pay. I deliver."

Haverland snorted softly. "Funny, that's what I thought the courier was supposed to do."

Jäger smiled to himself, amused at the irony. "Yes, we are not so different, he and I."

"You're more expensive."

Americanos, always the money. "I'm better."

"How much?"

Always the money. Always they wanted him to clean up their messes, do their dirty work, and then always they would try to cheat him out of his fair compensation. *Not this time.* "One million pounds. In advance."

"That's ridiculous."

"Yes."

"For something I could have had for fifty?"

"Yes."

Oddly, Haverland found the audacious demand somewhat comforting. Retnuh was the type who recognized a weakness and capitalized on it, a natural predator who would hunt down his victim for the pure pleasure of the kill. The million, of course, was easy—a bargain when compared to the potential loss. "Okay." A flash of triumph flickered through the peregrine eyes. "Half up front. The rest when you deliver the disks."

Either Haverland was not the fool he thought, or the disks were far more valuable than Jäger ever imagined. "So you think I would take your money and run?"

"It occurred to me."

Jäger pulled a card from the inside pocket of his jacket and slid it across the table. "Wire the money to this account."

Haverland nodded, noticing for the first time that Retnuh wore latex gloves that matched his skin tone. His caution, as well as his intentions when he walked into the place, were both encouraging and frightening.

"And file a report with the Swedish authorities that the disks were discovered missing when the researcher's files were . . . how do you say, *inventario?*"

"Inventoried?"

"Yes. Inventoried."

"Why would I want to do that?"

"A precaution. Should Leonidovich change his mind and decide to turn them over to the police."

"But they would want to know what's on them."

"They are encrypted, no?"

"Of course."

"So tell a nice story."

"Should I say they were stolen?"

"Absolutely not. But imply that something smells like the fish."

"You mean fishy?"

"Yes, this is what I said." Retnuh pushed himself up from the table. "You will have your disks."

At that moment Haverland would have bet his life on it. In contrast, he wouldn't have bet a nickel on the life expectancy of Simon Leonidovich.

CHAPTER FOURTEEN

Over the Atlantic Ocean

Friday, 15 November 16:57:16 GMT +0000

The flight steward smiled, the effort somewhat strained after thirteen hours in the air. "Would either of you like a snack?"

Simon shook his head. The woman in the aisle seat nodded enthusiastically, though she could easily have dropped two hundred pounds before needing a meal. "Is there a choice?"

"A fruit bowl or a sandwich tray. Each comes with a cup of lobster bisque."

The woman hesitated, as if struggling to make up her mind.

The steward cocked his head thoughtfully, as if her little maneuver hadn't been repeated half a dozen times since leaving New York. "Why don't I bring you both? That way you could sample a bit of each."

The woman's face lit up like a Japanese lantern, as if the suggestion came as a total surprise. "How sweet of you. That would be lovely."

The steward shifted his attention to Simon. "Nothing at all, sir?"

"Another bottle of Pellegrino would be great."

The steward nodded and moved down the aisle. Simon quickly turned back to his book of word puzzles, a hobby that helped pass the time on long flights, but the woman already had him in her sights. "Another bottle of water! I've never heard of such a diet. You'll be too weak to get off the plane."

He opened his mouth, ready to explain that it had nothing to do with diet, that it was just part of his jet-lag routine—no alcohol, no caffeine, lots of water—but she was already blabbering on about the "importance of good nutrition," a concept completely alien to her physiology, and he knew she wouldn't stop until the *snack* arrived. Just as he was getting back into the rhythm of nod and grunt, the phone on the seatback in front of him emitted a soft buzz. *Thank you, God.*

Of course, he knew God wouldn't save his irreverent ass from anything, so it had to be Lara, the only mortal soul who had his seat assignment. The only surprise was that she hadn't called sooner. He glanced down at his watch, 11 A.M. in New York, and snatched up the receiver. "*God Morgen*, Sissie."

There was a slight delay, the time it took for his voice to do the hop, skip, and satellite jump to New York, and for her response to somehow find its way back to his seat thirty thousand feet above western Europe. "There's nothing good about it."

"I take it the renowned Dr. Haverland didn't appreciate the news."

"Never showed."

That was not at all what he expected to hear. From the corner of his eye he could see the Snack Queen listening intently, making no attempt to hide her interest. He shifted the phone to his other ear, blocking her view of his mouth, and leaned toward the window. "I'm shocked."

"Then hang on to your shorts, Boris, you haven't heard the good part."

He had the feeling "good" meant "bad," the way teenagers always reversed the terminology. "I'm listening." He emphasized the word, hoping his seat mate would get the idea.

"Some other guy showed up. A Mr. Smith. Claimed to represent the company, but he didn't have a business card or anything."

"I take it you didn't believe him."

"I sure as hell don't think his name was Smith. He looked Bedouin: light-brown skin, dark features, late thirties or early forties, short hair, though he didn't have any accent I could identify. Actually kind of handsome, but there was something about him I didn't like."

"Something he said?"

"No, he was polite enough. Something about his eyes. The guy had evil eyes."

Simon turned to the Snack Queen, hoping to divert her attention with a pointed look, but she simply smiled back, as if waiting for him to finish so she could continue her discourse on the doctrine of diet. "You've just described half the lawyers in Manhattan."

"This guy was no lawyer."

"Evil eyes and he claimed to represent Bain-Haverland. Sounds like a lawyer to me."

"I don't think so. But he knew about the disks, that's for sure. Even knew you were on your way to

Stockholm. Insisted I page you the minute your plane touched down."

Though he realized anyone with good computer skills could track his reservation, the eerie music from *The Twilight Zone* began to echo through his head. Why would anyone be monitoring his movements? "Sure you didn't inadvertently mention it?" But he knew better, and knew her response even before it came snapping back.

"What do you think, *Boris*?"

"I think it was a stupid question. Anything else?" He knew the answer to that, too.

"I haven't even gotten to the fun part."

If *good* was *bad*, he had a feeling *fun* was going to be a real kick in the balls. "I'm listening."

"About ten minutes after Smith showed up, I got a call from the Swedish police. Seems the disks *were* taken without authorization from the company."

He wasn't totally surprised, but still believed Olin must have had good reason for what he did. "You don't have to sound so damn happy about it."

"Modesty prevents me from saying, I told you so!"

"Your restraint's appreciated, Sissie." The steward slid two plates onto the tray of the Snack Queen, diverting her attention. Simon shifted a little more toward the window, keeping his voice as low as possible. "So what did the police have to say?"

"In so many words, they'd like to have a *chat* with you."

"See how well that worked out? I show up, we have our little chat, I give them the disks, everyone's happy."

"Not exactly."

"What do you mean by that?"

"Smith made it clear *he* wants the disks. Says the company would prefer to 'handle the matter discreetly.' That they don't want to sully the reputation of their beloved and now very dead employee, Pär Olin."

"Very thoughtful. I don't believe a word of it."

"That's where he lost me. I didn't buy that benevolent bullshit for a minute."

"So what'd you tell him?"

"Before I could say anything, two of New York's finest showed up."

"Uh-oh."

"Yup. They asked to speak with me privately, and Smith couldn't have been more obliging in excusing himself."

"He scrammed?"

"Like the Road Runner in overdrive."

"And the cops?"

"Seems they got a call from the Swedish authorities about the missing disks. It's obvious they think you're involved in some kind of industrial smuggling."

That didn't surprise him. The police and customs officials always thought couriers were involved in smuggling. "Don't worry about it. I'm sure it'll be okay once I explain everything to the police in Stockholm." But despite his own words, he suddenly felt that invisible and cherished lifeline of American citizenship being stretched to the limit.

"I wouldn't be too sure about that. You haven't heard the best part."

Uh-oh. If *good* was *bad* and *fun* was a dropkick to the scrotum, he didn't want to consider how disagreeable *best* was going to be. "I can't wait."

"I got suspicious after Smith became so adamant about *not* turning the disks over to the police. Decided to do a little investigating."

"What do you mean by that?"

"You'll love this. I called the police in Stockholm and insisted on speaking to the detective in charge of finding the terrible person who ran over my dear Swedish cousin, Pär Olin."

"The Russian niece strikes again?"

"You got it."

"Very clever."

"I thought you'd approve."

"So?"

"Seems the police are interested in more than a couple of missing computer disks."

"What do you mean?"

"They think Olin was murdered."

The word *murdered* echoed from one side of his brain to the other. He glanced toward the Snack Queen, afraid that somehow the word had escaped the confines of his cranial cavity and burst through his ear canal. Seemingly unashamed at her obvious eavesdropping, she smiled at him through an open mouthful of mixed fruit.

"You hear me, Simon?"

He tried to return the smile as he struggled with the thought of murder and the ramifications attached to it. "Yeah, I heard. Why do they think that?"

"They found some radio-controlled gizmo on his car that cut off the ignition. They think someone purposely disabled the car, ran him down, then didn't have time to remove it when a farm truck happened by."

"Why do they want to question me about that? I wasn't in Sweden when it happened." But the answer was obvious, the police thought the murder had something to do with the disks, and if he had the disks . . .

"You really need me to answer that?"

"No. I'm sure I can straighten things out when I talk to them." But he didn't feel nearly as confident as he tried to sound. It was never easy to explain something to people who spoke another language. He could almost see their disbelieving eyes as he tried to justify why he accepted a package without a destination address, something he had never done before. It didn't take much of an imagination to see himself in a Swedish jail.

Lara's voice interrupted the nightmare. "I'm sure they have your name in the computer by now. I have a feeling you're not going to make it through customs."

"You're probably right."

"Want me to find a lawyer?"

"You'd better. No. That would only make them think I had something to hide. I think it would be—" A soft buzz echoed over the line, the familiar sound of the door buzzer, and he could almost see Lara turning to the small security monitor located above her desk.

"Aw, shit, it's that Smith character again."

"Don't let him in." He tried to speak calmly but could hear the panic in his voice.

"I can handle this joker. Maybe I can find something out. You call me the minute you know what's going on."

"No, don't—" but she had already disconnected. He wanted to call her back but knew she'd accuse him of being overprotective. He kept the phone to his ear, needing to think, and not wanting to face his seat mate and what he feared would be a barrage of questions. He continued the one-sided conversation for another ten minutes, easing it around to a casual brother-sister chat, until the steward began to clear away the plates, diverting the woman's attention.

"Anything else, ma'am?"

She held up a pudgy hand, her index finger and thumb about an inch apart. "Perhaps one little slice of cheesecake."

"Of course."

"And a little sherbet to cleanse the palate."

The young man's nonjudgmental expression never wavered. "Orange or pineapple?"

Her brow furrowed in distress. "Oh, dear."

"Why not a bit of each? They're both very good."

"What a splendid suggestion."

He turned to Simon. "And you, sir? Another bottle of Pellegrino?"

"No, thanks." What he needed was a parachute. In less than two hours they'd be in Stockholm, and he had this very ugly feeling he wouldn't be leaving the country anytime soon. "Do you know if we'll be arriving on schedule?"

"We're running about ten minutes late. But I'm sure they'll make it up on the ground if you're continuing on to Oslo."

"I thought this flight terminated in Stockholm."

"Technically it does. But the plane continues on to Oslo under a different flight number. About a third of our passengers continue on."

"Really? You wouldn't happen to know if the flight is full?"

"It usually is. A lot of businesspeople travel back and forth between the two cities, but we never know for sure until we land."

"Thanks." Before the Snack Queen could open her mouth Simon had his laptop open and his modem cord plugged into the phone. *A first,* if he could pull it off—making reservations to stay on the same plane he was already on.

CHAPTER FIFTEEN

Oslo, Norway

Friday, 15 November 20:50:45 GMT +0100

Stepping off the plane in Oslo, Simon felt a combination of guilt and relief, like an innocent man who had just broken out of jail: guilty for not facing the charges, but relieved not to be locked up in some cold and dreary cell. Not that he had any knowledge of the Swedish penal system, but in his mind all cells were cold and dark and he had no desire to test the supposition.

Unsure whether Interpol had him on some kind of hold-for-questioning list, or if such a thing even existed, he adopted his customary bored business-traveler demeanor and buried his nose in a paperback as the crowd of passengers pushed and jostled their way toward Customs. He knew most of the agents and cameras concentrated on nervous travelers "down the line." Appear anxious and they would analyze, scrutinize, and paralyze any chance you had to make it through without being searched. Act like you had nothing better to do than hang around four-hundred stinky and travel-weary strangers, and they would pass you through the inspection area fast enough to burn the soles off your shoes.

Slowly, not looking up from his book, Simon edged his way toward what looked to be the most bored-with-it-all inspector. The man didn't even bother to look up until Simon pushed his passport across the pulpit-type counter. He leaned forward on one elbow, as if happy to rest and chat. He considered a friendly "Howdy," but decided that would be carrying Americana a little too far, and settled on, "How's it going?"

The agent fanned through the tiny pages with all its attachments and stamps. "And for what is the purpose of your visit to Norway, please? Holiday or business?" Though accented, his English was clear and to the point.

Since "flight from prosecution" wasn't one of the choices offered, Simon avoided the question. "I work for an international delivery service." He held his breath as the agent began tapping his keyboard.

The man studied his monitor a moment. "You are coming here to pick something up"—he looked up, making eye contact for the first time—"or to make a delivery?"

Needing to avoid that question, too, and knowing the man would get to the package eventually, Simon pulled the plastic pouch from his security case and held it up. "Already made the pickup. Two computer disks."

The agent leaned forward, reading the pickup time, and nodded, as if the time between Sweden and

Norway made perfect sense, which it did, if you failed to notice the ten-day lapse in between. He picked up his rubber stamp and with a well-aimed punch centered it over one of the passport's small squares. "Enjoy your time in Norway." He spoke without inflection, his words as inviting as the sound of a running toilet.

Simon nodded, slipped the pouch back into his case, picked up his passport, and headed toward the SAS Executive Club, a facility he'd used on numerous stopovers, and the most convenient place to check his e-mail and use a phone.

It was 9:15 local time, the club nearly empty, most of the international flights having departed earlier in the evening. The decor was typical of flight clubs around the world: the carpet plush gray, a shade lighter than the walls, the furniture all glass and chrome and leather. A hostess—one of three, blue-eyed, blond, long-legged Scandinavian beauties—directed him toward a semiprivate corner with a phone and modem jack. Less than two minutes later he had his laptop connected, booted, and was downloading his messages. There were three: a where-are-you note from a member of his tech-chat group, his Tip-of-the-Day from *PCMag*, and one from Lara. He ignored the first two.

Subject: **Shhhhh**
   Date: **Friday, 15 November 2002 13:11:42 EST**
   From: **Lara Quinn <LaraQ@WorldwideSD.com>**
     To: **Simon Leonidovich <SimonL@WorldwideSd.com>**

Tracked your reservation change. Hope you made it to Oslo.

Smith is HERE waiting for your call. He seems nice enough (likes me I think), but he gives me the creeps and I don't want to see his reaction if you refuse to give him the disks. So, unless you've decided to do exactly that, DON'T call. He'll eventually assume the Swedish police have you and leave.

Call me LATER, once you decide what you're going to do.

Пока...........L

He had no idea what he was going to do, but he didn't like her being alone with a stranger and was tempted to call anyway. He sat back, trying to work it through his exhausted mind, but the more he tried to reason through the facts, the more confusing everything became. Why didn't Haverland show at the office? But why not, he could easily have been called back to California? The possible reasons were endless, along with the number of

Smith types to do his bidding. And why shouldn't he want his property back? No reasonable businessman would want his research tied up in a police investigation. The possibility that a man like Haverland, with his international reputation and billion-dollar bank account, would be involved in anything criminal seemed foolishly remote. In fact, the more Simon considered it, the more likely it appeared Lara might be right: Olin had been selling, or trying to sell, research secrets to a competitor. Maybe he changed his mind, tried to back out of his deal, and got himself killed in the process. *Made sense.*

So why didn't he believe it? As he tried to reason through the question, one of the hostesses wheeled a chrome and glass cart alongside the table. *"Goddag."*

He tried to remember an appropriate Norwegian reply, something he'd said a hundred times, but his brain felt like a gelatinous glob of overcooked oatmeal and the best he could manage was "Good evening."

She responded in English, her voice breathy and soft, as if she'd learned the language from watching Marilyn Monroe movies. "May I fix you a drink?"

He stared at the cut-glass decanters, the assortment of dark liqueurs and amber liquors, unable to make up his mind. It was a look she seemed familiar with. "Coffee, perhaps?"

That only seemed to complicate the problem. It had been over thirty hours since he'd last seen a bed, and if he ever hoped to figure out exactly what kind of mess he was in, and how to get out of it, he needed to sleep. "What I really need is a place to stay."

She smiled and glanced around, her voice dropping to an even throatier purr. "What exactly would you require?"

Was he hallucinating, or was this blond Amazon making an offer? If so, it was going to be a tragic waste of Scandinavian beauty. He not only lacked the strength, but had secretly pledged his foolish little romantic heart to one Pilár Montez, at least until she answered his e-mail. *Or not.* He pretended to miss the invitation. "How do you say here? *Pensión?*"

She nodded, showing no reaction to his rejection of her might-have-been offer. *"Vandrehjem."*

"Yes. Something nice. Close to the airport."

"Of course. You would like for me to make the reservation?"

"Please." Like any hotel concierge, it was a service most flight-club hostesses were happy to provide. He reached over and laid a twenty-dollar bill on the cart: ten for the service, ten for the fantasy of her company.

She flashed a knowing smile, appreciating the gesture. "How many nights?"

Another question he had no answer for. "Just tonight." But he didn't believe that, either. Without Olin to verify his story, he didn't dare return to the States with the disks. The week-old pickup date and the lack of a SHIP TO would only make him appear guilty of . . . ? Of what, exactly?

Holding stolen property?

Industrial espionage?

Accomplice to murder? The thought was almost beyond comprehension.

Almost.

CHAPTER SIXTEEN

New York City

Friday, 15 November 16:00:22 GMT –0500

Jäger glanced at his watch—4 P.M.—and added six hours. 10 P.M. in Sweden. Something had obviously gone wrong, he would have heard from his contact in Stockholm if the police had Leonidovich. Or the disks. He leaned back in his chair and scanned the street below, not wanting to be caught unaware by another impromptu visit from the police. Satisfied, he shifted his attention back to Lara Quinn, who continued to work at her computer. She seemed completely absorbed in what she was doing, as if unconcerned by his presence. The tension in her neck and shoulders told a different story.

He stood up, moving slowly as if to stretch his muscles. As expected, the woman's left hand slipped off the keyboard and into her lap, a few inches from the panic button located beneath the edge of her desk. Jäger smiled to himself, amused that the unexpected interruption from the police had given him the opportunity to locate and neutralize the security system. "Ms. Quinn."

She swiveled around, staring back into his eyes with unflinching boldness. "*Mrs.* Quinn."

That surprised him. Judging from the sequence of photos on her desk and the age of her children, the husband had disappeared from her life years before. "My pardon. I did not realize you were married."

"Widowed." She said it without bitterness or self-pity, simply a fact to be clarified.

He shook his head, hoping to appear sympathetic. In truth, he found her defiant, high-spirited attitude sexually arousing. Dressed in black jeans and a black ski sweater with a pattern of red and gray diamonds across the chest, she looked more like a model than a secretary. *Such a waste.* "Should not your Mr. Leonidovich have called by now?"

She shrugged, the gesture a little too nonchalant. "Not really. Not when he's out of the country."

Jäger knew better. Leonidovich had a reputation for unqualified reliability—his business depended on it. "Is this so?"

She nodded. "Sometimes I won't hear from him for a day or two."

Now he was certain she knew something. He looped the strap of his black nylon briefcase over his shoulder. "I would check back tomorrow, if this would be convenient?"

"Of course."

Though she tried to hide it, he read the relief in her eyes and knew she would never open the door to him again. He hated the additional complication, could tell she was not the type to give up anything without a fight, and had a feeling things were going to end up messy. Then he would have to kill her, another complication he preferred to avoid. But never before had he been given the opportunity to make a million pounds, an amount he expected to parlay into much more once he had the disks. Not a time to leave loose ends. "If I could use your facilities . . . ?" She hesitated and he gave her a tight smile, as if embarrassed at the urgency of his request. "I would be most grateful."

She nodded toward a door behind him. "Right there."

"Thank you."

Lara was certain her imagination had simply run amuck, but when Smith took his briefcase into the bathroom she began to question her judgment. The rational part of her brain insisted she was overreacting, but that ancient part of her brain still related to the lower animal species sensed danger. Not once in three years, since Simon first insisted she keep the tiny .25-caliber Beretta in her desk, had she touched the thing. It was an issue they squabbled about for weeks, and one argument she was now glad to have lost. Hiding the gun between her legs, she placed a small compact on top of the monitor and angled the mirror back toward the bathroom door. Whichever part of her psyche proved more reliable, she intended to be ready.

Jäger moved quickly, unsure what the woman might do once he was out of the room. It took him less than a minute to assemble the .22-caliber automatic from the innocuous pieces hidden among the contents of his bag. Though small, the gun was both deadly and lightweight, a rubber nipple over the muzzle enough to suppress all but the slightest sound. Most important, its plastic-composite parts allowed him to pass through airport security without detection. Ready, he pulled on a pair of skin-tone latex gloves and flushed the toilet. A rush of adrenaline, as powerful as heroin, burned through his veins. He slipped the gun into the side panel of his briefcase and opened the door.

The moment Lara saw the door move she pressed the silent alarm. If Smith left immediately—no harm, no embarrassment. But should her primal instincts prove reliable, cops would be swarming all over the place within five minutes. Smith stepped into the room, paused for a moment to adjust the strap of his briefcase, then started toward the door, his path taking him within a few feet of her chair. She swiveled around, ready to pull the gun when he smiled and stuck out his hand. "Your kindness is much appreciated. I hope my presence was not too much of an inconvenience."

Lara hesitated, then realized she was acting both foolish and rude and extended her hand. Not until she touched the man's fingers did she notice the gloves, and by then it was too late. She grabbed for the gun with her left hand, but he yanked her upright, the Beretta falling harmlessly between her feet.

"Mrs. Quinn, I am so very shocked." His lips curled into an amused half-smile. "What other treasures might you be hiding up there between your legs?"

Lara tried to hide her fear, but had the feeling she was staring into the eyes of the last man to see Pär Olin alive and could barely speak over the lump of panic working its way up her windpipe. "What . . . what do you want?"

"The disks, of course." Kicking the Beretta under her desk, he pushed her back into the chair and spun her around, pulling her arms around behind the seat-back.

"Why are you doing this?"

"A precaution," he said, binding her hands with a zip tie. "I wish not to harm you." He spoke with sincerity because he truly did not want to inflict any unnecessary pain. *Want*, of course, had no part in the equation. The degree of pain would be up to her. He reached forward and looped another tie around her legs, securing them to the base of the chair. Her helplessness aroused him, but he resisted the fantasy that began to play through his mind. Time enough for that later. "Where is Simon Leonidovich?"

She heard the huskiness in his voice and knew what it meant. *Five minutes*, that's all she needed, to keep him talking long enough for the police to arrive. "I don't know."

He stepped closer, straddling her legs. "I'll ask you one more time. Where is Simon Leonidovich?"

She could smell his excitement, could actually see his erection bulging against his dark slacks, and looked away to keep herself from gagging. He reached over and snatched a picture off her desk. "Such beautiful children. I would like so very much to meet them."

She felt as if he had sliced open her chest with a razor, reached inside, and grabbed her heart. How much time had passed? *Three minutes? Four?* Did she press the button hard enough? "They live in Florida with their grandparents."

"Florida?" His voice lifted in doubt. "Where in Florida?"

"Miami," she answered quickly, then realized how false it sounded, that she would so willingly give up the whereabouts of her children.

His brows drew together over his dark eyes, a look of angry disappointment. "I think not." With his fingertips he moved a strand of hair away from her face, the movement both gentle and frightening. "Let me show you something." He held up a beeper, the word CALL clearly visible on the tiny display. "Your security call."

She felt a terrible sliding sensation, a sweaty panic, like her first roller-coaster ride, scared to death and trying not to show it. "I don't know what you're talking about."

He tapped a button to clear the display, then reached over and pressed the panic button beneath the edge of her desk. Within a moment the word CALL began to pulsate across the display. "Forget the police. They will not be coming."

"How . . . ?"

"This is not important. Now where is Simon Leonidovich?"

It was all she could do to speak over the lump of fear wedged in her throat. "I think he went to Oslo."

"Oslo? Why would he go there?"

"He didn't tell me."

"He has the disks?"

"As far as I know."

He stepped back. "How would I contact him?"

She cocked her head toward the phone. "Top button on the right. His cellular."

He studied the console a moment, then pressed the SPEAKER button followed by the preset. "Please explain to Mr. Leonidovich how very much you would like for him to give me the disks."

She nodded, praying Simon would answer so she could do exactly that. The hollow sound of each unanswered ring seemed to grow louder and more ominous. Finally, after ten rings, Simon's voice echoed back over the speaker. "This is Simon Leonidovich. I'm presently unavailable. You may leave a message at the tone or call my office."

Smith reached over and punched the SPEAKER button. "How unfortunate."

She could almost hear the words *for you*. "I can send him an e-mail. Ask him to call immediately."

Ignoring her, he pulled a chair up to the desk, studied the icons on her monitor for a good two minutes, then pulled a CD from his briefcase and slipped it into the top bay of her 5-slot RW-DVD changer. A synthesized male voice reverberated from the speakers: "Password, please."

He sat back, staring at the screen like an owl that had suddenly flown from darkness into blinding sunlight. "Your password?"

He was angry, a man who clearly did not like surprises, and she knew better than to resist. "It's voice recognition."

"You will show me."

She nodded toward her headset. "I'll need my microphone."

He picked it up, examined it, flipped the toggle switch to COMPUTER, and held the point of the microphone up close to her mouth.

"Lara says—open CD." A dialog box instantly popped onto the screen, displaying the disk's hierarchy of files. Smith swiveled back to the computer, double-clicked an EXE file, then watched as a program began to install. Lara tried to see what was being loaded onto her computer, but the few words that streamed across the screen moved so quickly she couldn't read them. The installation took less than a minute. Smith retrieved the disk, returned it to his case, then began copying selected files from the computer's hard drives onto high-capacity zip cartridges. He worked quickly and efficiently, a man familiar with computers.

She had a feeling that unless he had some reason not to, he intended to kill her once he had everything he wanted. "Those files are worthless without me."

He swiveled around, boring into her with his eyes. She forced herself not to look away. "It takes a voice command to open any file. My voice."

"There is"—he paused, struggling to find the right words—"how do you say . . . a back door, eh?"

He was right, there was a password buried deep in the system, and she had a bad feeling he might have the skill to find it. "You're right, there is." The edge of his lips curled slightly. "The voice of Mr. Leonidovich."

"There is another."

She shook her head, holding on with her eyes.

He snorted softly and turned back to the computer. "This I doubt."

But doubt was exactly what she heard. When he finished copying files he turned and held the microphone up to her mouth. "Now you will send Leonidovich a message."

"What do you want me to say?"

"You will tell him not to give up the disks. He will be contacted." He gave her a hard look, as if his words were intended for her. "This is most important."

She nodded, understanding her life might depend on it. "Lara says—open mail—new message." A new-message window appeared on the screen. "To—Simon Leonidovich. Subject—disks. Message—Imperative you not give up the disks—period. I cannot emphasize this strongly enough—period. Do not give up the disks—period. Cap that." The last sentence instantly converted to uppercase. "You will be contacted—period. Lara Quinn."

Smith studied the message carefully. "This is how you sign? Lara Quinn?"

She knew he was testing her and could easily check her old messages. "Usually I don't include my last name."

"Change it."

"Select—Quinn. Scratch that." *Quinn* disappeared from the message.

"Everything is now correct? Is normal?"

Correct, yes. *Normal,* no. But she needed to take the chance, to let Simon know she was being forced. "Yes."

"Send it."

"Lara says—send message." A tiny envelope fluttered across the screen and disappeared into cyberspace.

Smith dropped the head-mike back on the desk. "Where is the safe?"

She hesitated, thinking of Simon's ten-thousand-dollar emergency fund, then immediately rejected the idea of lying. "Below the refrigerator."

He stretched out on the floor, examining the fake grill. "Alarm?"

"No."

"Where is the—" He rolled his hand in a circular motion.

"It's voice activated."

"From your computer?"

"Yes."

"Interesting." He retrieved the headset and positioned the microphone beneath her mouth. "Open it."

"Lara says—two, seven, Y, seven, two—open sesame." Instantly the grid began to slide off to one side.

"Clever." He dropped to his knees and carefully examined every inch of the reinforced-steel box before reaching in and picking up the bound stack of hundred-dollar bills. He fanned the edge, as if to confirm they were all the same denomination, then nonchalantly flipped the packet back into the safe. The arrogance of it, that a stack of hundred-dollar bills meant nothing to him, scared her all the more. What was so important about the disks? Why were they so valuable?

He stepped to the desk, retrieved the head mike, and again held it up to her mouth. "Close it."

Though she knew it was stupid, she couldn't stop herself. "Please, just take the money and leave. I won't even report it."

He laughed, the sound anything but humorous. "You think me a thief, lady? You think Eth Jäger is a petty thief?"

She wanted to forget the name as soon as she heard

it, knew it meant he intended to kill her. "I don't know *what* you are. I don't care."

He stared down at her, his face filled with self-righteous anger. "Your Simon Leonidovich is the thief. He took the disks. He is the one responsible. You will now close the safe."

She hesitated, but only long enough for the vacuous darkness of his eyes to suck away the last of her nerve. "Lara says—two, seven, Y, seven, two—clam up." The heavy steel grid moved silently back into place.

He nodded, a bemused look on his face, then pulled a small digital camera with flash attachment from his briefcase and began taking pictures, methodically moving around the room, shooting everything, from every angle, with close-ups of anything electronic, including the alarm pad next to the door. Whoever he was, whatever he was, the man was thorough.

When he disappeared into Simon's office, Lara considered screaming for help, but doubted her voice would penetrate the double-thick walls and decided it wasn't worth the risk of provoking him. Though she couldn't see him, she knew where he was from the constant snapping and flashes of light. Eyeing the small Beretta lying only a few feet away, she pulled and sawed back and forth on the plastic ties until blood began to run down her fingers, then abandoned the effort. Sick with fear, she considered trying to dictate and send a message, then dismissed the idea as too risky. But when she heard Smith start to go through Simon's desk, opening and closing drawers and rifling through the papers, she decided to take the chance.

Inching forward with her toes, she leaned down

until her mouth was touching the microphone, and whispered, "Lara says open mail new message."

PLEASE REPEAT COMMAND scrolled across the screen.

Shit. She took a deep breath and tried again, forcing herself to enunciate clearly and pause between each command. "Lara says—open mail—new message." A new-message window ballooned onto the screen. *Thank you, God!* She paused, listening to make sure Smith was still going through the desk, then whispered, "To—Simon Leonidovich. Subject—danger. Message—Smith is Eth Jäger." She glanced up at the screen and the words: Smith is death should our. "Damn." Unfamiliar with the name, the software had misinterpreted the words. Behind her she heard Smith moving toward the door, still snapping pictures, and realized she didn't have time to spell out a correction. "No time . . . hide kids . . . love you all . . . macro—signature one . . . Lara says—send message."

She had barely gotten herself back into position when Smith reentered the room. "You have an answering machine?"

She shook her head, trying to calm her racing heart. "The computer automatically transfers any calls to my cellular."

"And when you are not available?"

Not available, the words echoed through her head like a death sentence. She considered lying, but knew he would somehow test her answer. "We have an answering service."

"Activate it."

She gave him the code and he punched it into the phone.

"What is the security code for here?"

She struggled to understand, to jump ahead of his questions, to come up with some kind of plan, but everything was moving too fast, as if he were pushing her toward the edge of a cliff and she couldn't find anything to grab on to. "Here?"

"This office."

"Nine, six, seven, five, three."

"Say it backward. Quickly!"

"Three—five—"

"Faster!"

"Three, five, seven, six, nine."

"Again."

"Three, five, seven, six, nine."

"Forward!"

"Nine, six, seven, five, three."

He nodded, finally convinced the number was legitimate. "Now log off the computer."

"Lara says—computer—clam up." A large padlock bloomed onto the screen, confirming the lock-down command, then faded to black as the monitor shut down.

Standing in the middle of the room, Smith turned slowly around, his eyes sweeping the area like a cat searching for prey. By the time they settled on her she felt like a helpless field mouse. "It is the same, no?"

She didn't have the faintest idea what he was asking. "What?"

He gestured around the room with his latex-covered hands. "I was never here."

He was right, everything looked completely normal. And for some reason that frightened her. Very much. What did he intend to do with her? Some Pär Olin–type *accident* away from the office? He reached into his briefcase, retrieved a wide roll of skin-colored tape and tore off a strip.

A wave of nausea welled up from the pit of her stomach, burning the back of her throat. "Don't! Listen to me!"

"The time for talking is finished."

"Please! Mr. Leonidovich will do whatever you ask! I'm his—" The tape forced the word *sister* back into her mouth, and with it her last hope.

CHAPTER SEVENTEEN

Oslo, Norway

Saturday, 16 November 19:47:33 GMT + 0100

Simon rolled over and covered his eyes, trying to ignore the first beams of morning sunlight cutting through the shades. Never one to sleep during the day, he held on for only a few minutes, then gave up the battle. Without opening his eyes, he gathered the pillows up behind his head, pushed himself into a sitting position, and cracked an eyelid. Nothing familiar.

The feeling was not uncommon, not when you spent half your life away from home. It never took him more than a few seconds to figure it all out, but it always seemed longer and he enjoyed the experience— like stepping off a plane in a foreign country, not knowing exactly what to expect. Within seconds he had it: November 16th, Oslo, a small *pensión* near the airport. He glanced down at his watch—8:22—filling in the last detail of time and place.

The room was cheerful and cozy, snuggled into a corner of windows on the second floor, the furniture a farrago of pieces that didn't fit any specific period or theme but seemed to blend well. Aside from a small private bathroom, an uncommon amenity for European inns, there appeared to be no modern conveniences.

No coffeemaker.

No radio or television.

No phone, fax, or modem connection.

A technological vacuum of silence and sanity. Enough, Simon knew, to drive him crazy within minutes. He rolled over, snatched his cellular off the antique nightstand, and checked the display. The screen was blank, the battery dead. It was a mistake he rarely made, but in his exhaustion he'd forgotten to plug the damn thing in. Throwing off the puffy eiderdown, he scrambled across the cold floor to his security case, sequenced through the unlocking procedure, retrieved his spare battery, and jumped back into bed.

The phone beeped once as it powered up, the message "1 Missed Call" scrolling onto the screen. He pressed the MENU button to display the message or callback number, only to find another blank screen. He relaxed against the soft pillows, feeling better. If Lara had learned anything important from Smith, or had any kind of a problem, she would have left a message. He considered calling her anyway, but knew she'd only bitch at him for waking her in the middle of the night. After this fiasco, she was going to be hard enough to deal with.

I told you so, Boris. The guy was stealing company secrets.

I'm not so sure about that, Sissie. But he knew it was possible. Maybe Olin tried to change his mind. Maybe he tried to hold up his customer for more money. Whatever happened, he got himself killed in the bargain.

You should never have taken the shipment.

You're right, Sissie.

You should have turned them over to Bain-Haverland.

Should have—should have—should have . . . And she was probably right, he should have. So why didn't he believe it? Why should he worry about the motives of a dead man, simply because the guy looked honest and had a sweet picture of his kids hanging from the pocket of his lab coat? Simon didn't think of himself as gullible, but in this case . . .

He was half tempted to burrow down into the eider-down and disappear. If there was ever a day he didn't want to face, this was it. How did such a simple assignment turn into such a complicated mess, threatening both his livelihood and reputation? There were too many governments involved, too many innocent actions that could be twisted around to make him look devious. One thing was certain, no matter how long it took, he needed to solve the problem before leaving Europe. A person in his business couldn't afford to be persona non grata—not anywhere.

The thought was enough to give his internal battery a jolt of energy. In a blaze of movement, prompted by the room's Scandinavian temperature, he bounced out of bed, made a quick run through the bathroom, pulled on some clothes, and settled into an ancient, yet surprisingly comfortable spindle-back chair next to the window. Within a minute he had his laptop booted and was pounding away at the keyboard: writing a complete account of his meeting with Pär Olin, why he accepted the package, held it, and now wanted to turn it over to the Swedish authorities. If he hurried he could have the original delivered to the

Swedish Embassy by noon, along with an offer to meet their representative at the American Embassy to turn over the disks. Everyone else would receive a faxed copy: Bain-Haverland, Gotland Research, the New York Police. *Everything out in the open. No secrets.* He felt better having a plan of action, and confident the matter could be resolved before the day was over.

He worked nonstop for nearly two hours, hearing but paying no attention to other guests as they tromped down the stairs. By the time he finished and printed copies, the house was silent. Still too early to call Lara, he decided to appease the rumble in his stomach.

The proprietress, obviously attuned to the vibrations of her home, greeted him in the foyer. She smiled, a little tight-jawed, as if annoyed at his late arrival. *"God morgen."*

"God morgen. Am I too late for breakfast?"

"Nei." She turned and started down the hall toward the back of the house. "If you would this way follow, please." Despite the awkward syntax and heavy accent, her English was perfectly clear. She led the way past the parlor and formal dining room, the remnants of earlier diners still in evidence, and into a large country kitchen. A small table overlooking the winter garden was already set for one, offering a small compote of mixed fruit, a choice of blueberry or plain yogurt, apple juice, a tray of fresh pastries, and a thermo-glass carafe of dark coffee.

As the woman poured coffee, Simon glanced around the kitchen. The room was clean and bright, the walls the color of buttermilk. An array of fresh herbs in tiny pots covered the windowsill above the white porcelain sink. A huge island of butcher block, with an impressive array of kitchen knives attached to one end, dominated the center area. A profusion of brass, copper, and stainless-steel pots hung overhead. It didn't take a culinary genius to realize someone in the house liked to cook.

He gave the woman a hopeful smile. "Telephone?"

She nodded toward a tiny wall unit near the door. An obvious extension, it had no keypad or modular-jack connections. "If you would provide the number I would be most happy to make the connection."

A nice way of saying, "you're not sticking me with any long-distance calls," and he couldn't blame her for that. "Thanks. I'll let you know." For security reasons he normally avoided using his cellular for Internet connections, but had no choice if he wanted to e-mail a copy of his report to Lara before exposing himself to a charge of theft and smuggling, and the political clout of Bain-Haverland. Anxious to get on with it, he polished off the yogurt and three pastries in less than five minutes, popped a Mira-loss tablet, and headed back to his room. The woman stared openmouthed as he walked away, clearly overwhelmed at his impressive display of American gastronomy.

Settling himself into the spindle-back chair, he tapped out a quick message to Lara, asking her to forward a copy of his report to both his lawyer and the New York Police, and dialed his ISP. It took less than a minute to send the document and download his messages. There were four: the first from a generic Hotmail address he didn't recognize; two from Lara, and the last from Pilár Montez. He hesitated, momentarily overwhelmed with a fatalistic jolt of self-doubt. He could think of no reason why a beautiful woman like Pilár Montez would have any interest in a slightly overweight, just-turned-forty glorified delivery man. Certain he was about to get the old kiss-off, he took a deep breath and double-clicked the message.

Subject: **Hola**
   Date: **Friday, 15 November 2002 20:01:22 EST**
   From: **Pilár Montez <pmontez@elmundo.com.sp>**
      To: **Simon Leonidovich <SimonL.@WorldwideSD.com>**

Buenos días, Señor Simon,

Did you think I was ignoring your message? Not true—just flying. Now off for three days! What a funny job I have, but do love it.

Yes, I would have dinner with you (your charming sister convinced me you're harmless enough) but suspect that by now you've fallen for the last person to serve you an espresso with Monin and you've forgotten poor Pilár. Besides, you're in New York and I'm in Madrid. That doesn't sound promising. What would you suggest?

Must run—many messages to answer. Hello to Lara.

Pilár Montez

Simon smiled to himself, his self-doubt magically restored. She hadn't forgotten him, and she hadn't said "no." He leaned forward and clicked REPLY, wanting to answer before breaking his Internet connection.

```
Hello, "poor" Pilár. You're right,
I did "fall" for the last person to
serve me an espresso with Monin
(thank you for remembering), a
Spanish beauty with long legs, big
dark eyes, and a quick wit. As for
dinner, the prospects are more
promising than you might expect.
I'm practically next door. The same
time zone at least. Some business
to deal with but hope to have
everything cleaned up today. Dinner
tomorrow evening?
```

Too pushy? Too optimistic about straightening everything out with the Swedish authorities? He knew what Lara would say: *Go for it.*

```
Let me know. (I'd call, but don't
have your number.) You can reach me
on cellular at: 212 WORLDSD. Look
forward to seeing you again.
```

Was that going too far, expecting her to call?

```
WARNING: Despite what my sister
might have told you—I'm safe, NOT
HARMLESS.
```

Too glib? Too much of a dare? Before he could wimp
out and change his mind he added his name and hit
SEND. As the message dissolved into digital bits and
vanished into cyberspace, he prayed it didn't sound
too juvenile.

What if she called and he couldn't make a connection into Madrid? Clicking his TRAVEL icon, he typed in
his flight parameters, then waited as the wizard began
to search. There was only one direct flight, late in the
afternoon, with only a few seats still available. He hesitated, then scratched down the information on the back
of a business card and booked a seat, hoping the Pär
Olin fiasco would be over. His gut told him otherwise.
He terminated his connection and clicked the Hotmail
message, certain it was spam and wanting to dump it
before turning his attention to Lara's messages.

Subject:
  Date: **Friday, 15 November 2002 20:41:11
      EST**
  From: **Retnuh <retnuh@hotmail.com>**
    To: **Simon Leonidovich
      <SimonL@WorldwideSD.com>**

You have something I want. I have something you want.
Be smart, merchandise will not survive delay. Let's
trade. Contact retnuh at IM 12:00 GMT 17-11-02.

Retnuh? The name sounded like some kind of new-
age drug. A melodramatic twist to the Internet sales
game, he suspected, and was about to delete the mes-

sage when he realized how cryptic and personal the words might be. Most people didn't know the acronym for Greenwich Mean Time, and only Lara knew their shorthand code for Instant Messenger, the program they used for private on-line communication. *Let's trade.* A sudden chill ran through his body, making his skin pebble and the hair rise on the back of his arms. He moved his cursor over to Lara's first message and clicked it open.

Subject: Disks
    Date: Friday, 15 November 2002 16:36:21 EST
    From: Lara Quinn
          <LaraQ@WorldwideSD.com>
      To: Simon Leonidovich
          <SimonL@WorldwideSD.com>

Imperative you not give up the disks. I cannot emphasize this strongly enough. DO NOT GIVE UP THE DISKS. You will be contacted. Lara

---

Though the message originated from Lara's computer, he knew immediately that something was terribly wrong. She *always* signed her messages with the Russian word for "so long"—Пoka—and always abbreviated her name. And because she *always* used a macro signature, it couldn't have been an inadvertent mistake. Either she had been forced to write the message, or someone else had. Each scenario seemed equally bad. He clicked open the second message.

Subject: Danger
  Date: Friday, 15 November 2002 16:58:21
         EST
  From: Lara Quinn
         ≤LaraQ@WorldwideSD.com≥
    To: Simon Leonidovich
         ≤SimonL.@WorldwideSD.com≥

Smith is death should our damn hide kids no time love you all.
⊓oka..........L

Though unclear, the words "Smith is death" momentarily stopped his heart. He quickly punched Lara's number into his cellular, telling himself it was some kind of sick joke, but the murder of Pär Olin loomed like an evil harbinger, and he couldn't make himself believe it. The echoing silence of each unanswered ring only intensified his fear. Trying not to panic, he punched in the number of Lara's day-care provider.

"Oh, I'm so glad you called," the woman interrupted the moment he started to speak. "Lara never picked up the children. I called the hospitals and the police, but she hasn't been missing long enough and they won't do anything."

"You still have the kids?" he asked, working hard to keep the anxiety out of his voice.

"No, sir. When I couldn't reach you, I called their grandparents. They picked them up last night. I'm very worried. I think you should call the police."

"Thank you, I will," but knew that he wouldn't. They would want the disks and he couldn't give them up. *Not yet*. Not until Lara was safe.

Merchandise will not survive delay. Fighting to control his panic, he returned to Lara's last message, which she apparently had dictated surreptitiously, not taking the time to use punctuation commands. Hoping to discover some clue to what she was trying to say, he quickly divided the words into groups.

Smith is death
should our damn
hide kids
no time
love you all
⊓oka. L

The last four groups seemed obvious, each able to stand on their own. *No time*, that's why she couldn't say more. The thought of what might have happened a moment later made him sick, a palpable pain that spread across his chest and down his arms. He took a deep breath, fighting for control, and forced himself to concentrate. It seemed clear the software had failed to interpret the second group of words correctly—*should our damn*. Either Lara had mumbled or used words unfamiliar to her voice-recognition program, such as proper nouns. Of the two, he thought the second more likely: a name or a place.

He worked for over an hour, trying to phonetically break the three words into something reasonable, but couldn't come up with anything that made sense. At 11:45 GMT he logged back on to his server, sent a quick message to the company's answering service, directing all his business calls to another courier service, then initiated his Instant Messenger, and waited. Never in his life had he ever felt so alone and helpless. *You up there, God? I could use a little help. Not for me, you understand, I know better than that. But Lara, she's a good woman. Her kids need her. How about it? A little help here?*

At precisely 12:00 the name *Retnuh* appeared in the contact box, followed a moment later with the message:

> ▶ simon leonidovich?

Hoping the man didn't know about Lara's last message, Simon elected to play dumb.

> ▶ DIDN'T UNDERSTAND YOUR MESSAGE. WHAT DO YOU WANT?
> ▶ you know exactly what I want—yes or no
> ▶ SORRY, NO IDEA WHAT YOU'RE TALKING ABOUT.
> ▶ do not be stupid—play games with me you lose merchandise—a simple trade—yes or no

Simon realized it was useless to continue the not-knowing game. The man was obviously dangerous and unpredictable. *Merchandise.* Did he know Lara was his sister? His guess was *no*, and thought it might be best to keep it that way—at least for now.

> ▶ I NEED PROOF LARA QUINN IS OKAY.
> ▶ not interested your needs—last chance—merchandise perishable—yes or no

Perishable! The word stabbed at his heart like a blade of ice, and he knew the man who typed it was just as cold—a machine he couldn't argue with.

> ◗ YES
> ◗ I will send directions where to meet check back 1 hour

That, Simon suspected, was how Pär Olin ended up dead, meeting Retnuh at a location he picked.

> ◗ CAN'T MOVE AROUND. THE POLICE ARE LOOKING FOR ME.
> ◗ where are you?

He started to type Oslo, then thought better of it. The city was too isolated. He needed a place he could get in and out of quickly, then remembered his reservation to Madrid.

> ◗ MADRID.
> ◗ madrid no good—rome—I will e-mail location

Did that mean he had Lara in Italy? It didn't feel right—more like a trap than a trade.

> ◗ NO, MUST BE MADRID. OTHERWISE I COULD LOSE DISKS AT CUSTOMS. PLAZA MAYOR NOON TOMORROW.

One of the largest open-air plazas in the world, it was the most public place he could think of. A full minute passed before Jäger answered.

> okay—noon—come alone or . . .
> HOW WILL I KNOW YOU?
> I will find you
> I WANT PROOF LARA'S OKAY. A PRIVATE MES-
SAGE ONLY I WILL UNDERSTAND.

He waited, staring at the blinking cursor. A moment later two words flashed onto the screen.

CONNECTION TERMINATED

CHAPTER EIGHTEEN

Over the Atlantic Ocean

Saturday, 16 November 11:10:25 GMT –0200

Except for the glow of the laptop and the steady purr of the Lear's duel-fan engines, the cabin was silent and dark. Every fifteen minutes Jäger opened his eyes, checked the screen on his laptop to make sure nothing had changed, then slept for another quarter hour. It was something he had trained himself to do—to conserve energy, to wait for the right opportunity. With patience, it always came. And like all great hunters, Eth Jäger was a patient man.

Shortly after midday he felt a small, out-of-synch vibration as the sleek jet altered course. Cracking the sunscreen, he scanned the horizon—nothing but gray sky and blue water—then reached up and pressed the COCKPIT button on the communications console.

The pilot answered immediately. *"Sì?"*

"You have found a location?"

Sì. Sixty kilometers west of the city." His heavily accented Italian reverberated through the speaker. "The runway is only fifteen-hundred meters. No international traffic."

"Customs?"

"Arrangements can be made."

"How much?"

The pilot hesitated, but only a moment. "Twelve thousand. American."

Jäger suspected the man would pocket at least half, twice the usual fee, but knew he didn't have a choice. "Make the arrangements." The amount, of course, was meaningless. He already had more than half a million pounds of Haverland's money in his Liechtenstein account, and if things went as expected, he would soon have more.

He started to close his eyes when a yellow bar bloomed across the center of his monitor, the search engine finding its target. He leaned forward, reading the three lines of text:

```
>LEONIDOVICH/SIMON/NYC/NY/US
>HOTEL HUSA PRINCESA/MADRID/SPAIN
>AMERICAN EXPRESS/CORPORATE/APPROVED
```

Despite his reputation, Leonidovich was not a clever man. That, or the woman had fuzzed his brain. He called her *Lara*. Perhaps they were lovers. All the better; desperate men made foolish decisions, like using a credit card to reserve his room. A stupid mistake that would cost the man his life.

Jäger leaned back into the soft leather and closed his eyes. This was going to be easier than expected. The Plaza was risky: too many people, too many things that could go wrong. But a hotel room, that was private and uncomplicated, the perfect place for an accident. A slip in the shower? A fall from the balcony?

He could almost feel the disks in his hands. The only question was how much more he could squeeze out of Haverland. His willingness to pay a million pounds meant they were worth . . . ? The possibilities were staggering. What could be so valuable? Some new strain of virus? A biological weapon that could sway the balance of world power?

It didn't matter. The rich always survived, and by this time tomorrow Simon Leonidovich would be very dead and Eth Jäger would be very rich.

CHAPTER NINETEEN

Madrid

Saturday, 16 November 18:45:47 GMT +0100

The desk clerk smiled and with a pretentious flourish slid a registration card across the marble counter. *"Bienvenido* Husa Princesa."

Simon nodded, handed the man his passport and company credit card and began filling out the registration. It was a part of his life that had become routine, checking in and out of foreign hotels, and he almost missed the clerk's furtive glance across the lobby. The implication hit with a jolt, like touching the end of two live wires. *Dumb—Dumb—Dumb!* How could he have been so stupid, checking into a tourist hotel? If Retnuh wanted to catch him off guard, it would be the first place he would look. *But why?* Why not trade Lara for the disks, as agreed? Unless Retnuh had no intention of giving her up. Or worse, if she was already . . .

No, he refused to consider worse. Pretending not to have noticed the clerk's wayward glance, Simon forced his pen forward over the paper as he tried to think of a way to protect the disks without screaming *policía,* something he had a feeling would be akin to shoving a knife into Lara's heart. Running was out of the question, his body wasn't built for speed, and he didn't dare go to his room if he hoped to avoid a trap.

Jäger gave the clerk a withering look and turned back to his book. As if he, the world's greatest hunter, needed some slow-witted point dog to identify his prey. Fortunately, Leonidovich didn't notice the man's careless glance. Jäger tilted his book slightly, centering the courier directly beneath the crosshairs of the miniature camera embedded in the spine. It was the latest addition in his collection of surveillance gadgetry, the picture displayed on a two-inch LCD inside the book. Using the control pad hidden in his hand, he could rotate the lens 90 degrees, expand or narrow the view.

As the desk clerk finished, a bellhop jumped forward and scooped up the luggage, a well-traveled gray carryall and a black rectangular case with a fold-over top and shoulder strap. Leonidovich shuffled along behind, like a robot programmed to the task, too tired to think on his own. Not the sharp-witted adversary Jäger expected. Ironically, he felt cheated. Taking the disks from this middle-aged, pudgy delivery boy would hardly present a challenge.

When they reached the elevators Leonidovich hesitated, shook his head slightly as if unable to make up his mind about something, then extracted a folded-over pack of currency from his pocket and handed the bellhop a thousand peseta note with some kind of instruction. The man smiled and nodded, passed the smaller piece of luggage to Leonidovich, and stepped into the elevator. Leonidovich hefted the black case over his shoulder and began to trudge back across the lobby, a turtle exhausted under the burden of its own shell. Judging from the bag's size and obvious weight, Jäger felt certain it contained the man's laptop and valuables, including the disks. When he reached the north end of the lobby, Leonidovich veered into the cocktail lounge and collapsed at the first table, his chair facing the lobby.

Jäger crossed his legs, casually shifting his body around to hide his face. By the time he readjusted the camera angle and zoomed in, Leonidovich was staring down into a large brandy snifter. The man looked tired and depressed, no doubt thinking about the woman and feeling responsible. Not enough energy, Jäger thought, to put up much resistance.

Swirling his brandy, Simon studied the various people reflected off the film of liquor. He had to assume that anyone waiting would be alone or with no more than one other person. At one end of the lobby a group of American tourists were clustered around their local tour guide, a pretty college-age woman who spoke perfect English. She was laying out the various options for the evening's activities, and diplomatically trying to obtain a consensus. Typical of this part of the world, many of the finer restaurants didn't open for another hour, until eight, and one loudmouthed Texan wanted everyone within shouting distance to know exactly how he felt about it. "No damn wonder these people are always askin' for our help. Don't understand the basic principles of supply and demand."

The guide, who had to be offended by the remark,

gave the man a warm smile. "There is an American restaurant not far from here. I understand it's one of your most famous. If you'd prefer that . . . ?"

"Now you're talkin' there, little lady. Let's get us some real food for a change. What's the name of this here place?"

"McDonald's."

Suppressing a smile, Simon shifted his attention to the other people in the lobby. He quickly dismissed the only couple, a man and woman approaching octogenarian status, and four KLM flight attendants. That left only one possibility, a single man sitting in a high-backed lounge chair reading a book. He looked like a local, from his skin coloring to the European cut of his leather jacket. Though his face was partially hidden, there was nothing about the man that looked sinister. It was possible, Simon realized, even probable, he had misinterpreted the clerk's furtive look, but he couldn't be sure, and didn't dare make another careless mistake. If it *was* Retnuh, or someone who worked for him, he would eventually have to glance toward the lounge. For ten long minutes Simon stared down into the pool of amber liquid, never once diverting his attention from the reader's reflection, and never once did the man so much as glance up from his book. Feeling somewhat foolish at his overzealous imagination, Simon leaned back and drained the snifter in one long gulp, letting the cognac sear a path to his stomach. When he looked again the man with the book was halfway across the lobby, heading for the elevators.

The bartender, the only employee working the small room, leaned over the bar. "Another Napoleon, sir?"

Simon shook his head. "Check, please." Until he knew Lara was safe, he didn't need alcohol gumming up his brain. And something he couldn't quite identify kept tickling his receptors.

By the time he reached the elevators, the tickle had turned into an irritating itch. He glanced back, scanning once again each of the faces in the lobby. All tourists, nothing unusual. He closed his eyes, picturing the man with the book. Distinctively European— the only local in a tourist hotel. *Thin, Simon. Very thin.* But there was something else . . . ?

Something that didn't fit.

Something he should have noticed, but didn't. He concentrated harder, viewing the scene like a montage across the back of his eyelids. Then he had it—not what he should have seen, but what he didn't. In ten minutes the man had never once turned a page. *Still thin,* he could have been daydreaming, but it was all the motivation Simon needed to get his legs moving toward the exit. He was nearly to the front door before the desk clerk noticed and reached for the phone.

Ignoring a line of taxis parked under the portico— *too easy to follow*—he turned right toward the Plaza de España, then right again at the first corner. After ten minutes of weaving his way through a maze of commercial side streets, he was thoroughly lost, but confident no one had followed.

Exhausted and sweating, he stepped back into the dark entry of a small shop and tried to catch his breath. *Now what?* He couldn't check into another hotel without showing his passport and he didn't dare walk the streets at night with his security case. It was like a bad dream that kept getting worse. He felt himself losing focus, sinking into the depression he'd been trying to avoid since learning about Lara: fearing what she might be going through, or worse, having to face the possibility that she might be dead. He pushed the thought away, refusing to think about it. He needed to work on a plan, some way to protect the disks until she was safe, but his brain felt stuck. He tried to force his thoughts beyond the resistance, like pumping drain opener into a clogged pipe, but to no avail. He needed to sleep, to let his brain work on the problem while he wasn't looking. He needed a place to stay.

He needed help.

CHAPTER TWENTY

Madrid

Saturday, 16 November 19:28:51 GMT +0100

Hoping to appear less conspicuous than he felt, Simon casually shifted his security case to his left shoulder and started toward the TELÉFONO sign at the far end of the platform. Like most European subways, the area was brightly lit and spotlessly clean, not a gum wrapper or cigarette butt to mar the bright orange and blue tiles. The crowd was relatively thin—the lull between the working-class commuters and the more affluent throng of diners and theatergoers—giving him a somewhat schizophrenic feeling of exposure. He usually felt comfortable and safe in other countries, more so than in America, where any idiot could carry a gun, but now felt as if he had a sign hanging from his neck—*extranjero*—pointing out his foreign status like an animal in the zoo.

Leaning into the acoustical clamshell enclosure that served as a phone booth, he quickly read through the instructions, conveniently inscribed in both Spanish and English, dropped the required 50 pesetas into the slot, dialed the number, and immediately began having second thoughts. *Shouldn't involve her.*

"Hola?"

But he needed a place to hunker down, if only for a few hours, until he had a plan. "Pilár?"

She hesitated, as if trying to identify his voice. *"Sí."*

He glanced around, scanning the platform for the man in the dark suit. "It's Simon. Simon Leonidovich."

"Simon." She sounded surprised but pleased. "I didn't expect to hear from you before tomorrow."

"Something unexpected came up." *Unexpected,* a nice way to say the Norwegian police believed he was somehow involved in the murder of Pär Olin, that the American authorities wanted to question him about smuggling industrial secrets, and some maniac by the name of Retnuh had abducted his sister and was now looking for him. "I had to change my plans."

"Don't tell me you can't make it."

Hearing her disappointment gave him a surge of confidence, like a double shot of espresso directly into the cerebellum. "Actually I'm in the city. Thought I'd take a chance and see if you were home. Maybe join me somewhere for dinner?"

"Home, *sí,* but"—she paused, obviously struggling to find the right words—"how do you say—I don't wish to—"

"I understand." He tried to keep the disappointment out of his voice. "I shouldn't have called."

"I do not think you understand at all, Simon Leonidovich. I am always gone. Always somewhere else. This is my—"

"Really, you don't have to explain."

"But of course I must. You are a man, no? With the fragile ego? This is my most special somewhere. My *casa.* If you would join me here . . . ?"

That, of course, was exactly what he wanted, but faced with the opportunity he suddenly felt guilty at his lack of candor and worried that he might in some way involve her in his aggregation of problems. "That's really not necessary. I didn't mean to intrude."

As though knowing he needed a light in the dark, her voice became teasing, "I don't usually invite strange men into my lair, but your sister did say you were harmless."

He struggled to keep his voice light, to keep his thoughts of Lara locked away until he had a chance to deal with them. "I admit to neither. I'm not strange and I'm not harmless."

"I will take this chance."

"Okay, I accept. What about dinner, you want me to pick something up?"

"What, you do not think Pilár can cook?"

"I didn't mean—"

"Good, everything is settled. You will take a taxi, no?"

"Actually, I'm at the Argüelles metro station."

"Ah, so that is what I am hearing. I thought you were still at the airport. So you have checked already into your hotel?"

"Yes." *And out.*

"You are very close. Only a few minutes by taxi."

"I wouldn't mind walking." Most drivers recorded their stops, and though it seemed improbable, he didn't want to leave any trail that Retnuh might follow.

"Good. That will give me a few minutes to fix my face."

"Please, don't go to any trouble for me." Adding makeup to the face of Pilár Montez would be like trying to improve the Mona Lisa with fingerpaint. "I'd rather see you as you really are, Pilár Montez at ease in her *casa.*"

She groaned and laughed at the same time. "Okay, but you may be sorry. Do you have a pen?"

"Sure."

"Here is what you must do."

"Fire away." As she dictated directions, he scratched them down on the back of a business card.

The walk took less than thirty minutes, including the time it took to pick up a good bottle of wine and to double back a few blocks to make sure he wasn't being followed.

Pilár's *casa* turned out to be a six-story brick edifice facing the Casa de Campo, an immense public greenbelt five times the size of Central Park. Protected from the sun by a towering row of jacaranda trees, each floor appeared to have two apartments, each with its own canopied veranda and terra-cotta flower garden. A walkway of Spanish tiles curled through a sculptured courtyard to the entrance, a pair of thick glass doors overlaid with a filigree of silver patina. Either Iberia Airlines paid their flight attendants extremely well, or . . .

Sugar daddy? The thought left a bad taste in his mouth and he forced it away, disappointed in himself for glomming onto such a convenient and sexist explanation. As he pushed through the door, a distinguished-looking older man in a dark uniform appeared from behind a chest-high marble counter. As thin as a pencil and ramrod straight, he looked ex-military, his thinning black hair cut short with bare skin above the ears. *"Buenas noches,* Señor."

"Buenas noches. Señorita Pilár Montez?"

"Ah, sí, Señorita Montez." He gestured toward a large book on the marble counter. *"Su nombre, por favor."*

Simon signed his name, then waited as the man methodically checked his watch and noted the time. "Le-on-do-vich, Señor?"

"Le-on-o-vich."

The man bobbed his head. *"Gracias."* He picked up the phone, verified that Simon was expected, then escorted him to the elevator. *"Seis."*

Simon understood "six" but wasn't sure if the man meant floor or apartment. *"Casa número?"*

The man pointed at the top button. *"Seis."*

Still not sure but, with no more than two apartments per floor, knew he had a reasonable chance of finding the right door, and punched the button. But when the door slid open there were no choices to make or doors to knock on. Pilár was standing there, waiting for him, a glass of red wine in each hand. *"Bienvenida,* Simon Leonidovich, welcome to my *casa."*

It took a moment, a mind twitch between the time she spoke and the time it took to respond, to bring everything into focus—the fact that the elevator opened directly into her apartment and that it encompassed the entire top floor of the building. Decorated in wood tones and accented with soft yellows and oranges and reds, the central living area spread out behind her like an autumnal garden, cheerful and cozy and comfortable all at once. "Wow." *Brilliant, Simon.* He tried to think of something more profound, but standing there, under the scrutiny of her big dark eyes, his mind seized up. "Quite a place."

Her gaze shifted downward, to the case in his right hand. "And this? You assumed my invitation included . . . ?

"What? Oh, no. I mean—" He realized she was only teasing and took a breath, trying to compose himself. "It's my security case. I have to—"

She smiled, a hint of amusement in her eyes. "May I take your coat?"

A simple request, one any man should have been able to accomplish without difficulty, but whenever he wanted to impress a woman he came off feeling like an awkward high-schooler trying to pin a corsage to his date's bodice—or in this instance, trying to shed his coat and security case while juggling a bottle of wine back and forth from one hand to the other. In the back of his mind he saw Cary Grant turn over in his grave and groan. But Pilár seemed not to notice his awkward fumbling, or more likely, was accustomed to men making fools of themselves in her presence. She hung his coat, handed him a glass of wine, and graciously accepted the bottle. "Barolo. One of my favorites. *Gracias.*"

"Thank you for inviting me."

"But of course. And how is your charming sister?"

He knew it was coming, had mentally prepared himself, but it still took an effort not to show his worry. "Couldn't reach her today," he answered as nonchalantly as possible. "But I expect to speak with her in the morning." He hoped to God that he would.

"And you will pass on my greeting?"

"Of course."

"Good. And it is good to see you again, Simon Leonidovich."

He liked the way she said his name, the exotic cadence of her Castilian accent somehow turning what seemed formal into intimate. He raised his glass, hoping to make a comeback. "And seeing you pleases my eyes, Señorita Montez."

She laughed, the sound shiny and full of sparkle. "Then you must have very bad eyes, Señor."

In truth his eyes were perfect, one of the few parts of his forty-year-old body that had not yet started to deteriorate, and what he saw couldn't have been more pleasing. She looked natural and fresh, her olive skin smooth and makeup free, her dark hair pulled back in a way that seemed to accentuate the length of her slender neck. Dressed in a cream-colored wool sweater and tan slacks tucked into scuffed but fine leather boots, she looked even more beautiful than he remembered.

"Please make yourself at home. I must finish in the kitchen."

"Don't go to any special trouble for me."

She smiled, a playful, glittery flash. "I won't."

"Can I help?"

"You may open the Barolo." She nodded toward a small but well-stocked bar near the veranda. "You will find an opener there. I will not be long."

It wasn't until he stepped behind the bar and turned that he realized he wasn't alone. Across the room, nearly hidden among a mass of pillows, a frost-blue Siamese stared intently back at him. Despite his natural amity with animals, he had the distinct and immediate feeling this was not your typical friendly house cat. This beast was a killer, who very clearly had its prey locked beneath the crosshairs of its feral eyes. Having no desire to do battle with the household pet, Simon opened the wine, left it on the bar to breathe, and stepped onto the veranda, a glassed-in promontory that seemed to float above the branches of the jacaranda. The Casa de Campo was completely dark, except for a twinkling trail of gondola cars that stretched across the park from one end to the other. Feeling exposed, he started to step back when he caught the soft lemony scent of Pilár's perfume.

"It is most beautiful at sunrise."

Something he hoped to one day experience if he could somehow save Lara and survive himself. "I'll bet."

"You would like a tour?"

"Sure."

The cat immediately slithered out of its pillowy enclosure and began to follow, its eyes boring into Simon like a panther stalking prey. "I don't think your cat likes me."

Pilár glanced over her shoulder, her eyes warming at the sight of her pet. "Don't consider it as personal. Co-op hates all men."

"A sexist cat? How did that happen?"

The skin tightened across her cheekbones. "It is not her fault. Don't approach her, it will be no problem."

Whatever the explanation, it was obviously a sore point, and he knew better than to poke his nose where it wasn't welcome. "Co-op. What kind of name is that?"

"When I am flying she stays with my neighbor. So she's—"

"A co-op cat."

"*Sí.*"

"Cute."

Beyond the central living area the apartment was divided by a gallery corridor, the walls decorated with a mélange of watercolors. "It's one of the reasons I like my job," she explained. "I like to visit out-of-the-way places during my travels, trying to find local artists before the world discovers them."

"You have an eye. I like them all."

She led him down one side of the gallery and back up the other, letting him peek into rooms as they passed: bedrooms and bathrooms and a laundry room along the back; the dining room, master bedroom, and a combination office-reading room along the front. Everything was neat and clean, but in a comfortable way that made Simon want to sink down into one of the overstuffed chairs, grab a good book, and throw up his feet. And there were plenty of books to choose from, in every room—some in Spanish, some in English—everything from popular fiction to serious works by Gabriel Garcia Marquez and Don Miguel Ruiz. "Watch a lot of television, do you?" So far he hadn't spotted a single set.

Her body tensed slightly. "You like television?"

It was a loaded question, he could hear it in the edge of her voice. Somehow he had managed to touch a nerve, and had the feeling a wrong response might doom what little hope he had for a relationship with this fascinating woman. He considered, for just an instant, saying he never watched the damn thing, but occasionally he did, and knew he would never stand a chance with a woman like Pilár Montez if he compromised his integrity. "It's not my favorite form of entertainment, but I do like CNN when something important is going on."

"Good."

"Why good?"

Her gaze drifted away, like someone trying to remember the end of an old story. "My ex-husband. He was addicted. We had a set in every room and they all had to be on."

"You're kidding?" But he knew she wasn't.

"What was worse, I had to watch with him. If I went to another room or tried to read, it made him angry."

"Doesn't exactly sound like a match made in heaven."

She shook her head deliberately, as if to erase the memory. "A violent man."

"And the reason Co-op hates men?"

She nodded, tears welling in her dark eyes. "It was a game with him. He liked to pretend he was the great Pelé, with Co-op the ball."

"God, no wonder she hates men."

"She really is a sweety. She did her best to avoid him, but—" She took a deep breath, the memory obviously difficult, her expression asking if he was ready to hear everything. "One day he went too far."

Simon was almost afraid to ask. "Too far?"

"He decided I made a better target." Her eyes flashed with emotion: pain, disappointment, anger. "Co-op went right for his face. It was very ugly. If I had not pulled her away, he would have killed her."

"I'm sorry. I hope you threw his ass out the door."

"That very day." She smiled, a faint, tentative flash. "Along with his six televisions and universal *remoto.*"

"Did I mention how much I hate television?"

She laughed, her nostalgic trip to matrimonial hell seemingly forgotten.

"I do love your home."

She stared straight back into his eyes, a slow smile passing over her lips. "And you were wondering how I could afford such a place."

"No. That's none of my—" But of course that was exactly what he was thinking. "Yes, I guess I was."

"It was my settlement."

"Your husband must—"

"Not my husband. My family."

He had no idea what she meant, but knew it was none of his business. "Oh."

"My brothers, of course, they will receive the land and the factories."

Land and factories—plural. He had the feeling either was worth far more than her settlement. "Of course?"

"It is the way of my country." She said it without bitterness, simply a statement of fact. "Spanish machismo."

"Did I mention how much I liked your cat?"

She gave him a blank look, at first not understanding his subtle poke at male chauvinism, then her lips suddenly parted into a wide grin. "You are a funny *hombre*, Simon Leonidovich."

"Funny-strange, or funny ha-ha?"

"Funny good. You make me laugh."

"I like you, too."

She gave him a wink and turned toward the kitchen. "But will you still like me after you taste my cooking?"

Judging from the smells, he didn't have much doubt about that. He followed her into the kitchen, a chef's dream if ever he saw one, and the obvious heart and soul of Casa Montez. She motioned him toward a cozy table overlooking the park. "Do you mind if we supper here? It's my favorite spot."

"Looks perfect." And it did, the table already set with crystal and silver and a small vase of colorful flowers. Feeling comfortable, yet guilty at the way he kept pushing Lara to the back of his mind, he retrieved the bottle of Barolo and poured them each a glass. "What can I do?"

"Sit and enjoy the view."

He did as instructed, enjoying the view very much, though not the one she intended. And as he watched her cook, Co-op watched him, staking out a spot between them like a royal centurion guard, ready to do battle at the first sign of aggression against the Empress.

Moving quickly and efficiently, Pilár dropped a fistful of fettuccine noodles into a large pot of boiling water, pulled a sauté pan over the flame of a second burner, added olive oil and vermouth, and began to sauté a mountain of shrimp, sliced tomatoes, mushrooms, black olives, chili peppers, and garlic cloves. She looked completely at ease, a woman comfortable with herself and her surroundings, not someone who needed a man to feel whole. The kind of woman he admired and wanted, and could fall in love with in the time it took to sauté a pan of shrimp, but not the kind to abandon her home or way of life for any man. It seemed an impossible situation, as unmanageable as the distance between New York and Madrid.

She finished off the sauté with a generous ration of capers, the spicy aroma wafting through the air on a cloud of steam, sending palpitations of anticipation from his mouth to his stomach, reminding him that he hadn't eaten since breakfast. "Smells wonderful."

"Gracias. I like to cook."

"I like to eat." Almost without thinking he reached into his pocket for a Mira-loss tablet.

She glanced over her shoulder and smiled. "A match made in heaven, as you say. What's that?"

"A diet pill. I need to lose some weight."

"You are fine. All you need is for someone to cook you healthy meals."

He nodded, knowing exactly who he wanted that *someone* to be.

Within a minute she had everything on the table: the pasta, a loa of sun-dried tomato bread, and two small arugula and endive salads. *"Bon appétit,* Simon Leonidovich."

He raised his glass. *"Ch'i kulinarniye sposobnosti sposobna ztmit' tol'ko yeyo krasota."*

She cocked an eyebrow, studying his face over the rim of her glass. "Russian?"

"One of my few accomplishments."

"And you said?"

"To a woman whose cooking is outshone only by her beauty."

"Gracias. But you haven't tried it."

"Good nose. Perfect eyes."

They ate in companionable silence, neither sensing any need to force the conversation. Even Co-op seemed to relax, stretching out on the clay-colored ceramic and resting her head on one paw, her unblinking eyes fixed on Simon. Though he wanted desperately to enjoy the moment, Lara kept popping into his consciousness, and no matter how hard he tried to push the thoughts away, to avoid the problem for just a little longer, he couldn't. Slowly, but irrevocably, like a pebble drifting downward into a deep well, he descended into an abyss of dark thoughts.

"Simon, what's wrong?"

He was so deep, so far into the well, it took a moment to resurface. "Sorry. Guess I got lost in thought."

"I see that. You haven't taken a bite in over ten minutes."

He glanced down, surprised to see he'd finished only half his meal. "Sorry. It really is wonderful." To emphasize the point he began to twirl some fettuccine onto his fork.

"You avoid my question."

"It's—" He tried to say nothing, but couldn't bring himself to utter such a fatuous lie. Nothing in the world was more important to him than Lara. "It's complicated."

"Aaah. You do not think a woman—"

"No. I didn't mean it like that at all. Really. It's business." He tried to put a nonchalant shrug in his voice, hoping she'd let it go.

"No, I do not think this. It is Lara."

Her words paralyzed him, a forkful of fettuccine suspended halfway to his mouth. "I, uh—" He slowly lowered the fork back to his plate. "It's both. But how did you know?"

"When I inquired of her, you avoided that question, also."

"It's, uh—"

"*Sí*, complicated. You said that."

"Yes. And not something you want to get involved in."

"But if Lara has a difficulty, I would most certainly want to help. We've been—how do you say . . . chatting?"

"E-mail?"

"*Sí*. Almost daily."

"I didn't know that." But he wasn't surprised; that was just like Lara, always trying to *fix* his love life.

"I like her very much."

He shook his head emphatically, determined not to let her get involved.

"And I like her brother very much, also."

He somehow knew that to be "liked very much" by Pilár Montez was more meaningful than it sounded. He should have been elated, but the emotion was smothered over with worry. "I like you, too, but—"

She cut him off before he could say more. "Come." She reached out and took his hand.

She led him into the living room, directed him to a cozy sofa along one wall, and poured them each a snifter of cognac. Leaning back against the end of the sofa, she pulled her legs up beneath her like a schoolgirl and squiggled around to face him. "Okay, tell me everything." Her beautiful dark eyes demanded it. And he felt helpless to resist their power.

He started with Pär Olin, with the flight from Madrid that unknowingly had brought them all together only ten days before, and ended with his last flight from the Husa Princesa only a few hours past. He left nothing out, hoping she might discover some detail he had overlooked. She listened quietly, attentively, without interruption. Her first question, when it finally came, not only surprised him, but told him much about the character of Pilár Montez.

"What about Allie and Jack Junior? Are they safe?"

"Yes. They're with their grandparents."

"Do they know?"

He shook his head. "I called and made arrangements for a Disney World trip. They'll be too busy and excited to ask questions for a day or two."

"And you—" She hesitated and glanced away, her eyes glistening with moisture. "You think—" She took a deep breath, her voice faltering. "You think Lara is okay?"

He knew exactly what she meant. *Do you think Lara is alive?* The same question he had tried all day to ignore. "Yes, I believe that." To consider otherwise was unthinkable.

Pilár nodded and leaned back, tapping a forefinger against her pursed lips, the wheels churning behind her dark eyes. "And you do not wish to call the police?"

"Can't take the chance. Even if they believed me, which I don't think they would, I'd lose the disks. They're all I have to bargain with."

She seemed to think about that, then nodded. "I agree."

Oddly, those two small words bolstered his spirits immensely. If things went bad, that's what everyone would say, *you should have called the police,* but he didn't dare, and at that moment the only opinion he cared about was that of the woman sitting next to him.

"You have his message?"

"It's on my computer."

"And this is with your luggage, *si?*"

"No, it's in my security case."

She bounced off the sofa, retrieved his case, and was back within seconds. "Please, if I could see?"

He sequenced through the unlocking procedure—right latch toward the handle, foot lock one-half turn clockwise, left latch outward—the first time he'd done it with anyone watching so closely.

"Why could not someone just break the lock?"

"Ka-boom."

Her eyes widened. "You have a bomb in there?"

"A very small bomb." Actually it was only a dye bomb, guaranteed to turn the contents of the case, and any intruder who tried to open it, a nice glow-in-the-dark shade of pink. The explosive would also activate a homing transmitter and earsplitting siren, all of which could prove to be quite disconcerting for an unsuspecting thief. "Not big enough to hurt anyone."

"So why . . . ?"

"It's meant to draw attention. Most thieves don't like attention." He reached into the case and pulled out the security pouch. "This is what it's all about."

She leaned forward, studying the disks through the clear plastic. "They seem so"—she struggled to find the right word—"so insignificant."

"Well, there's something important on them, that's for sure. Important enough to kill for."

"Nothing is so important."

"Someone doesn't agree with you." Balancing the laptop on his knees, he quickly booted the machine and pulled up both Lara's and Retnuh's original messages, along with the string of back-and-forth instant messages between himself and Retnuh.

Moving in close, Pilár read slowly through each message before scrolling to the next. "This man is very dangerous."

"Yes."

"I do not think he is—how do you say? In poker?"

"Bluffing."

"Yes, bluffing. What is your plan?"

He hesitated, knowing it was weak. "A fair exchange. In the middle of the Plaza. Lara for the disks." Saying it out loud made it sound all the more senseless.

Her eyes said as much. "I do not think you should give up the disks until Lara is safe."

"And I don't think he'll give me Lara without the disks."

"You will need to give him one of the disks. A show of . . ."

"Good faith."

"*Sí.* He must then release Lara before you give him the second disk."

"And what's to prevent him from taking it at gunpoint."

"You won't have it."

He realized instantly where she was going. "No. I don't want you to get involved."

"I am a stranger. A local. No involvement. Someone paid to turn over the disk once you are gone."

He shook his head. "Too dangerous."

"You need help."

He couldn't argue with that. And she knew Lara. The pieces were all there, but no matter how he tried to twist and turn them into place, nothing seemed to fit.

Pilár stood up, as if sensing his entanglement. "We will think of something better in the morning."

He suddenly realized it was after two A.M. "I'm sorry, I didn't realize it was so late. Could you recommend a small *pensión*? Some place I wouldn't need to show my passport."

She reached down, took his hand, and smiled. "I do not think you should be alone tonight, Simon Leonidovich."

CHAPTER TWENTY-ONE

Plaza Mayor, Madrid

Monday, 18 November 10:00:41 GMT + 0100

Feeling exposed, Simon edged deeper into the shadows of the arched overhang. He had already walked the perimeter, familiarizing himself with the countless narrow side streets and nine major passageways that led into the immense open-air plaza. Though it was only ten o'clock, two hours before his meeting with Retnuh, he wanted to be prepared for any situation that might develop.

Trying to look like any other picture-happy sightseer, he used his camera to scan the square, a field of brick so vast it had once served as a bullfighting arena. Except for a small group of Japanese tourists surrounding the statue of Philip III, the courtyard was nearly empty. The shopping arcade, which completely encircled the area, was beginning to hum with activity, most of it along the northwest side where the sun hit first. With practiced efficiency, the coin and stamp vendors assembled their tables and laid out their collections. The artists filled in the leftover spaces with their easels and paintings. Almost immediately a wave of tourists swept down upon them, as if Sam Walton had just thrown open the gates to Bargain Heaven.

As the sun spread outward onto the courtyard, the *tapas* bars and cafés began to open their outside dining areas, each distinguishable from the next only by the color of their umbrellas. Like delicate flowers, their business was irrevocably tied to the weather and season, the tourists following the sun as it circumnavigated the courtyard and a new wave of umbrellas blossomed to life.

Simon shifted his camera quickly from one person to the next, searching for Lara or the man she had described: light-brown skin, late thirties, short hair, dark eyes. Features that matched half the men in Spain. He concentrated on the faces, hoping to spot what she had described as *evil eyes,* but without his telescopic lens the distance was too great and the details too obscure. He shifted his focus to the massive five-story structure that circled the plaza, an architectural wonder of balconies and steeples. Hundreds of windows and more apartments than he could count. He paused over a balcony at the north end, the second floor up, and the slim figure of Pilár Montez, the woman he now wanted to share his life with. He'd never been the kind to decide such important things in the middle of the night while making love, but he felt the rightness of it deep into the marrow of his bones, and had a feeling that she did, too. What had seemed so complicated suddenly seemed easy. New York was merely a dot on the globe. His business was international, his home a hotel. He could live anywhere. Nothing, of course, had been discussed. *Lara first,* then he could think about his own life.

He forced himself to move on, scanning past shuttered windows, pausing briefly over others, finding nothing. In less than thirty minutes the crowd had grown significantly. Tourists were fanning out over the courtyard with their cameras and digital camcorders and fighting their way through the shopping arcade with their pesetas and credit cards. The possibility of finding Lara or identifying Retnuh in such a mass seemed to grow more remote by the minute. He raised the two-way to his mouth and pressed the TRANSMIT button. The miniature radio barely covered the palm of his hand. "Any luck?"

Pilár's voice crackled back through the earpiece. "No. It is difficult from such an angle."

He knew what she wanted, to work the crowd herself, but he wasn't about to expose her to any more danger than necessary. "Are you using the telescopic lens?"

"Sí. It is still difficult."

In his mind he could still see Retnuh's words scrolling across his monitor: *I will find you,* and somehow knew it was true. "It doesn't matter, he'll find me."

"This is what worries me."

"That's why we're here."

"This is not a man to trust."

And he didn't, not for a moment. He didn't really believe Retnuh would show Lara before he saw the disks, and didn't believe he would take kindly to the idea of releasing her before getting them, but that's exactly what Simon hoped to accomplish. "He won't try anything as long as I have the disks." He tried to say it with confidence, as if he believed it himself.

"And after he has them?"

"Trust me, he's not getting anything until you've

got Lara tucked away in that apartment, all safe and sound. Just like we planned."

"You know that is not what I am saying."

Of course he knew. "He doesn't care about me. All he wants are the disks."

"And you will not do something *loco?*"

Again, he knew exactly what she meant. "Scout's honor, no heroic gestures to impress the damsel in the tower."

"You remember that, Simon Leonidovich."

"I'm more than ready to let the police handle it. You can call them the minute Lara's safe."

"Bien."

He glanced around, making sure no one was watching. "Can you see me?"

"No."

"Good." He studied his map, identified his position on the hand-drawn grid, then stepped forward out of the shadows. "Check area seven."

There was a long beat of silence, then a soft, throaty chuckle. "Nice hat, Señor."

Despite the situation, he couldn't help but smile. Along with the apartment and two-way radios, she had managed to obtain a green Tyrolean-style hat resplendent with travel medallions so she could find him in the crowd. "I feel like a dork."

"Dork? I am not familiar with this word."

"A fool."

"Ah, *sí*, very much like the *turistas*. Many dorks."

Laughing to himself, he retreated back into the shadows. "I'll get you for this."

She answered with another low chuckle. *"Sí."*

*   *   *

Attaching himself to a large tour group, Jäger circled the plaza, one more innocuous face in a sea of gawking tourists. He doubted Leonidovich would dare contact the police, but there was no need for chance, and the reason he had chosen not to carry a conventional weapon. The unconventional, that was his trademark. That's what set him apart. His imagination. And this, this would be his *coup de grâce*. Just the thought of it made his blood surge with excitement. Whatever Leonidovich had planned, and there was no doubt the man would have some kind of scheme, he would collapse in fear before he would dare try anything. Jäger could almost feel the terror sweeping through the courier's body, and could hear the screams of the crowd when it happened. *Perfect.* A perfect diversion. A perfect place.

It took him less than ten minutes to identify his prey. The man was an amateur, trying to act the tourist with his camera and funny hat, then slinking around in the shadows like a frightened rabbit. Confident but cautious, Jäger turned his attention to the crowd, methodically checking every couple and unattached single for *tells,* those tiny giveaways that always identified the fools of law enforcement: an ear piece on someone too young, shoes that didn't match the masquerade of dress, eyes that never stopped moving despite an immutable and predictable expression of boredom. It took nearly an hour, but by the time he finished canvassing both the courtyard and shopping arcade, he felt satisfied that neither Interpol nor the local police had been contacted.

Leonidovich had now worked his way halfway around the plaza, his behavior falling into a predictable pattern: scanning the crowd with his camera, then moving down two archways before repeating the process. Calculating the route and stops, Jäger found a suitable spot, a small gap between vendors, then moved ahead to wait.

Simon glanced at his watch: 11:45. *Fifteen minutes,* then he would have no choice but to walk out into the courtyard and wait to be found. Except for the vendors, the shopping arcade was nearly empty, the tourists having temporarily abandoned their quest for souvenirs in a mad rush for fortification among the courtyard restaurants. Trying to ignore the enticing smells, he wound his way through a maze of easels to his next spot. He started to scan the area when a different odor suddenly caught his attention, something acrid and vaguely familiar, yet distinctly out of place. Before he could put a name to it, it dissolved into the scent of Turkish tobacco and the realization that someone had stepped up close behind him.

"A beautiful place, no?"

Though he tried not to react, there was something about the ambiguous accent and impassive tone that sent a warning tremor rippling up his spine. "Sure is."

"The history, that is not so beautiful."

He turned, facing the man straight on. Despite the dark beard that covered much of his face, Simon knew by the eyes it was Retnuh or Smith or whatever the man called himself. "Oh?" He pressed and held the TRANSMIT button on the tiny two-way, opening the channel to Pilár. "Why's that?"

The man smiled, but without warmth, like an undertaker appraising his next client. "It is here they burned the heretics. During the Inquisition."

The words seemed to trigger some transcendental association in Simon's brain, attaching a name to the unknown scent that still lingered beneath the odor of tobacco: *napalm*. The word, and the memory it provoked—boot camp and the stench of a burning dog as it tried to escape the sick prank of a cruel drill sergeant—made Simon's skin crawl. Though he tried to stop himself, he couldn't, and glanced down. A thin sheen of gelatinous dampness covered his slacks and shoes. Retnuh raised his cigarette and blew across the tip, making it glow. "This, I believe, would not be such a pleasant way to die."

For an instant Simon considered running, but felt like all the blood had drained from his legs, every last drop, and realized any attempt to escape would be foolish and fatal. "I thought we were going to trade."

"But of course. This—" Retnuh raised a small aerosol canister and smiled. "Insurance. You give me the disks, I release the woman. Everyone is happy."

But his dark sadistic eyes told a different story. He wanted to do it, wanted to add one more blazing chapter to the history of Plaza Mayor. Determined not to show his fear, Simon swallowed back the lump of panic lodged in his throat and tried to speak with confidence. "First I need to see that she's okay."

"No. First you will give to me the disks."

Not believing the man would turn him into a Roman candle before getting them, Simon took a deep breath and shook his head slowly, as if nothing in the world could change his mind. "After I see her."

Retnuh stepped back, his index finger curling into his thumb, ready to flick the cigarette. "Do not be foolish."

Simon reached down and pulled up his left pant leg, revealing the disks, still enclosed in their plastic security pouch and taped to the inside of his calf. "Go ahead. But you can say goodbye to these."

The dark eyes flashed, like headlights clicking to high beam, then instantly shuttered down. "This is most unnecessary. We must trust each other if we are to do business."

Simon could hardly believe his ears; the man was threatening to turn him into toast and talking about trust. And he seemed utterly serious, as if spraying someone with napalm was normal and rational. More than dangerous, the man was *crazy dangerous*. "Guess we both felt the need for insurance." He tried to make it sound reasonable, as if they were just two businessmen negotiating a deal. "So—" He let it hang there, as if to say, I've kept my end of the bargain, now it's your turn.

Retnuh stared back silently, as if weighing his options, attempting to explore in advance every possible outcome before making a decision. Finally he turned slightly and nodded toward the opposite side of the plaza. "There. At the café."

Simon spun around, his held-in fears for Lara threatening to explode in a rush of exuberant hope. He spotted her instantly, sitting across from a man at one of the small tables in front of La Torre del Oro, the famous bullfighting bar. Though he could see only her profile, and the distance was too great to distinguish features, there was no denying the cut and color of hair, and most especially the distinctive ski sweater she frequently wore to the office. "Where?" He spoke as loud as possible, making sure the tiny radio would pick up his voice. "Is that her, with that man in front of La Torre del Oro?"

Immediately Pilár's voice whispered into his ear. "I am looking."

Retnuh dropped the silver canister into the side pocket of his leather jacket and extended his hand. "You will now give me the disks."

Simon frowned, trying to appear more unsure than unwilling. "I can't really tell if it's her," though he didn't have any doubt. "I need to get closer."

Retnuh shook his head slightly, once to the left, once to the right, a warning. "This would not be a wise decision."

"Cut the bullshit. You're not going to do anything as long as I've got the disks."

Retnuh snorted softly, as if amused, and calmly ignited a fresh cigarette off the embers of the first. "It makes no difference to me. The disks will be destroyed."

The words hit like a winter wind in the middle of summer. For some reason he assumed the data was valuable, but if the information threatened the reputation of Bain-Haverland, they might very well prefer to have it disappear in a shrieking ball of flame. Or was the man bluffing? "Then release her. You've got me and I've got the disks."

Retnuh shrugged and pulled a tiny cellular from his pocket. Using his thumb, he punched in a short text

message, then pointed with his chin toward the opposite side of the plaza. Almost immediately the man sitting across from Lara stood up, leaned over the table,
said something, then walked away. Retnuh dropped
his phone back in his pocket. "She has been told to
wait for you. Now you will give me the disks."

Overcome with relief, Simon couldn't think of any
logical reason to resist. The man had kept his end of
the bargain, though satisfying the terms of an agreement with a kidnapper hardly seemed to carry any
moral obligation. He knelt down and started to lift his
pant leg when Pilár's urgent whisper crackled in his
ear. "It is not her. I can see her clearly now. It is *not*
her. Do you hear me, Simon?"

Yes, every word, each one like a pistol shot to the
head. And between them, the same terrible thought:

she was dead . . .

she was dead . . .

she was dead . . .

He felt himself going soft, his muscles threatening to
dissolve into a gooey mass of protoplasm. The urge to
give up, to hand over the disks and melt into the
bricks of Plaza Mayor seemed overwhelming, but
somewhere deep inside his brain a single spark of
anger resisted the temptation. And with it came the
voices, Lara and Pär Olin, demanding justice and retribution. Bracing his hands on his knees, the material
sticky beneath his fingers, he pushed himself to an
upright position. "Whew, don't feel so good." He
turned his hands back and forth, as if disoriented.
"Must be the smell."

Retnuh stepped back, his dark eyes narrowing to a

slit. "If you care about your health, you will give me the disks now."

Trying desperately to think of something, Simon took a deep breath and nodded, as if to gather himself for the effort. He could run, but knew he wouldn't get more than two steps. He could grab the guy, send them both into the flaming hereafter, or . . . ? But there was no *or*—no other options. Then he saw her, from the corner of his eye, not running but coming fast, and before he could even think, Pilár was between them, thrusting a map in Retnuh's face and jabbering away in Spanish. Simon didn't hesitate.

Caught off guard, it took Jäger a moment to throw the woman aside when Leonidovich bolted. The man was like a crazed bull on the streets of Pamplona, running for his life and knocking down everything in his path. What caused him to run, Jäger had no idea—perhaps he realized the disks were the only thing keeping him from his glorious moment of martyrdom—but the *why* was unimportant; he now knew exactly where the disks were and had no intention of letting them slip away.

Hurdling through the field of fallen easels and pushing aside irrate vendors, it took Jäger only a few seconds to close the gap. He reached out and caught the back of the courier's overcoat just as he barreled into a knot of tourists. Everyone went down in a heap, including a table of coins, setting off a chain reaction of screaming and scrambling and cursing. Trapped beneath the mountain of screeching tourists, Jäger began to reel in his target. It took a moment before he realized the coat was empty, and by the time he unscrambled himself from the mess, Leonidovich had disappeared.

Furious, Jäger rifled through the coat's pockets, finding nothing except one of Leonidovich's own business cards. Scribbled on the back were directions to an address on Pintor Rosales, and a name: Pilár Montez.

CHAPTER TWENTY-TWO

Plaza Mayor, Madrid

Monday, 18 November 12:05:51 GMT +0100

Shifting his weight from one bare foot to the other, Simon glanced around the tiny kitchen—nothing like the cold, vacant chill of an unfurnished apartment to make a person feel miserable. And at the moment, he couldn't have felt worse.

Standing at the sink, washing the napalm off his shoes, Pilár glanced back over her shoulder. "I thought he would catch you."

He nodded, feeling awkward and self-conscious standing there in his Calvin Klein boxers and a T-shirt. Ironically, it was the napalm that helped him escape, the slippery goo allowing him to slide out from under the avalanche of bodies before Retnuh could extract himself from the quagmire of cursing tourists. "Lucky. Nothing but dumb luck."

She handed him a shoe. "One makes their luck, Simon Leonidovich."

Something he had always believed, and by diving into the crowd he did create the event that led to his escape, but he was lucky, too, one smoker and they'd all have gone up in flames, something he didn't think about until after the fact. "Maybe." Even to himself, he sounded bitter and defeated.

She gave him a penetrating look. "Stop that. Lara is okay."

"You don't believe that."

"But I do. You think this man would take Lara from your office if he wished to kill her?" She shook her head, answering her own question. "This would have been most difficult. A great risk. This man is not a fool."

"No, he's crazy."

"*Sí, loco* like a fox. The woman's hair was *perfecto*. Without Lara he would not have remembered that."

"Maybe."

"And the sweater. This you recognized?"

"Yes."

"So." She threw out her arms, a great expressive shrug, as if it was all so obvious. "You think he killed her and kept her sweater as a souvenir?"

It did sound ridiculous, the way she said it. "Then why the charade?"

"Because you might have called the *policía*. Why take the risk? Without Lara no one could connect him with her disappearance."

He wanted to believe her, wanted desperately to believe Lara was okay. "So you think he was just being cautious? That he was hoping to get the disks without exposing himself to a kidnaping charge?"

"*Sí.*" She glanced down and grinned. "No exposure."

"I caught that."

She fluttered her long eyelashes. "Caught what, Señor?"

Despite his anxiety, he couldn't suppress a chuckle. She had a way of making him feel better no matter what the situation. "If you're right, that only complicates things. If I go to the police now, I'll lose the disks. But if I don't, and Lara's alive—"

She interrupted, her tone sharp. "She is."

"Okay. Is. So I can't give them up. But if I don't go to the police and something happens to her, it'll be even worse. Catch twenty-two. You understand catch twenty-two?"

"Of course. Joseph Heller."

Having seen her library, he wasn't surprised. "So, what should I do?"

She didn't hesitate. *"Nada."*

"Nothing?"

She turned back to the sink and the cleaning of his other shoe. "He will contact you."

"Retnuh?"

"Sí."

"You're probably right. If he wants the disks bad enough."

She shook her head, the thick mass of dark hair, not so much in answer as disgust. "The disks have nothing to do with it."

"What are you saying?"

"I know this man. He needs to win." She glanced back over her shoulder, her expression remote and reflective. "You escaped his trap. He failed. Now he must beat you."

He realized then that she was talking about men in general, her ex-husband in particular, about macho and machismo and *mano a mano,* and all the other stereotypical baggage that identified the male species, and since most of it was true and he was standing there in his boxer shorts feeling humiliated and beaten, and wanting to bring down Retnuh nearly as much as getting Lara back, he knew she was right. "I don't like the idea of waiting. I feel like I'm letting Lara down, doing nothing while she goes through—"

"A day. No more. You will hear by then."

She seemed so sure of everything, while he felt naked and helpless and sure of nothing. "And if not?"

She turned, handed him the shoe, and smiled. "We will think of something."

It was such a simple thing, that word—*we*—but if a woman like Pilár Montez could find him attractive, anything seemed possible. "Okay, we'll wait a day."

"Good. I think it is now time for me to find you some pants."

"It's only been a few minutes. He might still be out there."

She made a face, waving off any suggestion of trouble. "He paid me no attention."

"But he wasn't alone, we know that. One of the others might have noticed you. We can't take any chances with these people."

"Okay, I'll wait." She narrowed her eyes in a grinning way. "You are the one shivering in your shorts."

"One of my favorite country tunes."

There was an empty heartbeat, then an amused chuckle. "You are a funny man, Simon Leonidovich. But"—her expression turned serious—"I think it's a"—she struggled to find the right word—"like a trick."

"A trick?"

"To hide your fear."

"Oh, you mean a ruse."

"*Sí.* A ruse. This is true, no?"

Of course it was true, something he'd done all his life without conscious thought. It was obvious that little escaped the sharp eyes of Pilár Montez. "To hide my *concern.* Men don't admit fear."

"This I understand."

And he knew that she did, the way she looked into his eyes and studied his face, like an old sailor reads the sea, knowing the secrets that lay hidden beneath the surface. But most of all, what he saw was acceptance, of all that he was. He reached out and pulled her into his arms. *"Gracias."*

Her dark eyes twinkled. "For what, Señor?"

"You saved my life."

She leaned forward and kissed the tip of his nose. "A selfish act."

"Oh?"

"Co-op likes you."

"Smart cat. What about her roommate?"

She pressed closer, covering one eye and then the other with soft kisses. "What do you think, Señor?"

"I think if you keep that up I'll embarrass myself."

Then she was kissing his mouth, and he felt a wild rush as her tongue touched his, his body suddenly aroused and aching with the sensation of life, aware that he should have been dead. She groaned and moved closer, rubbing her body against his as he kissed her with wild and almost painful abandon, each desperate for the other. His hands found the buttons of her blouse and he shifted his attentions, teasing her nipples with soft kisses. She arched her back and trembled, her breath coming in desperate short gasps and he knew that she wanted him. Right then, without blanket or bed, without thought or reason or logic.

He reached down, undid the tie on her skirt and let it drop. She pulled off her white panties and turned to the wall. "Hurry." She crossed her arms against the wall and leaned forward, laying her head on her arms and rising up on her toes, lifting her buttocks into the air. Holding her waist, he pressed his body into hers, feeling her warmth and flesh dissolve into his own. Unlike the night before—a long, slow, satisfying ride into the heavens—this trip lasted only minutes, a rocket blast that left them both exhausted and satiated. Simon backed away, his legs like rubber beneath him, and collapsed onto the cold, ceramic floor.

She stood over him, naked and smiling, with all the shameless candor of a child. "You are pleased, no?"

"I am your slave to the end of my days."

She laughed. "Then I wish you a very long life, Señor." She leaned down, planted a kiss on his forehead, then began to dress. "Now it is time to find you some clothes."

With his butt freezing to the tile, he wasn't about to argue. Pulling on his boxers, he managed to get his legs back under him. "Retnuh could still be out there. You need to be careful."

She ruffled her hair into a wild frizz, until it looked like she'd shaken hands with a lightning bolt, then slipped on a pair of dark glasses. "No one will recognize me."

He hardly did himself. "But I still don't like the idea of you coming back. And I don't want you anywhere around when I leave."

She cocked her head to one side, thinking, then her

face brightened as some internal lightbulb blinked on. "I know a small shop. The owner is a friend. He would be glad to bring you some things."

"That should do wonders for your reputation."

She shrugged. "This I can live with."

"I'm serious, what's he going to think?"

"He will think you have very nice legs, Señor."

"Very funny."

"He will understand."

"Understand what? That I'm just another crazy *turista* running around without pants?"

She smiled, a rueful, puckered flash. "Just another dork."

CHAPTER TWENTY-THREE

Madrid

Monday, 18 November 16:30:15 GMT +0100

Hidden behind the dark glass of his rental van, Jäger watched the tiny blips move across the screen of his laptop—up and back, stopping and starting, stretching out in irregular yet repetitive patterns as the woman moved from one room to another. Though small, the parabolic tracking antenna was state of the art, with software to match, transposing each sound into a dot of light, the dots forming chains of motion until he could clearly visualize the floor plan. The size of her apartment surprised him, the entire top floor of the building, but the lack of neighbors would make things easier if he had to go in. Growing impatient—an emotion completely alien to his psyche and potentially disastrous to his profession—he switched over to his search protocol, checking for any new hits on the name: Pilár Montez.

In four hours he had learned many things. A flight attendant for Iberia Airlines, she normally worked the route between Madrid and New York. Divorced. Lived alone. Well educated. From one of Spain's most prominent families. Most important, he knew with absolute certainty that Leonidovich was not with her. But what he didn't know, and needed to, was what connection she had to the man. *Friend? Lover? Client?* The search screen revealed nothing new.

Using his twelve-power scope, he zoomed in on a well-dressed couple as they entered the building. Though distorted by the thick glass doors, he could still follow their movements as they signed in with the security guard. The routine never varied. This was good, but there were still too many unknowns, and he hated to do anything without adequate preparation. He liked to plan for contingencies, to expect the unexpected—like that stupid woman who stuck a map in his face at the Plaza—the kind of unforeseen incident that could lead to disaster. He closed his eyes, watching the memory with growing anger as it played like a newsreel on the back of his eyelids. *Spagnolo bitch.* If not for her he would have the disks. He took a deep breath, forcing himself to focus, to contain his anger.

He leaned forward against the dark glass, checking the street for any sign of Leonidovich, but suspected the man had already left the city. *Most unfortunate.* Given a choice, he would have considered the situation too unstable, but he no longer had the luxury of time, and the woman represented his best opportunity of learning quickly where the courier had gone. Turning back to his laptop, he clicked over to the file of documents copied from WorldWide's computers and began to scan through them until he found a good example of the courier's signature. He zoomed in, until only the name Simon Leonidovich covered his screen, then began to practice. Within minutes he had every curl and swirl infused in his mind. Confident he could fool the security guard, as long as the man had never met Leonidovich, but not sure how things would play out with the woman, he transferred his .22-caliber automatic to the outside pocket of his jacket before leaving the van.

He pushed through the glass entrance door and headed directly toward the security desk, moving quickly and confidently, the step of a man who'd been in the building many times. The guard jumped to his feet, his youthful face frozen in an awkward expression of enthusiastic doubt, like a new employee not quite sure of his job. *"Buenas tardes,* Señor."

Jäger affected an impatient scowl, as if he'd been through this irritating routine a thousand times. "Señorita Montez, *por favor."* Without being asked he scribbled the courier's name into the registration book. As he did so, he noticed the courier had signed in the evening before but hadn't checked out until morning. *Lover.*

As the guard swiveled the book around, Jäger watched the man's eyes for any sign of recognition or surprise. The young man glanced at his watch, marked the time, then studied the name intently before picking up the phone. Jäger slipped his hand into his pocket, ready to pull his automatic should the woman raise some kind of alarm about an unexpected visit from the courier.

"Señor Le-ondo-vich," the guard announced, stumbling awkwardly over the name. He glanced nervously at Jäger, obviously embarrassed at his verbal assassination, then bobbed his head in answer to whatever the woman was saying. *"Gracias."* He hung up the phone and motioned toward the elevator. "Señor."

Without waiting for further instruction, Jäger stepped forward and punched the sixth-floor button. He waited until the door closed, then pulled his automatic and held it down next to his leg, ready for the unexpected. When the door slid open that was exactly what he got, the elevator opening directly into the woman's home. She was standing there, only a few meters away, waiting with a big smile that melted from her face like hot wax the moment she realized it wasn't Leonidovich.

Jäger recognized her at once, the woman from the Plaza, and understood immediately that her interruption had not been the accident he assumed. Her dark eyes glittered with outrage and anger, though she didn't scream or run as most women would have done, but in fact looked quite breathtaking in her beauty and wrath. A sight that aroused him instantly. "Please, do not be alarmed. I mean you no harm."

But her eyes had found the gun and she didn't believe him. "Is that what you told Lara Quinn?"

He ignored the question, though realized that was exactly what he had said. "I am a businessman. All I want are the disks."

"Then get out of my house. I don't have them."

He stepped forward, only one step into the room, not wanting her to bolt. "Where is Leonidovich?"

She shook her head defiantly, not in answer to his question, but in her refusal to say.

He admired that, the fact that she didn't lie and had the courage to resist him. He smiled and waved his hand in a vague, nonchalant gesture. "This man is not important." He realized his mistake the moment the words crossed his tongue, he could see it in her eyes, her feelings for Leonidovich, and for some reason it felt like a personal attack. What could such a beautiful woman find attractive about an overweight delivery boy? It made no sense.

"He *is* a man," she snapped, raking him with her big eyes, as if dismissing a heap of garbage. "You are nothing."

The acidity of her words landed with such force that for a moment he felt paralyzed, as if his body had been smothered in fossil resin, and that was the moment she chose to make her move. But rather than run she went straight at him, knocking him back into the elevator with such force that he fell to his knees. He reached out and caught her arm, pulling her down on the floor beside him, but not before she managed to hit the alarm. Overcome with fury, he ignored the high-pitched siren and smashed his gun down across the side of her face, crushing her cheekbone. *"Spagnolo* whore!"

As he raised the gun to hit her again, a strange, inhuman sound broke through his rage. He looked up just as a snarling blur of silver fur struck his face, its claws digging deep into his flesh.

Pausing at the bottom of the steps, Simon scanned the Plaza one final time before venturing into the minefield. He didn't expect Retnuh to suddenly appear out of the shadows, not after five hours, but with the money of Bain-Haverland fueling the search, he had to anticipate that others could be watching and waiting. Even so, he wasn't overly worried; Pilár had slipped away without incident, her friend having delivered a small duffel of work clothes less than an hour later.

The central courtyard was nearly empty, only a few young couples strolling arm-in-arm in the fading light, the restaurants having moved their business inside. The arcade area was equally quiet, the vendors and artists having packed up and vanished like a tribe of gypsies when the shoppers began to thin. Satisfied that no one appeared out of place, he hooked the duffel over his shoulder, pulled the brim of his new tweed cap low over his forehead, and started across the courtyard, right in the open, just another working stiff cutting through the Plaza on his way home from work. Not too fast; a man got tired after a day of manual labor. And not too slow, not when you were looking forward to a beer and a hot meal. The duffel, which contained his security case, his laptop, and his only hope of saving Lara—the disks—felt like an anchor. No matter what happened, running would not be an option.

Exiting onto Mayor, he reluctantly passed a line of taxis—cabbies kept records—and crossed over to Santiago, a route he had mapped and memorized before leaving the apartment. Keeping a deliberate pace, he turned first into one alleyway, then another. Finally satisfied that no one had followed, he cut north on Bailén, past the Palacio Real, which formed the southern end of the Casa de Campo. According to the map in his head it was only a short walk from there to Pintor Rosales, then a kilometer or so up the avenue to Pilár's building.

That's when it hit him, the moment he tried to recall her address. A sense of dread rippled through his body, making his heart momentarily lose rhythm. He rifled through his pockets, telling himself it wasn't possible, but could see himself slipping the card into his overcoat. Even so, he couldn't be sure Retnuh had gotten the coat, or if so, had bothered to search the pockets. But that was foolish and hopeful—if anything, the man was thorough. Fanatically so. If he had the coat, he would check the pockets.

He started to run, trying to hold back his panic with desperate prayer: promising to do better, begging for help, and finally threatening to become an avowed atheist if his plea for divine intervention went unanswered. Within minutes he was gulping air like a dying fish. He kept telling himself Retnuh couldn't have gotten past the security guard, but knew better. The man was too evil and clever to let some glorified doorman stand in his way.

The street curved around to the west, following the perimeter of the park, then straightened out, a cluster of red lights flashing in the distance. It could have been anything—street maintenance, an accident, a fire—but the more he tried to convince himself, the less he believed it. Everything in his life seemed to be spiraling downward, out of control, and there was nothing he could do to stop it. He tried to run faster, but his feet felt as if they were buried in sand, his heart threatening to explode.

Even before he was close enough to see the structure, he knew it was her building by the towering line of jacaranda trees. A half-dozen police cars, tiny Fiats with their lights flashing, were skewed chaotically about the street, blocking traffic from both directions.

A crowd of curious neighbors had gathered near the building's entrance.

Trying to control his breathing, Simon pushed his way through the crowd toward a group of detectives and police officers huddled near the front doors. Though he couldn't understand the hushed words that rippled through the crowd, he could tell by the tone of speculation that no one knew exactly what had happened. As he worked his way closer, he could see a detective interviewing a man just inside the first row of onlookers, but it wasn't until Simon edged his way up behind the man that he noticed the uniform and recognized the security guard from the night before. The detective was asking the old man questions and recording his answers on a hand-held microcassette recorder.

Before Simon could say anything, a uniformed officer interrupted, handing the detective the building's registration book. The detective rotated the book around so the old man could read it, and pointed to the last entry, a name Simon could see clearly. His name. His signature. Except that it wasn't, not quite. The old security guard nodded and the detective moved his finger up the column of names, to Simon's signature from the previous evening. *"Ruso?"*

The old man shook his head. *"Americano."*

The detective cocked an eyebrow. *"Americano? Está seguro?*

The old man nodded emphatically. *"Sí,"* then with a dramatic flourish of gestures began to detail what Simon realized was his description.

The detective smiled faintly, a pay-dirt smile, and Simon didn't need an interpreter to understand he was now the number-one suspect for whatever had happened. He wanted to step forward, to explain everything, but had the feeling he wouldn't be able to say three words before they hauled him away. And if Retnuh now had both Pilár and Lara, all the more reason he couldn't afford to give up the disks.

Jesus, Mary, he felt as if he'd stepped into a tornado and landed in Oz. He didn't understand the language, didn't know what happened, and didn't know what to do. Then, as if things weren't bad enough, an ambulance squeezed through the maze of police cars and began to back in toward the entrance. Like everyone else, Simon could only watch as the attendants unloaded two gurneys and disappeared into the lobby.

The minutes passed with agonizing slowness, until finally, like the opening of a play, the thick glass doors with their filigree of silver patina swung outward, and like any audience, the crowd murmured and went silent. The detective leaned forward, whispered something to the old security guard, then stepped to the ambulance as the first gurney was wheeled out, a body hidden beneath the green sheet. The detective glanced back over his shoulder, making eye contact with the guard, then pulled back the cover. It was a young man, no more than twenty, the collar of his security uniform momentarily visible before the sheet dropped back over his head.

The old man nodded. "Javier González."

The detective motioned for the second gurney as the first disappeared into the ambulance. Like a child's game of pass-it-on, a hushed groan moved through the throng, not for the person hidden beneath the green sheet, but for the dead cat lying at one end, its head twisted awkwardly to the side, its paws covered in blood.

For Simon, in that moment, the world seemed to spin off its axis. He wanted to turn away, but like passing the scene of a terrible accident, couldn't. The detective reached down, lifted the sheet, and the old man nodded again. "Señorita Montez."

CHAPTER TWENTY-FOUR

Taormina, Sicily

Thursday, 21 November 16:29:32 GMT +0100

It was one of those perfect days—the sun low in the south, pouring out bands of yellow and orange light. The faint outline of Italy floated like a ghost over the horizon, but for the first time since building his villa, Jäger took no pleasure in the view. There was something about seeing it through one eye that took away the enjoyment. The woman, of course, had paid for the unprovoked attack. And her *demente* cat. But it wasn't enough.

Simon Leonidovich, he was the cause, and must now pay with his life.

And Grayson Haverland. With his millions.

Just the thought made Jäger's heart pump faster, sending the blood pulsating through his veins and hammering away at the back of his dead eye. The pain was almost unbearable, and it took all his willpower to sit through it, to force his anger back under control and wait for the pounding to stop. Despite the cool temperature of the air, his forehead and shirt were soaked with sweat by the time the last

tremor passed. The housekeeper, he suddenly realized, was standing only a few feet away, waiting to be
recognized. He ignored her, her look of pitiful concern only aggravated him more. Taking a silk hand-
kerchief from his pocket, he calmly wiped his brow
and adjusted his eyepatch before acknowledging her
presence. *"Parlare,* Maria."

She pulled a small bottle of pills from her apron.
"Medicamento, Patron?"

No, he wasn't about to dull his senses with drugs,
not before making the call, something he couldn't
avoid much longer. He shook his head, slowly, not
wanting to awaken the demons. *"Nessuno.* I'm feeling
much better."

The wrinkles tightened across her forehead, a
motherly look of concern and disapproval. "Will that
be all, *Patron?"*

"Everything is prepared?"

"Sì."

"Grazie." He handed her an envelope containing
half-a-million lira, a considerable bonus for a peasant
like Maria. "A small *gratifica.* Have a nice vacation,
Maria."

She hesitated, obviously reluctant to leave him un-
attended after what she believed to be the unfortunate
result of a ski accident. "This *vacanza,* it is not necessary, Signore."

"Nonsense, my sister will be here tomorrow." He
forced a smile to cover the lie, as if he couldn't wait to
see her. "Did I mention she was a nurse?" The last
time he saw his sister—she was twelve, he was fourteen—she was selling her body to young boys and old
men on the streets of Beirut.

"*Sí.*" She handed him the bottle of pills and backed away. "Thank you, Signore."

He waited a good ten minutes, making sure she hadn't forgotten anything before setting the deadbolt. It was too early in California to call Haverland, so he took his time, eating a leisurely supper and enjoying a glass of twenty-year-old crusted port before descending to his workshop.

Typical of most wine cellars, the light was subdued and soft, the air a temperate 13° Celsius; but unlike most old-world cellars, everything else about the room was modern and hi-tech. Cobwebs and dust did not exist beyond the hermetically sealed door at the top of the stairs. The floors and walls were all finished in black slate, in sharp contrast to the polished aluminum bottle racks that circled the room from floor to ceiling, containing the best collection of red wine in all of Sicily. On the back wall, fitted tightly between two of the huge racks, a six-foot-wide stainless-steel cooler with glass doors offered a limited but exclusive assortment of white wine, champagne, and beer. The room contained no furniture, only a long glass table supported by swooping, orthometric legs of polished steel. Lined up in a row down the center of the table were four bottles of Chateau Pichon Pauillac, identical except for their vintage, and a silver tray containing a waiter's corkscrew, a white hand towel, and an Austrian-made lead-crystal decanter with four Bordeaux glasses.

Jäger paused at the bottom step. Everything was perfect and pristine, exactly as he demanded, but like everything else, seeing it through one eye somehow diminished its austere beauty. "Leonidovich." He spit out the name, an involuntary reaction to the stab of pain that burned through his eye socket. Dying would be too easy—the man needed to suffer.

He reached up behind the small wall sconce next to the stairway and touched the hidden button. Instantly the wine cooler began to move forward and turn—like the door of a bank vault, slow and hushed—exposing his workshop beyond.

Programmed to keep the exchange of air to a minimum, the huge cooler began to slide back into position the moment he stepped through the opening. Though similar in size to the wine cellar, and decorated in monochrome colors that suited his personality, the room was brightly lit and designed for work. Like any master craftsman, the tools of his trade were all there, within easy reach, arranged in neat rows above his workbench: miniature cameras and video cameras, close-surveillance binoculars and long-range telescopic sites, tracking cones and tracing bugs, mini tape recorders and micro listening devices, a telephonic voice modifier, and a hand-held G.P.S. unit with a high-resolution color display. The selection was endless.

There were no weapons—in the business of "hunt and find," violence was never the intention—and only a few innocuous restraints: packages of zip ties, coils of nylon rope, a 300,000-volt stun baton, and a small but effective assortment of disabling drugs. The larger items, everything from a laptop computer with parabolic antenna, to a mobile microwave transmitter with expandable dish, were stored beneath the workbench in shipping boxes marked:

PROPERTY OF: UNIVERSITY OF BRITISH COLUMBIA
GLOBAL-WARMING RESEARCH DEPT.

A nonthreatening activity from a nonthreatening
country, from a nonexistent department, which could
justify the need for any type of equipment.

The Planning Center, located along the adjacent
wall, was even more sophisticated and comprehensive,
including three computers and a library of CDs and
DVDs. The wall was covered in maps, the shelves
lined with atlases and almanacs from around the
world. A small file box, indexed by nationality, contained passports and identification documents from a
dozen different countries.

Jäger dropped into his chair and immediately
began to study the monitors of the three computers
grinding away on his long desk, each programmed
with a different set of search parameters. If
Leonidovich did anything—used a credit card or
wrote a check, reserved lodging or rented a car,
booked a flight or bought something, made a long-
distance call or used an ATM—the search engines
would find it. But so far—*nothing*. Three days and
not a blip. Either the man had gone into hiding or
was being held incognito by the police. Eventually he
would surface, they always did, but Jäger had hoped
for something before making the call, a matter he
could no longer avoid.

He leaned forward and selected one of the six cellular phones lined up like soldiers along the back of his
desk. Usually he kept a dozen at hand—it was possible
to run through six a day when he restricted their use

to one call—but his source for the reprogrammed units, a sexy young woman who could normally lift ten to twelve a day from unsuspecting male tourists, had been picked up by the police. Jäger had yet to find a new supplier. With practiced ease, he connected the tiny phone to a modem cable already attached to his main computer, activated his LINE-MONITOR and SCRAMBLER programs, and punched in Haverland's private number.

Despite the seven-thousand-mile microwave transmission, Haverland's voice came back as clear and arrogant and narcissistic as if he were sitting in the same room. "Grayson Haverland here."

Jäger pictured the man in his mind, a pompous ass with a mountain of money and a taste for young girls. "This is Retnuh," he answered evenly, hiding his disdain.

There was an extra beat of silence, longer than the normal transcontinental hiccup. "Give me a moment."

Jäger waited, knowing the man was shooing someone from the room or calling someone in. Twenty seconds passed, then a faint click as Haverland came back on the line. "You have the package?"

Jäger hesitated as the line meter jumped, indicating there were now two active phones on Haverland's end. He considered terminating the connection, but decided to continue when he saw no indication of a reverse trace. "There's been a complication. It will take longer than expected."

"That's very disappointing."

Disappointing! Grayson Haverland was not the type to accept delay so graciously. Why didn't he ask more? Demand details? There could be but two reasons: because he already knew, or because he didn't want to. Jäger considered quickly the ramifications of each. Not wanting to know: distance and deniability. *Acceptable.* But if he knew, that meant he would have talked to Leonidovich. Perhaps cut his own deal for the disks. *Not acceptable.* Either way, he knew how to find out. "Perhaps you'd like to terminate our arrangement?"

Haverland's response was immediate and emphatic. "Absolutely not."

"My expenses are higher than anticipated. I would understand if you'd like to cut your losses. I would be most happy to return your deposit." That, of course, was something he would never do.

"The money is unimportant."

That was all Jäger needed to hear. "I should know something soon." He glanced at the other two monitors, hoping, but finding nothing.

"Please keep me informed."

Please. A man like Haverland didn't say please unless he was desperate. "Of course." He disconnected the modem line and dropped the phone into the burn basket beneath his desk. *The money is unimportant.* The fool had no idea how much the eye of Eth Jäger was worth. And Leonidovich—did he know? He swiveled his chair around to face the woman. "Do you know?"

She stared back at him through unfocused, dilated pupils, her mind locked in zombie-like sleep. Lying naked on the narrow cot, the IV dripping a steady dose of Versed into her veins, she looked like a department-store mannequin carved out of pale wood.

"I think it is time to give your Leonidovich a nudge." As the idea took hold, Jäger chuckled to himself. "Perhaps he would like a picture." Keeping the woman alive had been a good decision. Leonidovich cared. That was his weakness—his Achilles' heel. Eventually he would stumble.

CHAPTER TWENTY-FIVE

La Jolla

Haverland punched the REPLAY button on his phone and listened again to the brief conversation. For the third time. He kept wishing he hadn't said what he had, that it would sound different in retrospect, but it was still there, as clear as crystal—his desperation. "What do you think?"

Tripp leaned back in his chair, his lips curled in a deprecating smile. "About what?"

"Don't be an ass."

The smug half-smile widened. "You're the one who told him money is unimportant."

"It isn't," though Haverland knew it was a mistake the moment he said it. Defending the remark only made it worse—he knew it, Tripp knew it—and that angered him all the more, the fact that Tripp would dare mention it. "You're the one who found this maniac."

Unfortunately, Tripp admitted silently, then shrugged as if he hardly cared. But of course he cared desperately. Forty-one more days until the first of the year . . .

Forty-one more days until the merger with Allen Labs . . .

Forty-one more days until he was rich and free of King Grayson and all his royal bullshit. But what he did enjoy—*oh, so much*—was watching the arrogant bastard squirm. "He may have gotten a little out of control."

"A little out of control!" Haverland shot out of his chair like someone had shoved a rocket up his ass. "That's the biggest fucking understatement I've ever heard! What are you going to do about it, that's what I want to know."

"As your lawyer—"

"Don't give me any of your legal crap."

Knowing Haverland was prone to recording their conversations, Tripp ignored the interruption. "I think you should go to the police and tell them everything before you're implicated in a murder." Of course he knew Haverland would never do it, nor did Tripp want him to—they were both involved up to their oysters, whether King Grayson realized it or not.

Haverland leaned over his huge desk and stabbed a finger at Tripp's nose. "I don't know anything about any murder."

Tripp was half-tempted to laugh, just to aggravate the bastard more, but decided to let it go, to leave the man with his self-serving illusion of deniability. "I didn't mean to imply that you did. I meant to say *wrongly implicated.*"

Haverland straightened up. "You hired Retnuh to find and recover our property. Nothing more."

You, not *we*—now Tripp was certain the conversation was being recorded. "That's true."

Haverland began to pace, back and forth behind his desk, ticking off his arguments one-by-one on his fingers. "We reported the theft to the police."

"Right."

"Both here and in Sweden."

Tripp tuned out the words, it was all bullshit, meant for the recorder. Like all kings, Haverland thought he was omnipotent, but Tripp knew better—there were too many things that needed to go right when everything seemed to be racing in the opposite direction. Eventually the police would find Leonidovich, then someone would start to put it all together:

the disks,

the death of the researcher,

the kidnaping of the courier's sister,

and now this . . .

He glanced down at the newspaper on his lap, folded over to the International Section, and the article about a double homicide in Madrid and the search for Simon Leonidovich of New York. *Nope*, way too much shit for King Grayson to bury beneath his billion dollars. And if Retnuh got lucky and found Leonidovich before the police, they'd have to deal with that crazy bastard—one person Tripp hoped never to meet. The room, he suddenly realized, was silent, Haverland waiting for some kind of response. He nodded thoughtfully. "You're absolutely right." About what, he had no idea.

Haverland resumed his diatribe. Like most monarchs, the man didn't talk, he lectured.

Now that he thought about it all, Tripp was half tempted to run. He had his emergency bag packed and ready but couldn't imagine starting over again with nothing. Not at his age. *Need to wait,* hope nothing would blow up before the merger. Then he was gone. Fuck Haverland and his *secret file,* none of it would matter once he was out of the country with a few million in his pocket.

Haverland dropped back into his ergonomically correct, king-of-the-world chair. "We've done everything possible to protect our shareholders—"

Tripp smiled to himself; considering that Haverland was the biggest shareholder, that was the first truthful thing he'd said all day. "Absolutely."

"And the well-being of our patients."

Patients—the man was delusional! Not only had he managed to absolve himself from any responsibility in a kidnaping and multiple murder, but had somehow forgotten what this was all about—the possibility that thirty-three million Mira-loss users would die! What he didn't want to believe, he simply decided wasn't true. The arrogant bastard hadn't assembled a Verification Team to confirm the research, and expressed no intention of doing so. That was more than Tripp could bring himself to endorse, at least verbally, so he simply shrugged.

Haverland leaned forward, his right hand hidden beneath the desk. "We need a plan."

"Plan?"

"How to deal with Retnuh."

Tripp didn't like the sudden change in tone and had a feeling Haverland had switched off the recorder. "What do you mean?"

"He'll try to blackmail us."

True, but Tripp didn't give a damn. "So what? Pay

him. It's not like you can't afford a couple million in hush money."

"I'm not worried about the money. The guy's crazy. There's no telling what he'll do."

"What are you suggesting?"

Haverland leaned closer, his voice low and conspiratorial. "You know."

Right, kill the crazy bastard. The great King Grayson still believed he could win the Nobel, and couldn't afford to have anyone around who might tarnish his overblown, self-promoting reputation.

"Think about it."

Tripp nodded, having no intention of doing even that. How long, he wondered, before Haverland would justify the need to eliminate Edgar Tripp from his life?

CHAPTER TWENTY-SIX

Amsterdam

Thursday, 28 November 08:48:42 GMT +0100

Like a bubble floating up from the deep, Simon slowly surfaced from his self-induced voyage into hell—a place so deep and dark and silent he couldn't hear the screams of his sister, or see the still, silent face of Pilár Montez. Rolling onto his side, he cracked one eye, trying to remember where he was, but the light was too much, exploding across his forehead like a bomb. It took another ten minutes of absolute stillness, waiting for his blood pressure to ease out of the red zone, before he tried again.

Slowly the blurred shapes began to solidify into objects, unleashing a mixture of vague memories: the long train ride across Spain and France and Belgium, trying to put distance between himself and the police. He couldn't fly or rent a car, anyplace he would have to use his passport. It took three days, using local commuters to avoid the main border crossings, but he finally made it to Amsterdam, a city known for its permissive atmosphere, where he hoped to disappear in the crazy jumble of humanity. He remembered renting the small houseboat, a cozy hideaway for romantic couples, but beyond that everything dissolved in a blur. He didn't know the time or the day, or even how many days he'd been there. From the accumulation of miniature Tanqueray bottles lined up like green soldiers next to his bed, it might have been a week. *Jesus, Mary!*

He had never been much of a drinker, had never tried to drown his problems in liquor, but from the hammering inside his head, that's exactly what he'd done. He remembered some of it, the crying and screaming and cursing, the terrible feeling of loss, but now all he felt was hollow—dead inside. Alone. And this was the moment, he felt it, he had to take control of his life, or risk falling into a pit so deep he would never be able to crawl out.

Gritting his teeth, he pushed himself into a sitting position. It was bad, everything he'd heard about hangovers multiplied by ten. He looked like a street bum, his clothes wrinkled and stained with perspiration—and felt worse, his skin clammy, his mouth full of cat fur, his head about to split down the middle, his stomach threatening to explode. By sheer willpower he made it to the bathroom before erupting.

By the time he pulled his head out of the toilet, he felt as if he'd gone twelve rounds with Mohammed Ali. Using the tiny stainless sink for support, he managed to pull himself upright. The sweaty, blotchy face reflected in the mirror was not anyone he recognized—or cared to know. He brushed his teeth, gargled for a good five minutes, then sat on the floor of the shower and let the water pound at him until it turned cold. It helped, but he still felt shaky and badly in need of nourishment. A bowl of warm milk and a piece of toast sounded surprisingly good—something from the memory bank of his childhood—but the only food he could find in the refrigerator was a container of raw herring and a thick bar of Droste chocolate, both of which made his stomach clench.

Fighting off waves of nausea and a bad case of the shakes, he managed to get himself dressed and up the street to a small grocery. The neighborhood was semi-residential, less than a ten-minute walk from Old Amsterdam, and offered a wide variety of bars, restaurants, and shops. Many of the warehouses along the canal had been converted into small hotels, so unless somebody had a camera hanging from their neck, it was impossible to distinguish the tourists from the locals. Loading up on an assortment of supplies and the latest edition of *The International Herald-Tribune,* he managed to make it back to the houseboat without drawing attention to himself.

Needing sun, he settled into one of the deck chairs and slowly ate his breakfast—two small croissants, no butter or jam, and a large coffee, heavily diluted with cream. He felt reasonably safe. He always carried a stash of emergency cash, and had not used a credit card since leaving Madrid, which he felt certain the police would use to track his movements. The owner of the houseboat had been more than accommodating—enthusiastically pleased to receive his rent in Euros, and unlike the hotels, could have cared less about recording any passport information.

Still feeling bad, but beyond the point of immediate death, he leaned back and reluctantly picked up the paper.

Thursday, November 28, 2002

Same year, same month—one week lost.

There was nothing startling in the headlines, just the usual mixture of tragedies, border disputes, and political hyperbole. He quickly thumbed through the pages, finding what he hoped he wouldn't in the European News section.

Madrid, Wednesday

Interpol has expanded its search for Simon Leonidovich of New York, wanted for questioning regarding a double homicide in Madrid.

The family of one of the victims, Pilár Montez, has offered a $400,000 reward for information leading to the killer.

It wasn't much, but that in itself indicated a continuing story with the details having been rehashed in previous articles. Everyone in the world understood the innuendo of "wanted for questioning," and with no other names mentioned, clearly implied Interpol wasn't knocking down doors looking for other suspects. That, and the offer of $400,000 would be enough to get every two-bit bounty hunter with a gun onto the street. He was half-tempted to turn himself in at the American Embassy and take his chances, but knew the long arm of Bain-Haverland would reach out and quickly reclaim their *stolen* disks. He couldn't allow that. Not that he had any illusions about trading them for Lara, the fantasy that she might still be alive had died along with Pilár. But unless he found out what they contained, no one would ever believe his story. More important, three people would have died for nothing. He owed them more than that.

He needed help. Someone with the ability to decipher encrypted files. Someone *willing* to do it. One of the people in his tech-chat group might have the knowledge, but aside from their sign-on names and the fact that they all lived in New York, he didn't know any of them: not their real names, who they worked for, or who he could trust. Still, he couldn't think of anyplace else to start.

Not daring to use his cellular, which would create an immediate record of his location, he updated the summary of events he'd written in Oslo with what happened in Madrid, copied it onto a floppy along with his address book and bookmarks, then set out to find an Internet café. He found what he was looking for in Old Amsterdam, near Rembrandt Square, not more than a fifteen-minute walk from the houseboat. Despite its location, it was anything but old, and hardly a café. Appropriately called easyEverything, the place was a modern-day, high-tech enterprise that looked more like a gymnasium, including bright lights and wooden floors. The huge space was divided into endless rows of computer terminals—over six hundred in all—each with their own keyboard, mouse, and fifteen-inch flat-screen display. It wasn't exactly cozy and private, the chairs barely three feet apart with no privacy screens between terminals, but none of the users seemed to have any voyeuristic interest in what anyone else was doing. Most of the customers were college age, many of them dropouts by appearance, out to see the world, save the world, or fuck the world. Interspersed among the youth was a mixture of business travelers and tourists.

A model of international bilingual efficiency, it took Simon only a few minutes to buy four hours of Internet access, usable any time over the next twenty-eight days, and select a spot among the cyber-masses. By the time he logged on using his new password, his files had been transferred onto the server and were available in his private locker.

"Very efficient." He didn't realize he'd spoken aloud until the young woman on his left glanced over and frowned, letting him know that speaking to one's screen constituted a breach of cyber-etiquette. "Sorry."

He clicked his MAIL link, then sat back to wait for his messages to download.

Getting New Messages
Status: Receiving: 1 of 94

Ninety-four! With his brain still functioning at dull speed, he decided to ignore the header information and open everything in chronological order to avoid confusion. He began to work his way down the list: deleting the spam and newsletters and jokes, and filing anything that required a reply in his PENDING folder. At least a third of the messages were from acquaintances and business contacts, expressing their reaction to news stories, everything from disbelief to condemnation. The most effusive endorsement came from the person benefiting most from his absence, the owner of the courier service receiving WorldWide's referrals, who sent a note conveying his gratitude, support, and "absolute faith in your innocence." Support, Simon had a feeling, that would last only as long as the phones kept pouring out business.

He had gone through more than half the messages before finding the one he knew would be there, and would require some kind of answer.

Subject: ????
   Date: Tues, 19 November 2002 19:01:13 EST
   From: **William & Lois Quinn**
   <w-lquinn@in.com>
      To: **Simon Leonidovich**
   <SimonL@WorldwideSD.com>

Simon, what is going on? Reading between the lines, the papers make it sound like you're involved in some kind of international smuggling operation. We don't understand this. Why are you avoiding the police?

Have you heard from Lara? Lois and I are distraught with worry.

Allie and Jack Jr. are fine, the trip to Disney World was a distraction, but they are now asking for their mother and we don't know what to tell them.

We are praying and waiting to hear from you.

Bill

Even they had doubts. Typical of their generation, they trusted authority without question and believed anything in print to be true. What could he say to shatter that illusion? And did he want to? The only thing that really mattered was Lara. But how could he give them hope when he had none? He moved the message to the top of his PENDING folder, clicked the café icon at the bottom of his screen, ordered a cappuccino from the list of drinks, then began to work his way through the remaining messages. He was down to the last ten when the waiter arrived with his drink.

"Cappuccino?"

Simon clicked the next message—a graphic file—to start the download before looking up. "You sound American."

The young man, not more than eighteen, with long blond hair tied in a ponytail, nodded. "Deee-troit." He leaned forward and placed a mug down next to the keyboard. The scent of marijuana, something that could be legally purchased in half the bars and brewpubs around the city, wafted off his body like cheap aftershave. "What about you?"

It suddenly occurred to Simon that his picture might have appeared in some of the international papers. "Canada." A provincial, apolitical country in most people's minds, it was his favorite place of origin whenever he needed to keep his citizenship hidden. A prudent precaution in many Arab states.

The young man bobbed his head. "Cool. That'll be four guilders."

Not wanting to encourage conversation, Simon handed the kid a five-guilder note and turned back to his monitor. The next message had finished downloading, but there was no message, only a small eyeball staring directly back at him from the middle of the screen. He wasn't sure why, but the image gave him a chill, a low-frequency hum that raised the hair along the back of his neck.

The header information didn't reveal much.

Date	Subject	Sender	Size
Thur, 21 Nov 2002 21:04	Guess who?	Unknown@hotmail.com	2149KB

The "Guess who?" sounded like a sales teaser, and the "Sender" name meant nothing, typical for that kind of message, but for some reason he didn't think it was spam. The clue was in the eye—such a tiny graphic wouldn't consume over two thousand kilobytes. He moved his cursor over the image, right clicked, and selected PROPERTIES. As suspected, the image contained a hidden EXE file. Normally, he made it a practice never to open an executable from an unknown source, but working on a public server with protection against worms and viruses, he could think of no reason not to.

Closing out the PROPERTIES dialog, he moved his cursor back over the eye and double-clicked. Like a time-lapse exposure of a blossoming flower, the image began to expand: exposing first one eyebrow, then the bridge of a nose. Then there were two eyes, and then he knew. *Lara.*

Unable to breathe, he watched as the camera slowly pulled away, the picture expanding outward as Lara's image receded and became smaller. Finally she was all there, looking small and vulnerable in the center of his screen—and naked. But alive. At least then, when the picture was taken. She was sitting very erect, in an ultramodern chair of polished steel and black leather and holding a newspaper. He glanced around, making sure no was watching, then edged forward on his chair, blocking as much of the screen as possible.

Five words—THROUGH A GLASS EYE DARKLY—framed the bottom edge of the picture, and beneath the words, a magnifying icon. He clicked the icon, then the newspaper, which immediately doubled in size. He clicked twice more, until he could read the date beneath the banner: Wednesday, November 20, 2002. For the first time since Madrid he felt alive, that there was still hope. He moved the cursor up past the newspaper, blocking his mind to Lara's nakedness, and zoomed in on her face. Her eyes looked glazed, drugged out, but moist—a good sign. He zoomed in closer. So close he could count the pores in her skin. So close he couldn't miss the edit marks if the photo had been altered. There were none. He took a deep breath, bubbles of relief bursting in his chest, then scrolled down past the picture, expecting to find a message. But there was nothing, only the picture and the five words: THROUGH A GLASS EYE DARKLY.

The words pulsated through his brain. *Through a glass eye darkly.* What the hell was that supposed to mean? What kind of game was Retnuh playing? Then it hit him, a memorized quote from his college days: "He saw nearly all things, as through a glass eye, darkly."

Nearly all things. What was he supposed to see? What did he miss?

He enlarged the paper until the screen was covered in newsprint, then began scanning through the various stories. Buried among a group of small articles just above the fold, he found it.

Where Did Simon Go?

Better be nimble,
Better be quick,
Or ....
Contact retnuh@hotmail.com

What a sick, demented bastard. The paper's style and print had been duplicated exactly, the edit marks hidden along the column lines. Why would he go to that kind of trouble? But as quickly as Simon asked himself the question, he realized the answer. To Retnuh it was nothing *but* a game—the ultimate game of hide-and-seek, winner take all—and he was simply making his opening move, measuring Simon as an adversary. In an odd way it gave Simon a renewed sense of confidence. At least now he understood the rules. The prize was obvious. And that meant Retnuh would keep Lara alive as long as she had value.

As long as I have the disks.

A trade was out of the question. After Pilár, he could never trust the man, and without the disks the police would never believe him. He needed an edge.

He needed to know what the disks contained. What
made them so valuable? Then he would have something to bargain with.

He quickly ran through the last few messages,
transferred the ones he wanted to save to his private
locker, then activated his Instant Messenger, letting
anyone in his tech group who happened to be on-line
know he was available. He didn't expect a response—
the group usually connected at night and it was now
early morning in New York—but within seconds a
message dialog ballooned onto his screen.

▶ Hello, Bagman. I just logged on
  to check my mail and caught your
  beep. Where have you been? Vic-
  TheQuick

Simon knew who it was even before reading the
name. Always precise and articulate, Vic was the sole
member of the group who never used Internet shorthand, always took the time to write complete sentences and punctuate properly. He was also, in
Simon's opinion, the smartest of the group. Never pretentious or pedantic, he always seemed to have an answer to the tough questions.

▶ OUT OF THE COUNTRY.
▶ Lucky you.

Yeah, lucky. Until that moment Simon had always
appreciated the autonomous nature of the group, that
they could communicate on a subject of common interest and never encumber the process with political

opinion or personal baggage, but now that he was
about to violate that unspoken rule, he wondered who
Vic was and how he might react when he found out
who he was talking to. For just a moment, Simon considered trying to avoid that bit of information, but realized there was no way around it.

▶ I NEED SOME HELP WITH A PROBLEM. KNOW
YOU'RE PROBABLY HEADING TO WORK—COULD WE
ARRANGE SOME CHAT TIME LATER TODAY?

▶ Don't know about you, Bagman, but
I make it a habit never to work on
Thanksgiving.

Jesus, Mary—Thanksgiving! What the hell had happened to his life?

▶ STUPID ME. FORGOT. NOT SOMETHING THEY CEL-
EBRATE HERE.

▶ So what's the problem? Hardware
or software?

▶ SOFTWARE

▶ My specialty. Shoot.

▶ IT'S KIND OF PERSONAL. WOULD YOU MIND
SWITCHING TO A PRIVATE ROOM?

This time the response took longer. It was the first
time anyone in the group had ever asked for a private
conversation.

▶ I don't understand, Bagman. We're
alone now.

▶ SORRY, BUT SOMEONE COULD LISTEN IN. PLEASE.

There was another short delay before the answer came back.

> ◗ Okay. Send me the location.

Simon quickly typed out instructions, then logged into the private chat room. Vic signed in seconds later.

> ◗ Before you say anything, Bagman, you should know there's something about this I don't like.
> ◗ UNDERSTOOD. APPRECIATE YOUR CANDOR. DO YOU KNOW ANYTHING ABOUT ENCRYPTED FILES?
> ◗ A little. Why do you ask?

Simon smiled to himself. When Vic knew *a little* about something, it usually meant he knew everything.

> ◗ I HAVE SOME ENCRYPTED FILES I NEED TO OPEN AND CAN'T.
> ◗ What are you saying, the encryption key failed?
> ◗ I DON'T HAVE A KEY. IS THERE A BACKDOOR?
> ◗ Why don't you have the key?

Simon had the distinct feeling he was no more than one wrong answer away from a disconnect.

> ◗ THE FILES AREN'T MINE.
> ◗ I can't help you.
> ◗ CAN'T OR WON'T?
> ◗ It makes no difference.
> ◗ IT MIGHT. ONCE I EXPLAIN.

▶ Okay. Explain.
▶ SORRY, PLEASE DON'T BE OFFENDED, BUT I
  DON'T WANT TO EXPLAIN UNLESS YOU HAVE THE
  ABILITY TO HELP.

This time the delay between messages grew exceptionally long, Vic obviously pondering whether or not
he wanted to expose that kind of information about
himself. Finally, after a full two minutes, his response
popped into Simon's text box.

▶ Okay, that sounds reasonable. Ex-
  plain.
▶ THEN YOU KNOW MORE THAN "A LITTLE" ABOUT
  THIS SUBJECT?
▶ Yes.

Though exactly the answer Simon hoped for, it
scared him. What kind of people knew anything about
encrypted files? Or how to crack them? Hackers. Law
enforcement. Neither choice sounded very appealing.
On the other hand, he didn't have time to go tippy-
toeing through the minefield, not with Lara trapped in
the middle, waiting for help. If there was ever a time to
put his head down and run . . .

▶ HAS THERE BEEN ANYTHING IN THE PAPERS THERE
  ABOUT SIMON LEONIDOVICH?

A short pause.

▶ Yes.
▶ YOURS TRULY.

▶ I hope you're kidding.
▶ NO.
▶ You don't need me. You need a
  lawyer.
▶ THE CIRCUMSTANCES ARE NOT WHAT THEY SEEM.
▶ All the more reason to get your-
  self a lawyer. Good luck, Bagman,
  you're going to need it.

Realizing he was about to get a disconnect, Simon knew he had to do something dramatic.

▶ I'M ATTACHING A PICTURE I JUST RECEIVED.
THE WOMAN IS MY SISTER. SHE'S BEEN KID-
NAPPED.

It was three minutes before a response came back.

▶ Okay, you have my attention. Ex-
  plain.
▶ THE CIRCUMSTANCES ARE COMPLICATED. I'VE
  WRITTEN A SUMMARY OF EVENTS WHICH I WOULD
  LIKE YOU TO READ. THEN, IF YOU'RE WILLING
  TO HELP I'LL SEND YOU THE ENCRYPTED FILES.
▶ Okay. Send the summary. I'll read
  it. No promises.
▶ UNDERSTOOD. THANKS. SUMMARY ATTACHED.
  LET'S RECONNECT IN THIRTY MINUTES. OKAY?
▶ Okay, thirty minutes.

Simon sipped his cold cappuccino and waited, never taking his eyes off the screen. Exactly thirty minutes later Vic's answer came streaming into the text box.

▶ Okay, I believe you. Or should say, I believe you believe it. That doesn't make it true. The connection between the disks and what's happened to your sister seems awfully far-fetched.

This was not, Simon realized, the time to argue. Considering what the papers might have printed, he needed to sound reasonable.

▶ I AGREE. BUT CAN YOU THINK OF ANOTHER EX-PLANATION?

A long minute passed before Vic responded.

▶ Okay, I'll look at the disks. Maybe I can open them, maybe not. BUT unless they confirm a reason for all this, I'll turn them over to the police.

▶ FAIR ENOUGH. THANK YOU. WHERE DO I SEND THEM?

There was an exceptionally long pause and Simon knew exactly what Vic was thinking. No one in his right mind wanted to give his name and address to someone wanted for murder. The answer, when it came, confirmed Vic's quick intelligence: avoiding both the use of his name and any way to trace him.

▶ Send to: V.H. (Postmaster, please confirm identity: last 4#'s of NY driver's license: 6281), General Delivery, Radio City Station, NY, NY 10101

▶ THANKS, VIC. YOU'LL HAVE THEM TOMORROW.

▶ Okay. Good luck. By the way, I get it.

▶ GET WHAT?

▶ Your handle. Bagman.

CHAPTER TWENTY-SEVEN

La Jolla

Grayson Haverland nodded and smiled and tried to memorize the names as Robert Maitland introduced "his team." It was hopeless, he could hardly remember the names of his own "team." It should have been one of those great days; the idea for a pre-merger reception had seemed so ideal just a few weeks earlier, a chance for the key players at Bain-Haverland to meet their counterparts from Allen Labs, but Haverland couldn't have felt worse—even in this opulent setting of wealth and power. He wanted to enjoy it, but couldn't, not as long as those disks hung over his neck like a guillotine.

How could Leonidovich have vanished so completely? And the sister? *Jesus,* a mother with two kids. What had Retnuh done with her? To her? But he couldn't ask—didn't dare get involved.

Maitland leaned close as the line started to thin. "Great idea, Grayson. This is perfect."

Haverland nodded, of course it was *perfect,* that's why he picked La Valencia, La Jolla's famous "pink palace," where nothing less would have been acceptable. Decorated in a Mediterranean motif, the room was ideal, not too large, elegant in a casual way. *Perfect* for a cocktail-hour reception and eighty guests. In addition to a roving bevy of waiters serving canapés from silver trays, hors d'oeuvre tables were strategically placed to keep the crowd moving, each table with its own chef and wine steward—the wine appropriate to the food being served at that particular spot. The first offering, a dazzling assortment of seafood just beyond the reception line, featured fresh Dungeness crab with mustard sauce and a nicely chilled Santenay Blanc. For those who preferred to start with red, both in wine and meat, the chef at the next table was slicing off rare pieces of prime rib and sliding the meat onto warm Viennese rolls while the wine steward handed out glasses of vintage Cabernet. Across the room, the small bar was being conspicuously ignored. Drinking hard liquor at such an event would have been considered professionally ill-advised, and no one did. Everyone seemed to be observing the same set of unwritten rules, their "casual cocktail" attire influenced by the same group of "in" designers: Ralph Lauren and Tommy Hilfiger for the men, Georgiou and Karen Kwong for the women.

Maitland observed the gathering with obvious pride. "You can just smell the synergy."

Haverland nodded again, but didn't see it that way. There was something awkward and stilted about the clustering groups, no one willing to share information, not sure which of the two companies would end up dominant. Allen Labs was older with more products on the market and more potential in the development pipeline, while Bain-Haverland was clearly a one-product company. But that product, Mira-loss, was a cash cow, one of the biggest in the pharmaceutical industry, and though both men were scheduled to share responsibility, most financial analysts believed one of the two would eventually emerge as top dog.

"Only a few more weeks," Maitland said, rubbing his hands together as if the fun was just about to start. "Nothing can stop us now."

Haverland wanted to believe it, but didn't, not as long as the disks existed. "Looks like everyone's here. We'd better mingle."

Maitland tipped Haverland a salute, finger to eyebrow. "You're the boss."

Haverland didn't buy the subordinate act for a second. Maitland wanted the merger for one reason—cash flow—and wasn't about to relinquish control without a fight. "That's what my wife always tells me. About a minute before she asks for money." He said it with a smile, like it was a joke, but letting Maitland know that Grayson Haverland wasn't anyone's fool.

He worked his way through the crowd, patting backs, dropping compliments, playing the good host. He found Tripp on the terrace, off to one side, staring out at La Jolla Cove and the sea beyond. Alone, naturally, with no twelve-year-old pretty boys to seduce. "Planning your escape?"

Tripp frowned, though that was exactly what he'd been thinking about. *Thirty-six more days.* Thirty-six days until he told King Grayson what he could do with his secret little file. "Waiting for you, actually."

Haverland stepped to the railing, turning his back on the people waiting for champagne and Bananas Foster at the dessert table. "I'm listening."

"He called."

Haverland didn't need to ask who.

Tripp lowered his voice a notch. "He found the courier."

"He has the disks?"

Tripp ignored the question, enjoying his opportunity to make the Majestic One suffer. "Actually, he hasn't really found him. Not yet. But he knows where he is."

Haverland's shoulders sagged slightly. "Where?"

"Amsterdam."

"Amsterdam's a big city."

"He'll find him."

"He'd better. We paid the bastard enough."

"Once you have the disks, you'll think it was cheap."

Haverland knew better; it wasn't just the disks. *Not anymore.* Now it was Retnuh and Leonidovich and the sister—they all knew too much. He glanced over his shoulder, at all the bright young faces. They depended on him. And thirty-three million people depended on Mira-loss. He had a responsibility, the needs of many over the needs of a few—an obligation. "What about the woman?"

"Now, which woman would you be asking about? The dead one in Madrid or the missing one from New York?"

Haverland glanced to the side, a look hard enough to shatter chrome. "Don't get smart with me."

"Right. We're not worried about the dead ones. They tell no tales. You don't really believe he's going to give the bitch a pat on the butt and send her running home with her story once he has the disks, do you? I don't think you need to worry about that."

"And the courier?"

"Dead man walking."

That's what Haverland thought, he just wanted to hear it. "And Retnuh?"

Tripp shrugged, as if the matter was no big deal. "I'll take care of him." Of course he had no intention of *taking care* of anyone.

"How?"

"I've got a plan." He hadn't even considered it. "You want specifics?" He knew Haverland would never ask, not as long as he still harbored illusions of deniability.

"No."

Tripp nodded. "No reason for you to sweat the details."

But Haverland knew there was one detail he would have to handle himself. The last link—Edgar Tripp, abuser of young boys. Eliminating him from the planet would be a humanitarian act.

CHAPTER TWENTY-EIGHT

Amsterdam

Despite the fact there was never anyone in the place over the age of twenty-five, Simon was starting to feel like a regular at the tiny café. Unlike the brightly lit, high-tech efficiency of easyEverything, De Muis—The Mouse—with its eight Internet terminals and eclectic group of young patrons, had its own special appeal. Dark and smoky with the pungent smell of cannabis and fresh-brewed coffee, it was the type of place a person could slip back into the shadows and disappear from the world. Best of all, it was only a short walk from his houseboat. He stopped by at least twice a day to check his e-mail, and made sure he was always at a terminal between noon and 2 P.M., when Vic promised to make contact whenever he had news.

Kaatje, the young woman who worked the day shift, cast Simon a vampy look as he came through the door. *"Hoi, Noordamerikaan,* you are back."

Simon nodded, waiting for his eyes to adjust to the dim light. "Just like MacArthur."

"MacArthur? Who is this?"

"Not important."

"I think you miss Kaatje, *nee?*"

"I miss her espresso."

"Ha." She pushed a tuft of blond hair back behind her right ear, an unconscious gesture she repeated at least once a minute. "You *Noordamerikaans, nee fantasie.*"

In the not so distant past he would have enjoyed her playgirl charm and flirted back, but that was another time. "You're right, I should live more dangerously. Make it a cappuccino."

He took a table along the back wall, at the only unoccupied terminal, and signed into the private chat room of Bagman and VicTheQuick. It had been six days since Vic's last contact, a brief e-mail confirming his receipt of the disks, and Simon could barely contain his panic—afraid he had made a mistake. Without the disks he had nothing. No hope of saving Lara. No way to convince anyone of his story. How could he have been so foolish, to give the disks to someone he didn't know? Disks containing something valuable enough to kill for. *VicTheQuick,* even the name sounded larcenous. The more he thought about it, the more foolish he felt. *Stupid—Stupid—Stupid!* He had a feeling VicTheQuick would never be heard from again.

Kaatje slipped out from behind the bar and glided silently across the smoky room, a panther stalking prey in her black latex bodysuit. "You have something else?" she purred, placing the cappuccino next to Simon's keyboard. "Something to eat?"

Her tone implied *anything,* but that was just her

way of trolling for tips, playing the sexual braggart by teasing her customers. He knew it—she knew he knew. And that being his only amusement in life, he rewarded the effort with twenty gilders. "I'm on a rigid diet. No sweets."

She frowned playfully, then glided back to her lair behind the bar. As Simon turned back to his terminal a message popped onto the screen.

▶ Hello, Bagman.

He took a deep breath and slowly tapped out a reply, not wanting to expose his concern.

▶ GOOD TO HEAR FROM YOU. ANY LUCK?
▶ Yes. Some good news,

Good news, he wanted to believe it but his mind refused. Like a worm chewing away at the inside of an apple, that part of his brain containing humor and hope and happy thoughts had been eaten away by all the terrible things that had happened.

and some bad.

That he believed.

▶ MIGHT AS WELL START WITH THE BAD.
▶ Retnuh may know where you are.

Though Simon didn't know what to expect, that wasn't it, the news enough to make the hair on his arms jump to attention, as if the room had suddenly filled with static electricity. Fingers frozen above the keyboard, he slowly scanned the room. All regulars. All young. He took another deep breath and forced his fingers to move.

▶ HOW COULD YOU POSSIBLY KNOW THAT?

▶ I checked the source code on the e-mail you sent—the one with the picture of your sister. There were two EXE files attached to the original document, one embedded within the other. When you clicked the eye, two things happened: the picture expanded and a message was sent back to the sender identifying your service provider.

▶ I WASN'T CONNECTED THROUGH AN ISP. I WAS AT A PUBLIC FACILITY.

▶ That's even worse. When you connect through an ISP a random number is automatically assigned to your computer. It changes every time you go on-line. If the computer is hot-wired into a public network, the number is static.

▶ MEANING IT COULD BE TRACED BACK TO AN EXACT LOCATION?

▶ Correct.

At least there was some good news in the bad. Retnuh might be in Amsterdam, but he'd be concentrating on easyEverything. *Time to leave Amsterdam.*

▶ I'M NO LONGER AT THAT LOCATION.
▶ Glad to hear it.
▶ SO WHAT'S THE GOOD NEWS?
▶ I broke the encryption. No problem.

No problem. That in itself made Simon nervous. Who was VicTheQuick and who did he work for?

▶ AND?
▶ A bunch of scientific data.
▶ COULD HAVE GUESSED THAT.
▶ Right. The data was meaningless to me.

Vic was holding back, Simon could sense it in the truncated responses.

▶ WHAT IS IT YOU'RE NOT SAYING?
▶ Sorry, Bagman. I was having a hard time believing your story and did something I knew you wouldn't like. That's why you haven't heard from me.
▶ I'M LISTENING.
▶ I have a friend. A research scientist. Very sharp. I asked her to look at the data. She just called. You're not going to like it.

So much for good news.

▶ SPIT IT OUT.
▶ The disks contain the results of a study on a drug called M-L One.

▶ NEVER HEARD OF IT.
▶ Right. That's its lab name. It took
  some work, but my friend finally
  identified the drug as Mira-loss.
  Are you familiar with the product?
  It's very popular.

Familiar—in three weeks the little pills had helped him shed ten pounds.

▶ YES. WHAT'S THE STUDY ABOUT?
▶ The data indicates the drug causes
  liver damage.

Jesus, Mary, he should have known there was no easy way to lose weight.

▶ WHAT KIND OF DAMAGE?
▶ Irreversible. Terminal.

The words popped onto his screen like bullets: *Irreversible—Terminal*, each one hitting his liver. He was almost afraid to ask the next question.

▶ WHAT PERCENTAGE OF USERS?
▶ 100%. Long-term users.

What constituted long-term? Not three weeks, he was sure of that, and he didn't have time to worry about it anyway. Finally he understood what Pär Olin was so worried about, and why Haverland wanted the disks so desperately.

▶ THAT EXPLAINS A GREAT DEAL.

▶ Yes. I did some checking. Bain-
Haverland is about to merge with
Allan Labs. They're probably trying to suppress the information
until after the merger.

▶ SEEMS MORE LIKE THEY'RE TRYING TO SUPPRESS
IT PERMANENTLY.

▶ They wouldn't dare. Millions of
lives are at stake.

That sounded familiar. *Most affected*, as Pär Olin
would say.

▶ AND BILLIONS OF DOLLARS. MY SISTER'S BEEN
ABDUCTED, THREE PEOPLE ARE DEAD, AND SOME
LUNATIC BY THE NAME OF RETNUH TRIED TO
TURN ME INTO A ROMAN CANDLE. THAT DOESN'T
SOUND LIKE A DELAY TACTIC TO ME!

This time Vic took a moment longer to respond.

▶ You're right. The FDA needs to
see this immediately.

Though Simon knew it was true—Lara's life paled
in importance to millions of others—he had to try
something.

▶ DO THAT AND MY SISTER'S DEAD.

▶ I understand. I sympathize. But
we're talking about millions of
people here.

▶ GIVE ME TEN DAYS.
▶ What good will that do?
▶ I'VE GOT AN IDEA.

Actually he'd been thinking about it for some time, but until that moment had never considered it seriously. It was complicated and crazy and dangerous as hell, but what choice did he have?

▶ PLEASE.
▶ Okay. Ten days. Anything goes bad I turn the disks over to the FDA.
▶ UNDERSTOOD. ONE MORE THING.
▶ What?
▶ I'M GOING TO NEED SOME HELP.
▶ Have I ever denied you anything?

Simon smiled to himself; at least the guy had a sense of humor. He was going to need it when he heard the plan.

CHAPTER TWENTY-NINE

Amsterdam

Monday, 9 December 11:50:52 GMT +0100

"Will that be all, Mijnheer?"

Jäger glanced out the window, making sure the view was right, then nodded and handed the boy ten gilders.

The young man smiled, giving Jäger a knowing, heavy-lidded look well beyond his years. "Amsterdam is very progressive. Whatever you require."

Not wanting to be bothered again, Jäger added an edge to his voice. "What I require is sleep." And it was true, after ten days of chasing ghosts and false leads, his mind felt thick and slow, but knew that he wouldn't sleep again until he had Leonidovich and the disks.

The young man dipped his head and backed into the hall. Jäger set the lock with a sharp snap, then quietly moved the vanity chair up next to the window and settled in to wait—the hunter's regimen. He had a perfect view, his vantage point high enough to see over the street traffic, the houseboat within easy distance of his Zeiss mini-scope. All he needed was confirmation.

Two hours later, shortly before noon, he had it. Nervous as a condemned man waiting for the needle, Leonidovich stepped cautiously onto the deck, locked the door, glanced back over his shoulder, then bent down as if to tie a shoe. Jäger zoomed in closer, watching with amusement as the courier slipped a small piece of paper between the door and jamb, leaving only a small corner exposed.

Though tempted to follow, he knew it would be too risky to take the man in broad daylight in the middle of Amsterdam. He quickly pulled on a pair of faded coveralls and rubber-soled shoes, the same as most of the laborers who worked the canals, then checked himself in the mirror. *Perfetto,* except for the dark, swept-wing glasses, but that was something he couldn't avoid. A man with an eyepatch would be too easily remembered. Carrying his newly acquired but well-battered toolbox, he quietly slipped down the back stairs and circled around behind the row of small tourist hotels that overlooked the canal. The traffic was heavy with lots of bikers and pedestrians, both tourists and locals. *Eccellente.* Just another face in the crowd.

When he reached the houseboat, he stepped confidently onto the deck—a workman with a job to do—and made his way to the far side of the structure, opposite the street. Using a miniature security sensor, he quickly scanned the largest window for contact switches. Satisfied there was no security, he drilled a small hole through the base of the frame, inserted a flexible surgical probe, and tripped the lock. The entire procedure took less than five minutes, from the time he stepped onto the deck to the moment he closed and locked the window behind him.

The living area was small and tidy and took less than fifteen minutes to scan and search, made easier with the curtains pulled and all the lights conveniently left burning. He found the courier's security case hidden behind a bag of trash beneath the kitchen counter, but it proved to be more difficult to open than Jäger anticipated. His scanner indicated a tight electronic grid beneath the black leather skin, making it impossible to open without activating some kind of alarm.

He leaned back against the counter and closed his eye, which tired quickly under the strain, and considered his options. He could take the case and open it elsewhere, but that seemed risky. He had no way to know if the disks were inside, or if the movement would set off some kind of homing device. Or he could wait and make Leonidovich open the case. The choice seemed obvious: he was The Hunter, the one who laid the trap, the one who waited. And he could then even the score for Madrid.

An eye for an eye.

Kaatje leaned over the bar, her off-the-shoulder gypsy blouse falling away from her body. "You are leaving Amsterdam?"

Simon nodded, ignoring her small but perfect breasts. "Maybe. I'm waiting to hear. Might have to leave pretty quick."

"You will be coming back to Kaatje?"

"Of course. But if I don't make it in to say goodbye, could you do me a favor?"

Her eyes narrowed as she pushed a tangle of blond hair behind her left ear. "A favor?"

"Send this message." He printed the message and

e-mail address on the back of a Heineken beer coaster and pushed it across the bar along with a hundred gilders. "It's important."

She glanced down, reading the note. "Veek?"

"Right. Vic."

"This is the message? *En prise?*"

"It's a chess term—a warning that one of your pieces is about to be captured. He'll understand."

She shrugged in her vampy way and slipped the coaster along with the hundred gilders into the back pocket of her black, skin-tight jeans. "This Kaatje can do."

He knew she would. Despite her teasing and taunting and trolling for tips, she was conscientious and trustworthy.

It was barely five when he reached the small canal and string of rental houseboats, but already dark. The lack of daylight, which lasted less than eight hours at this latitude at this time of year, was depressive. In what had become a familiar practice over the last few days, he ducked back into the entry of a vacant shop, first making sure he hadn't been followed, then trying to spot anyone who might be watching the houseboat. The lights were still on, just as he'd left them, glowing softly through the curtains. He waited thirty minutes, watching for any shadow movement beyond the thin material. Nothing. As a final precaution he checked the readings on his alert beeper to make sure no one had tried to breach his security case. The first number indicated a distance of 25.62 meters; the second—0000—locked and secure. Turning the beeper flat, he pressed the directional button and watched as the compass-like needle rotated toward the houseboat and stopped.

Satisfied that no one was watching or on board, he crossed the street, stepped quickly onto the deck, and glanced back over his shoulder. This was the moment, the place he expected it to happen, before he could get inside, with the water at his back and no place to run. He flashed his penlight at the doorjamb, just long enough to confirm the marker was still in place, then slipped his key into the lock.

In the second it took to close and bolt the door he became conscious of an odd tobacco smell and realized he wasn't alone.

CHAPTER THIRTY

Location unknown

Time unknown

Consciousness, when it finally came, was like waking up underwater, everything blurry and clouded, the sound muffled. The smell was still there, chloroform, stuck in his nostrils like a bad cold. He took a deep breath and struggled toward the surface, trying to clear his head. Slowly the blurred landscape began to form into highways and rivers and huge brown lakes. He struggled to make sense of it, to focus his attention. It came to him in a slow woozy way, like the end of a dream—he was on his back, staring at a high ceiling, the cracks a maze of highways and rivers, the stains a collage of dirty lakes. Streaks of pale light filtered through a long row of grimy and broken-out windows just below the roofline. The air was rank and fetid and damp, like an old tomb.

He tried to sit up but couldn't, and realized he was strapped down, completely immobile except for his head. He took a shallow breath, quietly, afraid to make a sound, and turned his head to the left. The walls and floor were concrete and stained with water rust, the vast space completely empty except for a jumbled stack of rotting crates piled against the wall, a good home for the spiders and roaches and rats judging from the accumulation of cobwebs and droppings. He was lying on some kind of hard surface, the size and shape of a narrow door, at least four feet off the floor, his arms bound to his sides by wide straps that covered his body. And he was cold. Very cold. And, he suddenly realized—naked. *Jesus, Mary.*

He closed his eyes, hoping it was all a dream, then turned his head to the right and opened them. *No dream*—the room was immense, some kind of abandoned warehouse, and he was right in the middle of it, stretched out bare as a newborn. Even more shocking, in sharp contrast to his grimy surroundings, was the shiny-as-a-new-dime seaplane sitting just inside the huge hangar-like door. A Seawolf amphibian, steel-gray in color, it had small pontoons attached to its wings, and wheels extending out from beneath the fuselage. Two men were sitting on folding chairs beneath one of the wings, a small table between them. They looked like a couple of fishermen, relaxing after a satisfying day on the water, sharing a bottle of wine and eating sardines from a tin. Even at fifty feet, Simon recognized one of the men instantly: the person who had been sitting with Lara—the fake Lara—at the Plaza Mayor. The other man, with blond hair and a patch over one eye, didn't look familiar.

The private plane at least answered one question, how they could move Lara from one country to another without detection. Careful not to make the slightest sound, he screwed his head around as far as he could, searching for some sign of his sister. Nothing. And no indication she'd ever been there. He tried to fight off the disappointment, telling himself it didn't mean anything, but afraid he was only kidding himself. He closed his eyes and tried to focus his thoughts. Where was he? How long had he been there? He rubbed his chin against the edge of his shoulder, testing his beard, and knew it couldn't have been more than a few hours—twelve at the most. By plane, in Europe, they could be anywhere in that time, but he had a feeling they were still close to Amsterdam. The temperature was right. And despite the stink of the old warehouse, the air felt the same.

So where was Retnuh? *Close*—he was sure of that. Not that it mattered. Nothing mattered as long as Lara was alive and Vic had the disks. Once he turned them over to the FDA, the game was over. Did Kaatje send the message? Too many questions—no answers. *Now's your chance, God. Show old Simon you're really out there.* He tried to clear his mind, listening for a Celestial whisper, some assurance God hadn't forgotten him. *Something. Anything.* But there was nothing. Only . . .

He strained to hear what he now realized had been there all along—the faint breath of another living creature. Close. Very close.

He twisted his head from one side to the other, noticing for the first time a hospital-like stanchion and IV drip bag a few feet beyond his right shoulder. Straining against the wide strap across his neck, he arched his head back as far as he could and followed the plastic tube downward to a thin bare shoulder and a flare of coppery hair. *Lara!* Though obviously drugged, she was still alive. *Thank you, God. Owe you one*. For the first time in weeks he felt as if he could breathe, as if an anvil had been lifted off his chest. But even before he could fill his lungs, the two men sitting by the plane stood up and started across the room. It was, Simon had a feeling, the beginning of a very long day.

Like a vulture staring down at fresh meat, the man with the eyepatch hovered overhead, his attention pure and focused. Despite the fact he was clean-shaven and had bleached his dark hair to a taffy-colored blond, Simon needed only to look into that one dark eye to know he had found Retnuh. Or, more accurately, that Retnuh had found him. A faint line of scratches below the eyepatch confirmed what Simon already suspected—that Co-op had not died without extracting some measure of retribution against the evils of man.

"So," Retnuh said, his voice low but triumphant, "he returns to the living."

The trick, Simon knew, would be to stay that way, and swallowed the impulse to strike back with his tongue. He needed to establish a pattern of give and take, to somehow make this psychopath believe he was the one dictating terms.

Retnuh leaned close, his breath heavy with the smell of sardines and tobacco. "You have caused much aggravation." When he spoke, nothing moved but his mouth, the hiss of his voice like a cobra: soft and deadly. "You think you are clever, eh?" He looked down, his single eye making a slow tour over Simon's naked body. "You do not look so clever to me."

The other man, a short ugly fellow with black hair and skin the texture and color of oatmeal, laughed like a hyena, the sound anything but humorous. Simon had read enough war stories and spy novels to know they were trying to break him down psychologically. A person without clothes will quickly lose their identity and self-confidence, and become more compliant. But even knowing that, it made no difference, that was exactly how he felt: exposed, vulnerable, and alone.

Retnuh turned to the shadow at his elbow. *"La bagaglio."*

The man hurried back to the plane, disappeared inside, then reappeared moments later with Simon's security case. Retnuh took the case and held it up so Simon could see it. "Give me the code."

Simon blinked his eyes slowly, as if trying to focus but barely holding on to consciousness. "Yes. Cold. Ver . . . very cold."

"Not cold, you idiot. Code!"

Simon feigned what he hoped to be a look of bewilderment.

Snapping open a switchblade, the little man with dark hair jumped forward and began waving the knife back and forth over Simon's eyes. *"Parlare!"*

Retnuh pushed the man away. "Code!" He slammed the case down on Simon's chest. "The code!"

Struggling to catch his breath, Simon stared at the case, then slowly nodded his head, as if he finally understood. "Special lock."

"How," Jäger snapped, "does—it—open?" He enunciated each word, as if trying to teach an idiot calculus.

"Right latch—" Simon tried again to look confused. "Turn in." He took a gulp of air. "Foot lock—" He shook his head slowly left to right. "Cold. Can't think."

Retnuh scowled, his dark eye full of scepticism, then as quickly as a chameleon changed colors his expression softened into one of concern. "A blanket." He snapped his fingers at the other man. *"Rapidamente."*

Simon hesitated, afraid he was about to make a mistake, but felt he had to take the chance. "Her, too."

And with those words Jäger knew Leonidovich was faking his confusion. Though tempted to retaliate immediately, he considered the value of playing along, to let the rabbit believe he could so easily outsmart The Hunter. "Eth Jäger is not an unreasonable man." He picked up the case and stepped back. "Cover them."

Pleased with his decision, Jäger returned to his chair and his glass of wine. *No,* he was not unreasonable. He would give Leonidovich a few minutes to play his game, then whatever happened would be on *his* head. The pilot, having finished his nursemaid duties, pointed the stiletto blade of his knife toward Leonidovich and spit. *"Mentitore!"* His disgust echoed through the vast space.

Jäger turned on the man, warning him with a sharp whisper. "Of course he lies. And if he understands *Italiano* he now knows that we know." The pilot opened his mouth, but Jäger cut him off. "You are anxious to go home, eh? This I am tired of hearing." He waved his hand toward the plane, a dismissive salute. *"Andare."*

The man shook his head emphatically, his eyes frozen with fear.

"Eccellente. The next time you speak above a whisper, I will cut out your tongue with that little knife and feed it to the rats. *Comprendere?"*

The pilot nodded, his head burrowing into his shoulders like a turtle. Jäger turned away, pleased with the response. Leonidovich would see the pilot's fear and think twice before he again tested the kind heart of Eth Jäger.

The moment Simon heard the name Eth Jäger he knew the man intended to kill him. It didn't matter, he expected that, the trick—*the plan*—was to save Lara. *Eth Jäger.* Why did the name sound so familiar? *Smith. Retnuh. Jäger.* He spun the names around in his head. Retnuh was Smith. Smith was Eth Jäger. Then it hit him, Lara's whispered message: *Smith is death should our . . .*

Smith is death. Death is Eth.

Should our—Jäger.

At least he knew the name of the man who would kill him. He closed his eyes, searching for a place so deep within his mind no psychopath could touch, and concentrated on his plan.

When he opened his eyes, the psychopath was there, waiting, the trace of a smile on his thin lips. "Warmer?" He gently tucked the blanket up beneath Simon's chin, then reached down, picked up the security case, and placed it lightly on Simon's chest. "We try again, eh?"

Despite the friendly tone, Simon heard the subtle warning and knew this was not the time to resist. "Turn the right latch . . ." He ran through the unlocking sequence, bracing himself for that moment when Jäger realized the disks weren't there. "That's it."

Obviously fearing some kind of explosive, Jäger stepped back, then reached out and flipped open the fold-over top. He waited for at least a minute, then stepped forward and cautiously peered into the case. Though his expression never wavered, it required no acute sense of hearing to detect the anger in his voice. "Where are the disks?"

Easy answer. "I have no idea."

A slow smile passed over Jäger's lips, the grin of a basking shark. "You wish to play games?"

"No game. I gave them to—" How could he describe Vic, a person he wouldn't recognize in a crowd of one? "Someone to hold."

"And the name of this someone?"

Good question, one Simon had asked himself many times over the last couple of weeks. "I don't know."

"You take Eth Jäger for a fool? You think I am crazy?"

Crazy, yes. Fool, no. "It's someone I met on the Internet."

"Why would you do such a thing?"

"I thought you might be getting close. I needed someone to hold them."

Jäger scowled in disbelief. "A stranger?"

Simon shrugged a shoulder, determined to make Jäger dig enough to make the story believable.

"This makes no sense."

"It makes perfect sense. You can't force me to tell you about someone I don't know."

"No?" His voice lifted in doubt. "I do not believe you would give something so valuable to a stranger."

"Valuable? I don't even know what's on the damn things. And unless you agree to my terms, they're not going to be worth anything to anyone."

"Terms!" Jäger laughed, a tight bark that sounded forced. "What terms?"

"It's simple. You release her—" He motioned with his head toward Lara. "The disks will be sent. Wherever you say."

"This woman is of no importance."

"She's important to me. She's my sister."

Though he tried to hide his surprise, Jäger's expression seemed to lock in place, as if his face had been flash-frozen.

"And unless," Simon continued, "she walks out of here, you're never going to see those disks." He held on with his eyes, letting Jäger know that nothing this side of death would change his mind. "That I promise you."

For a moment Jäger simply stared back, as if trying to measure Simon's resolve, then with a show of indifference pulled a slim gold case from the pocket of his leather jacket and extracted a cigarette. "And why would I agree to such a thing?"

"For one thing, you'd still have me—" He let the sentence hang, forcing Jäger to dig.

"You said one thing." He gave the cigarette two sharp raps on the case. "There is another?"

"And unless she's released within forty-eight hours of my disappearance, the disks will be turned over to the police." He glanced up at the long row of broken windows, as if trying to measure time by the fading streaks of light. "How long have I been here?"

Jäger shook his head and smirked, as if he'd finally

discovered the lie. "You could not have made such an arrangement. You had no way to know I would find you."

"You're right, I couldn't be sure." He took a deep breath and played his ace. "That's why I made it easy."

CHAPTER THIRTY-ONE

Location unknown

Time unknown

Simon came awake with a scream—the pain pulsing through his body like a high-powered laser, up the backs of his legs, along his spinal cord, and into his brain. The top of his head felt as if it were going to split open, and he almost hoped that it would—anything to make it end. And then it did, as quickly as it started.

He laid there, choking and shivering and waiting for his heart to regain its rhythm. The light was thin, yellow, and cold—early morning. Jäger was standing over him, a cruel smile on his thin lips. He leaned forward, his voice sharp and deadly, like an ice pick out of the dark. "I think now you will tell me everything. Where are the disks?"

It was all Simon could do to shake his head.

Jäger frowned impatiently and nodded toward the foot of the table. Instantly another lightning bolt ripped through Simon's body, the pain so sharp and unyielding it felt like his insides would liquify before it finally stopped. This time it took him longer to recover, not because the pain was worse, there was no way to measure such agony, but because he realized he was going to die an excruciating death unless he thought of something very fast. So he gagged and gasped and groaned for a good two minutes as he struggled to organize his thoughts.

"That was just a taste," Jäger said, "of what you'll get if you fail to answer my questions." He pointed toward Simon's feet.

With an effort, Simon lifted his head off the hard surface. The blanket had been pulled aside, leaving him naked and exposed except for the wide straps that held him in place. Despite the cold air, every inch of his skin was covered with oily perspiration. Just beyond his bare feet, the pilot grinned and held up a small black box. It was a simple device: one wire in, two out, with a lever to open or close the circuit. The single wire, a thick black cable, disappeared beneath the table. Connected to a very large battery, Simon had no doubt. The other wires, thinner with the insulation stripped away at the ends, were attached to his feet, one wire taped to each ankle.

Jäger smiled with malicious enthusiasm. "You wish to see how it works?"

No, he knew very well how it worked, but he also knew he would have to endure a few more jolts to convince the crazy bastard that he didn't care. "Fuck you."

Another surge of current ripped through his body, just a quick shot, but enough to send his heart flying into another fluttering spasm. Jäger leaned in close, his dark eye as flat and dull as old paint. "Again?"

Though Simon wanted desperately to spit in the man's face, his heart was quivering so rapidly it felt like it was about to explode out of his chest, and it took everything he had just to speak. "Crank it up."

Jäger straightened, his expression suddenly suspicious. "Ah, so you wish to die?"

Simon gulped down a lung full of air, gathering himself for the effort, then let it out in one breath. "No, but you're going to kill me anyway, along with my sister and your sadistic little buddy"—he pointed his chin toward the pilot—"once you've got what you want." It was only a guess, but he had a feeling *no one* lived for long once they'd seen the face of Eth Jäger.

Jäger's stunned expression, like a bug that had just gone headfirst into a windshield, seemed to confirm it. "This is not true." He glanced at the pilot, as if to assure him. "All I want are the disks." The little man returned a tight smile, then dropped his gaze—an abused dog, afraid of a boot in the ribs if he didn't respond properly.

"Excuse me if I don't look convinced," Simon said, knowing another jolt might send his heart into fibrillation heaven but also knowing he had to take the chance. "But you're as full of crap as a Christmas turkey." He clamped his teeth together, preparing himself for the next shock.

But Jäger took a step back, apparently more intent on proving him wrong. "People get only what they deserve. No more—no less. It is the law of nature."

Though tempted, Simon resisted the impulse to mention Pär Olin and Pilár Montez. Jäger was clearly psychotic, able to justify whatever he did by applying his *law of nature* theory. "Doesn't really matter, does it? Either we play *Let's Make a Deal* or you give me another jolt."

Jäger looked away, as if mentally chewing through his choices, measuring the risks and rewards before deciding on a course of action. "If I release the woman—"

"You'll get the disks. I told you that."

Jäger nodded slowly. "Yes, you told me." He turned, his expression dark and dangerous. "And I will remember your words. No man lies to Eth Jäger and lives."

It was more than a threat, it was a promise, and Simon believed it absolutely. An unappealing thought since he had just lied to the man.

It was becoming increasingly hard to keep everything straight. It was night. Again. Or it might have been the same night, just later. He suspected Jäger was screwing with his mind, manipulating his body clock with drugs, knocking him out for short periods of time, then waking him up—purposely trying to confuse him.

It was working.

He tried to count days, couldn't, then tried to measure the length of his beard against the blanket, but someone had given him a shave. He cranked his head around to check on Lara, then vaguely remembered them taking her out. *When?* He couldn't be sure, the hours and days had all melded together into one great hallucinatory dream.

Yesterday? It felt like more.

Not more than three days, he was sure. *Almost sure.* His thoughts skidded off in another direction, absorbed in the contradictory muddle of *sure* and *almost*. Nothing could be sure if it was almost. Nothing almost if it was sure. Could anything in life be sure? Each question led to another, then another, with no end in sight, until some circuit breaker in his brain tripped the connection and everything faded into darkness and dreams.

The drug-induced nightmares were always the same, bizarre combinations of memories and people—family and friends, people he knew and people he didn't—everyone talking at once, telling him what to do, their voices blending into a cacophony of screams that would eventually wake him, his mouth dry as ashes, his tongue stuck to the roof of his mouth.

He took a deep breath, waiting for the images to fade, then slowly turned his head. *Another day?* The warehouse was dark except for a small lantern hanging below the seaplane's wing. Jäger was alone, sitting directly beneath the circle of yellow light, a laptop on his knees. Judging from the rapid tap of keys, the man knew his way around a computer. Despite the distance, there was enough light to distinguish the silver logo of WorldWide SD on the laptop's dark cover. Searching, Simon was sure, for some clue to Vic's identity. Anticipating this might happen, he had overwritten all their correspondence, making sure it couldn't be retrieved using a recovery program, then created a series of bogus messages between himself and Vic that would seem to validate the story he had given Jäger. To add credibility, he buried the messages in a file deep on the laptop's hard drive, knowing if Jäger found them he would buy the story. The man was too egotistical to believe anyone could manipulate him. At least, that was the flaw Simon was betting on—with his life.

The rhythm of keystrokes slowed and then finally

stopped as Jäger turned and stared into the darkness, as though he could sense that Simon was awake and watching. Knowing what would happen next, Simon closed his eyes and waited. He heard Jäger set the laptop aside and stand up, then nothing. The man had a way of moving, like a cat through tall grass, you never heard him coming, but by measuring the intensity of lantern light through his eyelids Simon could always tell when the ghost was hovering, and he also knew it was useless to feign sleep. "You always sneak up on people?"

"This is what I do."

Which confirmed what Simon already suspected— that Jäger didn't work for Bain-Haverland, but was some kind of freelance bloodhound. A human hunter. *Hunter*. The letters dissolved and swirled through his mind in an anagram tornado, searching for some common denominator and finding only one: *Retnuh*—Hunter spelled backward. "Sounds interesting." *And sleazy.*

Jäger didn't respond, his thoughts hidden behind an impassive mask as he pulled the now-familiar black case from the inside pocket of his jacket. About the size of an eyeglass case, it contained a glass vial of clear liquid and a hypodermic syringe. As he carefully drew 20cc's of fluid into the hypodermic, Simon tried not to think about all the bad things he could get from having a dirty needle jabbed in his arm. "Guess you must be worried."

Jäger looked up, a slow, curious glance, as if he had to retreat from thoughts so distant he needed time to reorient himself. "Worried?"

"How long's it been now . . . ?" He paused, hoping for some kind of response.

The corner of Jäger's mouth curled slightly, amused by such an obvious attempt to get information, but said nothing as he looped a rag tourniquet around Simon's upper arm.

"Maybe I was wrong about Vic. Maybe he decided to keep the disks for himself."

The amused smile turned smug. "I can find your Vic the Quick."

Simon acknowledged the slip with a startled expression, though he realized instantly the *mistake* had been intentional. The man was too clever for such a blunder, but couldn't resist letting Simon know he had found the hidden files. Which was exactly what Simon needed to know. "Yeah, maybe. But not before the merger is finalized."

"Maybe you talk too much."

Simon ignored the warning, intending to hammer away with *maybe* until the bastard became paranoid with possibilities. "Maybe Haverland forgot to mention the disks were worthless once the company merged with Allan Labs." It sounded reasonable, enough to make Jäger crazy with doubt no matter how much Haverland denied it. "Maybe he didn't even tell you what was on the damn things." Something, Simon was sure, Haverland would never do. "Maybe he didn't trust you with the details."

With an aggressive twist, Jäger pulled the tourniquet tight. "I know enough."

But there was a slight hesitation in his voice, his response half a beat late, and Simon knew he'd planted the doubt. "You only know what Haverland wants you to know. He's going to keep you dancing till they play the wedding march." He chuckled softly, as if the thought amused him. "And you're the one who gets left at the altar."

Jäger glared back his response, then plunged the needle into Simon's arm.

Consciousness, when it finally came, hit like a lightning bolt, a great flash of white light, hot and painful, burning through his veins like hot lead, and then it was over, leaving him panting and breathless and perfectly lucid. Unlike the first time Dr. Strangelove gave him a "hypodermic wake-up," it didn't scare him nearly as much, though he realized the drugs might eventually kill him. *Should I live so long.*

The light was dull and gray, the sky the color of hammered pewter beyond the row of broken-out windows. *Another day.* But whether it was five or fifty he had no idea.

Jäger leaned forward, dangling one of WorldWide's see-through security pouches a few inches beyond Simon's nose. "This you recognize, eh?"

Of course he recognized it, it was the same pouch he used to secure the disks, his signature still visible alongside Olin's. The plastic skin had been sliced open an inch below the adhesive seal and contained only one disk. That came as no surprise, but the fact that Vic had sent it meant Lara was safe and a copy of the data would soon be on its way to the FDA. At least that part of the plan had worked—*Thank you, God*—though he knew better than to expect any divine intervention on his own behalf. "Sure. I told you he'd send it."

"No," Jäger said, swinging the pouch back and

forth like a pendulum, "you said 'you'll get the disks.' This I remember quite clearly."

"Okay, that's what I said. So . . . ?"

"There is only one."

Simon stared at the pouch, trying to affect a surprised look without overdoing it. "I don't believe it." He glanced at the pilot, hovering in his subservient position a few feet beyond Jäger's shoulder. "Maybe your buddy decided to go into business for himself."

Jäger shook his head, once to the left, once to the right, then back to dead center, as though disgusted with the need to explain something so simple. "One disk." He held up a small index card with printing on one side. "And this." He turned the card around, holding it off to one side, toward his good eye. "'Buy one, get one free.'" He looked at Simon. "How do you say in America, come and get it?"

Simon nodded, his surprise no longer an act. "A come-on."

"*Sí,* a come-on. He wants two-hundred thousand American for the second disk."

And with those words Simon felt his life slipping away, like grains of sand between his fingers. The plan had been simple, an even trade, his life for the last disk. Either Vic had gotten greedy, or for some reason had changed the plan. The answer seemed obvious. "He's bluffing. He's just trying to see if they're worth something."

"Of course." Despite the setback, Jäger seemed amused. "We have already agreed to a more reasonable accommodation."

"You're going to pay?" He could hear the desperation in his voice.

Jäger waved his right hand in a vague gesture of indifference. "The amount is insignificant."

Insignificant. A good word, Simon thought, to describe the value of his life at that moment. Though he already knew the answer—*Simon says: Bend over, you're about to get screwed*—he couldn't resist asking, "And me?"

"You he does not mention." Jäger grinned, clearly enjoying the irony of the double-cross. "A very clever man, this Vic." The smile dissolved. "Perhaps a little too clever."

"What do you mean?"

"He demands I wire the money. What do you think, *Bagman*"—he emphasized the tag, letting Simon know that all his secrets had been uncovered—"should I trust this Vic the Quick?"

Simon resisted verbalizing his first thought—something akin to self-copulation—realizing what he said and how he said it would probably determine whether he lived beyond the next minute. It was possible, now that he thought about it, that Vic had merely refined the plan—something that would appeal to Jäger's sinister nature and deflect any thoughts he had about being outwitted. *Or* Vic was looking to score, a more likely scenario. Either way, Jäger needed to believe in the double-cross, true or not, if Simon hoped to survive. "Absolutely, send him the money. And I hope he fucks you good. You deserve each other."

Jäger nodded, taking no offense. "I think you are right. This Vic is not a man of character."

"Like I give a damn what you think."

"But you should." He exchanged a look with the

pilot, some inside joke passing between them. "I have volunteered your services."

Simon hesitated, not sure he wanted to know, but unable to resist. "What do you mean by that?"

Jäger shrugged, an Italian shrug with both hands, as if it were all so obvious. "You are the Bagman, eh?"

CHAPTER THIRTY-TWO

La Jolla

"Good morning, Dr. Haverland."

"Good morning, Helen." He kept moving, as if he didn't have a moment to spare. God knew he had enough to do; the work had been piling up for more than a week, but he couldn't seem to focus on anything.

"Coffee?"

He shook his head, avoiding eye contact. He had seen enough of her sympathetic looks. "Hold my calls." He knew what she thought—*problems at home*.

He closed the door behind him and headed straight for his desk and his bottle of Valium. *Problems*, the woman had no idea! His world, his company, the well-being of his patients, they were all threatened, like sand castles lined up on the beach, and all he could do was pray the next wave wouldn't wipe them out.

Problems at home, that was the least of it, but he had those too: a spoiled eighteen-year-old daughter and a thirty-one-year-old trophy wife who couldn't understand why he didn't want to go out, didn't want to invite anyone in, and suddenly couldn't get it up.

I think you should see a doctor, Gray.

"I am a doctor."

Well, of course you are. She gave him that benevolent, condescending smile he hated so intensely. *I meant a—*

He cut her off before she could say *real* doctor. As if he needed some fucking idiot with an M.D. behind his name to explain the causes of erectile dysfunction. "It's only temporary."

Of course it is. That smile again.

Goddamned bitch. It wasn't enough that he gave her everything she wanted, she just *had* to remind him how old he was. As if her firm tits and hard ass would defy gravity forever.

She prattled on, never tiring of the endless social minutia that consumed her life. *Natalie, that's the new decorator I told you about. She found the most marvelous tartan on her trip to Scotland. I think I'll have the chairs in the billiard room redone. What do you think?*

As if he had time to even think about such trivial crap.

The Burdens invited us to spend a week at their chalet in Aspen. Doesn't that just sound divine?

He nodded, hiding his feelings. He didn't ski, didn't want to learn, and didn't want to be reminded of his age by some Nordic-God ski instructor by the name of Sven.

The La Jolla Beach and Racquet Club is hosting a fund-raiser for the Special Olympics. It's only $5,000 a seat. I told them we'd take a table of twelve. Okay?

Sure, why not? *Grayson Haverland—billionaire.* What difference could sixty thousand make? And after the merger he'd be worth another half billion. That or broke. It didn't matter if Olin's research was flawed, which of course it was; if the information slipped out, he'd never get a chance to prove it. The FDA would pull Mira-loss off the shelves pending one of their endless investigations, and the price of Bain-Haverland would plummet, leaving him with over twelve million shares of worthless stock. The thought made his stomach churn, pushing a huge bubble of gas up against his heart. Shaking two of the tiny green tablets into his hand, he popped them into his mouth and leaned forward on his elbows, trying to calm himself.

The piles of unfinished work stretched across the back of his desk like a mountain range, imposing and impenetrable. Everything was sorted and stacked and prioritized by date and level of importance, bottom to top. Helen had already opened, categorized, and added that day's mail to the appropriate mountain. One item, he noticed, had not been opened: a heavily padded, D.H.L. express package marked CONFIDENTIAL. He reached out and pulled it close, his heartbeat rising. The sender's name was a hieroglyphic scribble, but it came from Amsterdam and he knew it had to be the disks. *Finally!* He slowly turned the package over in his hands, squeezing and savoring the moment as if a kid at Christmas. *Had to be.* He couldn't remember ever feeling so euphoric, as if he'd just taken a shot of heroin directly into his brachial artery. He damn well wouldn't have any problem getting it up that night.

His exhilaration was shattered when Tripp came barging into the room, waving a newspaper in front of his face as if to deflect a swarm of angry bees. "You won't believe this." He dropped the paper—a section of *The New York Times*—onto Haverland's desk and pointed toward a small article near the bottom of the page.

MISSING WOMAN FOUND

Lara Quinn, missing for nearly a month, mysteriously showed up at her home in Queens yesterday evening. When questioned by police, she claimed to have no memory of her whereabouts or the circumstances surrounding her disappearance, nor could she supply any information that might help in the search for her brother, Simon Leonidovich, who is being sought for questioning regarding a shipment of missing research material.

Though it made perfect sense, in light of the package he was clutching in his hands, it wasn't what Haverland expected. "I thought sure Retnuh had"—he couldn't bring himself to say *killed*—"done something to her."

Tripp sank down into one of the leather chairs, his head barely visible above the mountains of paper. "I can't believe she got away from that son of a bitch."

"She didn't get away. He released her."

"Released her! Why the hell would he do that?"

Haverland held up the package. "Looks like her brother negotiated a trade."

Tripp popped out of his chair like Jack out of his box. "You got the disks?"

"That's what I was about to find out." He picked up his gold-plated X-acto knife—a Christmas gift from

Helen, embossed with his initials—and sliced open the top edge of the package. "But what else could it be?" He reached inside, found the first disk among the layers of foam, pulled it out, and went back for the second. Nothing. Trying to hold down his panic, he emptied the package onto his desk, the scraps of white foam unraveling like a nest of albino snakes.

Tripp reached over the mountains of unfinished work and began rifling through the pile of serpentine debris, his expression frozen somewhere between hope and disbelief. "Maybe there's a note."

Haverland shook his head, too angry to speak.

"Maybe he sent them separately. For security or something."

Haverland knew better—knew exactly what it meant. "The bastard wants more money."

Tripp slumped down in his chair. "He must know something."

"He doesn't know anything. We offered him a million pounds for the damn things; it doesn't take a genius to figure out they're valuable."

"Maybe he broke the code."

That was a thought Haverland didn't care to consider. "He's just seeing how far he can push." He picked up the disk, slipped it into the optical drive of his computer and clicked the shortcut at the bottom of his screen. A security dialog bloomed onto his monitor. He nodded, hiding his relief. "Still encrypted." He typed in his eight digit alpha/numeric password and pressed ENTER. A large hourglass appeared on his screen while the document deciphered and converted to English. Thirty seconds later it ballooned onto his screen, the manifestation of all his problems. He scrolled down a few pages, making sure everything appeared to be in order, but purposely not reading the data; it was flawed, Karl Langerkvist had assured him of that, and there was no reason to believe otherwise. "Never been touched." He reached down, extracted the disk, and slipped it into the floor safe beneath his desk.

Tripp stared back over the stacks of paper, his eyes appraising and skeptical. "You're sure?"

He nodded, though he wasn't, and didn't dare give the disk to anyone with the expertise to tell him. "Absolutely."

"Now what?"

"He'll call—we'll pay." It wouldn't be that simple, there were too many loose ends, but he didn't want Tripp to get all freaky and run. He was the loosest end of all.

Jäger glanced at his watch and subtracted nine hours. "It's time. Get me a phone."

Like a trained dog, the pilot scurried away. He was back in seconds, extending the phone like a retrieved stick.

"It's clean?"

"*Sí.*"

Jäger quickly linked the small cellular into his laptop, activated his scrambler and line meter, and punched in the numbers. He watched his monitor and the string of dots trace their way across the Atlantic and west toward the Pacific. When the line reached San Diego, the last dot blinked three times, followed by a soft click and the now-familiar response, "This is Grayson Haverland."

The asshole didn't sound so arrogant this time. "You know who this is?"

"Yes. I was expecting your call."

"So, you received my gift."

"Gift! I'm paying you a million pounds."

"Truly a bargain. The second disk will not be so cheap."

"You—" A silent *son of a bitch* hung in the air.

Good. Now he would find out how valuable the disks really were. "Five million."

The line hummed with silence for a good ten seconds. "Pounds or dollars?"

Jäger smiled to himself. At least the *Americano* knew when he was beaten. "Pounds."

"When and how? And don't think I'm going to give you anything before I get the disk."

"*Certo.* It will be my pleasure to deliver it personally." It was an offer he knew Haverland didn't expect or want, and the silence confirmed it.

"Give me a minute."

"Take two," he said, curious to see who Haverland would make the patsy. A man like him always had one.

It only took him thirty seconds. "Mr. Tripp will handle the transfer. I'll put him on the line."

"This is not necessary. I will contact him."

"But . . . but we need to make arrangements."

Arrangements. What amateurs. Did they really think Eth Jäger was stupid enough to walk into a trap? "Arrange to have the money."

CHAPTER THIRTY-THREE

Location unknown

Time unknown

Simon tried to estimate how long they'd been driving, but it was hard to calculate scrunched down on the floor between the front and backseat with a stocking cap pulled over his eyes and his brain still clogged with drugs. One thing he knew for sure, the Volvo was a rental—a Hertz—didn't matter where in the world you picked it up, they all used the same I'm-a-new-car air freshener.

Jäger reached over and pulled off the cap. "Sit up."

Simon pushed himself off the floor, squinting against the midday light. They were parked alongside a wide canal, the banks lined with silent warehouses. It looked like an old movie set, before color—the buildings bleached with age, the washed-out sky, the gunmetal-gray water with clouds of fog floating off the surface and drifting away like ghosts. Though nothing looked familiar, it was obvious they were still in Amsterdam, somewhere in the industrial part of the city.

The pilot, sitting behind the wheel, swiveled around and handed Jäger a small two-way radio with an earplug-microphone extension. Jäger clipped the unit to his belt, ran the wire up beneath his leather jacket, slipped the pea-sized receiver into his ear, then carefully attached the tiny microphone to his collar, directly beneath his mouth. *"Bene?"*

The pilot tapped his ear and nodded. *"Sí."*

Satisfied, Jäger turned to Simon. "Everything is clear, eh?"

"Clear?" Though his brain felt like an oversoaked sponge, he wanted to hide the fact it was getting drier by the minute. "About what?"

"It's simple. You will not speak. Do what I say and hope this Vic does not"—he paused, searching for the right word—"how do you Americans say? Screw up."

Simon nodded, hoping the same, but doubted Jäger intended to let him walk away, whether he got the disk or not.

As if to confirm the thought, Jäger pulled a pair of radio headphones from his duffel, the kind weekend joggers wore, with a little aerial coming off one side. He slipped them around Simon's neck and connected the ends with a thick line of monofilament so they couldn't be removed. "You see this?" He held up a small silver box, about the size of a cigarette pack, and flipped open the cover, exposing a small red button and telescoping antenna.

A sudden chill traced a finger down the middle of Simon's back. "A transmitter?"

"Sí. Insurance. Nothing of concern."

Right, and if you believe that . . . "Insurance?"

"In case you would try something stupid"—the corner of his mouth curled slightly—"and lose your head." Then he laughed, a sadistic chuckle cold enough to freeze alcohol.

Simon tried not to react, but the thought that he had a bomb strapped to his neck made it hard to breathe. Was the man crazy or bluffing? *Crazy—yes. Bluffing—no.* The man was certifiable, and crazy people didn't bluff.

Jäger slipped the transmitter into his pocket, checked the Velcro strap on the money belt beneath Simon's jacket, then opened the door. "We go."

Using the doorframe for support, Simon pulled himself upright. His legs felt like two wooden stumps, heavy and hard and unresponsive. Similar, he had a feeling, to what an amputee experienced the first time he strapped on a prosthesis.

A slow-moving barge passed by, sending waves of dark water slapping against the canal wall. Jäger gave the captain a friendly wave, then placed his hand under Simon's arm and began to steer him down the sidewalk. Simon shuffled along awkwardly, not wanting to expose how quickly the cold air was clearing away the mind fog he'd been living in for at least a week. The unaccustomed movement had a less sobering effect on his stomach, which felt ready to erupt. "Need to sit."

Jäger nodded in the direction of a water taxi as it angled toward a landing area a hundred meters ahead. "Rest there."

Vic might be a computer genius, but meeting Jäger on a water taxi seemed about as smart as stepping onto a small island with Hannibal Lector. "We're meeting him on a boat?"

"This Vic the Quick is very clever." Somehow he made the word *clever* sound stupid.

The boat edged up to the landing, but with no one waiting and no one getting off, it immediately pulled back into the channel. Simon wasn't sure if he should be relieved or disappointed. "Missed it."

Jäger pushed him toward a metal bench near the ramp. "We miss nothing."

Simon slumped down on the cold seat, as if his legs couldn't carry him another step, and slumped forward, resting his head in his hands. The earphones felt like a hangman's noose made of lead. The moment Jäger glanced away he reached down and gave the plastic filament a hard tug. The headband, cut into the back of his neck, and he realized the headphones would probably explode before the monofilament gave way. He needed a knife, but had a feeling God wasn't about to drop one in his lap. He tried to tell himself it didn't matter, that Vic would make the trade and everything would be fine, but his mind refused to believe it. He couldn't be sure whose side Vic was on, whether he was playing the game for himself or had simply refined their original plan.

Insurance. Nothing of concern. He didn't believe that, either, not from a man who had tried to turn him into a human torch. He tried to focus, to come up with a plan, but the drugs kept diverting his thoughts, sending them into vacant channels of darkness. By the time the next boat arrived, his toes were numb and his backside frozen. Jäger gave him a warning glance. "You will not speak."

Besides the captain, there were only four passengers, all men, all sitting inside under the clear Plexiglas cover. Jäger purchased two day passes, then pushed Simon toward one of the open seats near the bow.

"Outside?"

"Silence." He pulled a tiny cellular from his pocket, glanced at the display, then stuffed it back into his pocket.

Simon lowered himself onto another icy seat and studied the blurred faces beyond the Plexi-shield. Though he wouldn't have recognized Vic if the man sat on his lap, all four of the passengers had that pale Scandinavian look, and none of them seemed interested in two fools sitting outside in the cold. He glanced around slowly, looking for . . . What? If there was help anywhere close, he didn't see it.

They traveled north for a good twenty minutes, the warehouses gradually replaced by massive eighteenth-century brick homes overlooking the canal. They were moving toward the center of the city, picking up passengers as they went, most of them tourists and holiday shoppers. Simon ignored the women and families, concentrating on the men, hoping for eye contact or some indication that Vic had found him. Nothing. From snippets of conversation, he determined that Christmas was less than a week away. And that meant—he struggled with the math, his brain stuck on dial tone—*twelve days! Was that possible*—strapped on his back for nearly two weeks? No wonder his legs felt like wood. The picture of what Jäger planned was growing sharper by the second, coming into focus like a bad movie.

The setup: lull Vic into believing everything was okay.

The hook: make the exchange and let Simon walk away.

The finale: BOOM!

That was one thing Simon didn't doubt for a second, that once Jäger had the disk, he would push the button, if only to witness the result of his devious little invention.

As they moved closer to the central part of the city, the homes gave way to commercial buildings, their walls covered with graffiti and political posters, their doorways cluttered with bikes. From time to time Simon caught sight of the Volvo as the pilot worked his way between bicycles and cars, trying to keep pace with the boat. Jäger seemed to miss nothing, his single eye tracking every movement like a hungry hawk. As they pulled into a landing beneath the Nieuwe Doelenstraat bridge, his cellular emitted a sharp chirp. He pulled the phone from his pocket, glanced down at the display, scowled, and jumped to his feet. *"Andare."* He pointed toward the ramp. "Go."

They crossed the bridge, heading north toward the central part of the city, then turned left, skirting around the Allard Pierson Museum. At each turn Jäger would whisper into the microphone at his collar, keeping the pilot informed of their location. Vic had clearly done something unexpected, and for the first time Simon felt some hope that the man would not go skipping blindly into a trap. But the more he considered the situation, the more certain he became that whatever precautions Vic took, it would never be enough. Even if he noticed the earphones, he would never understand their significance.

When they reached the Grimburg wal Landing they

caught another water taxi heading north on the Oude zijds Voorburg wal, a small canal skirting the Wallen, Amsterdam's infamous Red Light District. The boat was nearly full, mostly tourists, loaded down with cameras and backpacks and the omnipresent bottles of mineral water. Jäger commandeered two seats near the bow, where he could see everything.

A few meters away, a half-dozen teenagers, equally satisfied with their place in the cosmos, huddled together beneath a wispy cloud of smoke, the pungent smell of marijuana wafting back over the deck. *Amsterdam,* you had to love the place—no one seemed to care what anybody else did. An old man, oblivious to the crowd, squatted on the deck and methodically began tamping a load of tobacco into his meerschaum pipe. Finally satisfied, he turned his back to the wind and fired it to life with a disposable lighter set to blowtorch level. He took a deep breath, savoring the moment, then closed his eyes—a man at peace with the world.

Simon leaned forward, resting his head on the rail as if exhausted from the fast walk, and scanned both sides of the canal for the Volvo. The streets were crowded with bikes and taxies and private vehicles, but there was no sign of the ugly green rental. Jäger was obviously thinking the same, his attention shifting back and forth between the street, the passengers, and the display on his cellular. "This Vic the Quick likes to play games."

"Maybe he just wants to be sure you don't have any surprises planned."

"I am a man of my word." Though spoken in a whisper, the words sizzled with self-righteous indignation. "All I want is the disk."

"Is that what you told Herr Olin?"

"A weak man. It is the law of nature."

No, murder was the law of man—nature was never so discriminate. "What about Pilár Montez?"

Jäger stabbed a finger toward his eye patch. "She deserved it. You would have done the same."

Though he didn't appreciate being drafted into the world of psychopaths, Simon realized this was not the time to deny his membership in Club Crazy. Going over the side seemed a better option. He glanced down at the dark water and considered his chances. The water might kill the explosives. *Might,* but a long shot. *Wishful thinking.* He turned his attention to the other passengers, looking for a knife, a nail clipper, anything sharp enough to cut the noose from his neck. And if he spotted something . . . ?

The boat slowed and angled in toward another landing, a popular drop-off point for tourists venturing into the Wallen. Most of the passengers began to move toward the ramp. A few feet beyond the bow, on a pedestrian bridge that crossed over the canal, a young woman leaned over the rail, her breasts threatening to burst out of her pink tube top. Her short skirt not only showed off a pair of shapely legs, but advertised her profession as well. She smiled flirtatiously at Jäger. "Hey, *schatze,* I've got something *speeeecial* for you." The way she said *special* made the word sound wicked and full of erotic promise.

Jäger made a little sound, like spitting a bug off the tip of his tongue. "You've got nothing I want."

She cocked her head to one side, giving him a vampy look. "You think?" She extended her right arm over the railing and dropped something. It fell about three feet, then hung there, spinning slowly on a string a few feet beyond the bow: a clear plastic bag containing the disk. "Mr. Veeek, he promised you would like it."

For a brief moment Jäger's mouth went slack, as if caught unexpectedly between expressions, then he reached out and tried to snatch the bag before she could pull it away. She grinned and yanked back on the string, letting the prize dangle a few inches beyond his reach. "Not so queeek, *schatze.* You have—" She rubbed her thumb against the tip of her fingers, that universal hand sign for *show me the money—the moolah —the scratch.*

Jäger reached down, jerked Simon to his feet, and pulled open his jacket, showing her the money belt. She hardly looked, her big eyes boring into Simon's with such intensity he felt like an animal caught in the headlights. "You have seen it, *ja?*"

Simon nodded, though he realized the question was perfunctory and meaningless, that if Vic cared about the money, he would have wanted more than "You have seen it," he would have demanded the woman get some kind of verification. The money was only a ruse, a trick to distract Jäger and force him into a situation where he didn't have time to think or improvise, where he had to make up his mind quickly or risk losing the disk. And by using a prostitute as a go-between there could be no negotiation, the girl would do only what she was paid to do—no more, no less. *Very clever.* Only Vic didn't know about the bomb.

The woman turned back to Jäger. "He is to leave the boat."

Jäger glanced toward the passengers waiting to get

off, then back to the girl. "How do I know you'll give it to me?"

She shrugged, the tops of her breasts jiggling provocatively. " 'Cause that's what I do, *schatze.*" Then she laughed, amused at her own wit, and held up a wad of Euros. "I got mine."

Jäger hesitated, glanced again toward the ramp, then made up his mind and shoved Simon toward the crowd of passengers waiting to get off. *"Andare!"*

For a moment Simon considered resisting; if he stayed close, Jäger wouldn't dare push the button, but then realized that would only delay the inevitable. *More wishful thinking.* He lurched toward the crowd of passengers, wondering how far he could get before Jäger had his hands on the disk. How strong was the transmitter? *Strong enough;* he could feel it down into the marrow of his bones.

He pushed his way past the group of teenage pot-smokers and into the crowd. He could feel Jäger's dark eye itching across the back of his neck. Afraid to move his head, he glanced around with his eyes, trying to hide his panic. "Anyone have a knife?" He tried to sound casual, but in his effort to keep his voice low it came out sounding nervous and desperate. No one said a word, but he could read their expressions and realized he looked like a whacked-out street bum, not the kind of person you wanted to share sharp objects with. He squeezed forward, between a young couple with backpacks large enough to set up house, and into a wall of bodies. To his right, the old man with the pipe puffed and waited, in no hurry to get anywhere.

"Excuse me," Simon said, an idea popping into his head. *"Spreekt u Engels?"*

The old man nodded, very slowly, as if challenged by the question.

"May I borrow your lighter?"

With some effort—they were packed in like subway commuters—the man retrieved his lighter and handed it over. Scrunching down as low as he could in the crush of bodies, Simon gritted his teeth, snapped the lighter, and without hesitation directed the flame toward the monofilament stretched across his neck. For a moment there was only the soft *whoosh* of the blowtorch flame, then the pain hit, like a dental probe going into a rotten tooth, and it was all he could do not to pull the lighter away before the plastic thread finally snapped. He yanked off the headphones, realized he couldn't move his arms enough to throw them beyond the crowd, so pulled them down next to his leg and handed the man his lighter. The old man stared back in disbelief, smoke leaking from his mouth and curling upward past his nose and bulging eyes. Fighting to control his panic, Simon gave the man a shrug—*no big deal, that's the kind of crazy thing us foreigners do all the time.*

It took an effort, but he resisted the impulse to glance around to see if Jäger had seen anything. What he couldn't resist was the disconcerting thought that, instead of his head, it was his balls that were now in danger of being blown into tiny bits of useless protoplasm, which, in an odd sort of way, seemed worse. Some egotistical male thing, he was sure. *This is it, God,* your chance to emasculate Simon Leonidovich, your irreverent servant.

The crowd began to move forward, squeezing over the ramp and spreading out like sand through the neck of an hourglass. Simon edged his way toward the outside, to a place he could drop the headphones in the water. *Almost there,* and resisted again the impulse to look back.

He stepped onto the ramp and glanced up at the street, expecting Vic to leap forward and shout triumphantly: *"Hey there, Bagman, it's me, VicTheQuick."* But it was the pilot who was waiting, leaning casually against a lamppost, his left hand cupped over his left ear, his right fist down at his side, the silver nub of his switchblade visible between his thumb and forefinger. The bomb or a shiv in the gut—*nice choice.* Either way, in less than ten seconds it would be over. His life would be over. *Ten seconds.* In that moment time seemed to stop, the world taking on a strange density, as clear and thick as water, and he knew exactly what he needed to do. *Eight seconds.*

Shielding the headphones with his leg, he fell in behind a family of tourists as they headed toward the street. *Seven.* The engine of the water taxi rumbled as it pulled away from the landing. *Six.* Without looking, he could see Jäger stretching for the disk. *Five.*

He headed directly toward the pilot, the seconds dissolving like quicksand beneath his feet. *Two.* Before the man could react, Simon flashed a disarming, great-to-see-you smile and without breaking eye contact flipped the headphones. Like an infielder caught off guard by a hard liner, the man instinctively reached out and snatched them out of the air. Instantly Simon veered to his left—

WHUUUMP.

The sound was surprisingly muted, the shock-wave no more than a breath of warm air across the back of his neck. He didn't want to look, but like the repulsive allure of an expressway pileup, couldn't stop himself. The pilot was standing in the same spot, a bewildered expression on his face, staring down at his hands—or where his hands had been a moment before. There was no blood, not yet, just two blackened stumps extending from the shredded sleeves of his coat. Then a woman screamed, but Simon had already turned away.

CHAPTER THIRTY-FOUR

La Jolla

Monday, 23 December 17:28:24 GMT −0800

Moving quickly—he hated to miss the "top of the news"—Tripp slid his briefcase onto the bar, dropped his keys, picked up the remote, snapped on the television, clicked over to NBC, grabbed a bottle of sauvignon blanc from his eighty-bottle cooler—a 1999 Simi, one of his favorite before-dinner wines—pulled the cork, poured a glass, and settled into his leather armchair just as Tom Brokaw flashed onto the screen. *Perfect.* It was his favorite time of day, when he could sit back with a good glass of wine, enjoy the news and for thirty minutes forget about King Grayson.

But before Brokaw had finished his first sentence, the phone screeched. *Mother-fuck!* He hit the MUTE button on his remote and snatched up the receiver, ready to blister the ears of whichever telemarketing asshole had been unlucky enough to pull his number. "This is Edgar Tripp," he snapped, letting the person know he wasn't a man to trifle with. "Who's this?" He liked to throw them off with a question before they could jump into their spiel.

"The money is ready?"

The soft voice made the hair on the back of his neck prickle. He took a deep breath and counted to five, trying to sound more confident than he felt. "Absolutely. You have the disk?"

The soft voice took on an edge. "Of course."

Of course, as if getting the damn things hadn't taken six weeks, three murders, a kidnaping, and . . . ? *Better not to know.* "Where do—"

"The zoo. Two o'clock tomorrow."

Tripp forced himself to breathe. "The zoo's a big place."

"Koala exhibit."

"How will I know you?"

"It is enough that I know you." *Click.*

Jesus-fuck, just the thought of standing eyeball to eyeball with that maniac was enough to make his bowels seize up. He could run, before the merger and without his fuck-you money, but the thought of starting over at this point in his life was unimaginable. He drained his glass in two long gulps, then leaned back and forced himself to relax, to focus, to think, to find a way out of the box. In front of him, in silent narration, Brokaw described the kaleidoscope of images that radiated off the screen, the history of the day, interrupted by commercials selling the future: the next vacation, the next computer, the next movie . . .

That's when it hit him, so simple and obvious he couldn't stop himself from giggling. *The Score,* one of his favorite movies, it had the perfect ending, Robert De Niro blazing into the sunset *with* the money.

It was perfect.

Prophetic.

All the pieces were there; all he had to do was shuffle them around a bit. He picked up the phone and dialed Haverland's private number.

"Grayson Haverland, here."

"He called."

There was an extended moment of silence. "And?"

"What you think? He wants his fucking money."

"He's got the disk?"

"Of course." *Jesus, now I'm saying it.* "Why else would we pay him?"

"He's in town?"

"Be here tomorrow." He made a quick calculation, being careful to leave himself plenty of time. "Ten o'clock. At the zoo."

"The zoo! That was stupid. Couldn't you have arranged something a little more private?"

Stupid, he'd find out soon enough who was stupid. "You don't like the arrangements, you meet him." Something he knew Haverland would never do.

"Don't get smart with me, Edgar. You don't have a choice."

"Fuck you, Grayson. I've had it with your ultimatums. Wait'll that lunatic shows up at *your* office. I'm outta here." He slammed down the phone, then slowly began to count off the seconds. *One motherfucker. Two motherfucker. Three motherfucker. Four . . .* It took less than twenty for the royal-ass motherfucker to realize who it was that didn't have a choice. Tripp let the phone ring for nearly a minute, making the arrogant bastard sweat before picking up. "Yeah?"

"Okay, Edgar, what do you want?"

"You know damn well what I want. The file. All of

it." Of course he didn't care about any of it, not anymore. It was only the bait.

"And you'll get it. Take care of Retnuh and you'll get everything."

What a load, the lying son of a bitch would have multiple copies of everything. He hesitated, as if trying to make up his mind, then gave in with a reluctant, "Okay."

"And you'll—"

"Yeah, yeah, yeah, don't worry about it. I'll take care of that crazy son of a bitch. You just have the money ready by nine o'clock. I'll meet you at the office." He disconnected and immediately dialed his travel agent. *Five million pounds.* He quickly made the conversion. *Seven and a half million dollars!* And he'd be out of the country before Retnuh or King Grayson even knew he was gone. *Fuck 'em,* they deserved each other.

Jäger snapped off the recorder, pulled the mini receiver from his ear, and smiled to himself. *Fools.*

He pulled on the red Santa cap, letting the white ball hang down jauntily over the side of his face, obscuring his eye patch, then checked himself in the mirror. Satisfied, he pushed open the rear door of the rental van and stepped out onto the street. Every home in the quiet cul-de-sac twinkled with identical white Christmas lights. *Americanos,* they were like sheep. He took a moment, carefully checking his blue I'm-a-delivery-man uniform to be sure nothing was out of place, then tucked the Express package under his arm, picked up his clipboard, and started up the walk. *Crazy son of a bitch.* Señor Tripp was about to find out who was crazy. He pressed the doorbell and offered a cheerful smile for the security camera over the door.

Tripp's voice echoed over the intercom. "Who is it?"

"Delivery." He affected a Mexican accent. "Overnight package for Señor Edgar Tripp."

The door swung inward. "That's me."

Jäger held out the clipboard, then patted his breast pocket. "You have a pen, Señor?"

"Sure, let me grab one."

The minute he turned, Jäger stepped inside and closed the door.

Tripp whirled around. "What do—" His voice faltered, as if an internal lightbulb had just blinked on in his head, bright enough to hurt. "You're . . . you're Retnuh?"

Jäger smiled and dropped the accent. "Ho ho ho."

"I—uh—" Tripp's gaze skidded around the room as if searching for an escape route. "I . . . uh—"

"You *do* have my money?" Jäger asked, watching with amusement as the man squirmed and stuttered.

Tripp licked his lips, two tiny beads of sweat glistening at the corners of his nose. "It's at the office. You don't keep that kind of money lying around the house."

"Then we go to the office."

"We can't . . . I mean . . . it's in Haverland's safe."

"Call him."

Tripp hesitated, a man caught on the precipice, not sure whether to leap or step back, then made up his mind and jumped. "He's out of town. Won't be back until tomorrow."

"How disappointing. I did hope to conclude our business tonight."

"There's really nothing I can do."

Jäger nodded slowly, disappointed but resigned. "Tomorrow then. Two o'clock."

"Right, stick with the plan." He tried to hide his relief, but it oozed from his voice like sap from an old maple. "I think that's best."

Jäger started to turn, then paused as if he'd just noticed the bar. "Perhaps we could have a drink?"

Tripp bobbed his head enthusiastically, his eyes telling a different story. "Uh, sure. A quick one. I'm expecting friends."

Jäger smiled to himself, reading the lie. "Yes, very quick."

CHAPTER THIRTY-FIVE

La Jolla

Exhausted from the long flight and beaten down by the unending questions, Simon struggled to keep his eyelids from going the way of his brain, which had shut down somewhere over the Atlantic. Being stuck in the back of a van with three Federal agents and enough equipment to heat Madison Square Garden didn't help. Antonio Torres, the Special Agent in Charge—SAIC—either satisfied or equally tired of repeating the same questions, scribbled something in his notebook and turned away. Handsome, with salt-and-pepper hair and penetrating blue eyes, he exuded the quiet confidence of an old sea captain, a man who knew how to survive a storm.

The agent controlling the surveillance cameras—a baby-faced young man whom everyone referred to as The Kid—swiveled around to face his boss. "We've got company."

Torres glanced up at the row of twelve-inch monitors. "That's Cantrell." He reached over and cracked the van's side door, then turned to Simon. "Don't let

him get to you. He's stubborn and likes to bark, but
he's a good guy and a smart cop."

Outside, a man with massive shoulders glanced
around cautiously, then gave the camera a one-
fingered salute, slid the door open, and stepped inside.
"Channel 28," he snorted, mocking the van's descrip-
tive camouflage. "Ain't no Channel 28 in San Diego.
Whatchu think, people are stupid?"

Torres smiled, making it clear that was exactly
what he thought, and motioned the big man toward a
small fold-down seat, the only place left to sit in the
overcrowded compartment. "How you doing, Jimbo?"

Cantrell scowled, showing no inclination to sit.
"How the fuck you think I'm doing? I was just about
to do my Christmas shoppin' when you beeped me."

"At eight in the morning?"

"Best time. Malls open early the day before Christmas."

"One of those leave-it-to-the-last-minute guys, uh?"

"No," Cantrell snapped back defensively, "I'm one
of those wait-for-the-sale guys. I don't make the bucks
you Feds do."

"Sorry," Torres said, no apology in his voice. "You
want to pass this off to somebody else?"

Cantrell shifted his gaze from Torres to Simon, then
to the two agents at the control console: The Kid and a
squatty-body audio technician by the name of Abner
Katz, who wore headphones and never looked away
from his panel of high-tech equipment. "And miss the
chance to work with you sleazy bastards again?" He
hitched up his khaki slacks and lowered his huge
frame onto the tiny seat. "Whatcha got goin'?"

Torres grinned, just a little. "Knew you couldn't resist." He nodded toward Simon sitting on another fold-down seat attached to the van's permanently sealed rear door. "Jim, say hello to Simon Leonidovich. Simon, this is Lieutenant James Cantrell, our liaison with San Diego PD and the grouchiest son of a bitch in the whole damn department."

Cantrell nodded, not taking his eyes off Torres. "Now I suppose I gotta say something nice about you." He made a show of checking out the vast array of monitors, video cameras, tape machines, scanners, and microwave receivers. "Nice equipment." Then he grinned, a quick flash. "And I ain't talkin' about your little weenie, Tony."

Torres feigned a look of shock. "Your wife's never complained."

Cantrell snorted a laugh. "She didn't want to hurt your feelings. You Feds are so damn sensitive." Before Torres could respond, Cantrell turned his attention to Simon. "You're new."

"Actually," Torres cut in, "Mr. Leonidovich is in custody."

Cantrell's mouth went a little slack. "Oh, yeah?"

"It's complicated."

Cantrell frowned and glanced at his watch. "Let's start with the Cliff Notes."

"A couple of days ago Mr. Leonidovich walked into our consulate with a very interesting story."

"Consulate?"

Torres nodded. "Amsterdam. A multinational pharmaceutical company, headquartered here in La Jolla, has accused Mr. Leonidovich of stealing proprietary research material." He glanced at Simon. "Mr. Leonidovich claims they're actually trying to destroy the material."

"Their own material?"

"Right."

Cantrell leaned forward, his face a knot of confusion, like a man straining on the toilet. "And that would be wrong because . . . ?"

"Because if what Mr. Leonidovich says is true, a few million people are going to die."

"A few mil— You're kidding?"

Torres shook his head, an emphatic one-sided horizontal move.

Cantrell sat back, crossed his arms over his huge chest, and leveled his eyes on Simon. "Better tell me everything."

Everything. The last thing Simon wanted to think about was everything. He didn't want to think about Pär Olin or his children, he didn't want to think about Lara and what she had gone through, and most of all he didn't want to think about Pilár Montez. How could he face that—how could he ever face that? How could he ever forgive himself? And though he tried to ignore the thought, he had a feeling that God held him responsible—that in His celestial ledger of credits and debits, of good and bad deeds, Pilár's life had been charged against the account of Simon Leonidovich. He took a deep breath, closed his eyes, and forced his thoughts back to the beginning.

It took thirty minutes and he didn't begin to tell *everything.* Unlike the earlier interrogations, where they interrupted, harassed, and intentionally tried to confuse him, no one said a word until he finished.

Cantrell looked at Torres. "And you believe all that?" It was obvious he didn't.

"The FDA is evaluating the data. They won't know

anything definite for a few more days. But yes, we're inclined to believe his story."

"You got anybody who can corroborate?"

"We're working on it. Of course we've talked to the sister—"

"Sister." He might as well have said *bullshit*. "Whatchu expect her to say? What about this Vic character?"

"We're trying to track him."

"Track him?"

"All we have is a Web-based e-mail address."

Cantrell turned back to Simon. "Thought this guy was your buddy?"

"He saved my life. That qualifies."

"So where is he?"

Simon shrugged. It was a question he'd been asking himself for two days.

"Ain't that convenient," Cantrell snorted, as if he'd just proven the story was nothing more than a defense against criminal charges. "Come on, Tony, you don't really believe a man like Grayson Haverland would get involved in something like this? He's a personal friend of the mayor, for God's sake." He glanced up at the monitors and the close-in views of the palatial Spanish-style estate three-hundred yards to the west. "You go after a man like that, you're gonna end up pushin' paper clips around some igloo in Alaska."

"But—" Torres leaned forward, the posture of a man wanting to share a confidence. "If it's true"—he cocked an eyebrow, as if to say the matter involved far more than Cantrell realized—"it's going to be big. *Very* big."

The other two agents exchanged a knowing glance,

clearly understanding the meaning of *very big*—a once-in-a-lifetime career boost.

Cantrell tapped a finger against his lip, as if considering what a high-profile case might do for him. "You still need evidence."

"That's why we're here, Jimbo."

The big man studied the monitors, his gaze shifting slowly from one screen to the next. "And what exactly you hopin' to see from here?"

"At some point there's got to be an exchange," Torres answered. "Haverland's got the money. Jäger's got the disk."

"Even if it's true. If . . . if . . . *if,*" Cantrell repeated, emphasizing each word more emphatically than the last, "Haverland's not going to stand out there on the front lawn and play Dollars for Disks. He'd have some flunky make the exchange." He snapped his fingers, three quick pops, as if to jump-start his brain. "Like this Tripp character you mentioned."

"I sent another eyeball over to his place early this morning." Torres swiveled toward the agent wearing headphones. "Abe, Eyeball Two check in yet?"

Katz nodded. "Everything's quiet."

Cantrell shook his head, the exasperated look of a man struggling to do a jigsaw puzzle while blindfolded. "I just don't see how we can move on a guy like Haverland without some really solid evidence."

"And we won't," Torres assured him. "Not unless he takes possession of that disk. That would validate at least part of Leonidovich's story."

"Don't tell me we're sitting out here the day before Christmas hoping he's stupid enough to make the exchange in front of your cameras. Crissake, Tony, let's get real."

Torres narrowed his eyes in a grinning way. "We think the disk is wired."

"A tracking device?"

"That was the plan," Simon answered, trying to sound more optimistic than he felt. "Vic was going to try and embed a microchip beeper into the disk."

"Try?" Cantrell cocked his head in disbelief. "You got a signal or not?"

Simon forced himself not to look away from the man's unrelenting gaze, not to be embarrassed or apologetic for what he still believed was a good plan. "It doesn't work that way. We were afraid Jäger might scan the disk and pick up the signal. The beeper won't activate until someone tries to access the data."

Cantrell exhaled long and loud, as if he'd just endured a long-winded joke only to discover there was no punch line. "This gets better and better." He turned to Torres. "You're dreaming, Tony. If half this shit is true, Haverland would burn that disk the minute he got his hands on the thing."

"Eventually," Torres agreed, "but would you pay for something without first verifying it was real?"

Cantrell hesitated, as if searching for a rebuttal, then gave up the quest. "So you get a beep. Then what?"

Torres pulled a search warrant from the inside pocket of his jacket. "Good to go. Provided we get a signal."

Cantrell shook his head slowly, as if trying to convince himself. "Murder. That's a big line for a man like Haverland to cross."

"You're right," Simon agreed, trying to sound objective. "And I doubt that's what he intended. I'm pretty sure Jäger was only hired to find the disks."

"Probably," Torres said, picking up the thought, "he's some low-life private investigator looking to make a score. We're checking the local agencies. He shouldn't be hard to find."

Simon knew better. Jäger might be a psychopath, but he wasn't some local-yokel, low-life private investigator. "Trust me, you're not going to find this guy in the Yellow Pages. And you're not going to find him under the name of Retnuh or Eth Jäger."

Cantrell leaned forward, his eyes fixed on Simon the way a psychiatrist studies a patient, hoping to glean some empirical information from an inadvertent word or gesture. "Why you say that?"

"I did some research on the flight over. In German, *Eth Jäger* means 'The Hunter.' *Hunter* is a unique word in the English language. The *only* word comprised of those six letters."

Torres looked from Simon to Cantrell, then back to Simon. "You lost me."

"*Retnuh*'s an anagram. *Hunter* spelled backward."

Cantrell smiled, just a little, a new respect in his eyes. "You don't say."

Torres slipped a small leather-bound notebook from the inside pocket of his coat and made a note. "That's a hell of a coincidence."

"It's no coincidence," Simon continued. "This guy promotes himself as some kind of great white hunter. Actually sees himself that way. To him it's a game. I think he was hired to find the disks and things just got out of hand."

The Kid swiveled around in his chair. "Heads up, boss. Somebody's leaving the house."

Everyone turned to the monitors, watching as the security gate swung open. A moment later a silver-blue sports car shot through the opening and turned south on La Jolla Farms Road. Even at a glimpse, Simon recognized the tan face and steel-gray hair. "That's Haverland."

"Oh, man," said The Kid scrambling into the driver's seat, "I'd give my left nut for wheels like that."

"What is it?" Torres asked, climbing into the passenger's seat.

"Aston Martin DB7 Volante. Zero to sixty in five point seven."

"Well, don't lose him," Torres warned, "or you won't have any nuts to give up."

The Kid grinned and gunned the engine. "Where you suppose he's going in such a hurry at eight-thirty in the morning?"

Torres glanced over his shoulder. "What you think, Jimbo? Christmas shopping?"

Cantrell snorted. "Yeah, that's how he got so fuckin' rich. Bargain hunting."

The Kid had barely gotten the van up to speed when Haverland turned right, toward the coast, then left on a private boulevard leading to the Bain-Haverland Research Center. The huge building seemed to float over the Pacific in a vapory cloud of early-morning mist, the parking lot empty except for a white Toyota pickup.

"Over there," Torres ordered, pointing to the side of the road. "We'll stand out like a whore in church if we go in there."

The Kid wheeled the van onto the gravel, then scrambled back to his video station. With the skill of a teenage gamer, his hands flew from one joystick-type controller to the next, adjusting and focusing his cameras. "Looks like they're closed for the holidays."

Cantrell pulled his cellular and leaned in close over The Kid's shoulder. "How 'bout giving me a close-up of that Toyota's plate." Despite his previous skepticism, it was obvious from his expression that his adrenaline was up, and he was now firmly entrenched on the team. "Let's see who's waiting for that son of a bitch."

Torres glanced over at his audio man, "Abe, any problem picking up a signal from here?"

Katz shook his head. "If that disk peeps, I'll hear it."

Torres's gaze slid toward Simon. "Let's hope your buddy Vic wasn't just bragging when he said he could wire that thing."

Simon nodded, hoping the same, but not taking his eyes off the screen and Grayson Haverland as he walked toward the building's entrance. Whatever the circumstances, he appeared pleased with himself, his easy gait almost a swagger.

Cantrell snapped the flip closed on his cellular. "If he's meeting someone, they're not here yet. That Toyota belongs to the security guard."

CHAPTER THIRTY-SIX

La Jolla

Tuesday, 24 December 08:34:05 GMT –0800

Haverland slid his key card into the reader, waited for the beep, then pressed his thumb against the scanner. He was feeling better than he had in weeks, and very relieved to escape the preparations surrounding his wife's Christmas Eve soirée: an intimate gathering of two hundred *friends,* all hers, half of whom he didn't like and the other half he barely knew. There was a second beep, an audible click as the lock released and the lobby door slid open. "Good morning, Henry."

The guard jolted to attention. "Mr. Haverland, sir. I didn't expect to see you today."

"I have a meeting with Mr. Tripp. Is he here yet?"

"No, sir—" Henry looked down at his monitor. "Oh, yes, he is. Came in through the garage about thirty minutes ago." He touched a button on his control panel, and the image changed to a wide-angle view of the underground parking area. "Yep, that's his red Mercedes, all right. Only car down there." He glanced away, a little shame-faced, like a school boy caught skipping class. "I should have noticed."

Yes, that's what you're paid to do, Haverland thought, but they were closed and it *was* the day before Christmas. He reached into the side pocket of his briefcase and pulled out one of the prewrapped fountain pens he carried for just such emergencies. "Thought of you when I saw this, Henry."

The guard's face flushed with surprise. "Thank you, sir."

Pleased with himself, Haverland turned and started toward the elevator. "Happy holidays, Henry."

"You, too, sir. Merry Christmas."

Oh, yes, it was going to be a *very* Merry Christmas. The nightmare with Retnuh was nearly over, and in less than a week the merger would be complete. *Happy days are here again.*

The Administrative Floor was blissfully silent, the reflection of early-morning light casting a warm glow over the empty cubicles and desks. *The skies above are clear again.*

He gave Tripp's door a "heads-up" rap as he walked past—*So long sad times*—and turned into his office. *Go 'long bad times.* He snapped on the light and sang out the last line: "Happy days are here again!"

He had barely taken a step when he noticed the connecting door to Tripp's office had been left open, the room beyond dark and silent. Then a faint smell, or the memory of a smell, skipped across the edge of his brain. It came like a radar flash, one tiny blip, there and gone, between one step forward and the next. He stopped and took a deep breath, hoping desperately that his mind was playing games, but his nostrils immediately confirmed what his brain had already whispered: *Turkish tobacco.*

He wanted to run, but his legs felt like two disconnected appendages, and all he could do was watch helplessly as the high-backed chair behind his desk swiveled around. Retnuh, his left eye covered with a black eyepatch, grinned back at him, his expression rueful and ghoulish behind a thin cloud of smoke that leaked from his mouth. "Happy days, uh, Doc?"

Struggling not to show his fear, Haverland forced himself to return the man's unblinking stare. "Where's Mr. Tripp?"

Retnuh smiled again, as if the question amused him.

"I know he's here. One of the guards"—he tried to make it sound like security people were everywhere—"told me he checked in through the garage."

Retnuh simply stared back, as if his silence carried some kind of warning he wanted Haverland to pick up.

Though Haverland knew he was babbling, he couldn't stop himself. "You couldn't have gotten in the building without him."

Retnuh brought his latex-covered fist up from beneath the desk and slowly uncoiled his fingers, exposing Tripp's perfectly manicured thumb. It was all Haverland could do to keep his knees from buckling—not because of Tripp; the man was a deviant and deserved whatever he got—but because he was now sure of his own fate. "You're"—he could barely speak, his voice lost somewhere deep in his trachea—"going to kill me."

Retnuh barked a one-note laugh. "You think I am stupid? You are my privata *banca.*" He took a drag on his cigarette, then stood up and crushed the butt into the top of the desk. *"Comprende?"*

Haverland nodded, bubbles of relief bursting in his chest. *Money.* That's all the bastard wanted. An endless supply. "Yes, perfectly."

"Eccellente, then we understand each other." He pulled a disk protector from the inside pocket of his jacket, the Megneto storage disk clearly visible through the plastic. "Now we do business, *sì?"*

Like a moth drawn to an irresistible glow of light, Haverland stepped forward and reached for the disk, but Retnuh warned him away. "Money first."

He hesitated, knew Retnuh might still kill him once he had the money, but what choice did he have? *None.* "Quite right. Money first." Barely able to control his panic, afraid he would get a knife in the back the minute the safe opened, it took him three tries to get the combination right. As he reached inside for the small red-and-blue duffel, he threw out the only bargaining chip he could think of to save his life. "Plenty more where this came from."

Retnuh smiled, just a little, as if to confirm the bargain, then stepped to the small conference table and began to scan the bag's nylon surface with a device similar to the hand wands used by airport security. After carefully examining each side, including the bottom, he opened the bag and dumped the contents: one-hundred separate packets, each totaling fifty-thousand English pounds. With the dexterity of a bank teller, he stacked and counted the bundles, fanned each to make sure they were consistent, then snapped the paper band on one and counted the bills. Apparently satisfied, he scooped everything back into the bag, then casually slid the disk across the table and into Haverland's hands.

Katz suddenly leaned forward and flipped a switch on his console. "Bingo!"

Torres looked at his audio man in disbelief. "What? You pick up a signal?"

"Beep, beep, beep. He must have had the disk with him."

It took Simon a moment to grasp the implication of "had the disk with him," then realized they had missed Jäger. He shouldn't have been surprised—the man was a ghost, always a step ahead—but the realization left him feeling hollow and defeated. As long as they both inhabited the same planet, it would never be over.

Torres frowned, a ditch furrowing down the center of his forehead. "They must have made the exchange last night." His shoulders drooped in defeat. "We're screwed. He'll turn that disk into toast before we ever get to him."

Cantrell, so reluctant earlier, now seemed completely unwilling to pull back. "Bullshit, you don't know that. I say we go."

The Kid bobbed his head.

Katz tapped his headphone. "Loud and clear."

"On tape?"

Katz frowned, clearly offended, and pointed to a pulsating green band on his digital-frequency display. Torres nodded slowly, a man struggling to convince himself. "I suppose that would validate the warrant."

"Damn straight," Cantrell snapped, as if that settled the matter. "Let's get that rich motherfucker."

"Okay, let's do it."

As The Kid scrambled into the driver's seat, Torres began passing out radios and issuing instructions, his tone suddenly commanding. "Abe, you and The Kid come with me." He turned to Cantrell. "Your boss is gonna have a hernia when he hears we made a move on Haverland. You stay here and—"

"Bullshit! You're not calling me out the day before Christmas just so I can sit on my duffer and watch you Feds have all the fun? I'm—"

Torres crossed his index fingers, as if to ward off the devil. "Okay, okay. I don't have time to argue. Abe, you stay with the van." He cocked a thumb at Simon. "And keep an eye on him." He looked at Simon and shrugged helplessly. "Sorry, but if we don't catch him with that disk . . ."

Jäger watched the monitor as Haverland typed his eight-digit decryption password. Instantly the indecipherable mixture of letters, numbers, and symbols reconfigured themselves into comprehensible columns of text and numbers. What it signified, Jäger had no idea, nor did he care. All that mattered was value. If the disk had been compromised, the value would disappear. *"Accordo?"*

Haverland shifted nervously, the vein at the edge of his hairline pounding like a tom-tom. "I don't understand."

"The disk? All is in order?"

"It looks—" He leaned forward and studied the screen. "It looks okay. Why? You think . . . ?" His words trailing away.

"The courier is not a man of principle. I thought

perhaps—" He shrugged, such things required no explanation. "He has not contacted you?"

"I—" His mouth opened and closed and opened again, like a dying fish. "I assumed—"

Jäger smiled to himself, knowing exactly what the man assumed. *No,* Leonidovich was not dead. *Not yet.*

Haverland leaned back in his chair and took a deep breath, feeling as if a giant weight had been lifted from his chest. Never again would he allow that maniac to get close—even if he had to surround himself with an army of bodyguards. Though he didn't believe in God or the vagaries of fate, he realized in some cosmic sense he'd been given a second chance. It was an opportunity he didn't intend to waste. *If*—and he didn't believe it was possible—*but if* there was a problem with Mira-loss, he would fix it. He would personally review Olin's research, find the flaw, and correct it. No one would ever know. *Nothing to worry about.*

Still, somewhere deep in his mind he had that vague feeling of something forgotten. *Tripp? No,* the man was dead—another complication eliminated. Then it hit him, the record of Tripp entering and leaving the building. *After* he was dead. How could he explain that? Absorbed in trying to form some logical explanation, he didn't hear the men approach until Henry was standing in the door. "I'm sorry, sir, they wouldn't let me—"

Another man, middled-aged with steel-gray hair, moved the guard aside. "I apologize for the interruption, Mr. Haverland." He held up a small fold-over wallet with identification. "I'm Antonio Torres. Federal Bureau of Investigation."

FBI! Afraid his reaction might reveal some inappropriate expression, he didn't dare to even blink. Why would the . . . ?

No one knew what was on the disk.

No one knew he had it.

He hadn't done anything.

He hadn't authorized anything.

Tripp hired Retnuh.

Then, like the gears of a stubborn transmission, all the cogs slipped into place. *Tripp.* They had found his body. It was one of those rare moments that came along once in a lifetime, a split-second crack of clarity in which all the answers to his dilemma were revealed. He looked flushed and shaken, he could feel it, but that, too, was good. Tripp was dead. If the FBI killed Retnuh . . . It was almost too perfect.

He leaped to his feet. "Thank God you're here!" He could read the surprise in the eyes of Torres and the men crowding the door behind him. "There was a man here when I came in! My God, it was terrible! I think he's killed Edgar Tripp, our lawyer."

Torres held up his hand, trying to cut the flow of words. "Stop right th—"

But he couldn't stop, he needed to convince them before Retnuh got away. "He robbed me!" He pointed to the open safe. "I thought he was going to kill me!"

Torres glanced at the safe, his expression doubtful. "You recognize this person?"

Haverland shook his head emphatically. "No, I would have remembered. He had a patch over one eye."

The expression on Torres's face changed instantly, his doubt replaced by a sudden excitement.

*   *   *

Simon tried not to think about the past two months, about Pilár Montez and Pär Olin and all the things that had happened, but could think of nothing else. He told himself Jäger didn't matter, that he was an insignificant player in the drama, that if they never caught him it wouldn't make a difference, but the more he tried to convince himself the less he believed it. More than anything he felt cheated and alone, nothing more than a witness to a car wreck waiting to give his statement.

"Abe!" Torres's tinny voice burst from Katz's two-way radio. "Jäger was here. He's coming out through the underground garage. The ramp's on the north end of the building. Stop him."

Katz snatched up the radio, his face suddenly pale, as though the tan had run out of his face. "Stop him? How am I supposed to do that?"

"Try using your gun," Torres snapped back, his voice flat with sarcasm.

"I haven't used my gun since I left the Academy."

"Just block the damn entrance. We're on our way."

"Ten-four."

Simon scrambled into the front passenger seat as Katz cranked the engine and turned the van toward the north end of the building. "I'm not a field agent." His voice piped and cracked with nervousness. "I'm not a field agent."

Despite the circumstances, Simon couldn't keep from smiling. He suddenly felt like more than a specta-tor. And if Torres was right, they still had a chance to catch Jäger. He pointed to the ramp as Katz came around the side of the building. "There."

Katz eased up to the edge of the incline and

stopped, letting the engine idle. Barely wide enough for one vehicle, the narrow tunnel-like ramp slanted downward for twenty feet before leveling off, the view into the garage obstructed by the overhang. Round convex mirrors at each end provided drivers a clear view of any oncoming traffic before proceeding. Katz fumbled awkwardly as he pulled his revolver, an old-fashioned snub-nosed thirty-eight. He glanced at Simon, as though just now realizing he was there. "I'm not really a field agent."

Simon nodded, feeling sorry for the guy. "Could have fooled me."

"What do you think?"

"About what?"

"You think he's still down there?"

"Let's hope so."

Katz nodded, the anxiety in his eyes suggesting the opposite. "Maybe I should take a look."

When it came to ideas, Simon couldn't think of a worse one. Abner Katz was not the man to go up against Eth Jäger. "What about the cameras? I noticed a couple of them had extension arms."

"I've never used them. I'm an audio specialist."

"Why don't I try?" He jumped into the back, not waiting for an answer. "I was watching The Kid."

The cameras were all sensibly labeled, each with its own set of toggle switches so the operator could direct the image to any one of the van's monitors. The joy-stick controller operated similar to a computer game Simon played with his nephew, and it took him less than a minute to get the front-view camera extended down the ramp. The camera was preset to wide angle, giving a full view of the garage, which appeared empty except for a sporty red Mercedes parked near the loading platform at the far end of the cavernous space. "I've got a picture."

Katz pointed to a small monitor on the dash. "Can you throw it up here? The screen is marked S-1."

Simon flipped the toggle marked S-1. "How's that?"

"A little dark. Can you lighten it up?"

"No." He scrambled back to the front. "The camera was easy. That's mechanical. The visual enhancements are controlled by computer. If I start playing around with that, we might lose the picture."

Katz nodded and opened his door. "I'd better take a look."

"This isn't someone you want to fool with."

Katz frowned, a trace of indignation in his voice. "I know what I'm doing,"

Or not, Simon thought, keeping one eye on the screen as Katz edged his way down the ramp. Just as he reached the bottom, a man carrying what looked like a gym bag appeared on the loading platform. Even in the dim light, Simon recognized Jäger immediately. Katz ducked back behind a cement column.

Not good, Simon thought as his heart rate edged toward the red zone. Then he noticed Katz's two-way on the dash. *Worse.* He grabbed the radio and pressed the TRANSMIT button. "This is Leonidovich, anyone hear me?"

Torres response was immediate. "Where's Katz?"

"He's in the garage. We've got the ramp blocked. Jäger's just getting into his car. A red Mercedes sports coupé." He tried to sound calm, but could hear the anxiety in his voice. "I think you'd better hurry."

"He disabled the elevator," Torres answered. "It'll take us a few minutes to get there."

"Okay," but he had a feeling it wasn't. "Ten-four," *or whatever the fuck you people say.*

Jäger, with his headlights on, and apparently in no hurry, followed the marked route through the empty garage toward the exit. Simon moved into the driver's seat, not sure what Katz would do but wanting to be ready. When the Mercedes was only about fifteen feet from the ramp, Katz stepped out from behind the column, gun in one hand, identification in the other. "Stop! FBI!"

Simon could see the surprise on Jäger's face. The car slowed, as if to stop, then lurched forward directly at Katz. The agent momentarily froze, then tried to dive out of the way, but too late, the left fender knocking him aside just before it smashed into the column.

Jäger was out of the car almost before it stopped, an automatic in his right hand. He glanced around, making sure there was no one else nearby, then stepped up to Katz lying unconscious a few feet away, and calmly pointed his gun at the agent's head.

Instinctively Simon slammed down on the horn.

Jäger leaped behind the column, then crouching, leaned out and peered cautiously up the ramp. Seeing he was trapped, he retrieved the gym bag from the front seat of his car, then hugging the wall, started up the incline. Trying not to panic, Simon stepped down on the brake and shifted into reverse. About halfway up the ramp Jäger stopped, as if trying to assess the situation, his dark eye auguring into the van's windshield. Then he grinned, like a jackal that had just found his next meal, and in one quick motion brought his gun into firing position. Simon ducked and stomped on the gas as the windshield exploded into a thousand fragments. The van lurched backward, swaying wildly from side to side as he tried to control it from the beneath the dashboard. By the time he stopped, about a hundred yards back from the building, Jäger had disappeared back down the ramp.

Now what? Then he heard it, the fan clattering against the smashed-in grill of the Mercedes as Jäger tried to start the engine. It turned over, ran a few seconds, then stopped. A moment later he had it going again, the fan screaming like a banshee as he revved the engine and backed away from the column. From the corner of his eye, Simon saw Torres and Cantrell come tear-assing around the side of the building, but it was obvious they weren't going to make it in time.

Don't even think about it, he told himself, *just do it.* He reached down, yanked the seat belt tight across his chest, set the emergency brake, stomped down on the floor brake, then revved the engine until the van was straining and lurching against the brakes. Over the sound of the engine he could still hear the high scream of the Mercedes's fan and knew the moment Jäger started forward. Instantly Simon released both brakes and pushed the accelerator to the floor. "Simon says: You're not getting away this time, you bastard!"

He hit the top of the ramp just as the front of the Mercedes popped into view.

He opened his eyes slowly, afraid he might be dead, and if so, where God had decided to deposit his irreverent ass. He could see almost nothing, the van leaning slightly cockeyed with the roof smashed up against the top of the ramp. Cantrell came through the side door, crawling forward on his hands and knees. "You okay, buddy?"

Buddy. Now they were pals? "Yeah, think so." He really didn't know, but didn't see any blood. "Air bag worked I guess."

"Lucky you. That was some stunt."

"Stunt! It sounds like you can't wait to write me up for reckless driving."

Cantrell laughed. "Naw, I saw the whole thing. You definitely had the right of way."

"Where's Jäger? Did he get away?"

Cantrell laughed again. "You're sitting on his car. Damn near took his head off."

"He's dead?"

"No. Hell, no. Hardly a scratch. But it's gonna take some work to get him out of there."

"Abe?"

"Coupla broken ribs, my guess. He'll live. Knowing the Feds, they'll give the little twerp a medal and early retirement."

Torres crawled in behind Cantrell. "I heard that." He looked at Simon. "You okay?"

"Depends."

"On what?"

"On whether you got Haverland."

"Oh, yeah. The Kid's got him inside. He's already screaming for his lawyer."

"Did you get there in time? I mean—"

Torres grinned like an old tomcat about to get chow and held up the disk.

CHAPTER THIRTY-SEVEN

New York

Thursday, 2 January 08:57:01 GMT –0500

Simon glanced at the meter—$12.40—and slipped a twenty through the Plexi pass-through. "Keep the change."

The cabbie flipped him a salute, finger to eyebrow. "Thanks, Mac. Happy New Year."

Simon nodded—nothing could be worse than the last—and stepped out onto the sidewalk. The air was cold and crisp, the sun fighting to break through the morning overcast. Everything looked the same: the street, the old brownstone, the unknown people rushing to unknown places and jobs—but everything felt different. It was creepy, like the world had tilted slightly in the time he'd been away.

Despite Lara's poking and prodding, he had refused until now to go near the office. He needed to decompress, but knew it was now time to face the reality of *normal*. He started toward the elevator, then turned and headed toward the stairs. For the first time in ten years he'd gotten his weight below 190, the hard way, and wasn't about to let it creep back without a fight.

No more Mira-loss, no more quick-and-easy diets. This time he'd do it the old-fashioned way: diet and exercise. *Ugh.*

By the time he reached the door to his office, his legs felt as if they'd run out of blood. He hesitated, his mind a complete blank as he tried to recall his security code, but his fingers, which seemed to have a memory of their own, tapped in the familiar sequence. He took a deep breath and pushed open the door.

Lara, hunched over her desk reading *The New York Times,* jerked upright, her eyes wide with alarm. "Damn you, Simon! That's not funny, sneaking up on me like that!"

"Sorry." It was useless to plead innocence, despite her claim of being *just fine,* it was obvious she was still struggling with everything that had happened. "I thought I told you to take the week off."

"I have too much to do."

"Right." It was obvious what she was doing, suppressing her feelings with work, but he wasn't about to argue—that's the way she'd work it out. It might take awhile, but her eyes still flashed with that indomitable spark, and he knew she would eventually be okay. He glanced around, surprised how normal everything looked. "So, we're still in business?"

She frowned impatiently, as if to say *no thanks to you.* "We've lost a few accounts."

And he didn't care. He wanted to stay close for a while, to be there for her, whether she *thought* she needed him or not. "Good." He leaned down and kissed her cheek. "You've been telling me to cut back for years."

"I've been telling you not to take on *new* clients. There's a difference."

But not one worth arguing about, he thought, and shrugged off his overcoat. "So what else is new?"

She shuffled through the paper until she found the Business Section. "You see this?" She pointed to the headline.

GRAYSON HAVERLAND FOUND DEAD—APPARENT SUICIDE

"Heard it on the radio. Guess he couldn't handle the thought of spending his golden years in a six-by-eight cell."

"Seems like half the stories in here are about Miraloss. The doctors are overwhelmed with patients. Everyone wants to have their liver tested."

"That's good." It was something he considered doing himself, but didn't think he'd been taking the stuff long enough to do any damage. "I'm glad people are taking it seriously."

"It's the lawyers. They're pushing everyone to get checked. They say it's going to be the biggest class action in history."

He wasn't surprised. "No one can turn chicken shit into chicken salad faster than a lawyer."

She flipped over to a group of articles in the National Section. "And then we have the crazies."

"Crazies?"

"Listen to this woman from Dallas. 'My momma didn't raise no dummy. I bought a year's supply before the recall took effect.' "

"You must be kidding."

"Apparently there are thousands of people who would rather be thin than alive. There's already a huge black market for the little killers."

He leaned over her shoulder, scanning the head-lines. "Anything new on Jäger?" Too late he realized the foolishness of his question.

Her face seemed to shift and resettle in a kind of wave, as if a bad memory had rippled through her body. "Nothing new. Refuses to speak. Won't even admit he understands English. They don't have a clue who he is or where he's from."

"It doesn't matter, they caught the son of a bitch with a dead man's thumb in his pocket. He's gonna get a needle in his arm whether he talks or not." He turned toward his office, eager to change the subject. "Did I tell you, I finally reached Pilár's brother?"

She jumped up, following. "How'd that go?"

"Good. A really nice guy. Perfect English. We talked for nearly an hour."

"And . . . ?"

"And he agreed immediately when I suggested the reward money go to Olin's children." He dropped into his chair, the soft leather comfortable and familiar. "That and the hundred grand from the money belt should be enough to give those kids a pretty good jump on life."

"The FBI agreed to give you the money?"

"As long as no one else makes a claim."

"That's obviously not going to happen." She plopped down into a chair and shifted back and forth in the seat, as if burrowing in for a long stay. "Any other little gems you haven't shared?"

"I heard from Vic."

"Well, hallelujah. What's his story? Where's he been? What took him so long to show up?"

"I don't know. He didn't say. I couldn't ask. All I got

was an e-mail. But I have a feeling he was skating on pretty thin ice when he decoded those disks. Probably works for some government agency. Anyway, I'll know soon enough. We're meeting at Clark's for lunch." He reached out, pulled the huge stack of mail up close, then glanced up with what he hoped was a look of excitement, as if this wonderful idea had just popped into his head. "You should join us."

She shook her head empathically. "Too busy."

Too busy—code-speak for not wanting to hear the name *Eth Jäger* ever again. As much as he wanted to help, he knew better than to argue. "Suit yourself."

"How will you recognize him?"

"My picture's been all over the papers. I'm sure he'll find me."

"Or not."

"Then I'll find him. How hard can it be? The guy's a computer geek, you know the type: squinty eyes, thick glasses, milky-white skin, lives at home with his mother."

The bar was packed, most of the crowd waiting for a table in the back dining room. Except for the faces, nothing ever changed at Clark's—a place that defied the trends, with authentic brick walls and real hardwood floors. It was a favorite for bankers and brokers and ultra-thin models who crowded together in small clusters to discuss the direction of the market and debate the most current political scandal. Everybody seemed to be talking at once, drinking and laughing among themselves, having a good time. The real drinkers were at the bar, all men, lined up like crows on a wire, stealing glances at every woman who walked through the door.

Simon noticed a few looks in his direction, as if trying to place him, a common experience since having his picture splashed across the front page of every newspaper in the country, but no one seemed more than curious and no one approached. He was starting to think Vic was a no-show when someone from behind spoke his name. "Simon Leonidovich?"

He turned, not recognizing the woman's voice. She was tall and slim, mid-thirties, with short jet-black hair that spiked out in every direction, and big intelligent eyes that seemed vaguely familiar. "I'm sorry, I know we've met but . . ."

"No, not exactly." She smiled, a slightly teasing grin that left him hanging there in one of those awkward tongue-twisting moments when a man comes face-to-face with a beautiful woman he doesn't know.

Not exactly? His mind shifted from low to overdrive as he struggled to connect the face with a name. Then it hit him, the woman on the bridge in Amsterdam—the prostitute. "You're—"

She stuck out her hand. "Vic."

He was struck completely and absolutely mute—not simply by the unbelievable realization that Vic was a woman, but by her pure and absolute beauty. In that moment before his mouth found a connection to his brain, he tried to recall every e-mail, everything he'd written that would have marked him as just another ignorant, chauvinist male. And all the things he'd asked her to do, all the risks he'd asked her to take—things he would never have dreamed of asking a woman. "I . . . I . . . you're a woman." *Brilliant.*

Her big eyes sparkled with amusement. "You are a clever one."

He shook his head, almost afraid to say anything, afraid he might blurt out something *really* stupid.

"It's Victoria. Victoria Halle." Then she laughed, a deep throaty laugh full of sparkle and light, like diamonds flung high in the air.

And then they were laughing together.

**POCKET BOOKS
PROUDLY PRESENTS**

BAGMAN

JAY MacLARTY

**Coming soon in paperback
from Pocket Books**

**Turn the page for a preview of
Bagman. . . .**

CHAPTER ONE

Galápagos Islands

Saturday, 3 November 16:02:59 GMT –0600

Once clear of San Cristobal, Kyra disengaged her autopilot and banked southwest toward the southern tip of Santa Cruz, gradually reducing altitude. Her butt felt like petrified wood, as if all the blood had drained into her legs. *Long day. Long, long day.* From Bogotá, where she spent the night, to Guayaquil, where she topped off her tanks, to this Pacific archipelago—twelve total hours when you counted the flying, the filing, the fueling, and the fussing with customs. She silently added one last F to the list, then reminded herself it was for a good cause, and had given her time to think, to work on *the problem.*

Not that anyone at the Charles Darwin Research Station —the *Center,* to all current and previous employees—needed a zoologist from Washington to tell them what everyone already knew about the expanding population and the effects it was having on the biogeochemistry of the island. They had plenty of experts to sing that tune, her voice would add little to that overcrowded chorus, but what they *really wanted* was Dr. Kyra Rynerson-Saladino, daughter to one of the world's richest men, and her ability to raise money. But what they *truly wanted,* at the very top of their fantasy wish list, was that her father, Big Jake Rynerson, *businessman and billionaire*—God, how she hated that over-used tabloid description—might become a benefactor. He wouldn't. Not that her father was insensitive toward a good cause, but they rarely spoke and she would never ask.

Never ask—never take.

It was a pledge she had made to herself years before, on the very day Big Jake dumped her mother for trophy wife Number One, a sin Kyra would never forgive, in sharp contrast to her mother, who seemed to harbor no ill feelings toward her former husband—something Kyra had never been able to understand. It was an old argument, but the familiar words never seemed to change.

"Kyra, you can't expect a man like your father to be satisfied with one of anything. Including women."

"Hardly an endorsement for Husband-of-the-Year, Mother."

"Get past it, dear. I have. He misses you."

But she couldn't, though she never really tried. Why should she? She hated everything about him: his money, his lifestyle, his wife—he was now on trophy wife Number Three. "I can't stand to be around that woman—she's younger than I am."

"And how's your marriage, young lady?"

The memory of that question stung. She reached down and touched her stomach—still flat, but it wouldn't remain that way for long. She needed to make a decision. *Soon.*

She banked Babe toward Baltra and tuned her VOR receiver. The airport's Morse code identifier came back instantly, followed by a recorded weather report: clear, 28° Celsius, winds ENE 5 mph. *Normal,* Kyra thought, remembering her time on the island.

Thirty minutes later Babe was on the ground, tied down in a cordoned-off area reserved for private aircraft, chocks under her wheels. A customs officer arrived five minutes later, wrote Kyra's name on a clipboard and departed without giving Babe so much as a perfunctory look-through. She had just removed her carryall and garment bag from the luggage compartment when an open Jeep with no doors came barreling across the tarmac and skidded to a stop not more than three inches from Babe's right wing. "Doctor Rynerson?"

Kyra suppressed her irritation. "You found me."

"I'm Kelly Anderson, your driver." He was young, obviously American, dressed in a T-shirt and cut-offs, with an Angels baseball cap and Raybans. He looked like a California surfer on a good day: not more than twenty-two or -three, golden tan, dazzling white teeth, big smile.

Fresh out of college, Kyra thought, serving his internship at the Research Station, just as she had done. "Hello, Kelly. Mind grabbing my bags?"

"You bet." He came around the Jeep in an exuberant rush. "Sorry I wasn't here to meet you." He snatched up the canvas carryall and nylon garment bag. "Nice plane. Yours?"

"Someday. Right now the bank owns most of it." He gave her a look, a mixture of surprise and disbelief, something she had seen a million times. Why would the daughter of Big Jake Rynerson owe money to a bank? Not about to explain, she retrieved her laptop from the cockpit, locked the cabin door, and climbed into the passenger seat as Kelly strapped her bags onto the Jeep's open bed.

"Ready?" Kelly asked, his eyes making a quick, admiring tour over the contours of her body. "Seat belt on, tray table in its upright position?"

Okay, she wasn't too old to enjoy a little flirtation from a younger man. "All set, Captain Kelly."

He hit the accelerator, and the Jeep leaped forward. "Your father's Big Jake Rynerson?"

Typical. That was the question everyone asked first. "Sure is."

Kelly nodded, as if this confirmed the stories he'd heard. "Must be nice."

She was tempted to ask, *why,* but knew exactly what he meant: your father's a billionaire, your life is nothing but champagne and caviar. When she was young and foolish she had tried to correct the misconception, but no matter what she said, everyone had their own fantasy about what it would be like to have a billionaire father, so she learned to let it go. If anything, life as the daughter of Big Jake Rynerson was nothing more than a bloody curse. Along with the name came the expectations and celebrity-by-association, something she didn't ask for and didn't want. "Yeah, real peachy." *Peachy!*—did she actually say *peachy?*

"When did you work at the Center?"

Good way to learn her age, Kyra thought, though the question seemed part of his inquisitive patter and without guile. "About 15 years ago."

His pupils popped and she could see the wheels turning behind them. "Thirty-five," she said, providing the answer to his unspoken question.

"Oh." He seemed to deflate, his fantasy balloon leaking air. "You don't look that old."

She laughed. "Well, I don't know how old you *think* I look, but until this moment I didn't exactly consider myself long in the tooth."

His cheeks flushed, his eyes darting back and forth between her and the road. "I didn't mean you were old. I meant—" He glanced back at the road, as if searching for a cliff to drive over. "You look so young. I mean you *are* young, but—"

She held up a hand, cutting him off before he fumbled his way into adolescent purgatory. "I understand. Thanks. I'll consider that a compliment."

"You bet. You should. Yes, ma'am."

BOOM—her own balloon exploded. Nothing like the word *ma'am* to make a woman feel ancient.

Thankfully for both of them, the remainder of the trip passed in relative silence, normal conversation precluded by the wind howling through the open Jeep. "You'll love this place," Kelly said, as he pulled up to the front of the Red Mangrove Adventure Inn.

Surrounded by wild red mangrove trees and perched on the edge of the sea, the shell-pink structure reminded Kyra of La Valencia in La Jolla, where she once vacationed as a child with her mother and father, in those wonderful days before Big Jake had gone and ruined their family. "I'm sure. It looks wonderful."

Kelly started to pick up her bags, but she caught his arm. "I can take it from here, thanks." She didn't want to have to push him out of her room, in case he might be harboring fantasies about seducing an *older* woman.

"Oh sure, okay." He took a hesitant step back. "Dr. Marshall said to remind you about the reception."

Ugh, just what she needed, smiling and chatting and acting bubbly to a roomful of potential donors. "Looking forward to it. See you there?"

He gave her a jaunty little salute, finger to eyebrow. "You bet."

Her room was large, overlooking Pelican Bay, with white adobe walls and a great hammock for lounging, but most important, it had a private bath, an oddity for that part of the world. Hoping to squeeze in a nap before the reception, she stripped down and turned on the shower. Waiting for the water to heat, she took a hard look at herself in the mirror, something she hadn't done for a while, and tried to imagine herself through the eyes of Kelly Anderson. Was he just another horny graduate student, marooned on Santa Cruz without female companionship, or could she still attract men, something she might have to face sooner than later? *Ugh, dating.* The thought of it turned her stomach. It was something she had always hated—did they really like *her,* or were they simply attracted to the Rynerson name and wealth?

Tall and slim, she could see no sign of that foreign object growing inside; she didn't want to think of it as human, a baby boy or girl—that would make things too difficult. Her breasts were small but firm, something that had never bothered her—*Better than big and saggy*—and her skin was still smooth and unblemished, though darkened by the sun to an unfashionable golden brown. Her shoulder-length blond hair, solar streaked in shades ranging from platinum to dark honey, looked like she had just stepped out of a tornado. *Not bad—for a ma'am!*

* * *

She waited until 7:45, putting off the inevitable as long as possible, then took a taxi to the reception. The party was already in high gear, the locals clearly determined not to miss any part of the festivities, social events being somewhat rare on the island. A small lecture hall had been converted into party central: the walls decorated with poster-size pictures of the island's unique animal species; the ceiling awash with lanterns made of mulberry paper and imbedded with natural leaves and petals, casting a warm glow over the party-goers. An impressive hors d'oeuvre buffet had been laid out down the center of the room, with drink stations strategically located throughout. Kyra was barely in the door when Elsworth Marshall swept down upon her. He was a man of average height and unremarkable features, but his expression was wide and friendly, with Santa Claus eyes that made a person feel good just to be included in their twinkling gaze. "Kyra, my dear, you're more beautiful every time I see you."

At least she wasn't a *ma'am* to older men. "No wonder they're putting you out to pasture, Elsworth, you've become senile."

He laughed heartily, a booming HEHHH, HEHHH, HEHHH, from deep inside. "No, it's true, it's true, you look fabulous." He took her by the shoulders, holding her at arm's length, admiring the view. "Or maybe it's because I've never seen you in a dress."

She had to admit, she didn't look half bad in the dress: a simple black sheath with matching sling-back heels. "Doctor Marshall, that sounds positively risque!"

"I mean—" He laughed again. "Oh, you know what I mean."

"You probably didn't even notice that I was a female when I was your A-Number-One pupil."

His emerald eyes sparkled, the lecherous twinkle of an old man who had not yet lost his memory or appreciation for a younger woman. "Oh, I knew."

"You better be careful, Elsworth, I might just take you up on that unspoken offer."

The sparkle faded from his eyes. "Things are not well between you and Anthony?"

She shrugged.

He shook his head slowly and sadly. "And your father? How are things between the two of you?"

She shrugged again. "The same."

"I'm very sorry to hear that, my dear. I hoped things might improve between you."

This was not a subject she cared to discuss. "Let's party."

"That's the spirit." He reached down and took her hand. "Come, my dear, there are many people I want you to meet."

The party-goers were exactly as Kyra expected—academics, alumni, previous donors, and new pigeons—most of them gathered in small coveys, everyone eating and drinking and talking at once. Elsworth guided her from one group to another, introducing her as "Doctor Kyra Rynerson-Saladino from the National Zoological Park in Washington. A former resident here at the Center."

The response was always the same, the questions familiar. Kyra offered up her best smile and did her duty, avoiding the personal questions with long-established answers, schmoozing the pigeons, and sipping white wine to help her get through it.

"Oh, you're the Rynerson girl. I just love your father."

All the world, it seemed, knew Big Jake Rynerson, and everyone always spoke as if they knew him personally. It wasn't his fault, Kyra told herself—Big Jake was news, always good for a memorable quote or a spicy story, and the press was always there to record it—but for some reason she still blamed him. "He's a classic."

The most popular question, and the one that irritated Kyra the most because of its disingenuous nature, was the *contrived realization.* "Rynerson? You wouldn't be related to Big Jake Rynerson, by chance?"

By chance, as if they didn't know.

As if she didn't realize she was that evening's celebrity.

As if she couldn't hear the buzz of conversation as Elsworth escorted her around the room. The real celebrity, of course, was her father—Big Jake Rynerson, *Billionaire*—but it hung around her like a net, trapping her in its web, refusing to let her go no matter how hard she struggled to escape.

They had pretty much worked the crowd, up one side and down the other, when Elsworth introduced her to a man standing alone near one of the drink stations. "Kyra, I'd like you to meet Señor Luis Acosta, one of our newest benefactors. Señor Acosta, Doctor Kyra Rynerson-Saladino."

Kyra flashed her best smile. Though she could tell by the change in tone that this was someone Elsworth wanted to impress, there was something about the man that didn't quite fit the mold of *benefactor*. Short and stocky, mid-forties, small dark eyes, with skin the color and texture of wet sandpaper, he was wearing a tan Panama suit that didn't quite fit his body—or more accurately, Luis Acosta didn't quite fit the suit. Though his nails had been filed and cleaned, there remained a thin, dark line around the edge of his cuticles, the kind of dirt that builds up over years of labor and couldn't be scrubbed away with a boxcar of borax. "Señor Acosta, I'm very pleased to meet you."

The man bowed, his movements somewhat stiff. "My pleasure, Doctor."

Elsworth clasped an arm around Acosta's shoulders. "Luis has just pledged twenty-five thousand dollars to our Save the Island fund."

"That's wonderful," Kyra said, working hard to sound enthused, the long day and the wine beginning to take their toll. "The work is so important, and so few people understand the problem."

Acosta shifted his weight from one foot to the other, embarrassed. "It is only a small thing."

"Well, I can assure you, it's a very big thing for the Center. What kind of business are you in, Señor Acosta?"

"Agriculture."

That made sense, and would explain the dirt around his nails—a man not afraid to work with his hands—something to be admired, but for some reason he made her feel uncomfortable. Some undefined, unreasonable prejudice, she was sure, and that made her angry—at herself. "Really? What kind of agriculture?"

"Corn and potatoes," Elsworth answered quickly, as though wishing to show his interest in the affairs of such an important contributor. "Luis has a plantation along the Mantaro."

"In Peru?"

"Sí."

"I love your country. It's beautiful."

For the next five minutes they talked about the Center and the work being done. Kyra let Elsworth carry the conversation as she struggled to keep her eyelids above avalanche level. Just when she thought she couldn't last another minute, Captain Kelly swooped in for a landing. He bobbed his head awkwardly toward Kyra and Señor Acosta before turning to Elsworth Marshall. "Sorry to intrude, Professor, but I was about to leave and remembered that I promised Dr. Saladino a ride back to the hotel."

Escape, nothing could have sounded better, but Kyra still didn't want to mislead Kelly into thinking she might be interested in anything more. Elsworth misread her hesitation and supplied the push she needed. "Kyra, you've done enough. Let Kelly take you back to the hotel."

It was true, she had done her duty: promulgated, proclaimed, and publicized all the fine work done by the Center, and all the wonderful things it had done for her—she had oiled the pigeons' wallets, and if she could get some sleep, would clean their nests in the morning. What more could they expect? "It has been a long day." She turned to the South American. "Señor Acosta, if you wouldn't mind . . ."

He reached out and took her hand. "It has been a great pleasure, Doctor." He bowed, his lips lightly brushing her hand. "I look forward to your lecture."

Though the kiss was a common gesture in South American society, Kyra sensed an awkwardness in the man's movements, like an actor rehearsing an unfamiliar scene. "Thank you," she said, forcing out one last smile. "I promise not to make it overly long."

Thankful for the rescue, but determined not to mislead her savior, Kyra turned on Kelly the minute they were outside. "I hope you don't think—"

He interrupted her with a big, flashy grin. "Don't worry, Doc, I got the idea this afternoon."

"Then why . . . ?"

"I thought you were about to take a swan dive off those heels. Someone had to save you."

"Oh no." She couldn't suppress a groan. "That obvious?"

Kelly shook his head. "Nah, I'm probably the only one who noticed."

"And why would you be the only one to notice, may I ask?"

"I said I got the message—that doesn't mean I can't admire the messenger."

She laughed, surprised that a young man's words could make her feel so damn good—so attractive. "Well, thank you for the rescue, Captain Kelly. *And* the compliment."

"No sweat." He gave her a wink. "My pleasure."

Despite her exhaustion, Kyra was up at 5 A.M.—daybreak—a habit that had stayed with her since college and a three-month internship into the Amazon rain forest to study the effects of deforestation on the indigenous wildlife. A place where you worked as long as you could see, then crawled into your tent and slept until the sun came up.

She made a quick sprint through the shower—in and out, three minutes—pulled on a T-shirt and shorts and was ready to hit the day running, though she had no intention of doing anything so literal. Setting up her laptop on the terrace and using her cellular to make the connection, she logged into her office network, downloaded her messages and went to work.

At 6 A.M. she called the restaurant located directly beneath her room, the Bay Café, and ordered breakfast;

whole-grain cereal, fresh papaya, and a large carafe of *strong* coffee. *Another long day,* she was sure of that.

She had finished breakfast and was making a sizable dent in the coffee when someone began rapping on her door, insistently and hard, as if thinking they needed to wake her. "Kyra! Kyra!"

She recognized the voice immediately and pulled open the door. "Elsworth, what's the problem?" He was panting, cheeks flushed. "You okay?"

He took a quick breath. "The stairs—" He waved a hand, indicating it was nothing. "But we do have a problem."

"Come in. Let me get you some coffee."

He sank down into one of the rattan chairs, across the table from her spot on the terrace. "Thank you." He took a large gulp, then winced as the hot liquid hit his throat.

"What's wrong?"

He ignored her question. "When are you leaving?"

She hedged, not wanting to sound like she couldn't wait to rush off the moment she finished her speech and the last pocket had been picked. "Well, I'm not sure, exactly." *True.* "Once my part is done and they've given you the golden boot, I guess. Why?"

He stared back at her with a bemused, knowing expression. "Can't wait to go wheels-up in that little bird of yours, right?"

"It's not that, it's just that—" But she couldn't explain, couldn't tell him she was pregnant and her marriage was about to go up in flames.

He held up a hand. "No need to explain. I understand."

He didn't, of course, but it didn't matter. He was a good friend, and good friends didn't require an explanation. "What's on your mind, Elsworth?"

"There was a man I introduced you to last night . . ."

For some reason she knew exactly whom he was referring to. "You introduced me to a lot of men last night."

"Yes, of course. He was alone. And uh—"

"And he had just made a *significant* pledge."

"Yes. Luis Acosta. You remember him?"

"Of course. He didn't seem—"

Elsworth nodded deliberately, as if he understood precisely what she meant. "The right type."

"Exactly. What about him?"

"He came to my house just a short time ago. Quite frantic. His four-year-old daughter was bitten by a Bushmaster."

"Oh my God, that's terrible! When did this happen? How many hours ago?" With proper treatment an adult might survive a Bushmaster's attack, but it was nearly impossible for a child's small body to overcome the snake's deadly venom.

"It's only been a couple of hours. She's been stabilized for the moment, but—" He spread his hands in a helpless gesture.

"That's terrible, but why are you telling me this?" Not that she didn't have a good idea.

"Well, of course Luis wants to get home immediately. He can make connections in Guayaquil, but there's no flight off the island until late this afternoon. He tried to charter a plane but there was nothing available." Elsworth shook his head slowly, squeezing out the words like the final breath of air from a balloon. "She's not expected to survive the day."

Kyra didn't like it, but wasn't exactly sure why. Luis Acosta was clearly a good man—had proven it with his concern and contribution. So why did she hesitate? Some prejudice because he didn't fit the mold of the typical dilettante benefactor? It was only a four-hour flight to Guayaquil, and not out of her way. Had he said anything wrong? Anything offensive? *No.* It was more what he hadn't said that bothered her. He was the type of person who would drop her father's name in a heartbeat, but the name Rynerson had never once crossed his lips.

Elsworth leaned forward, reading her trepidation. "You don't have to do it, Kyra. He doesn't even know you have a plane."

That too surprised her. "He doesn't?"

"I never mentioned it. Told him I might be able to arrange something and would have to make some calls."

"It's not that I don't want to help. It's just that there was just something about him that made me uncomfortable."

Elsworth bobbed his head. "I know. I understand. He's not the type we're used to."

Not the type we're used to. That made her feel even worse, as if she had looked at the outside of Luis Acosta and judged what was inside the man. That was *not* the type of person she wanted to be. "You said he made a pledge. He hasn't actually given you the money?"

"No, but I too had reservations so I had someone in the office make a few discreet calls."

"And . . . ?"

"Luis Acosta is the biggest landowner in the Mantaro Valley. He's a very rich man."

So there it was—a well-known businessman, perfectly legitimate—how could she even consider not helping the man? His daughter was dying. She stood up. "Give me a few minutes to get my stuff together. Have him meet me downstairs."

Elsworth put a hand on his knee and levered himself to his feet. "I'll have him there. Kelly will drive you."

"Looks like you're going to miss my open-your-wallets-and-do-the-right-thing speech."

"Aaah." He exhaled through puffed cheeks, making an exaggerated sound of relief. "That I can live without."

"Me too. But I do hate missing your big sendoff."

"And I'll miss having you there." He reached out and gave her a hug. "You were always my favorite."

"You say that to all the girls."

"True, but with you I mean it."

"You'll make my apologies?"

"Of course. I'll make you a hero. By the time I'm through telling everyone the story, the money will be pouring out of their wallets and into our Save the Island fund."

She packed quickly, grabbed her bags and headed for the lobby. She still didn't have the best feelings about Luis Acosta, but realized she was being silly. It wasn't like she was going off with a complete stranger—Elsworth had checked the man out, and would know who she was with and where she was going.

Kelly was waiting with his Jeep outside the hotel, Luis Acosta pacing nervously alongside. The man rushed forward to take her bags, his hurried, waddling gait reminding her of a duck. "Doctor, I feel so terrible about this, taking you away from the conference. Your work here is so important."

"Señor Acosta, I'm nothing more than frosting on Dr. Marshall's retirement cake. Getting you home to see your daughter is more important than my presence here."

"I told Elsworth that I could wait for the afternoon flight, but he was most insistent that I leave now."

"And he's right. Let's go."

The trip to Baltra was made in silence, Luis Acosta obviously thinking about his daughter, and Kelly having the good sense not to shout over the wind. Kyra closed her eyes and tried to reconcile her misgivings about Luis Acosta. She had been around the rich and successful all her life and had come to recognize certain characteristics—the nouveau riche, never missing an opportunity to let everyone know how much they had; or the inheritors of old money, exuding a confidence that only great wealth could bestow—but new money or old, they all seemed to share one characteristic, whether real or imagined, that most other people lacked: an aura of superiority. A trait alien to Luis Acosta. *Why?* She couldn't explain it, not beyond the *exceptions-to-every-rule* rule.

A customs official, having received a heads-up call from the Center, was waiting when Kelly pulled alongside Babe. While Kyra completed her pre-flight walk-around and filed her flight plan, the man stamped their passports and cleared them for departure without looking at their bags.

Kyra leaned forward, gave Kelly a sisterly peck on the cheek and whispered, "Thanks, Captain Kelly, I do appreciate your dash to the rescue last night."

"Anytime, Doc. Come back and see us."

"I will," she replied, though she had a feeling that with

Elsworth gone she would not be returning to the Galapagos anytime soon.

"Ready?" she asked, as she fired up Babe's dual Continental 300-hp engines. Sitting beside her in the co-pilot's seat, clutching his briefcase like a parachute, Luis Acosta nodded. "Want me to stow that in back?" she asked, indicating his briefcase.

He shook his head, as if afraid to open his mouth for fear of what might come out.

Conversation, she decided, was not to be encouraged.

It wasn't until Kyra began her descent into Guayaquil, over four hours later, that Luis Acosta finally spoke. "There's a small landing strip four nautical miles south of Milagro. We will refuel there. Please adjust your heading to 071 degrees."

Stunned, Kyra could only stare at the man, who suddenly appeared completely at ease, his expression one of arrogant self-confidence. Smiling, he snapped the locks on his briefcase—*click, click*—and pulled open the top. It was empty except for two items: a pilot's aeronautical map and a steel-blue revolver.

That was the moment Kyra knew she was in trouble. *Serious trouble.*